Best Wishes,

Peggy,

Claire Gilbeau

Gather No Moss

Gather No Moss

Claire Janvier Gibeau

VANTAGE PRESS
New York

This is a work of fiction. Any similarity between the names
and characters in this book and any real persons,
living or dead, is purely coincidental.

Cover design by Polly McQuillen

FIRST EDITION

Copyright © 2007 by Claire Janvier Gibeau

Published by Vantage Press, Inc.
419 Park Ave. South, New York, NY 10016

Manufactured in the United States of America
ISBN: 978-0-533-15693-1

Library of Congress Catalog Card No.: 2006910303

0 9 8 7 6 5 4 3 2 1

To my wonderful husband, Billy;
49 years of marriage,
the best years of my life

Rove on, oh rolling stone,
living life for you alone.

Commitments you do avoid,
though by many you're employed.

Rove on, oh rolling stone,
ending life so all alone.

It's your loss, your loss,
to gather no moss, no moss.

Preface

The stories about the main character of this novel, Oliver Janvier, are based mainly on the colorful family lore that was passed on to me by many family members who knew him well.

The *Larchmont* disaster, his fathering a male child out of wedlock, and Oliver's propensity for roving the states are all factual, as are the wrestling events of my Uncle Frank, who became the welterweight wrestling champion of the world in 1923.

My dad, Joe, the baby of the family, was in the Merchant Marines during World War One and became a well-known percussionist. He was also the owner of Haverhill, Massachusetts' Snow White Laundry.

My weaving of imaginary dialogue and happenings with these facts, are a blend of truth and fiction.

I am grateful to my brother, Russell, for furnishing me with copies of many newspaper clippings pertaining to our Uncle Oliver's terrifying experience on the sinking of the *Larchmont*, and also of Uncle Frank's wrestling career.

I also thank my cousins, Russell Gagne and Lorraine Janvier Tylock, for supplying me with an insight as to the character of our uncle.

I am most thankful to my husband, Bill, who helped me with the French phrases, and for all his encouragement and patience.

I extend my gratitude to Dr. Roger Bennet, Richard Terravechia, Fev Porter, and Ron Moorse for helpful suggestions.

All family names are real. Many of our friends gave the okay to use their last names, in which cases I invented first names, making the characters fictional, and any similarity to any other person or persons is purely coincidental.

Gather No Moss

One

The seas of possibilities and opportunities before him awakened in him the urge to seek new vistas; but he didn't always flow with the tide. Going back to Oliver Janvier's beginnings may bring understanding as to why he chose paths not fitting the molds expected of him.

Oliver's parents were born in the French province of Quebec, Canada. After their marriage, they moved to Lawrence, Massachusetts where his father, Isaiah, opened a blacksmith shop.

"Janvier" translated to English means the month of "January." It has been told that *Azilda Parent* married *Mr. Isaiah January* in the month of *January,* and their first child, *Oliver William January,* was born the following year in the month of *January.* He died in the month of *January* after many years of searching for something forever elusive.

Oliver was born in 1886, the same year as Ty Cobb, and the same year of the dedication of the Statue of Liberty. He was a citizen of the United States by birth, and his parents were naturalized some years later. The Janvier children grew up with many of the French Canadian traditions which Isaiah and Azilda had brought with them to America.

The New Year was the most celebrated holiday; it was a day for family reunions. Gifts were exchanged, and the usual meal consisted of Tourtieres, which are pork pies made with ground pork and beef, chopped onions, mashed potatoes, seasoned with salt, pepper, nutmeg, and allspice, all cooked together and baked in a pastry shell. A pork spread used on crackers or bread was called Gorton, which was often eaten along with a French favorite: pea soup.

Non-French kids would teasingly chant in rhythm: "Pea soup and johnny-cake make a Frenchman's belly ache. Pea soup and johnny-cake make a Frenchman's belly ache."

The nineteenth century was replete with prejudices, and because of the lack of understanding the French language and culture, insensitive bigots called them "dumb Frenchmen, frogs, and brook jumpers." Many of the French Canadians had little book learning but were skillful in many trades, such as bread making, tailoring, carpentry, and other skills

1

requiring physical strength and endurance. Many had the courage and foresight to start up private businesses such as blacksmithing, laundries, and bakeries.

Most women of Canada had outdoor ovens for baking bread, but the immigrants found that baking breads in the ovens of their large iron stoves worked out just as well, if not better. These iron stoves were fueled by coal or wood for both cooking and heating their homes.

The fare for Christmas was often Boudin, blood sausage. The casing was made from animal innards, then filled with the congealed blood of the animal, mixed with special seasonings. The Canadians also brought with them a flair for music and dancing.

They danced Quadrilles, a square dance for two or four couples, consisting of five movements. The music was usually chosen from familiar music of the day.

Homemade wines were often featured at French gatherings and most of the men had their own wine cellars.

In the winter months, they made maple syrup candies by pouring boiled syrup on fresh snow. Those who were fortunate enough to have maple trees, owned their own "La Cabanne aux sucre," a maple shack. Toffee pulling parties were also seasonal. Canadians were used to hard work, and during harvesting season, those with gardens were kept busy canning fruits and vegetables.

*   *   *

The Janvier home on May Street, was in a section of Lawrence known for its many French speaking inhabitants. Most of the homes, built in the mid nineteenth century, were unassuming two-story structures with third floor attics and small front porches.

The Janvier abode was modestly furnished; the kitchen provisions consisted of an old black iron stove, circular oak table, and many unmatching chairs.

A parlor, adjacent to the small kitchen, was furnished with an old faded green velvet sofa and two stuffed chairs that had seen much wear. The Hubbard lamp, sitting on Azilda's prized carved walnut table, had held its patina in spite of the antiquity of the piece.

There were two small bedrooms on the second floor, separated by an extremely narrow hallway. The parents occupied one, and their two daughters, the other. The tiny bathroom, across from the parents' bed-

2

room, contained old lead pipes, visible under the tiny sink, and in full view up to the flush-box above the commode and along the wall by the tub. The unfinished attic served as a bedroom for the boys where there were two old iron beds with lumpy mattresses, and a large oak bureau. These austere possessions suited the needs of the Janvier family.

*   *   *

St. Anne's Catholic church served the religious needs of the many French Canadian immigrants whose children also attended St. Anne's parochial school on Haverhill Street. The school curriculum was taught in French by the Good Shepherd Sisters and Marist Brothers from Canada, and several lay teachers who made up for the lack of available nuns.

*   *   *

Oliver showed his propensity for humor at an early age. One day in first grade, he appeared to have a swollen jaw on the right side of his face. Sister Cecilia asked if he had candy in his mouth. "No Sister," he lowered his head and mumbled as if in pain.

"Do you have an infected tooth?" she asked with concern. He just nodded.

Oh the poor child, she thought . . . but when she took a second look at him, his left cheek was swollen, not his right. He had transferred the large wad of paper from the right to the left side of his mouth. The very young nun was just a novice and hadn't learned lessons in sternness. She wanted to laugh, but thought it best to help him dispose of the paper, guide him to his seat with nothing more said.

When she related the story of Oliver's behavior to an older experienced nun, she was advised to nip that kind of behavior in the bud, or "experience more problems with that child." Sister Cecilia was determined to keep a watchful eye for further antics.

Some of the children in the first grade class, which consisted of only boys, already knew their letters. Oliver didn't. The inexperienced teacher moved ahead at a pace catering to the needs of the more advanced boys, which left a number of pupils behind. Things got so perplexing that Oliver cried, not wanting to return to school. Sister Cecilia was advised of the problem. The only way fit to remedy the situation, she was told by the principal, was to tutor the slower students after school each day, which made for a long tiring day for pupils and teacher alike. However, it didn't take long for Oliver to catch up to the more advantaged boys. He was a bright kid, who hadn't been taught anything of a scholastic nature at home. He still pulled off his little pranks, which the kids loved; he often created disruptions. As a result, he found himself sitting in a lonesome corner of the classroom, repenting as he felt the repercussions of his silliness.

After a few days of second grade, he contrived a way to test his new teacher by arriving to class with a black patch over his left eye. Under the advice of an eye doctor, Blanche, who had one eye that was slightly askew, wore the patch over the stronger eye until the weaker eye had improved. That happened some time before Oliver was in second grade. Oliver "borrowed" his sister's eye patch.

"Oliver, can you see well enough out of your right eye?" asked Sister Bertha.

"Yes, sister," he answered with much innocence.

Class went on, but halfway through the reading lesson, Sister Bertha questioned herself . . . "was that patch over his left eye . . . or his right?"

Oliver got away with the switch because the nun became confused. The children delighted in the prank. They could always count on Oliver to brighten up their day.

However, his antics didn't exactly brighten up his teacher's day. When he was in the third grade, he waited for the last child to be seated in the classroom before purposely tripping over the threshold, falling flat on his face and enjoying the reaction of his fellow classmates. Sister Marie had difficulty suppressing her laughter while reprimanding him.

"When you return to school tomorrow, you will write a penance on the blackboard ten times! You have many lessons to learn, young man!"

On the way home from school, he taught the kids how to hold a blade of grass between two thumbs, blow into it as one would blow into a reed instrument. The shrieking sounds delighted the children, and a mingled joyous laughter followed each piercing noise. They all liked this silly kid.

The next day, he was obliged to write on the blackboard, in front of his fellow students: "God doesn't mean for me to be a silly boy." Sister hushed the chuckling of Oliver's classmates.

After that chore was completed, the religion class wasn't holding Oliver's attention, so without much thought, he blew into his Catechism.

4

Like the blade of grass, the startling sound unnerved the class and angered Sister Marie into taking drastic measures.

"You, Oliver Janvier, go down to the first grade and spend the rest of the day there!"

Oliver was too humiliated to obey, and quietly and quickly exited the building. He told Mama: "They let us out of school early today."

He confided in his sister Eva, that he departed school unnoticed . . . but lied to Mama. The two siblings were close, and never revealed the secrets they shared. Easter vacation was coming up and Oliver thought that his ill deed would be forgotten and not reported by his teacher.

Two

Papa had surprising plans when he announced to his family: "Pendant l'école ajournement pour les Pâques, nous visiterons mes cousins, Raymond et Jeanette à Berwick, Maine, pour deux jours, et mes autres cousins, Pierre et Annette à Manchester, New Hampshire pour trois jours."

(During school vacation for Easter, we will visit my cousins, Raymond and Jeanette, in Berwick, Maine, and my other cousins, Pierre and Annette, in Manchester, New Hampshire for three days.)

Oliver and Eva were so excited about this news that they both declared almost in unison, "Oh Papa! ça sera le premier fois que nous envoyerons par chemin de fer!" (Oh Papa! this will be the first time that we will take a train ride!)

Blanche and Frank were a little young to understand what the excitement was all about. Oliver told them, "We go choo choo," and all four children formed a line, holding onto each other's shoulders singing "Choo choo, choo choo." Mama and Papa laughed at their children's happy sounds.

The day of their departure, Papa's blacksmith helper took them to the train station by horse and buggy and promised to meet them upon their return.

The children were told to address Raymond and Jeanette as aunt and uncle. They were happy to see that these new acquaintances had three young children of their own. They were typical Canadian transplants who had all the same ethnic customs as the Janvier family. Their French community also had a Catholic church and parochial school. The only difference was that Ray and Jeanette encouraged their kids to speak English, which shocked Isaiah and Azilda.

"We're in America, so we want our kids to talk der language them," Ray was proud to announce in his Canadian accent.

"But, dey will, (how you say?) forget der talk French them," Isaiah argued haltingly.

"No, no, they get 'nough French in school. Der nuns, them, don't know much English, them, so our kids keep up der French," Jeanette added.

All Azilda could say was, "Mon Dieux, c'est triste!" (My God, it's sad!)

All the while these conversations were going on, the six children were having a marvelous time in the yard, playing on the homemade swings, seesaws, and wooden trucks. Ray was an expert carpenter.

At night, space was a bit cramped with three girls in one bed, and three boys in another. While the parents played cards, they were often distracted by the giggling of little girls and the rowdiness of the boys pushing each other out of bed. Unnoticed by Isaiah and Azilda, Ray and Jeanette rolled their eyes and tightened their lips as if to say, "We can't wait for these people to leave." And two days were enough for the visitors. However, they parted cordially and the Janviers extended reciprocal invitations.

✳   ✳   ✳

They were off on the next leg of their journey: Manchester, to visit Pierre and Annette. The children were again advised to address Papa's cousins as uncle and aunt.

At the risk of displeasing his parents, Oliver chirped, "But, Papa, they aren't our aunt and uncle."

"Children, it's a matter of showing respect." Oliver couldn't quite grasp that, considering that if he called them cousins, that wouldn't be so disrespectful. *After a while, we won't know who our real aunts and uncles are*, he pondered, but he reluctantly acquiesced.

Pierre met the Janvier family at the train station and rode them to his home in a rather exquisite carriage, pulled by two bay horses.

"Business must be good, Pierre," said Papa, in French, of course.

"You yourself know that, Isaiah; we're in the same business."

"Yes, business is profitable. That's why I could afford a few days off with my family."

"Well, we're glad that you could come. We'll have a good time. Remember the fun we had growing up so close in Canada?"

"It seems like yesterday, but things are always changing."

Isaiah often thought about all his children, and Azilda's attitude toward his advances; she feared another pregnancy. He didn't feel that he had the comforts that he deserved.

7

Annette greeted her husband's cousins with enthusiasm.

"Welcome to our home," she said in French.

"It's good that we won't have to struggle with the English language while we are here," said Azilda as they kissed each other on each cheek.

They kiss like plungers, thought Oliver. *Too much, too wet!* He was glad when the salvos were over with, and so were the other three children.

Annette escorted their guests to their rooms. The Victorian home was elegantly furnished, a little too formal for the Janvier kids.

"We won't be able to horse around in here," Oliver whispered to his siblings.

There were four spacious bedrooms on the second floor, including a master bedroom, a room for their teenage daughter, and a guest room for Isaiah and Azilda. The children were led to the third floor rooms that reminded them of their rooms at home, lumpy mattresses and old quilts.

"Only grownups get the best," Oliver told the other kids.

Dinner was served in the stylish dining room. Annette showed off her finest china, on which was served a sumptuous seafood meal of Maine lobster, scallops, shrimp, and haddock. The children were frightened by the huge red things that looked like oversized bugs . . . all except Oliver, the oldest bravest kid. Uncle Pierre showed him how to open the claws and dip the meat into melted butter. He had never tasted anything so "yummy!"

"You don't know what you're missing," he announced to the others, but they chose to eat the scallops. Azilda helped Annette and Marie, her daughter, clear away the dishes.

Annette announced that she had someone to come in to do dishes.

"You have a maid?" exclaimed Azilda in disbelief.

"That's what happens when you don't have so many kids."

"That's what you can afford!" cackled Isaiah.

All laughed except Azilda.

*   *   *

That night after everyone had gone to bed, Isaiah announced to Azilda, "Let's have some loving, my dear wife."

"Not in someone else's home; they'll hear us."

"Not in our home, not in someone else's home, not then, not

now . . . when Azilda, when?"

She did love her husband, but had such a fear of another pregnancy that she held back. Isaiah was determined to win her over, and asked for a good night kiss. He kissed her with such passion, she was electrified and gave in to his lovemaking with more pleasure than she had ever experienced.

"My Azilda, why can't it be like this more often?" She didn't reply, but wondered herself. She asked herself, *Could this be because I'm not making meals, not doing laundry, not dressmaking, not burdened with never ending work? How nice it must be to have a home like this, and a maid besides!*

✳   ✳   ✳

"Mama and Papa look so happy this morning, they seem to like this place," Eva told Oliver.

After breakfast, Marie took the children to a nearby park where there were slides and swings. In spite of the fact that she had reluctantly agreed to "babysit" the Janvier brood, she found that it was fun pushing swings and hearing mirthful laughter. The joyous mood was contagious and she found herself wishing that she had brothers and sisters.

That night, the Janviers were mesmerized by the powers that Annette displayed in her clairvoyance trances.

"Annette," a disturbed Pierre admonished, "you know that Father Petit told you not to do that! He said that you could be excommunicated from the church. It's of the devil!"

"That's what he thinks! I think I have a gift from God! What about the time the little Godette boy was lost, and I saw him in my mind's eye playing by the river. His parents got there in time to save him from falling in. And what about the time Marie was horseback riding with her arms outstretched, not directing the horse with the reins. When she got home safely, I said, 'Marie, never ride your horse like this.' She replied, 'how did you know?'

"I know lots of things because of this gift. Maybe if I did it to get paid, that would be wrong."

Annette surprised her guests by telling them about things that had truly happened in their lives, but they were anxious to learn what lay ahead for them. Annette closed her eyes and went into a deep alpha state, but quickly opened her eyes with a distressed look on her face. Her guests were disappointed when she sputtered, "That's all for today. It is stressful at times, and I must rest now."

That night, Pierre asked his wife what she had seen. He knew that it must be something negative for her to call off the session.

"Oh Pierre, I hope that it does not come to pass, but I see Isaiah leaving his family after their next child is born. I could never tell them what I saw!"

"Annette, I beg of you to give up your clairvoyance practice. There may be other negative revelations that you will regret seeing. Please, please give it up!"

"After tonight, I'll give it serious thought. It can be frightening. I don't want to be prophesying negativity."

The next day, Annette accompanied her husband and their guests to the train station.

There were many thanks, kisses, and hugs before the Janviers boarded the train for Lawrence. All agreed that it was a memorable vacation, a new experience for the children.

Three

After being home for a week, Eva said to Oliver, "It just feels like we never left home. Things are back to the same, same old routine. Get out of bed, eat, go to school, come home, eat, do homework, and go to bed."

"Come on, Eva, you know it's not all that bad. I've seen you out jumping rope with friends. But I do agree, it does seem like we never went away. Some day, I'll go away and travel to lots of places, see lots of things . . . maybe I'll come home once in a while."

"You'd have to be all grown up to do that, Oliver. I'll miss you. Will you miss me'?"

"Yeah, I guess so." But then he thought, *I just might be too busy to miss anybody.*

*   *   *

Sympathy was something not doled out often in the Janvier family. When Oliver scraped a knee, or an elbow, the only comforting words offered were: "C'a ne tu ferrat pas du mal le jour de ton noce." (You'll never feel it on your wedding day.) It was a phrase laughable to the adults, but never to the child. Eva and Oliver comforted each other.

"Oliver, what do you want to be when you grow up?" asked Eva.

"I don't know. I'll have to see what's out there in the rest of the world. Do you know what you want to be?"

"Girls don't have much choice. I guess I'll get married and have children. That's all there is for girls."

"Look at Aunt Anna Parent; she never married."

"But Mama says she's an old maid. I don't want to be called an old maid."

"Well, we have a few years before we have to decide."

Oliver and Eva played together and sang together, harmonizing French tunes such as " Frère Jacques," or "C'est La Belle Françoise," and several Christmas carols.

Eight years old wasn't too soon to begin to earn a little money. Oliver took it upon himself to get a job selling newspapers. That's what began his interest in learning to read English and he wanted to be informed of the news. He could always tell his mother where the food bargains were:

PUBLIC MARKET
BEST RIB ROAST 12 cents a lb.
CHUCK ROAST 6 to 8 cents a lb.
Corned Beef is cheap.
Vegetables are cheap also.
We have them fresh every day.

"What does this headline say?" he would ask the circulation worker.

He had many willing helpers as he began reading the *Tribune* papers that he sold on Essex Street, Saturdays and Sundays. The following story from the July 9 *Tribune* was one of his favorites:

The Dream of a Smart Boy

"Pop," said young Phillip Gratebar to his father, "I had a dream last night." "You don't mean it!" said Mr. Gratebar. "Yes I do," said Phillip. "I dreamed I was going along the street, and I got awful thirsty, and I went into a drug store to get some soda water. The soda fountain there was the biggest one I ever saw and the man tending it was a giant. He looked down on me and asked me what I'd have, and I said I'd like strawberry with ice cream in it.

"The giant set out on the counter a glass about two feet high and he put in it a lot of strawberry syrup, and then he took the cover off of an ice cream freezer that was pretty near as big as a barrel and scooped out about three platefuls of ice cream and put that in. Then he put the tumbler under the soda water spout and whirled the wheel around and the soda went zz-z-zz! zz-z-zz! and then the giant pushed the glass over in front of me, full, and the thick creamy foam running over the tap, and I didn't touch it."

"What!" said Mr. Gratebar.

"No," said Phillip, "I didn't touch it. I felt in my pocket, and I found I hadn't got a cent."

Mr. Gratebar understood.

Then Phillip went forth in search of a fountain, not of the fountain he had seen in his dream, but of one as nearly like it as he could find in actual life.—*New York Sun.*

Oliver told the story to his sister Eva. They were always making up songs together:

> Phillip dreamed about an ice cream soda
> but he didn't have a cent.
> So, he found a real ice cream fountain,
> and he and his father went
> Oh Phillip, did you make up that dream?
> Did Dad catch on that it was just a scheme?

"Ha, ha, let's sing that one for Mama and Papa."

But their parents didn't understand what the song was about, so all was lost in the translation.

The children were learning English at a pace which perplexed Mama and Papa. They were told "Parlez en français" (Speak in French) but they quickly learned that they had something like a code between them—the English language.

More and more frequently, Oliver and Eva heard the discordant tiffs of their parents. They loved both Mama and Papa, and it upset them dreadfully to hear the arguments and to see Mama with tears running down her cheeks.

"I'll be glad when I'm old enough to travel to see the places I've read about in the newspapers and in our geography book. I want to *go go go*, then I won't see Mama cry."

"Oliver, I'll be sad to see you go . . . then *I'll* cry."

"Sometimes, I wonder why Le Bon Dieu put us on this earth. I've got to figure that one out."

"Maybe you should study to be a priest, then you'd find out what the good Lord wants you to do with your life."

"I don't want to be a priest. As far as I can see, they're in a world all their own. I'll bet they don't even know what's out there. They try to tell people how to live, but what experiences do *they* have? Some of them go to the seminary right after the eighth grade. What have they learned about life outside of their world?"

"Oliver, your thinking is sinful. Priests are close to God. God must tell them what to do or think. Be careful, Oliver. I want you in heaven when I go there."

13

"Well, I try to be good, and there are lots of good people in the world. How can anyone believe that good people will be thrown into hell just because they don't believe in a certain religion?"

"Let's drop the subject, Oliver. You give me doubts and it scares me."

"You mean that it makes you think?"

*   *   *

During the summer months, the weather was often humid, and steamy. On such days, no one felt any inclination for physical activity. It was no wonder that when the neighborhood children saw the horse-drawn ice wagon coming down the street, they would flock to where the iceman was making a delivery, and beg for ice chips to cool them off. Sometimes the wagon would be followed further to other deliveries in hopes of more refreshing coolness.

While the iceman was in a patron's house, Oliver often jumped up on the wagon, chipped more ice in larger pieces for his friends and himself. But then, the transgressors would have to disappear before the man returned to his wagon. Summertime was usually the time when young boys were . . . well, boys were often mischievous. If they ever dared to sneak ice chips from their kitchen ice boxes, there would be a price to pay, maybe sent to bed with no supper. On the days of extreme heat, one could hear the constant dripping of the melting ice into the pan under the ice box.

Four

Oliver still sold newspapers on weekends, and when cooler weather came, he almost welcomed the inevitable: back to school.

Occasionally, he would go to his father's shop after school. Isaiah let Oliver work the bellows which blew air under the fire. At eight years old, he found that turning the crank wheel to work the bellows was a strenuous task. *Hard work was something my boys have to learn*, reasoned Papa, as he let Oliver sweat it out.

On one of these occasions, the lad showed his father a picture he had cut out from the *Tribune*. It showed a muscular man lifting weights to enhance body strength. The advertisement stressed the importance of building the male body by lifting "dumb-bells," which could be purchased by mail order.

"Papa, see how strong this man is. Just look at those muscles! If I had some things that they call dumb-bells, I could get stronger and stronger."

"Where do you think you can get those things?" asked Papa.

"Papa, you're teasing me. You know that you have everything here to make me a set. Please, Papa, *please?*"

There was no answer, but his father planned to make a set of iron dumb-bells for the boy's ninth birthday.

It was a big surprise and a happy day when Oliver experienced a wish come true. Little six-year-old brother, Frank, insisted on trying to lift the weights.

"Stay away from those. Those weights are *mine!*"

"*No!* Mama, Oliver pushed me!"

Mama took the dumb-bells and hid them, after which a tussle between the two boys ensued on the kitchen floor. Azilda pulled each one up by an ear, sat them at the kitchen table and said, "Souffez juste pour vivre!" (Breathe just enough to live!) She had had enough!

Papa took it upon himself to resolve the little sibling dispute by making a smaller set of dumb-bells for Frank. From then on, the two brothers exercised together to become strong like the man in the picture. When

Oliver showed his little brother a newspaper article with illustrations of wrestling holds, Frank decided then and there that one day he would become a famous wrestler. The boys practiced all the holds shown in the newspaper article.

✻   ✻   ✻

Oliver continued to read and sell the *Tribune* on the weekends, progressively improving his English reading skills and adding pennies to his savings. Working the bellows at his father's shop did not increase his stash; he was told, "C'est pour gagner ton pension." (It's for earning your board and room.) Oliver was now ten years old and learning the hard lessons of finances.

He was also learning about nature, not from his parents, but from his peers.

"See what those two cats are doing?" Jerry pointed to two mating animals.

"That's how they get kittens. And my big brother told me that's how people get babies. That cat under the other one is going to get big and fat, and then the kittens will be born."

"How does your big brother know that?" asked Oliver.

"He said my dad had a talk with him. He promised Dad that he wouldn't tell me 'cause I'm too young to know that stuff . . . but he told me anyhow."

"So you're telling *everyone?* Wow! All the kids in our class must know!"

This was some kind of discovery for Oliver, who had recently noticed his mother's distended belly. He shared the startling information with Eva, and they both observed their mother becoming more and more burdened with her weight.

On September 13, 1896, all four children were brought by horse and wagon to Uncle Ben's farm in Dracut, a town near Lowell, Massachusetts. Oliver and Eva whispered that it must be *that* time. The next day, September 14, the children were told that they had a new baby brother born that very day, and he was to be named Joseph Clovis Janvier.

"So close to my birthday!" lamented Frank, whose special day was September 13. He felt sad that it was almost forgotten this year. But Aunt Anna, the old maid, Uncle Ben's sister, did bake a cake for seven-year-old Frank.

Oliver went out into Uncle Ben's yard and sat under the old maple tree pondering the latest news of a new sibling. He had learned that God makes babies, but he reveled in the thought that man had a part in the process. Oliver often sought out places of solitude to just think and wonder about things.

The children were brought home two days later, giving Azilda enough time to get out of bed to resume family duties. Oliver, Frank and Eva were the only ones who noticed how pale and worn Mama appeared. There was a lot of stifling and hushing because, "L'enfant dorme." (The baby is sleeping.) Once a routine was formulated, the children knew what to expect. Oliver found it easier to be somewhere else, rather than at home. Much was expected of Eva, being the oldest female offspring. She helped care for "tse boy, (little boy)," the name the family began calling the baby. Both Eva and Blanche were assigned such chores as moping and dusting all the bedrooms, and scrubbing the bathroom and kitchen floors. Boys were never expected to do domestic chores; they were given the responsibilities of keeping the hod by the stove filled with either wood or coal and disposing of the ashes created by the burnt fuel.

For about five months after the arrival of the baby, Oliver and Papa had a grand time riding his father's two Morgan horses. Papa had told his son that Morgan horses, though appearing to be a little smaller than some other breeds, were the sturdiest animals and their stamina could outdo other breeds.

"They are truly an American breed," Papa told his son.

Papa taught Oliver how to saddle and ride, and Oliver was a happy lad when perched in the saddle atop one of his father's prize horses.

He worked with Papa more often, but began noticing that his father was becoming more and more drawn into himself, sharing little or no conversation with his son.

"Is something wrong, Papa?" Oliver would ask, thinking that maybe it was his fault.

"Ne demandes pas des questions. Ce n'est rien de ton affaire." (Don't ask questions. It's none of your business.)

Oliver developed a sense of rejection which was difficult for him to understand, and Eva's attempt to console him was to no avail. His unhappy feelings were heightened the day he went to his father's shop and found Papa working frantically to hoist blacksmithing paraphernalia onto a large wagon outside of the shop. The building had been emptied of all equipment. Isaiah's two Morgan horses were harnessed to the wagon.

Papa never used his prize horses in that fashion, thought the distraught boy.

"Papa, Papa, what's happening?" The only reply that Oliver heard was, "Ne demandes pas des questions." Papa seemed upset and angry.

After all the gear had been packed securely on the wagon, Papa, with tears in his eyes, said, "Je vais loin. Tu es un bon fils. Adieu, mon fils." (I'm going far away. You are a good son. Good-bye, my son.)

Oliver stood motionless, in disbelief, as he watched the wagon on the way to God knows where. When he could no longer see Papa, he ran home to find his mother tearfully explaining to the other children that Papa would be happier elsewhere.

Oliver flung himself on his bed and moaned, "I have no Papa! I have no Papa!"

That night he kept repeating the phrase, "I have no Papa," until he finally fell asleep, only to dream a most disturbing dream . . . or was it a nightmare?

In this dream, he was on his way to school, All the boys from his class were chanting: "Ollie has no fa-ther, Ollie has no fa-ther, Ollie has no fa-ther. Boo-hoo-hoo, Boo-hoo-hoo." The cruel kids repeated their chant over and over again. When he finally got to school, all the nuns, brothers, and priests were singing the same chant.

The exhausted child refused to go to school the next day. Mama let the children stay home and lectured to them about being brave and going on with their lives. That's what she would do, she claimed. But the children could sense that she struggled to be optimistic.

They all did go on with their lives bravely, and in time the boys were wrestling again, and Eva and Oliver were sharing more secrets, making up humorous songs, and singing old French songs that they had heard Mama singing while sewing. There was a certain amount of normalcy that entered their lives, in spite of being without a father.

When cousin Pierre heard the news of Isaiah leaving Azilda, he recalled what his wife had said about a forewarning she experienced as a clairvoyant woman. He had felt relieved that she finally agreed not to pursue the trances ever again. When Pierre informed Annette that her prediction was right on the mark, she said with much sadness, "It was bound to happen."

※　　※　　※

After Isaiah's departure, Oliver was more determined to prepare himself for his future. He saved every cent of his earnings selling newspapers, and he continued to gain proficiency with the English language. In 1896, he read the news about Utah, becoming a state of the United States. He was always going to go to the places he read about—*some day I'll go there*, he thought. William McKinley was elected 25th president. I like what I've read about him. He'll be good for America. Oliver was especially interested in the article announcing the first modern Olympics that were held in Athens, Greece. More and more, world affairs caught his attention. The story of the Klondike Gold rush made him daydream about a voyage to Bonanza Creek, Canada. He mused that in 1897, he would be eleven . . . one year closer to his dreams of adventure.

In January, 1897, Oliver bought himself a birthday present: Kipling's newest book, *Captains Courageous*. He sat reading by the kitchen stove.

In the wintertime, all other rooms were closed off. Hods of coal had to be kept by the stove, which had to be continually lit for warmth in the kitchen. During the day and evening, family members huddled in this one comfortable room of the house. At night, they had to wear warm night dresses and woolen night caps to sleep soundly in the cold bedrooms.

✻   ✻   ✻

Through all the distractions of the family activities, Oliver focused his attention on the young boy, Harvey Cheyne, depicted in Kipling's book. He began comparing his beginnings with Harvey's. Oliver thought, I'm only eleven and know what hard work is. Harvey was born rich and didn't have to work, but because he fell overboard from the ship bound for Europe and was rescued by a fisherman, he was forced to learn what hard work was all about on a fishing trawler. Now he's as poor as I am. I think they call that "eating humble pie." He was no longer the arrogant, spoiled-rotten rich kid.

If I suddenly became rich, I wonder how I'd handle it. I think what I would do first of all is buy Mama a house that is warm in *every* room. Oliver read on: Poor "Penn," he thought, what a horrible thing happened to *his* family; his wife and four children had been drowned when the dam broke in Johnstown, Pennsylvania. The Captain's brother got him work on the fishing trawler, but the Captain's son, Dan, told Harvey all about Penn. "He ain't no wise dangerous, but his mind's give out."

Wow, no recollection of having a family, pondered Oliver. Poor Penn can't remember that he once had a family, but the accident wasn't *his* fault. Papa lost his family, too . . . but it was *his* doing . . . wonder if he has forgotten us.

Oliver struggled through the book, remembering that he had been told that the language in the book was written in mostly broken English.

"Kipling wrote it that way to make the seamen of many nationalities seem more real," he was told.

*　　*　　*

Oliver became interested in a special section of the *Tribune* that featured gems of wisdom. He bought himself a notebook, cut out famous quotes of outstanding people and glued the clippings on to the pages of his "scrapbook." The only glueing method that he found to work was by mixing a paste of flour and water; its adhering quality was amazing. Even when he became an adult, he would often refer to these quotes as they would apply to specific happenings. They became his moral code.

Oliver felt "grown-up" at eleven, and he became anxious about his life's goals. None of the family knew how much money he had saved since he had begun selling papers three years before, but he could account for every penny. Once in a while he would empty his box of change and secretly count and write down his holdings, trying to figure out how much he would have when he finally was able to leave. He calculated that if he sold fifty papers and was paid one cent for every five papers sold, his earnings would be ten cents. Some weekends, he had earned as much as twenty-seven cents and more! People frequently paid him a little extra for their papers. He felt lucky when he had saved as much as fifteen dollars in one year. In three years, he had close to forty-five dollars, less the sixteen cents he had paid for *Captains Courageous*.

Five

"Mama, pourquoi les soeurs n'enseignt pas l'anglais? Je veux parlez et faire des études dans la langue anglais." (Why don't the sisters teach English? I want to speak and study in English.)

"C'est important que t'études en francais parce que autrement, tu vas oublié ta langue." It's important to study in French because otherwise you will forget your language.)

"Pourquoi est-elle *ma* langue? Nous sommes aux États-Unis. Nous devrions parler la langue Américaine." (Why is it *my* language. We are in the United States. We should talk the American language.) Whenever Azilda became frustrated, she would shake her head, knit her brows and exclaim, "Mon dieu, Mon dieu." (My God, My God.)

✻   ✻   ✻

Oliver's fourth grade studies went well for a time, but he thought that Sister Anne was too stuffy and rigid. He held that picture of the nun in his mind, until he tried capturing his impression of her in a drawing, a very unflattering picture. One day, it slipped out of his notebook, onto the schoolroom floor where Sister had found it. In trying to ascertain who would have drawn such a thing, she confronted the class with the words, "Who drew this?"

Oliver was shaken when he saw his artwork on display, and involuntarily called out, "Not me!"

His speaking out in class proved to be a sure give away. This time, he was escorted to the first grade where he spent the rest of the day in humiliation.

✻   ✻   ✻

It was in Sister Pauline's fifth grade class that Oliver would ask all kinds of questions that had the nun anxious to ship him off to the sixth grade where he could be straightened out by a male faculty member of the order of Marist brothers. But, she still had to contend with this young nonconformist for several more months.

"Sister, we're in America; why don't we speak American?"

Being a French Canadian, without a full command of the English language, Sister Pauline haltingly tried to explain to Oliver that if he was unhappy with lessons being taught in French, then he should be enrolled in public school. He told her that his mother wouldn't allow it.

"C'est regrettable." (That's unfortunate.) For her sake, it was.

Sister Pauline felt the need to put some fear into the boys in her classroom, especially Oliver. She told them about the never ending suffering in hell:

"Toujours ici. Jamais, jamais sortir." (Always here. Never, never to leave.)

Oliver's hand shot up in the air.

"Oui, Oliver?"

"If they could never leave hell, who came back to tell *you* about it?"

Sister was saved by the dismissal bell. The children filed out of the building leaving a most aggravated nun. She sought out a sympathetic ear in Sister Therese.

"Ce garçon me fait mal." (That boy gives me a pain.)

"Je serai contente l'année prochaine quand il sera avec les frères!"

(I'll be glad next year when he will be with the brothers.) But it was a long year for the fifth grade teacher.

Julien, the boy whose desk was to the rear of Oliver's, whispered to him, "I don't like this teacher."

Oliver, turned his head toward Julien, and whispered, "I don't either."

Sister Pauline called Julien to the front of the class and said, "Julien, tell the class what Oliver said to you."

Julien, with bowed head, said, almost inaudibly, "He said that he doesn't like you."

There were snickers heard in the classroom, which made the nun more infuriated. The recess bell rang and Sister Pauline dismissed all her students but Oliver. She crisply commanded, "Stay at your desk. Put your hands together, bow your head and pray to God for forgiveness. Do not change this position until the other boys return from recess."

"But, Sister, Julien didn't tell the truth."

"Be quiet, Oliver, or I'll send you to Mother Superior."

That would be worse than bowing his head in prayer. He acquiesced.

During the history lesson, Sister Pauline wanted to point out how important it is not to lie; she chose the story about George Washington who admitted to his father that he chopped down the cherry tree and said, "I cannot tell a lie."

Up shot Oliver's hand, which was hard for the nun to ignore when he began waving it frantically. Sister said, in a slow, uneager voice, "What is it, Oliver?"

"I read somewhere that *that* whole story is a *lie*. Maybe he chopped down the tree, maybe he didn't. Who knows?"

"Oliver, why must you question everything we teach here? This story is in your history book!"

"That just proves that we can't believe *everything* that's in print!"

Sister Pauline finished the day's itinerary with another headache, which she attributed to "Ce garçon la!" *That boy!*

☼   ☼   ☼

At the age of twelve, he was entering the sixth grade at St. Anne's school. From that grade on, he would have a man teacher whom they called Brother. Brothers were in a religious organization, much like the nuns. Brother Pierre was Oliver's teacher.

The boys were not allowed to take slingshots to school, but one day Oliver was shot at by a lad breaking the rule. The boy was shooting bubble gum, and the sticky glob landed on Oliver's clean shirt. He wasn't about to tattle to Brother Pierre, but decided to handle things his own way. The following day, with his slingshot concealed in his trouser pocket, he was ready to retaliate. The wad of gum flew a distance across the schoolyard, striking the intended target. *Oh, oh,* Oliver said to himself, as he saw Brother Pierre coming toward him with a menacing look on his face.

"Young man, you come with me," spoke Brother Pierre, with a threatening look in his eyes.

Oliver obeyed and humbly followed him into the school building. He thought that the good man of the cloth would ask him why he did such a thing. *Then I could explain,* thought Oliver. This man wasn't looking for an explanation; he believed that corporal punishment would keep his students in tow. He took away the slingshot.

"Put your hands in front of you, palms up," he said, and then proceeded to whack each hand ten times with a wide ruler.

The terrible stinging sensation made Oliver wince, but he didn't cry. The brother wasn't too happy with the outcome, so he repeated the performance until his misbehaved student cried in pain. Oliver had heard of children getting what was called "the rat hand" in public school, but he had no idea that it would be that painful. His hands stayed red and swollen most of the day.

❊   ❊   ❊

"Eva, did you ever get 'the rat hand' for a punishment in school?" Oliver showed his hands to his sister.

"You must have done something bad."

"I got back at a kid for shooting me with his slingshot. He didn't get caught, but I did!"

"Did you tell Mama?"

"Heck no! She would find an extra punishment for me."

"The nuns and brothers won't want to see another Janvier in their classes. You just might be spoiling it for the rest of us. Sister Pauline told my sister that you gave her a hard time in her class. She just might expect the same from the rest of us Janviers."

"For some reason, I'm always the one to be blamed for disruptions in class. Though I think that I've given the good nuns some things to think about," Oliver spoke with a haughty attitude.

"Hey brother, take that chip off your shoulder. You're no authority."

"Well, when you do a lot of reading, it makes you think and wonder more about other people, other beliefs, other ways of living. Don't you ever think about things like that?"

"I probably will, after hearing you. Did you ever see the picture of the statue called, The Thinker? It was sculpted by a French guy named Rodin. That's how I picture you, just sitting there, thinking, looking lonely. Maybe you should plan on what you will do with your life and be a *doer* . . . besides a thinker."

"Hey sister, you're the one I depend on to talk things out with . . . don't turn against me!"

"Oh, Oliver, you know I wouldn't do that; you're my special brother, but I wish you wouldn't make things difficult for our teachers."

24

At recess time, several days later, a few of the boys showed Oliver their squirt guns.

"They sell them at the corner store for only two cents," the kids told him.

Oliver decided that two cents wouldn't break his bank, so he bought one. The very next day several more boys, plus Oliver, had their guns filled with water, ready for battle. They separated into two fighting battalions. They named one group, "The Angels," the other group, "The Devils." If a person became wet from being targeted, he was "dead," and could no longer fight. At the end of the game, Oliver, one of "The Devils, was the only "live" fighter left.

"Give me that gun! So all this was *your* idea, Oliver Janvier?"

"Oh no, Brother Pierre. Please believe me. Almost all the boys took part in the game."

"If they did, then why are so many boys wet and *you*, the only one with a squirt gun, *are dry*?"

"Here Sir, take my gun and collect the guns from the others; that should prove that they were in on it."

"Line up, boys," the brother announced.

The boys did as they were told, and lined up against the school building near the rubbish barrel.

"Boys, turn your pockets inside out, and give me what you have in them."

Oliver couldn't believe his eyes; not one gun turned up!

"Now what do you have to say for yourself?" Brother Pierre asked, as he took Oliver by the ear and led him to the building.

"Brother, can we look into that barrel for the guns. I know that they had them."

For once Oliver wasn't the only condemned culprit; the evidence had been discarded into the receptacle.

Each boy was given extra homework which included a hundred word essay on why he should follow school rules. Not one boy got "the rat hand."

At a time when the class was supposed to be reading silently in their French grammar books, Oliver's mind was elsewhere, thinking about what he might write for the essay.

"Oliver," called Brother Pierre.

Awakened out of his thoughts, Oliver answered, "W-What . . . I'm not doing anything!"

"That's the trouble." Brother Pierre shook his head in frustration over his defiant student not following directions.

"You may add another fifty words to that essay," each word enunciated and pounced upon by Brother Pierre.

* * *

Oliver was promoted to the seventh grade into Brother Paul's class. The new instructor was a blond, blue-eyed, robust man who would have made a formidable football player. Just his size alone should have been enough to keep the most pesky kid in tow.

"Tomorrow afternoon, you boys will file in double lines and walk to the church where Father Devon will hear your confessions. Prepare yourselves well. Think about how you have offended God, and be prepared to tell the priest how many times you have sinned. After confession, you will kneel at the altar, say your penance with sincerity, then you will be dismissed.

"Remember, we have a holy day coming up, and you will be unfit to receive the blessed sacrament if you don't make a *good* confession. I will be there to make sure that all you boys perform your duty to your maker."

"Oliver, what are you going to tell the priest tomorrow?" asked Oliver's friend, Gerald.

"I don't know, Jerry. I don't know what I've done that's wrong."

Jerry said, "I disobeyed my mother a few times, but I didn't keep track of how many. Do you suppose that we should keep a sin notebook so that we'd know the exact numbers?"

"Gee Jerry, that's a big problem, but I would think God would know the exact number and if we don't remember I don't think he'll write up a big punishment in his 'big black book.'"

"Then you don't think we should worry about it?"

"I'm not going to . . . a couple of times, I lied to my mother. It was just a little white lie. Do you think that's a sin?" Oliver worried a tiny bit about that one.

"Gosh, I don't know, Oliver; it seems that just about every time we turn around, we're sinning. I'd be scared to go to hell, but I think God would be fairer than our teachers. They seem to be really afraid."

26

"Yeah, doesn't it make you wonder what *they've* done?" asked Oliver.

"You mean that teachers go to confession . . . wow . . . they seem so perfect!"

"I know some kids who make up sins to tell the priest, just so they'll have something to say."

"If only we knew that the hell business is for real. I believe in doing what is right whether there's a hell or not, but if we knew, we could relax and enjoy life on this earth without getting uptight each time we make a little mistake. If someone could come back and say, 'hey kids, watch your step, it's for real,' then we would know for sure."

In Oliver's scrapbook, he found these words: "Sin makes its own hell, and goodness its own heaven," written by *Mary Baker Eddy.*

*   *   *

On November first, All Souls' Day, a holy day of obligation, all the children in every class took on the appearances of holy angels, with praying hands held together in saintly form, in perfect rows, approaching the altar to receive the Holy Eucharist.

"The children are so well-trained. What a satisfying procession," whispered the teachers among themselves.

Each Sunday, students of St. Anne's school met in the schoolyard at seven-thirty in the morning to walk in silent procession to the church for eight o'clock Mass.

It was seven-fifteen on a blustery day when Oliver and his sister Eva were walking down Haverhill Street dressed in their Sunday best clothes to attend the eight o'clock Mass. The wind took Eva's hat, whirling it into the muddy street into the path of the milkman's wagon. The two children could see that to retrieve the hat would be useless.

"What can I do?" cried Eva. "I won't be able to go to church!"

"Just don't worry about that. Maybe your nun won't notice . . . anyhow, God still loves you whether you wear a hat or not."

"But it's a church law! Girls and women all must wear hats or you don't go into church!"

"I wonder why the rules are different for us boys and men. They seem to think that it would be insulting to God if we wore hats!"

Before entering the church, Sister Pauline pulled Eva out of the line and asked, in her most pedantic manner, "Young lady where is your hat?"

After hearing Eva's explanation, the nun dug deeply into her skirt pocket and out came a large handkerchief which she placed on Eva's head and prompted her to take her place in the usual row with her classmates. This gave Eva about the most awkward feeling . . . having to walk down the aisle alone and find her place . . . and besides, having to put up with hearing a few snickers. *If only the floor would open up and swallow me,* she thought.

*   *   *

On one particular Sunday, Father Lucien's sermon had Oliver's full attention.

Translated: "Someone told me that he hated his father. I will tell you what hate does, not only to the soul, but to the body of the one who hates. Hate does not hurt the person who is hated, but it hurts the person who hates. It sends poisons through the hater's body and causes him to become ill. We pray 'forgive us Lord, the way we forgive others.' How can we expect forgiveness if we ourselves cannot forgive? The message today is for a healthy soul and body, love everyone and forgive those who have hurt you ."

*   *   *

"Are you lost in thought, Oliver?" Eva asked as they walked toward home after Mass.

"Huh?" he was awakened from his reflections.

"What's weighing on your mind?"

"It's Father Lucien's sermon. I felt as if he was speaking just to me. Did you ever feel that you hated Papa for leaving us?"

"Hate is a pretty strong word, though I have felt some resentment toward him, I guess. It's hard to deny how we feel."

"How can we work on forgiving him? My heart feels heavy when I think of what he did. Could it possibly make me sick, as the priest says?"

"Maybe we should just pray that God will help us find forgiveness. I can't think of any other way. I wonder if Mama holds any resentment in *her* heart."

"She wouldn't tell us if she did . . . who knows, maybe she was affected by that sermon, too."

Not another thought was expressed by the two siblings. They each walked in silence . . . both lost in thought. *Maybe I could speak to my new eighth grade teacher, Brother Emile,* reasoned Oliver.

When Oliver reached home, he took out his "wisdom" scrapbook and read: "Folks never understand the folks they hate," *by James Russell Lowell.*

Maybe when I get older, I'll understand Papa better, he reflected.

✻ ✻ ✻

Oliver was torn between getting a job in a mill, or continuing his education. He consoled himself with the thought that in one more year he would be on his own . . . out in the world. He pondered the necessity of his taking chances in life. If I look for a new way to live, I might discover that there are things worth taking risks for. Oliver lived in hopes and dreams of finding something, or some place that would be worth searching for.

Brother Emile counseled him on the importance of remaining in school. Here is a teacher who *isn't* anxious to get rid of me. I'll probably like his class. He seems older and more fatherly. I'll stay.

Oliver looked on his new teacher as a mentor, someone who was kind, yet demanding of the students in their studies. Once in a while, the good brother would sneak in little lessons which were not in the text books.

"When you blame and point a finger at someone, there are three fingers pointing back at you."

"Brother Emile, you might say that I've been pointing a finger at my father and blaming him, and actually hating him for leaving our family. Can you show me the way to forgiveness?"

"Well Oliver, when someone has wronged you, it *is* difficult to look kindly upon that person. I can understand how unhappy this has made you. Life is full of tests and hurdles, and as we go through these sad experiences and accept them as *obstacles to overcome*, we're on the road to becoming better persons. You might call it, going through the school of hard knocks. Be kind to everyone; you don't know what hardships they have experienced."

After this quiet talk with his teacher, Oliver felt a certain amount of peace, and was more determined to study hard to please this fatherly man.

Geography and History lessons held Oliver's attention more than

29

other subjects. As he studied the maps, he became amazed at the vastness of the United States . . . places yet unexplored. When I grow up, I'll go to these places, he promised himself. But he would still complete the school year, and learn many lessons from his favorite teacher. During his last school year, Oliver made every effort to further any talents he might possess. He wanted so much to take part in the annual talent show, so he bought himself a ukelele. Every spare moment was spent in learning chord positions and songs from a Stephen Foster album.

Oliver's performance of "Old Folks At Home," "Ring, Ring The Banjo," and two French songs, that beckoned the audience to sing along, received a rousing response.

Brother Emile's encouraging words, "I knew you had it in you, Oliver," couldn't have pleased the boy more. *Maybe I could be a performer*, he mused. After the talent show, he entertained all kinds of dreams of artistic achievements.

Achieve, he did. His mother was both surprised and elated with his impressive report card. Oliver must be growing up. There were no marks against behavior.

After graduating from St. Anne's school, Oliver pondered, now is the time to "pack up my troubles in an oaken bag and smile, smile, smile." According to the old song, he felt that he would have a lot to smile about, being on his own. His optimism was not contagious as far as his mother was concerned.

Six

"Mais, mon fils, tu' n'as pas encore seize ans!" ("But my son, you are not yet sixteen years old.")

Oliver's mother had been in America since her marriage, but had never mastered the English language. She presented herself with dignity in countenance and mannerisms. Her tall willowly stature, classical roman features and red hair lent a picture of a graceful, confident person. She hid well her true feelings of inferiority, which her English speaking customers never detected. However, they did find it necessary to develop a certain sign language to help her understand just how they wanted their custom-made clothes styled.

Azilda had learned so few English words, which made it possible for Oliver to get away with the use of some naughty words he had learned from unprincipled kids living in the neighborhood, words that would not have been tolerated by his mother if she had known the meaning of them. Brother Emile had straightened him out on that count.

Oliver was leaving home to extend the orbit of his experiences. He frequently mulled over the prospects of remaining in this old mill town of Lawrence, Massachusetts. Where do I fit in here? he asked himself. He was convinced that there was something better for him elsewhere, but he didn't know what or where. He daydreamed about going west and staking his claim on acres upon acres of land, where he could raise thoroughbred horses and ride the plains. This dream felt so real and foreseeable that he actually believed it would happen some day.

※　　※　　※

It was five years since Isaiah had left, and Azilda at last learned of his whereabouts through sad circumstances which she didn't immediately reveal to her children. A divorce decree was mailed to her from Providence, Rhode Island. The document came to Azilda as something unexpected, something unheard of for such a devout Catholic. It pained her and she felt such shame that she held this information to her aching

31

heart, revealing it only in later years when she felt that it was only fair for her children to know the whereabouts of their father.

Joseph was five years old at the time that Oliver was leaving, but he was just a babe in arms when Isaiah absconded from all responsibility of family life and moved to Rhode Island. Azilda supported her family by sewing dresses for women who could afford her meager fees. The old treadle machine could be heard throughout the night, into the wee hours of the morning.

Oliver was a precocious child, but of an independent nature. He felt that there was so much more to be learned out in the world, rather than what the nuns or the brothers had to offer at St. Anne's School, Brother Emile being the exception. The fifteen-year-old Oliver was seeking adventure.

*   *   *

Before his departure in June of 1901, Oliver cautioned his siblings not to make trouble for "poor Mama." He felt compunction for one of his dishonest pranks, the time when old Mr. Goldberg, with his horse and wagon, was on his regular route yelling, "*Old rags and bottles. Old rags and bottles.*" (He earned his living by buying old rags and bottles, and reselling the rags to paper mills and rug makers at a profit, an early form of recycling.) Young uncouth pranksters would steal a bag from the back of Mr. Goldberg's wagon while a customer was being tended to, then the little imps would sell the ragman his own product. Oliver was one of them. A difficult lesson was learned when a policeman spotted Oliver pulling the bag off of Mr. Goldberg's wagon. The other boys quickly disappeared, evading punishment. Officer Lamond, instead of bringing the young "French kid" to the station, brought him home where Azilda doled out the punishment: Ten whacks on his bare behind with a Sears Roebuck yardstick, which snapped in half in the process.

Oliver's smarting rump didn't hurt as much as his aching heart. He lamented the fact that his sweet mother had done this to him, and wondered if, at times, he might have warranted more. But, it did make him realize that responsibilities for ill deeds must be met. He was grown up now and beyond those days of impish pursuits.

Seven

Oliver packed his few belongings in an old worn valise, arose at four-thirty the next day, ate his breakfast hurriedly, kissed his sad mother good-bye, and left their May Street family home with a feeling of liberation, and a bit of apprehension. What does the future hold for me? he reflected as he wended his way to the South Station, across Central Bridge.

The six-o'clock train was on schedule. He seated himself in the first car, in back of the engine, and wondered why most people opted for the cars furthest from the engine. They were well on their way when he realized that his clean clothes were becoming sooty. *So, that's why,* he thought. Oliver was able to find his way to a rear car, and as he settled in for the hour's ride to Boston he recalled riding this very train with his mother when he was only seven years old. But, they were on a very different mission then, a most painful one.

As a small child, Oliver had been susceptible to sore throats. His mother was taking him to Dr. Talbin to have his tonsils removed, a torturous experience Oliver would never forget.

"Open wide, young man," said the doctor, as he proceeded to swab Oliver's throat with a burning, foul-tasting substance. Oliver refused to open his mouth the second time after seeing the tong-like tool the doctor had in his hands. The nurse and his mother had to hold Oliver as he fought for his life. They finally subdued him enough for the tool to reach his tonsils and rip them out. Oliver was sure that he was dying as his convulsive vomiting cleared most of the blood from his throat. Two hours later Oliver and Mama were riding the "agony" train back to Lawrence.

This morning, the B & M railroad train arrived at Boston's North Station at 7:15, Oliver had a long wait at the South Station for the nine-forty-five train to New York. With so much time to spare, he decided to take a small tour of the big city known as "The Hub of the Universe," Boston. First he bought his ticket to New York City, stowed his luggage in a locker, then ventured to the famous Quincy Market, ate a few treats, took a look at the outside of Paul Revere's birthplace, and read the

33

plaque. He felt disappointed that the historic home wasn't open until later in the day . . . he couldn't miss his train.

Oliver headed back to South Station, picked up his luggage, bought a newspaper and a candy bar before boarding the train to his destination. Once seated, he opened the newspaper and read: "THOMAS EDISON RECEIVES THREATENING LETTER"; then the news article went on to tell about the contents of the letter. The potential kidnapper said that he would "steal" Edison's daughter, Madeline, if Edison didn't leave a certain amount of money in a designated place. Oliver wondered if Madeline was ever stolen.

He also read about the treaty regarding the construction of a canal in Panama, "to be built under the supervision of the United States," and another story about someone by the name of Marconi who transmitted telegraphic messages from England to Newfoundland.

Oliver found the newspaper advertisements entertaining and sometimes humorous:

DON'T MARRY FOR MONEY!
The Boston man, who lately married a sickly rich young
woman, is happy now, for he got DR. KING'S NEW LIFE
PILLS which restored her to perfect health.

LYDIA E. PINKHAMS VEGETABLE
COMPOUND
The great woman's remedy for woman's ills.
CASTORIA
Harmless substitute for Castor Oil.

Oliver was determined that he would always carry his "book of wisdom" no matter where he would go. On the subject of travel, he read: "There are three wants which never can be satisfied: that of the rich, who wants something more; that of the sick, who wants something different; and that of the traveler, who says, 'Anywhere but here.'" *(by Emerson.)*

Emerson sure did have a window into human nature . . . I guess I've said "Anywhere but here," . . . so, I left my home town, looking for what? reflected Oliver.

Enough of that, he thought, folding the newspaper, and replacing his scrapbook into his baggage. Then he took out the clipping he had put into his pants pocket; he had cut it out of the *Lawrence Tribune* a few days before his departure. It read: WANTED: STRONG YOUNG MEN

TO WORK ON LAKE ERIE SHIPPING DOCKS, BUFFALO, N.Y.
SIGN IN AT DOCK #6 WHERE YOU WILL FIND MISTER JAKE
RONAN AT THE FOREMAN SHACK. YOU WILL BE HELPED IN
SECURING LODGING."

*   *   *

The longest part of the journey was ahead for Oliver. From the
Boston South Station to New York's Penn Station would take nine hours.
At noon time, he ate the lunch that his mother insisted he take with him,
walked the aisles, then sat and read the *Boston Globe* again. Oliver was
an avid reader of newspapers, and he still took a keen interest in current
events. At five o'clock, he went to the dining car and had an adequate
meal for the price of forty-five cents. It was there that he met Dominick
Abati. The two rather lonely boys struck up a conversation. Each was
happy at the prospect of companionship during the rest of the trip.

"Where are you going, Oliver?"

Oliver showed Dom the newspaper clipping that had inspired him to
leave home.

"Wow, that's the same ad that was in the *Haverhill Gazette* a couple
of weeks ago! That's where I'm headed for."

"You mean that you're from Haverhill?"

"Yeah, my family lives on High Street. I'll be staying with an uncle
and aunt on Columbia Street in Buffalo."

"You're luckier than I am. I don't know anyone there and I don't
have a place to stay either."

From Penn Station, with a slight wait over, the two new buddies took
the 8 P.M. train to Buffalo. By the time they arrived at the Buffalo Station
it was far too late to see Mr. Ronan. Dom was able to reach his uncle by
phone and "Uncle Nicky" told him that he should take the trolley to the
corner of Market and Scott Streets where Nicky would wait for him with
his horse and buggy.

"I'm going to stay at the station for the night. I'll see you at dock six
in the morning, Dom."

"Oliver, you ain't gonna sleep on a bench if I can help it! Hey, you'll
like Uncle Nicky and Aunt Molly. I'm sure they'll have an extra couch you
could bunk down on."

Uncle Nicky and Aunt Molly were particularly warm and cordial.
They had immigrated from Italy in 1887. After enduring many hardships,

35

they never failed to help others. They furnished a blanket and pillow for Oliver, who rested his exhausted body on their den couch. Morning came much too quickly for both boys. After a hearty Italian breakfast of eggs, spicy sausages, toast and coffee, Uncle Nicky took them in his horse-drawn buggy down to Dock #6.

They were each assigned to a different stevedore who was to teach each boy "the ropes."

Oliver stayed in the Foreman's shack while Jake phoned a Mrs. Kelleher about the one room she had said that she would be willing to rent.

"Ya still 'av that room for a young lad, Lizzie?"

"It depends, Jake. What's 'is name?"

"Oliver Janvier."

"What kinda name is that? He ain't Irish!"

"It's a French name, Lizzie!"

"French! I ain't aboot taking in no frog. Ya know I 'av me fourteen-year-old gal, me Meghan, and me five-year-old Tommy. No, Jake, I'll take in a nice Irish lad, but no frog!"

"Lizzie, you know ya need the money since Pat died, and this here young un seems like such a fine lad. I'd take im in me self if I 'ad room."

"Well, send 'im over and I'll judge fer me self."

Jake wrote down the directions to Mrs. Kelleher's house: "Go up Michigan, cross the bridge, take the second right, then take a left to East Mark Street, number 30."

It was, by no means, a short distance from the docks, but Oliver found his way. Most of it looked familiar . . . just one street away from where Dom was to live. The houses on East Mark Street were basically the same: Brown shakes on the second stories, and beige clapboard below, the foundations were of red brick, very usual structures for laborers' abodes. However, number 30 had a more attractive appearance; spring blossoms, below the rather large front porch, added the personal touch that showed someone really cared.

Oliver used the door knocker, which was answered rather quickly by a portly woman in her forties. Mrs. Kelleher led Oliver into her parlor, where she proceeded to interrogate him. His answers seemed to satisfy her. She then led him to his prospective room, while firmly admonishing him about the many rules for her boarders; she had just one other boarder, Tim Cronin, her nephew. Most of the rules, she had thought up just since Jake's call.

"There's to be no cussin'. Ya must clean the tub after usin' it. Don't leave no clothes hanging around. Make ya bed every morning. Breakfast is at five-thirty ... ya late, too bad for you. Ya make ya own lunch the night before. Ya better buy ya self a lunch pail.

"When ya git home after work, hang ya key on the rack by the door. Dinner is at six forty-five, an ya help Tim Cronin clear the table after the meal. Me Meghan will take it from there. If ya goin' out after dinner, ya better be in by ten. And mind ya lad, no makin' eyes at my Meghan!"

All Oliver could say was, "Yes ma'am."

They went up the narrow stairway to his room. The small bedroom was neat. Across the room from the doorway was one single bed covered with a colorful quilt. An old chiffonier stood next to the door, an old rocking chair beside it. A small chair before a writing table had been placed in front of the only window. A cool breeze was blowing the lace curtain. The room seemed impeccably clean and airy. *Mama would approve*, thought Oliver. He left his valise on the floor to be unpacked later, and headed back to the dock with a few misgivings about all the rules of his new domicile. Jake was relieved to hear that Lizzie had accepted his new employee.

Oliver had read as much information as he could find about Buffalo, before he had set out on this adventure. He had learned that Buffalo was "The Queen City of the Great Lakes," and the second largest city of New York. It was considered an international port, handling large quantities of coal and grain.

Oliver was introduced to Stan Lefkowitz, his trainer on the dock. His first day of lifting the heavy burlap bags of grain left him exhausted. Oliver was quite muscular for his age, having lifted weights with his brother Frank, who aspired to be a wrestler; the two boys would often spar with each other, though their mother viewed this "fighting" with disfavor. The workouts strengthened both boys, but Oliver found that handling the large grain bags for so many hours, was a strain on his whole being.

"You'll toughen up to this job," Stan reassured his neophyte.

"Each day, you'll become more and more used to the work and your body will adjust."

Maybe I'll look for other work, thought Oliver. The quitting horn sounded at six o'clock, which was not too soon for the new long-shoremen. As the two buddies, Dom and Oliver, hoofed it home, they compared aches and pains.

"What do you think, Dom? You gonna stick it out?"

"Maybe we'll get used to it, Oliver; it ain't the fun I thought it would be." The boys parted at the corner of East Mark Street, each hurrying home, looking forward to his prospective dinner.

The fare of the evening was Irish stew with Treacle bread, and as Oliver entered the house, the fragrance of the meal made him forget his weariness. He quickly made his way upstairs to wash before dinner. The seating arrangement at the oblong table was to be constant, all were told. Mrs. Kelleher, with little Tommy to her left, Meghan sat at the other end of the table, next to Tim Cronin, and Oliver's place at the table was to the right of Mrs. Kelleher, where she could keep an eye on him and observe his manners. The mistress of the house announced that it was their custom to say "grace" before each meal.

"Bless us, Oh Lord, and these thy gifts which we are about to receive from thy bounty, through Christ our Lord, Amen."

They must be Catholic too, thought Oliver. (In Oliver's home, the same grace was recited in French.)

Conversation seemed somewhat strained . . . *It's all in getting to be more acquainted,* thought Oliver. The hearty repast was most satisfying. Homemade rhubarb tarts topped it all off. Oliver did his part in clearing the table and left to sit on the porch. It was a balmy evening and so relaxing to just sit and enjoy the scent of honeysuckle which climbed the porch post. Little Tommy came out and sat on the top step.

"I have a little five-year-old brother at home. His name is Joey."

"If I had a big brother, I wouldn't like it if he left home! Why did you leave?" Tommy asked.

"Well, would you like to be one of three boys, all sleeping in one bedroom? I also have two sisters . . . the house was too crowded."

Tommy thought about that . . .

"Well, I guess one sister is plenty for me. Meghan bosses me a lot."

"Yeah, girls can be like that. Look Tommy, see that little humming bird at those red flowers? He flies to Mexico when the weather gets colder."

"How does he know his way?"

"Well, you just keep watching his wings, and if they slow down a little, maybe you'll see a little compass under there."

Meg had been eavesdropping from the screen door.

"You shouldn't tell my little brother such lies, Oliver! Those ruby throat humming birds have their own built-in system to help them find

38

their way as far as two thousand miles . . . That's without a compass, Oliver."

"Oh, I was just teasing him . . . and how do you know all that, any-how?"

"I can read, Oliver!"

"I guess that I read different things than you do. I read newspapers and know what's going on in the world."

"Well good for you. La de dah," was Meg's sarcastic reply as she slammed the screen door behind her. *She doesn't seem to like me much*, thought Oliver . . . she sure is kinda cute, though.

"You'd better come in and get ready for bed, Tommy," Meg called from the door.

"See, what did I tell ya . . . See how she bosses me? Gees!"

After Tommy left, Tim Cronin came out onto the porch.

"How was your first day out on the dock?" he asked Oliver.

"Long and tiresome, but I'll toughen up to it. What kind of a work do you do?"

"I'm an apprentice typesetter at the Roy Croft Company in East Aurora. It's a commune for craftsmen that was founded by Elbert Hub-bard."

"Oh, I have a few good quotes attributed to him in my scrapbook. He was a very wise man."

"He certainly did a lot for people wanting to learn a trade. Some day, I want to work for a newspaper publishing firm."

"Is it very far from here?"

"Nah, I could stay at their rooming houses near the plant, but I pre-fer to stay with Aunt Lizzie. I take the trolley to East Aurora each week day. It's like a school and you can be a student of most any trade, and get a small pay while you learn."

"I'll have to look into that in case things don't work out at the dock."

"Yeah, but that might be sooner than you think . . . have you ever thought about the winter snowstorms we have here? You'd have to get another job, Oliver; the docks close down!"

"How do the flour mills keep going?"

"They keep their silos pretty much filled up . . . and then there's the other means of transportation . . . the railroad."

"Oh, I see what you mean! Do they teach blacksmithing at the Roy Croft place? My father is a blacksmith, and when I was a little kid, I used to work the bellows for him . . . that was before he moved away."

Oliver contemplated his own last remark with a saddened facial expression; he was only ten years old when his father moved to Providence, Rhode Island, and he could never fathom out why his father could leave the family . . . Joey was just a few months old. It put a damper on the life of every family member.

"Sure, they have training for blacksmiths. Want me to get information for you?"

"Thanks, that would be helpful. Tell me what typesetting is like. What purpose does it serve, other than for newspaper work?"

"We set up print for school books. There are new methods for even printing pictures; we're learning to use phototypesetting machines. I want to learn all the newest methods. It's a far cry from the ancient times, when documents were written by hand on papyrus sheets. This work fascinates me and the methods are always improving."

*   *   *

The sun was setting and the air outside had cooled. Both boys went back into the house and Oliver prepared his lunch for the following day, and readied for bed early.

He read just one quote by Grover Cleveland, "Honor lies in honest toil."

Toil I must, he pondered. *Going to school was a lot easier...I made a choice, and like it was once told, "once you make your bed, you lie in it."*

But this isn't exactly my permanent bed. He lay down and worked on the dock all night long in his dreams.

Morning came all too soon again. Getting up before dawn became a regular routine, and routine was something that didn't set too well with Oliver . . . the free soul. But, he rationalized that it was too soon to move on. He needed to save some money, even send a little to his mother to help out. He wrote letters home and got news from his family. Frank, who was four years younger than Oliver and still attending St. Anne's school, wrote short little schoolboy notes. Sometimes, his sisters Eva and Blanche wrote. Eva was just one year younger than Oliver; Blanche, three years younger; and Joey, the baby, was ten years his junior.

Oliver's first letter home gave an account of his trip to Buffalo, meeting Dom Abati, being hired by Jake Ronan, and about the family he lived with; he enclosed two dollars. His family, reading between the lines,

40

detected a note of unrest and agreed, "He'll be on the move again; that's our Oliver . . . itchy feet." Three weeks later, a letter arrived for Oliver:

Dear Brother,

Your letter made Mama happy. Mrs. Boulet gave us her old piano, and Mama says that I can have lessons with Sister Marie; she charges twenty-five cents a lesson. Mama says your two dollars will help, and she sends beaucoup de mercis, et elle envoye ses amities.

Have you tried the new cold cereal called Shredded Wheat? On the package, it says that the inventor of the stuff is named Henry Perky, and he opened a bakery at Niagara Falls, not too far from where you are. Mama thinks it's healthy stuff. It really isn't all that bad.

Blanche says that her school teacher, Sister Mary Louise, told the class that anyone who steals will go to hell; she's scared for you, Oliver, because you stole a rag bag from Mr. Goldberg . . . Blanche says that she'll join the convent to pray for your soul. She has a long wait 'til she's grown up enough. I hope your soul is safe! I'm teaching the 'tsi boy his letters; he'll go to school next year, maybe he'll have an easier time than we had if he knows his letters before then. Frank wants to write to you.

We miss you,
Eva

Oliver,

I'm still working out with the dumbbells . . . I can feel myself getting stronger. I miss our wrestling together. The kid next door tried wrestling with me . . . but he's a weakling. Some day, I am going to be a famous wrestler!!

Wish you'd come home,
Frank

Eight

It was late June, 1901, and Oliver was sorry to have missed so many of the events at the Pan American Exposition which was being held in Buffalo. He wanted to hear the Phillip Sousa Band, which appeared in the Temple of Music on June third, through the eighth. He was determined to mark his calendar so as not to miss hearing the Brooke's Marine Band which was performing September second through the fifteenth. There were many more "best known bands" of the Western world. There were even seventy-three organists hired for recitals in the Temple of Music.

Oliver had heard about the main attraction: the 375-foot electric tower, called "the goddess of light" which was set on top of the tower. Oliver felt that he just had to get there; after all, his home state, Massachusetts, had appropriated $15,000, its share with other New England states, for the erection of a building, displaying their resources and industries. He often read about the midway concessions advertising "Village Glass Factory, Trip to the moon, Beautiful Orient, Colorado's Gold Mine, Moving pictures, Water sports, Miniature Railway," and many more things of interest. *What an opportune time to be in Buffalo!* thought Oliver.

The months of July and August were humid and uncomfortable on the docks; more heavy loads of grain to haul from the ship to wagons, headed for the nearby flour mill. Oliver decided to look into a job at the flour mill, since in another couple of months, the inevitable blizzards of Buffalo would be upon them. He gave Mr. Ronan his notice, and was to begin his new work at the mill in mid September.

"You're a good worker, Oliver. I'm counting on you to come back to the docks next spring."

"Gee, Mr. Ronan, I really can't promise you that I'll return. I appreciate your offer, and thank you for the letter of recommendation to my new boss at the flour mill."

On September 5, after reading about William McKinley's impressive speech, which he had given at the Pan American Exposition in Delaware Park, Oliver and his friend, Dom Abati, made plans to take a trolley to the exposition the next day, September 6, 1901. They didn't want to miss seeing President McKinley, who was to have a public reception at the Temple of Music building.

The lines of well-wishers were long, but Dom and Oliver finally shook the President's hand. Afterwards, they stood on the sidelines watching, and thinking that it was a proud day, one they could tell their grandchildren about. *They shook hands with the President of the United States of America!* While they reveled in their excited thoughts, little did they realize that they would have much more to tell their grandchildren. A gunshot startled them out of their euphoric mood. President McKinley fell to the floor. Mayhem broke out; the perpetrator was quickly apprehended, and the crowd was immediately dispersed by security guards.

The next day, they learned that someone by the name of Leon Czolgosz had been in line with a concealed weapon and offered no excuse for his criminal deed. Dom and Oliver were shaken by this turn of events. Neither was old enough to vote, but they both agreed that if they had been, William McKinley was their man. Oliver kept abreast of the news, and learned that Theodore Roosevelt, McKinley's Vice President, was told that the President would survive. So the avid outdoorsman went to his camp in the Adirondack Mountains where he and a few cohorts climbed Mount Tahawus. A guide caught up to them with the news that the President had taken a turn for the worse and wasn't expected to live.

Roosevelt had to hike ten miles to the nearest road, then rode by horse and buggy for forty more miles. At five-thirty in the morning, a special train was waiting at the station to rush Roosevelt to Buffalo. He took the oath of office at a friend's home. It was said that his life was filled with typically dramatic events; this was one of the biggest dramas he was yet to experience. Roosevelt was in time to witness McKinley's last words: *"It is God's way. His will, not ours, be done."*

"Life goes on for the living," lamented Oliver after reading of McKinley's death. The guy with the "itchy feet" felt that there was nothing dramatic occurring in his life; he yearned for more adventure. *I need to save some money before moving on,* he told himself. *I'll have to keep my appointment with Mr. Van Dreel at the flour mill.*

The foreman of one section of the flour mill, Henrik Van Dreel, explained a little about flour milling to Oliver. Oliver had no idea that the processes could be so involved and extensive. He listened attentively as his new boss explained things.

"These here machines remove foreign materials. When the grain is cleaned, it is tempered by adding up to as much as eight percent of water; it rests in these bins up to twenty-four hours. To remove the germ, it's put through the degerminator machines. These steel cylinders grind the wetted grain, which removes the bran. These large boxes, here, rotate at high speeds to sift the ground grain . . . and that's about all I can tell you about the processes in my department. Your job, for the present, will be to work at the machines that clean the grain. Keep your eyes peeled, and be extremely careful; we don't want any accidents here."

Oliver found that he still had to handle many heavy bags of grain; the only difference being, that he had to empty the bags into the cleaning machines.

Oliver decided that a celebration for getting a new job was in order, and on his way home from his first day at the flour mill, he bought a quart of ice cream; thirty cents was a lot of money to him, but he wanted to share his joy with Mrs. Kelleher and family. After all, he would be getting a lot higher salary than he got on the dock . . . a dollar and twenty-five cents more a week!

Mrs. Kelleher appreciated Oliver's ice cream dessert, and immediately placed it near the block of ice in the ice chest. She looked forward to the day when she could afford one of those new electric frigidaires. It certainly would alleviate the bother of the iceman tracking up her kitchen with the block of ice dripping from the man's leather-covered shoulder. She even feared that the ice might slip from those formidable looking tongs.

"We'll have to eat this up quickly; unfortunately, the ice cream won't stay solid for long," she lamented.

At the dinner table, conversation was flowing much better these days since all were more comfortable with each other.

"Gee, Oliver, I got you the information that you asked for at Roy Croft . . . you know, about blacksmithing . . . you changed your mind?" Tim asked, not hiding his disappointment.

"Yeah, I do want to learn blacksmithing some day, but they don't pay enough at Roy Croft. Later on, I just might look up my father in Providence, Rhode Island, to see if I could learn from him. I don't think they even have a blacksmith shop in Fredonia, the next town from here. Maybe after I learn the trade, I'll come back to New York to open up a shop." He glanced at Meghan as if to say, "Yeah, I'll be back . . . but for more than one reason."

Meghan brightened up as she sensed his unspoken words. Mrs.

Kelleher, who had become to regard Oliver as almost family, did not seem to disapprove of his "eying" her sweet daughter. As time went on, Oliver was allowed to take Meghan to the ice cream parlor, and to some Sunday afternoon band concerts in the park. Oliver didn't mind Meghan correcting his "Frenchy" accent; though he knew that Mama wouldn't like it if he lost all signs of his ethnic background.

Even his sister, Eva, was learning that there was another world outside of St. Anne's school . . . and the teaching of the "Sisters of the Good Shepherd," whose mother house was in Canada. In Eva's last letter she had said,

"I've been reading with the Sullivan kids who go to public school, and would you believe that the word "T-H-E" is not pronounced THUR!" Should I dare to correct the good sister, during English lessons? Also, the Sullivan's are learning about Sir Walter Raleigh . . . our nun made him Irish, "Sir Walter Riley! I asked Mama if we could go to public school, and all she could say was, "Mon Dieu!"

My piano lessons are getting more interesting since I've changed teachers. Sister Marie can't play any better than I can. It's funny how the sisters take just a few lessons on an instrument and then they think that they're qualified to teach! My new teacher plays so beautifully, I hope to learn a lot from her.

So, you changed jobs. After that, what's next? Are your little itchy piggies itching again? Write soon. We worry about you.

Eva

＊　　　＊　　　＊

1902, and Oliver had visited most of the towns surrounding Buffalo. It was the year that the United States acquired control of the Panama Canal, the year that a man named Bacon crossed the English Channel in a balloon, the year that Oliver turned sixteen and thought that he was man enough to kiss his girl, Meghan.

They had gone to the ice cream parlor for a soda. Sitting across from each other, their eyes locked and their hearts thumped as they sipped their drinks.

"Gosh Meghan, your eyes are so pretty!" Oliver had been told by other boys that if you want to kiss a girl, you should say lots of things that she would like to hear.

"Do you really think so, Oliver? I like blue eyes better, but I guess the brown eyes go better with my auburn hair."

"I think that big brown eyes are more expressive, and your hair is very pretty, too. My mother's hair is redder than yours, but she has hazel eyes like mine. None of us kids got the red hair."

"I thought that your eyes were green."

"Yeah, watch out for me . . . I'm the green-eyed monster . . . grr." Oliver raised his arms, clawed his fingers, and mimicked an evil creature.

"Oliver, you couldn't look ugly if you tried. You're pretty good looking you know."

Hmm, he thought, *this won't be as difficult as I thought; I don't think she'd turn me down for a little kiss.*

They finished their sodas and left the ice cream parlor hand-in-hand.

"Want to walk over to the park?" he gestured toward the tree-lined path that led to where there were children playing ball, women pushing baby carriages, men sitting on benches reading newspapers, and a maze of tall hedges that were fun to get lost in.

"How do we get out of here, Oliver?"

"Let's try this path here . . . oops, that's a dead end." They both laughed as they tried to figure out which path led to the exit of the maze.

"I've figured out how to get out of here," said Oliver with eyes that betrayed a bit of mischief. Then in a slow mysterious voice, he said, "It's a magic formula . . . we hold hands like this," taking both of her hands in his, "then we close our eyes, turn around three times, kiss . . . and there you have it."

"Have what? You clown . . . I'm not falling for your 'magic!'"

"Aw Meg, let's try it."

They were like five-year-olds, playing "ring around the rosy," turning in circles with eyes closed and laughing and laughing, then "smack," their very first kiss.

"Meg, can we kiss again . . . a little slower?"

"All right," she said shyly. They embraced and kissed more intensely.

"Hmm, now that's what I call magic, Meg, real magic."

"It was magic for me too, Oliver."

And there at the end of that path was the exit to the maze. The young couple walked through a wooded area, hid behind a tree and smooched some more.

"I'm telling Mama," bellowed Tommy, who had been playing ball in the park with friends.

"Where did you come from?"

"I was out in the ball field and saw you two go behind this tree."

"What should we do, Oliver, I've never kissed a boy before," Meg whispered.

"You're the first girl that I've ever kissed . . . and wow, I want to do it again!"

"If Tommy tells on us, my mother will be angry and she won't let us go anywhere together!"

"Tommy, come here," called Oliver. "Now why would you want to be a tattle-tale? There's no harm in a little kiss."

"I'll tell Mama that was a humunguous smacker . . . boy, Meg, are you in trouble."

"Tommy, are you trying to bribe us into paying you to keep your mouth shut?"

"Hey, that's a pretty good idea. What's it worth to you?"

"How about a dime?" asked Oliver.

"A quarter, and Meg has to promise me that she will never boss me around again."

They shook hands on that hard bargain, but wondered if his keeping a secret was worth the subsequent problems.

Meghan had helped her mother with the dinner that evening while Oliver and Tommy played ball outside.

"Meghan, call Oliver and your brother in for dinner," said Mrs. Kelleher.

Oh oh, thought Meghan, *Tommy will think I'm bossing him*. She opened the screen door and announced, 'Would anybody out here like dinner, which is on the table now?"

Oliver understood the reason for her posing a question instead of a command phrase such as, "Come in for dinner, Tommy."

During the meal, the urge for the couple to tell Tommy to wipe the silly grin off his face, had to be suppressed. Tommy had the upper hand.

When it was time to tell her brother that he should get ready for bed, Meghan didn't want to do it.

"Mom, now that Tommy is getting a little older, I don't want him to resent me for telling him what he should do. He can tell time now, and he knows when to come in."

"Ya know, Meghan, he won't be cummin' in less he's told to. You call 'em in now."

"Tommy," Meghan called, "it's seven-thirty."

"So what! Are you bossin' me?"

"Oh, I wouldn't do that, but I think that it is time for you to ready yourself for bed."

"I knew you wouldn't keep a bargain...*Mama*," he called, "Meghan kissed Oliver behind a tree in the park...I saw them with my own eyes."

"What's all this fussin' aboot out 'ere. What ya yellin' aboot, son?"

Meghan had Tommy by the shirt collar warning him to "shut up," but he ranted and yelled the news so loudly that neighbors could hear. Mama had a worried look on her face.

"I'll be talkin' with you two after this young un goes ta bed." She directed her remark toward Oliver and Meghan.

"Aw gees, I want to hear you bawl them out."

"That's enough, son, you get your hide up those stairs before I redden ya bottom."

"Tommy's oot of the way. Now, tell me wuts goin' on with the two of ya?"

"Ma, he just stretches things. We just had a little kiss. What's wrong with that?"

"Well, I'm not against a little show of affection, but that's to go no further. Do you understand?"

The young couple just nodded shyly, thinking that nothing more would be said. They weren't "bawled out," as Tommy had hoped.

"And Meghan, I want to see you in your room."

Oh oh, it's not over with. Oliver's and Meghan's thoughts were in congruence.

Mrs. Kelleher spoke softly to her daughter.

"Ya much too young to be involved with any boy. Such behavior could be the start of something ya cud be sorry fer later. Now, boys is different from girls. Girls get romantic ideas, and boys get other kinds of ideas. A strong girl can refuse advances; a weak girl can lead the boy to go much further. Now, I trust you to be strong, Meghan."

"I'll be strong, Mama, but I don't think that Oliver is that kind of boy."

"Ho ho, young lassie, all boys have one track minds. Believe me!"

Meghan's "Thank you for your trust, Mama," ended their one-sided discourse.

Oliver was anxious to let his sister know about his love interest.

Dear Eva,

I have a girlfriend named Meghan. Her mother, my landlady, is letting me take Meg walking in the park when there are band concerts Sunday afternoons. She must feel that there is safety in numbers . . . there are lots of music lovers strolling the grounds, some sitting on the grass, listening to the music.

Well, last Saturday, Meg and I went to the ice cream parlor, and after we finished our sodas, we went to the park, hid behind a tree and had our first kiss. Hmm nice, and I think she liked it too. Now, we have a problem. Her kid brother Tommy spotted us and now he's bribing us so that he won't tell their mom. Have you kissed a boy yet?

Meg wants to go to Normal School to be a teacher. She's practicing on me, helping me to get rid of double negatives and gradually getting rid of "thur *h*accents on thur wrong sy*lab*le." She's a good English teacher, but if I didn't like her so much, I just might resent all her corrections.

Don't tell Ma. Just give her a hug and say that I sent it with kisses.

Oliver

The next Saturday afternoon found Oliver and Meghan back at the ice cream parlor.

"I've decided that when we come out like this, I'll let you kiss me just once before we go home.

"We had a lot more than that last week; why the rationing?"

"Mama says it's safer that way."

"What's so unsafe about a few kisses?"

"Well, my mother knows more about boys than I do, and she explained that boys want to go further and further."

"Honestly, Meg, I wouldn't take advantage of you."

"That's what I told Mama, but she warned me . . . she said that *all* boys are the same."

Their smooching behind the tree amounted to more than one kiss, but Meghan was strong and reluctantly walked away from their hide-out. From then on, she proved herself to be the strong girl, worthy of her mother's trust. In spite of Oliver's frustrations, he had a great respect for Meghan.

Oliver wanted to "advance in the direction of his dreams," as in the quote of Henry David Thoreau: "If one advances confidently in the direction of his dreams, and endeavors to live the life which he has imagined, he will meet with success unexpected in common hours . . . If you have built castles in the air, your work need not be lost, that is where they should be. Now put the *foundations* under them."

Oliver wanted to find something that would offer him a new exciting career, something that would lay a foundation he could build on. He had been working at the flour mill for over a year, and could see that advancements with the company were not in view.

Oliver hadn't told Eva about his plan to move on. An answer to his last letter came two weeks before his new adventure.

Dear Oliver, the guy bitten by the love bug,

That bug stings with corrections and you put up with it?? I hope she's worth it. But dear brother, it might be worth it all. I'm getting a few corrections myself from the Sullivan kids. I'd still like to go to public school but Ma says no.

Did Tommy squeal on you, or are you paying him to keep quiet?

Maybe you should leave . . . you know, scratch your itchy feet. Take off for greener pastures . . . That's what you want, isn't it?

Little did Eva know . . . she was on the right track . . . how well she knew her brother!

Nine

"Go West, young man," was an intriguing invitation. He dreamed that living the life of a cowboy would be romantic, but where to go? He had read about the frontier of Montana and had saved an advertisement about Miles City, on the Montana ranges. It might take some traveling getting there, but the adventurous pursuit will be well worth it all, he reasoned.

Before making my travel arrangements, I'll talk to Meghan, so she'll understand that I have a need to find something I'm suited to. Also, I feel the need to get the roving addiction out of my blood, before settling down. I guess that's not putting "foundations" under my dream castles . . . but who knows what the future holds. Charles F. Kettering had said, "We should all be concerned about the future because we will have to spend the rest of our lives there."

The rest of my life in a flour mill . . . NO. The rest of my life on the docks . . . NO. The rest of my life as a cowboy?? Who knows?

Meghan couldn't hide her disappointment; she was heartbroken when she learned that Oliver was leaving, but as her mother pointed out, she was far too young to think of a serious relationship, and needed to pursue her ambition to be a school teacher. Study would get her mind off of Oliver. It never did, though, especially after his first letter from Miles City:

Dear Meg,
    You wouldn't believe how picturesque this place is! I'm in a different world. The horses here are a different breed than the ones my father owns, they are wiry animals called "Broncos." They run wild for two or three years before being trained. There are too many steps to explain about their training, but the final test is to saddle the critter and let him wear himself out trying to throw off the saddle. After a few days of this kind of training, a bitless bridle is slipped on the horse's head, a blindfold placed over his eyes, then the bronco buster gets into the saddle, and when the blindfold is removed, the bronco goes wild and tries to throw the buster.
    The horse I was given was trained two years ago, and I feel comfort-

51

able in the saddle. I still have training to go through, driving, roping, and handling cattle; I know that I can do it!

The cow hands are wonderful guys. We have a great time at night, sitting around the camp-fire telling stories and singing cowboy songs. I'm glad that I brought my trusty Ukelele with me.

The cooks aren't all that bad. Their chuck wagon rides ahead of the steer and cowboys, and when it's time for a meal we hear them yell, "Come and git it," and boy do we all move fast . . . we get as hungry as heck!

Please write soon, Meg, I really miss you and some day I'll settle down when I set up a blacksmithing shop in Fredonia. Be patient with me, Meg, I care about you a lot.   Oliver

Meghan's and Oliver's exchange of letters became more frequent. They learned a lot about each other and each felt: He's *the* one." "She's *the* one" Each living in the fantasy world of youth.

It wasn't often, but Meghan, in her pedantic way, corrected Oliver's grammar.

Oliver, I hope that you won't be offended by a little grammatic correction. In your last letter, you mentioned you had met a new friend and you said, "Rusty gave the ropes to Ed and *I*." Think of it this way. Rusty gave the ropes to Ed . . . that's OK. Rusty gave the ropes to *I* . . . oops . . . do you get what I mean? So, the correct grammar is: "Rusty gave the ropes to Ed and *me*."

Oliver wasn't too thrilled with Meg's corrections. *I guess I still have a lot to learn about the English language,* he thought as he shrugged his shoulders. Meg thought that his next letter was a little late in coming. He did put some thought into it though, purposely breaking about every law of grammar.

Dear Meg,

How you be? I be fine! Me still cowboy . . . me roam the prairie . . . me and Ed go with Rusty and I. When the moon she shines on the faraway mountains, me thinks about me love, Meg. Is you thinking of I? How be my grammar? She be living in Canada so my Mama and Papa tells I.

Thanks for the lesson, Meg. It didn't bother me one iota. It is not easy being brought up in one language and then switching to another. French is a language that can't be translated word for word. For instance in French, if I say, "Jai soif," translated word for word, you might say "I have thirst." It really is saying, "I'm thirsty." In many instances, French puts the cart before the horse. It's like the old French farmer who is trying to speak English and says, "I threw the horse over the fence some hay."

Give my best to your Mom and Tommy. Write soon. Je t'aime . . . word for word, I you love . . . true translation, I love you.

Oliver

It wasn't long after that Meghan wrote to Oliver.

Dear Oliver,

I hope you don't mind that I let my mother read your last letter . . . you are a true clown and we laughed ourselves silly over it! Your letter did convey the message of language difficulties. I certainly can understand this. In my French class, as you say, we're learning to "put the cart before the horse," and it can be confusing at times. I'm hoping that when you return to Buffalo, you and I can converse in French . . . then you can correct my French grammar. Tell me more about being a cowboy. Do they have cowgirls? Have you met any? Could I get a job there, too? . . . 'cause I miss you! Je taime, aussi.

Meg

Dear Meg,

Don't worry about cowgirls . . . there aren't any here. And if there were, I want you to remember that I only have eyes for you.

I would like to be a fly on the wall during your French class. I'd get a chuckle out of hearing an Irishman trying to pronounce French words. I've known of some high school French teachers in Lawrence who were Irish, and the students' pronunciations were hilarious! You needn't worry . . . I won't laugh at you.

No, I didn't mind that you showed my last letter to your mother. Give her my best regards and say "hi" to Tommy for me.

There's more to being a cowboy than I thought. I'll tell you more about it when I can do the roping and things a lot better . . . gotta go practice.

Je t' aime beaucoup.

Oliver, who was more accustomed to the English saddles, had to practice putting the forty-pound Western saddle on his horse, and getting the girth of woven cord under the horse's belly and securing the second flank.

He practiced sitting straight-legged, with his feet in the heavy stirrups. Oliver was dressed in a cotton shirt and heavy woolen trousers, and wore a big handkerchief tied around his neck; this protected him from the sun, and could also be pulled up around his nose and mouth when dust was thick.

He also wore a broad-brimmed felt hat. Oliver felt important and was so sure that he would become an expert cow hand. He dreamed of the long days in the open, riding with the cattle, gaining self-composure. However, he ended up having the most disagreeable job, riding in a huge cloud of dust behind the hundreds of hoofs ahead.

There were the "swings," two riders, one on each side of the herd; further behind the "swing" rode two more riders, called the "flanks," and bringing up the rear were the "drags," the lowliest of all. Oliver and another rider were with the drags. The slow and lame cattle were in the drag, and it was a tiresome job moving these beasts forward; they mustn't be separated from the herd.

At noon time the cattle were stopped and allowed to graze. The cowboys eagerly approached the chuck wagon when they heard the call from the cook: "Come and git it!" Oliver frequently built up a huge appetite; eating and enjoying the camaraderie was his favorite activity . . . he was still like a school kid, looking forward to and enjoying recess.

The day's travel was close to fifteen miles; the herd drank at a nearby water hole and then grazed some more. After the evening meal, guards were sent off to their posts, working all night in four shifts of two hours each, watching the herd. Other men sat by the campfire, joking, laughing, and singing. Oliver had a few jokes that had the men bent in two with laughter. They were pleased to have this likable "clown" in their midst; the funny guy who also entertained them with a few raunchy songs. Then, beds were unrolled and the tired cowhands slept under the stars.

There was little time off from herding the cows, but one fun occasion arose when a few of the men had time off to go to a barn dance. Locals called it a hoe-down. Two people playing fiddle, and one playing banjo furnished the lively music; they played "Texas Star," "Swing That Girl Behind You," "Skip to Ma Lou," many other tunes, and closing with a few finales such as, "Twistification," "Ladies Doe," and "Grapevine Swing."

"What an evening of fun!" Oliver exclaimed to Sally, the pretty young thing he had ended up with on the barn dance floor.

Looking at him, with her sweet smile and sparkling eyes, seemed to be sending him an encouraging message.

"It doesn't have to end here," he whispered in her ear, in his flirtatious way.

"Oh, yes it does," she told him, as she headed toward her parents who had escorted her to the dance.

There'll be other opportunities, thought Oliver, as he trudged his way back to the ranch, trying to rebuild his deflated ego. The cowhands didn't help, with their teasing him and slapping him on his back.

"So ya ended up with the prettiest gal at the dance. You ain't the first guy to find out that her mommy and daddy are afraid to let their kid come here alone!" said one cowboy in his drawn out western accent.

With a couple of beers, good camaraderie and a few good poker hands, he had forgotten his disappointment. Gambling, gambling . . . Ma would disapprove . . . so did George Washington when he said: "It (gambling) is the child of avarice, the brother of iniquity, and the father of mischief" . . . but it did help Oliver to forget his disappointments. But how could he have forgotten his first love, Meghan?

Oliver withstood his lowdown dusty job until he felt that he no longer cared to cope with it; he liked and got along well with all the riders, but could see that the more advanced jobs were not in the cards for him. It was again time to move on so he informed the foreman that someone else can bite the dust, "I'm moving on."

Gee, I thought that I might belong to this kind of living, he weighed. *What in heck is right for me? Why do I feel the urge to move on again? Maybe I just can't take life...sticking to one blasted thing. I don't know anyone else like me.*

Ten

The chuck wagon cook gave Oliver a few important pointers on cooking large amounts of grub for huge numbers of hungry dudes. Oliver had been self-sufficient as far as preparing dishes that were pleasing to his own palate, but never preparing food for a great number of guys. His new frontier would be Texas!

It was 1904, and Oliver's family always knew what part of the country he was in, because he would send a sheet of popular music to his sister Eva. She noted the postmark, and had some inkling as to where he was. Eva was becoming quite a pianist and even had a pupil or two.

Won't they be surprised to get a music piece from San Antonio, Texas, imagined Oliver, and they'll be still more surprised to learn that I have a job as a cook on a ranch!

He had learned some things about cooking at home. His mother tutored him in some form of culinary techniques, so that he and his siblings would become self-sufficient while she tended to her dressmaking business. The ranch hands appreciated the hearty meals prepared by their three cooks.

Oliver, being one of them, became adept at dressing and roasting venison, raccoon, rabbit, and any meats brought in by the hunters; of course, on alternate days, the usual fare was ham and beans. Oliver enjoyed his new job, and found that he had time to do a little exploring in San Antonio. "I'm anxious to tell Meghan all about this place. I'll send just a card first."

Hi Meghan,
Can you read the postmark on this card? Yeah, that's *San Antonio, Texas* all right. Can you believe . . . I'm a cook at a ranch. No more herding cows for me! I had to change trains three times, so it took a while to get here. Here's my new address: Bar X Ranch, Paso Road, San Antonio, Texas.
Je t'aime, beaucoup.

Oliver

Meghan was both astounded and disappointed to learn of Oliver's change of jobs, and he was even further away!

Hey Mister Traipser,

When are you going to stay put? It's difficult to keep track of all your meanderings. I thought that you liked being a cowboy . . . and now you're a *cook?* How do you qualify for that job? You never told me that you knew how to cook! I hope that the people you cook for stay healthy!

Are you aiming to be a man of all trades? . . . I should start calling you *Jack.* I know that this note is short, but I have to study for lots of exams coming up. Write soon, I want to hear all about your new job.

Much love,
Meg

Oliver's most memorable journey was to the Alamo, which had become a state park. He spent a long time at the monument, dedicated to the heroes who had died there. He contemplated the fierce battles, and remembered what he had read about the role his favorite frontiersman, David Crockett, had played as he helped the Texans in the siege that lasted twelve days. Oliver vowed that he would always "Remember The Alamo."

He would always remember Lorie, too. How could he forget their first and last meeting? Oliver attended a raucous entertainment establishment named Pedro's, catering mostly to leering men. The stage show was akin to burlesque: long-legged chorus girls, scantily dressed, doing what they got paid for, and exciting the men who yipped and yelled, "Take it off, take it off."

The bouncer forced his way over to the most boisterous guy and said, "Listen here, buddy, it ain't that kind of a show."

A fight ensued, the girls ran off the stage, got dressed hurriedly and exited the rear door. Oliver wanted no part in the fracas and left unnoticed. Outside of the establishment, he saw a girl whom he recognized as a member of the chorus line. He told her that he was sorry about what had happened inside, but then asked, "Why do you work in such a place; you look too nice for that joint."

"What else can I do? I have to earn a living somehow!"

Young naive Oliver asked: "Would you be willing to go to the town ice cream parlor and tell me about yourself?"

She shyly agreed, and over a soda, poured out her heart to Oliver. It was indeed a sad story; he felt so much compassion for Lorie, that he dug deep into his money belt and gave her a goodly sum for a trip home to Nevada to care for her ailing mother. Later, he presumed that he could walk her home.

"Oh no, you mustn't do that; I live with a bunch of girls, and I wouldn't want them to see me coming home with a man."

It seemed a little strange, but he agreed to part, and each went his and her own way.

The next day, Oliver told one of the cooks, Jose, about the ruckus at Pedro's and how he met a pretty young girl, who had a very compelling story. Jose startled Oliver with his clamorous laughter.

"Is this dame's name Lorie?" he asked, trying to contain his hilarity.

"Yeah."

"Did her old man die, and her sick mother needs her care in Colorado, but she doesn't have enough money to get there?"

"No, her mother is in Nevada."

"Maybe her mother will be in Canada, next. Can't you see through it all, pal? You've been had. Did you see where she lives?"

"No, she said that she lives with a few girls, and didn't want to be seen taken home by a man,"

"That's one true thing she told you. Yeah, those girls she lives with serve many a customer in Señora Dondero's bordello." Jose was bent in two howling with laughter.

"How could anyone who looks so sweet and innocent work such a scam?" Then he recalled the old saying, "Don't judge a book by its cover." *She seemed so mighty sweet though*, he mused.

Oliver would be forever cautious after that experience. He figured that it was safer to go out into the woods with his trusty rifle, and hunt animals. With a few tips from hunting companions, he became a better and better marksman, contributing to a varied menu at the ranch.

Oliver began an introspective examination, questioning his particular brand of lifestyle. *Is this all that life has to offer? What am I aiming for? For what am I searching?*

Am I alienating myself from something more important?

I am alone and anxious...but I am a free man!

Could I possibly be living in anomie? Still I get along with people. I can still laugh. But what is missing? What am I looking for?

These thoughts plagued Oliver from time to time, and when he couldn't stand them any longer, he had to move on.

He never did give up his ambition to be a blacksmith. He still mulled over the idea of possibly buying a shop for blacksmithing in Fredonia, but first he had to learn the business.

Eleven

Oliver quit the cooking job. He was never fired from a job, but once he made his decision to go elsewhere he wasted no time in making his move. He arrived in Providence in the summer of 1905. His father, Isaiah, who had adopted the name Joe, welcomed his eldest son with open arms. Joe was an expert in his field, and even took pride in his Morgan horses which he often used in Sulky racing. There was more to blacksmithing than Oliver remembered from his childhood.

His father was steadfast about safety, and insisted on every precaution: Long leather apron, to protect against hot metal and sparks, heavy shoes, safety glasses, leather welding gloves, and at times, ear muffs to muffle heavy hammering sounds. He was introduced to the essential equipment: cast-iron hearth, blast, anvil, bench and vise, water trough, power driven bellows, and fuel container. Horse shoeing was the most difficult to learn.

First, Oliver managed to learn to remove the old shoes . . . all eight nails in each, without damaging the hooves. Then, he watched Joe pare down each hoof with a knife, cutting away unwanted growth.

"There must be a good clean flat surface to prepare for the new shoe," Joe told him.

Then Oliver watched as his father heated the iron, and bent the hot iron around the horn of the anvil. Joe bent the ends up and welded a clip to the front topside of the shoe.

"The clip keeps the horse's hoof from slipping."

After the roughly finished shoe matched against the hoof to Joe's satisfaction, he heated it again and hammered until it was smoothed and flattened. He then punched eight nail holes into each shoe and "voilà," they were ready to nail to the hooves, nailed at an angle, then the sharp ends of the nails were pinched off. Joe only let Oliver learn shoeing, one little step at a time.

Blacksmiths had to be Jacks of all iron trades. They repaired hinges and plows for farmers, made baking pans and ladles, shovels, and buckets. They also made and repaired iron fences.

Oliver, thanks to the close scrutiny of his father, became more and more adept at all the needed skills of his trade.

* * *

In 1907, after two years of honing his skills, Oliver felt the impulse to move on, and looked forward to owning his own blacksmith shop in Fredonia, New York, and possibly settling down with his first love, Meghan Kelleher.

I hope she's a good cook, I'm tired of eating those Post Toasties for breakfast most every morning. That pamphlet that comes in all the packages named Wellville, "*The Road to Wellville*," is a lot of bunk, mused Oliver. He had grown tired of preparing his own meals.

It was 6:30 P.M., February 11, 1907 when Oliver left Providence, Rhode Island aboard the *Larchmont*, a Joy Line two-masted steamer. Before leaving, his father said, "You'd better wear your long johns, son; it'll be mighty cold out on the waters."

It was extremely frigid, with gale winds thrashing both the sea and the ship. Oliver shared a cabin with another young man who had become miserably seasick. Most of the passengers retired early, but Oliver decided to go up on deck where he was pleasantly surprised to find that the ship was brilliantly lighted. A little after ten P.M., he and other passengers caught sight of a three-masted schooner. The schooner was traveling at a swift clip, abetted by the thrust of the gale winds. The passengers on deck couldn't believe their eyes, and stood aghast at the sight of the schooner headed directly toward the *Larchmont*. The two ships collided. The steamer was struck on the port side and all lights were extinguished. Water began pouring through the gaping hole. Oliver rushed down to his cabin to warn the other occupant, but the young man vehemently refused to budge. Oliver struggled to pull the young man out of his bunk, but the sick fellow fought him with all his might. He had no will to save himself.

"You've got to get up on deck or you'll go down with the ship."

"I don't care if I live or die. Leave me alone."

When Oliver spotted the water that was beginning to flood the cabin, he grabbed some clothes and rushed up to the deck where he heard the blood-curdling screams of terrified passengers. Some, who jumped overboard, drowned quickly in the freezing water. Oliver managed to get into a lifeboat with ten other people.

The *Larchmont* sank rapidly, and much of the wreckage and the lifeboats were swept by the gale winds toward Block Island, Rhode Island. It was eleven P.M. when the lifeboat, number six, drifted away from the *Larchmont*, in the rough waters; its occupants becoming colder and more arctic as the splashing waves covered them with icy water.

"Try to stay awake; don't let yourselves fall asleep, or you'll never wake up," one man cautioned.

Someone, who swam near the boat, yelled for help.

"The boat will sink if we pull in another person," warned the same man. No one made an effort to save the swimmer, and soon the cries for help ceased. Oliver reverted to the language of his childhood, as he pleaded to God:

"Notre Pere, qui est au ciel, . . . sauvez-nous, s'il vous plait."

Oliver, some time later, described his plight to an interviewing newspaper reporter:

"We drifted from 11 P.M. until 7:30 the next morning. It was below zero and I watched all the others freeze to death. I prayed all night. One of the men was a barber; he slashed his throat, and later, lifeguards found ten razors on his person."

Oliver recalled how the boat drifted to shore near the Block Island lifesaving station at Sandy Point.

"I saw the men coming toward us, but I could neither move nor speak. One of the men called out that here was a lifeboat filled with dead men.

"'No,' cried another, 'there's a little fellow blinking his eyes.' The little fellow was me. I remembered them saying, 'Be careful, his legs may fall off,' and then I lapsed into unconsciousness."

Investigations, delving into the cause of the disaster, uncovered the fact that there was the failure of both vessels involved in the collision to burn rockets or make other distress signals.

This neglect was doubtless the result of great confusion on board the *Larchmont* and the swiftness with which the stricken vessel had sunk. Also, the schooner, the *Harry Knowlton* drifted away after the collision; its crew members were totally unaware of the extent of the damage the schooner had inflicted on the *Larchmont*.

The scene of the disaster was not more than three or four miles from the mainland, which, the records showed, was patrolled by members of the lifesaving service. Signals would have been seen offshore, since the night was clear. It was possible that someone would have observed signals burning by either of the vessels. Many of those who had died could have been rescued. There were nineteen survivors among 150 passengers.

*   *   *

Oliver was well taken care of by the Marine Hospital Service which was stationed on the island; his frozen clothes were cut off his numbed body; he was placed in a drum of oil, then gently wrapped in warm blankets. As he became aware of the blood beginning to flow through his body, he found that the numbness was subsiding, but being replaced by unbearable aches and pains.

On the thirteenth of February, Oliver was among the survivors carried to the western side of the island and placed aboard the Joy Line steamer, *Kentucky*, which carried them to Providence. His father met him at the dock and Oliver was brought to a local hospital where doctors suggested that his ears should be cut off. Joe vehemently opposed the doctors, and took Oliver home for further recovery.

"Well son, you must have followed your old man's advice and worn your long johns; you're lucky to have survived. Are you still determined to open a shop in New York?"

"Well, Pa, maybe I'll stay here a little longer, but when I do go to New York, I'll travel by train."

*   *   *

Oliver resumed work with his father and began noticing, and finding such a disparity in his fathers lifestyle, comparing it to the poverty with which he and his siblings were raised, back home in Lawrence. He couldn't seem to drum up the courage to ask, "How is it that you live so well, and you left Mama to fend for herself and the rest of your family?"

Joe seemed to have close friends with whom he enjoyed socializing, riding horseback, going to races and shows. He had a lady friend, too. She was introduced to Oliver as Anita.

Papa with a girlfriend, shrugged Oliver. Joe was carefree, perhaps in denial of the way he had handled his family affairs.

"Why couldn't you have helped out your family?" Oliver wanted to ask his father.

*   *   *

Joe, seemingly the type to have few concerns, almost lost his certitude when crowds were doing a run on banks during the "Panic of 1907." After reading about J. P. Morgan's effort to put a stop to the panic by importing one hundred million dollars in gold from Europe, his fears were allayed.

What power this Morgan possesses, thought Joe, puzzling over the thought that any one man could be so rich. He didn't resent the fact that Morgan was "rolling in dough." The country needs more Morgans to bail out the little fellows, mulled Joe.

Feeling flush, he celebrated by taking his son out to dinner, having his usual rare, bloody T-bone steaks, and then going to the Nickelodeon to view a presentation of two old films: *A Trip To the Moon*, and *Great Train Robbery*. The charge for admission was a nickel, hence the name of the storefront theater, Nickelodeon.

"Thank you, Pa; it's too bad that Mama and the kids don't have the money to do things like this." Oliver's remark fell like a hammer on the anvil with nothing to shape. Joe was forever reticent about any mention of family. Father and son parted, each going to his own abode. When Oliver arrived home, he found a letter waiting for him. It was from Frank.

Dear Brother,

Ma was sick with worry when she learned of your plight on the *Larchmont*. Please phone her as soon as you can. I couldn't convince her that you are all right. How are you making out living near Pa. I heard that he lives with a woman. Does he really?

The other day, I was standing in the Lawrence Unity Cycle Club on Broadway with three of my buddies when a man shouted, 'Who's the best one to throw one another?" None of us budged until the man said the magic words: "Whoever wins, I'll give him a quarter." How about that, Oliver? . . . My first pay day!!! I licked them all! I keep telling you . . . some day, I'm going to be a famous wrestler. Do you believe me now?

Frank

Thereafter, Oliver frequently received newspaper clippings about his wrestling kid brother: JANVIER DEFEATS OPPONENT AT FRANCO-BELGIUM CLUB . . . JANVIER WINS AGAIN AT SACRED HEART IN SOUTH LAWRENCE . . . JANVIER GAINS ANOTHER VICTORY AT ST. PATRICK'S. Frank is really serious about a wrestling career, reflected Oliver, he's definitely on a roll.

Oliver spent the rest of the evening scanning a section of the newspaper that featured "Newsworthy Remembrances of the Year 1907."

He was determined to read some of the works written by Rudyard Kipling who had recently won the Nobel Prize for Literature.

Ah, he thought, another ship for the wealthy bigwigs. That S.S. *Lusitania* made good time from Queens Town, Ireland, to New York. They broke a Transatlantic record by taking just five days and forty-five minutes.

Yeah, the Pope's encyclical condemns Modernism. What is Modernism, anyhow? I wonder if it's just living with the times!

Oh, here's a good idea to honor mothers. The second Sunday in May has been declared officially as Mother's Day.

Well. it's too late this year, thought Oliver, *I'll make it all up to Mama by visiting family during the celebration of her day next May.*

*   *   *

It was May 1908 and again it was time to bid adieu to his father. This time, he was traveling by train. En route, he read "The Secret Agent," by Joseph Conrad. The mystery novel made the time flee and he was back to familiar turf before he knew it.

The excitement of meeting his family at the Lawrence South Station became emotional. Mama, Eva, and Blanche showed their elation, smiling through tears. They held on to Oliver as a child would guardedly hold on to a favorite teddy bear, never wanting to let go.

"We're here too, Mama and girls. Give *us* a chance to greet our brother!" Frank grabbed Oliver almost in a wrestling hold. Joey, who was now almost fourteen, wasn't so little anymore, though his sisters still referred to him as "tsi boy." The youngest Janvier boy had not seen his brother since he was five years old; he just stood by, observing the others with their excited greetings, feeling like a stranger and thinking, *who is this guy?* Joey shyly shook hands with Oliver and slunk away into the background. Oliver was aware that his youngest sibling was uncomfortable, and made a mental note to devote meaningful time to him.

A neighbor had loaned his horse and buggy for the occasion. Oliver thanked the gentleman and helped his mother and sisters into the wagon. On the ride home, Mama asked a question that had been weighing on her mind.

"Vas-tu a la Messe chaque dimanche?' (Do you attend Mass each Sunday?)

"Oui, Mama," Oliver lied.

He had problems with some of the Catechism teachings, such as missing Mass on Sunday, eating meat on Friday, being equated with the horrendous sin of murder . . . all Mortal sins! and what about "Original" sin . . . would he be responsible for his own father's sins? Why should he be responsible for the sins of Adam and Eve . . . he didn't do it! He couldn't argue with his dear Mama, who was a daily communicant at St. Anne's Church.

Oliver had almost forgotten that Mama was such a wonderful cook. Good nourishing home-cooked meals is what he had missed most in his travels. If I stayed home, he pondered, I just might get fat.

After a family meal, Eva dodged the chore of cleaning up by playing the piano in accompaniment to her brothers singing the popular tunes of the day, many of which were sent to Eva by Oliver. Surprisingly, Joey joined in.

Maybe he's warming up to me, thought Oliver.

The family closeness, the singing, the card playing, the conversations, and especially the food warmed Oliver's heart.

The following week, the family visited Uncle Ben Parent in Dracut. Mama's other brother, Albert, was also paying a visit from Canada. When he told Oliver about his job as Forest Ranger in the Canadian woods of the Province of Quebec, a spark of interest was ignited in Oliver. It didn't take much prompting from Uncle Albert to have Oliver accompany him home to Canada. His family was disappointed that his visit was cut short.

"I'm just getting to know my brother and will miss all the humor he has brought to our family," sulked "tsi boy."

Mama Azilda cornered her brother Albert and whispered: "Find a nice French girl for my son. He's too interested in an Irish girl in Buffalo."

"I'll do that avec plaisir, Azilda."

*   *   *

Oliver enjoyed sauntering through the Canadian woods, riding horseback with Uncle Albert, and helping to plant seedlings. He loved their hunting conquests; they had many meals of roasted venison, rabbit, and wild turkey. Uncle Albert was impressed with Oliver's marksmanship. Oliver especially enjoyed the horses.

"These animals are so mellow compared to the broncos ridden by

Montana cowboys," Oliver told his uncle, as he related his experiences as a herdsman.

Albert enjoyed his nephew and listened to every intriguing adventure story with enthusiasm. However, he had not forgotten to keep a promise to his sister; he introduced Oliver to Juliette Comeau, a neighbors attractive daughter.

Oliver hadn't conversed at length in French for several years, and found conversation rather faltering. He found Juliette to be pleasant and proper, but felt no chemistry toward her. Her parents liked Oliver and tried to encourage a romance by inviting him to dinners, and attendance at church functions. Oliver accepted their invitations but his lack of interest was interpreted as shyness, which they considered an attribute in a young man.

As winter approached, Oliver's interest in forestry, and especially his social life soon waned. The frosty Canadian air proved to be intolerable to him, especially since being frost- bitten in the *Larchmont* disaster.

He traveled back to his family in Lawrence, just in time to help with their move to Dracut, near Uncle Ben's farm. The weather wasn't that much warmer than in Canada, but the warmth of family members comforted him.

Oliver and "tsi boy," who preferred to be called *Joe*, worked clearing the fields of dried corn stalks, and all other remnants of dried plants for their aging uncle. He stayed in Dracut with his family until heading for Buffalo.

Oliver was introduced to his future brother-in-law, Joseph Gagne, a likable red-headed guy who was engaged to Eva. The special event was in the planning for 1910. Oliver observed that they seemed well-suited to each other.

His other sister, Blanche, had just joined the Sisters of St. Joseph's Convent in Biddeford, Maine. She would be forever known as Sister Marie Gerard.

Wow, thought Oliver, *after Eva marries that will leave just Frank and Joe with Mama! Moving close to Uncle Ben will be good for them all.*

✻   ✻   ✻

Indian summer, like warm embers of a dying fire, inspired Oliver to walk to Uncle Ben's nearby farm and sit under the old maple tree, where long ago he had contemplated many decisions.

Comfortably leaning against the tree, with a long piece of straw in his mouth, he recounted his life's experiences, then asked himself: What have I accomplished? What does it all amount to? He glanced to his right where he saw a mound of healthy green leaves, then chuckled as he thought, does it all amount to a hill of beans, or a pile of manure? Now his mood had shifted from solemnness to nonsense. He rose to his feet and went to his mother's new residence.

"Eva, it's almost 1909 . . . then I'll be twenty-three years old. Most men my age know what they want out of life, most are married and have families, I get kind of mixed up when I think about my future. What do you think I should do?"

"Find a steady job, look for a nice girl to marry, raise a family . . . what else is there?"

"What else is there? . . . *that*, I need to find out for myself. I have a nice girlfriend in Buffalo, but she's getting really educated. If I marry Meg, after a while I might feel inferior to her and then she'll tire of me. I read an article of advice somewhere, it said 'just take things as they come,' whatever that means. Maybe I'll just wait for things to come to me. That will eliminate a lot of searching. I'll think about your advice on the train to Buffalo."

They both began to sing, "Shuffle off to Buffalo," which set them both off in one of their silly fun loving moods. Azilda, who was working in the kitchen, had her attention geared to the uplifting sounds from the parlor and pondered, "Quand mes enfants sont heureux, cela me fait heureuse, aussi." (When my children are happy, it makes me happy, also.) She wished that her eldest son would remain with her, but she knew that it was not to be. She resolved to enjoy each moment they had together before Oliver took off again. It was such a rare occasion to have all her children, all except for Sister Marie Gerard, home for the holidays.

They enjoyed the festivities, celebrating in the French Canadian ways, feasting on Tourtieres, Gorton, Boudin and participating in the family sing-alongs. Oliver stayed home until late February. When he left he felt exhilarated, all from the warmth and laughter expressed by his family. It was a jubilant time indeed!

Twelve

Oliver settled down for the long train rides bringing him to Buffalo. As usual, his supply of newspapers and books kept him occupied during his travels.

The important news headlines that Oliver had read in 1908 consisted of William Howard Taft being elected the 27th President of the United States. Then there was the horrible earthquake where one hundred fifty thousand people were killed in Sicily. Former President Grover Cleveland had died. But there was good news about Americans winning fifteen firsts out of twenty-eight in track and field at the Olympic games in London.

The lighter reading which Oliver enjoyed, was a newspaper advice column written by a Tennessee woman who adopted the pen name of Dorothy Dix. She advised against any woman marrying any man who did not have a sense of humor.

One young woman wrote, "I'll be getting married soon and would like to know if I should tell my fiance that I have false teeth."

Dix replied, "No, marry him and keep your mouth shut."

It was March, 1909 when Oliver arrived in Buffalo. It was a blustery day. The snow storms were still hitting the big city hard, and the clean-up was a big problem for the politicians meeting expenses without again raising taxes.

In spite of the blizzard, Oliver was met at the station by his heart throb, Meghan Kelleher, and also his buddy, Dom Abati. They both plied him with questions about his distressing experience. He filled them in with brief accounts of the calamity . . . but refused to go on. After all, he wanted to hear about their lives, especially Meghan's.

They had not seen each other for a long four years, but through frequent letter writing, they felt that they had gotten to know each other better. Oliver was twenty-three now, and Meghan, twenty-two . . . and, he observed that she was more beautiful than ever, with long auburn hair, lively brown eyes, cheeks like Macintosh apples, with those freckles across her little turned up nose, creating an impish look . . . Oh, he was smitten. Dom realized that the two love birds could only see each other. Meghan noticed that Oliver had grown an inch or two . . . was more handsome than ever. She loved those expressive green eyes, his deep dimpled cheeks that only showed with his broad smile, displaying his even white teeth. His light brown hair shone with reddish highlights.

He did tell me that his mother was a "carrot top," Meghan remembered. If we marry and have children, they'll all be redheads. I hope that he means it, when he tells me that he is ready to settle down after he opens his new blacksmithing shop in Fredonia, thought Meghan. Will he ever be content to stay put?

Oliver rented a room in Fredonia, a short distance from the small building he was able to purchase. After he equipped his shop with the necessary smithing apparatus, his business, being the only one like it in town, took off lickety-split; it was just what the town of Fredonia needed.

The Ford Motor Company had been selling their Model T cars since 1908, which was somewhat of a concern for Oliver, but in Fredonia, the horse-drawn carriage seemed to be the main means of non public transportation. For the present, Oliver reasoned, my new venture is safe. Not many people can afford a "Tin Lizzie" at the cost of eight hundred fifty dollars. The Studebaker brothers' horse-drawn vehicles are still in use, he mused, and the David Dunbar Buick cars are very expensive. Indeed, his business did flourish. Oliver was kept extremely busy and was only able to see Meghan on Sundays. He became a Sunday regular at the Kelleher dinner table.

＊　　＊　　＊

In late May, the weather had become considerably warmer and Oliver was able to shed his winter woolies. Meghan and her mother prepared the meals while Oliver and Tommy played ball. The boy, who was now fourteen years old, aspired to be a professional baseball player. His ambition was to be a paid player for the Cincinnati Red Stockings; he had read that they were the first ball club to pay their players.

"But then," he said, "I don't know whether I want to be in the National League or the American League. What should I do, Oliver?"

"If I were you, I'd just keep practicing, Tommy. You might change your mind a hundred times before you're old enough to make any decisions, but you know that the 1908 world series was won by Chicago, of the *National* League; they beat Detroit four to one. If you're good

70

enough, you'll be chosen . . . not the other way around."

On the next pitch, Tommy hit the ball with such force that it landed in a neighbors yard three houses away.

"Home run!" yelled Oliver.

"Dinner is ready," called Meghan.

"Aw gees, just when I'm getting warmed up!"

"Well Tommy, you'll have your seat warmed up plenty if you hit a ball through someone's window," warned Meghan.

"Aw gees," pouted Tommy as he and Oliver followed his sister into the house.

"See how she treats me, Oliver . . . as if I'm a little kid!"

The seating arrangement was changed, and now Oliver was able to sit next to his girl. Tim Cronin had moved on to become an editor for a small newspaper in a small New York town. Mrs. Kelleher's new boarder, Patrick O'Hearn, had immigrated from Ireland and was working for Jake Ronan.

He's too young to give me any competition with Meghan, thought Oliver.

Meghan seemed to monopolize the conversation, telling about her work as a fourth grade teacher; she had completed the two years of Normal school, which qualified her to teach in the lower grades of public school. She was proud of her work, and talked about the progress of her young students, which was a source of annoyance to Tommy; he had heard it all before. He wasn't interested in hearing anything about school.

"Hey Meg, Sunday is a day off from school; don't spoil it!"

The conversation turned to current events.

"A new commercial product called 'Bakelite' has been manufactured; it's a hard substance which can be used for several things, like telephone wires and receivers," said Oliver.

"They'll be using it for electric insulators, too. That should make electricity safer," piped in Tommy . . . much to everyone's surprise.

Tommy wanted to add more to the conversation, being proud of things he had learned in the eighth grade.

"Admiral Robert Peary reached the North Pole," he proudly exclaimed.

"Now, who is this school kid, who doesn't want to be reminded of school on a Sunday?" his sister asked, and quickly changed the subject and suggested to Oliver that they go to the park where the local band was performing at three o'clock.

"They've been playing some of the latest songs, besides Sousa marches, and tunes from Victor Herbert's 'Babes in Toyland.' The music gets better with every concert,"Meghan announced.

"That sounds swell. Let's go!"

Mrs. Kelleher said, "You two go along to the concert. Tommy and I will clean up the dishes."

"Aw gees, Ma," pouted Tommy.

*　　*　　*

Because of the warmer than usual May weather, people were out in great numbers at the park. Oliver and Meghan walked hand in hand through the maze of paths, while the band played "My Sweetheart's the Man in the Moon, I'm Going to Marry Him Soon." "Daisy, Daisy, Give Me Your Answer, Do." They both knew all the words, and sang happily together while holding hands, swinging arms to the rhythm of the music, and strolling cheerfully.

When the band began, "Peg O My Heart," Oliver stopped, turned Meghan towards himself and sang, "*Meg* O My Heart, I Love You. Never to Part . . . " He leaned forward and kissed her on the mouth.

"Oh, Oliver! Not in public!"

"Who cares where! I want you to know that I love you and want to marry you."

She really cared deeply for Oliver, but tried to convince herself that she wasn't interested in marriage . . . well not at the moment. After all, she had just begun her career as a teacher, and once a woman married, she was no longer in that chosen profession. Those who remained were looked upon as "old maids;" she wanted to get married some day, but thought . . . *it's too soon.*

"Oliver, you're building up a business, I've just begun a career in teaching . . . we both need time."

"Need time? Time!" wearing a quizzical look on his face. "I thought we had a long four years pass us by . . . but we need *more time?*"

"Oliver, you never mentioned marriage in your letters. I will admit that our exchange of letters did get a bit warm and chummy, but you've been back for such a short time, I don't think that it would be wise to make a jump decision."

"Think it over, Meg. We'll talk about it again next Sunday."

After Oliver left Meghan to return to Fredonia, a mother-daughter tête-à-tête followed.

"He asked me to marry him, Mom!"

"Did you say 'yes'?"

"I'm confused, Mom, especially since I've been seeing Sean Ronan . . . I didn't tell Oliver about Sean, I assumed that he had been seeing other women, because he never mentioned an engagement, and never even suggested that we go steady, and then he just pops the question out of the blue. What should I do?"

"Honey, it's such a big decision; I cannot be makin' it fer ya."

"Mom, I can't help thinking about all the jobs that Oliver has had, all the roaming around he's done. Is a person like that stable? I want equilibrium in my life. What if, after we'd marry, he decided to take off again?"

"I 'av thought aboot the very same questions, Meghan; he seems kind and considerate, but on the other hand . . . flighty. Sean seems so steady and dependable, and to top it off honey, he's Irish. It's best to marry yer own kind."

"Sounds like you've made my decision, Mom."

"Oh no dearie, you'll be makin' yer own choice."

"What if Sean doesn't get serious? . . . Mom, I don't want to be an old maid . . . a spinster, like a lot of the other teachers at school, but I do want more time."

"Now, child, you sound worried. 'Aven't ya heard about the number of fish in the sea . . . they'll be many more; there's nothing for a pretty girl like you to be concerning 'erself aboot. How ere, don't be keepin' Oliver on a string, ya must be tellin' 'im next Sunday."

Oliver's week fled by. He catered to many demanding customers without time to think about his proposal to Meghan. It was Sunday again when the reality of his carried away emotions hit him.

Me, a married man? he thought, with many a doubt creeping into those thoughts.

He took the usual train to Buffalo, while nervously fiddling with his keys, and feeling that he arrived at his destination all too soon. Again, he played ball with Tommy while Meghan and her Mom worked on the Sunday dinner.

"Are you really flighty, Oliver?" asked Tommy.

"What brought that on, Tom?"

"Well, I heard my mother and Meghan talking about you. I'd like to have you for a brother-in-law, but they think that you are too flighty. I

73

heard them talk about Sean Ronan, to."

"Who is Sean Ronan?" Oliver asked.

"Oh, he's Meghan's other boyfriend. They usually go out on Saturday nights, but he hasn't asked her to marry him."

That bit of eavesdropping on Tommy's part had Oliver too mentally occupied to continue playing ball. He sat on the front steps, realizing that he was about to be dumped by his first love. I should have kept my trap shut, he scolded himself.

"Dinner is ready," called Mrs. Kelleher, rather lifelessly.

That's a switch, thought Oliver, *usually Meahan calls when dinner is ready. She does seem sort of standoffish today.*

It wasn't St. Patrick's Day, but the fare of the day turned out to be "bacon and cabbage," or, what Americans call, "corned beef and cabbage." *It must be a farewell meal*, thought Oliver. There seemed to be tension all around the table . . . next to no conversation, and the food going down with extra weight . . . or was it weight in his heart?

Boy I really blew it, thought Oliver . . . *things might have worked out just keeping our relationship platonic.*

"Does the concert in the park still begin at three?" he forced himself to squeak out.

"We won't be going today, but I would like to have a talk . . . how about on the porch?" Meghan gulped.

Tommy's "Aw gees," was heard when his mother said that he and she would be clearing the table, and washing dishes, so that Meghan and Oliver could sit on the porch for their talk.

＊ ＊ ＊

"I've gotten your answer to my question I posed in the park last Sunday . . . I got it loud and clear, Meghan."

"I don't want to hurt you, Oliver, but you did take me by surprise, and since then I've been in such a quandary. I've liked you since the first day you came here.

"While you were away we exchanged letters, and I actually imagined myself in love with you, and I could hardly wait for your return. Well you're here, and reality has set in. I ask myself, why is he so compelled to take off? What is he looking for? Will he ever stay put?"

"You needn't say any more, Meghan. I understand how you feel. I don't regret the roving I've done. I've seen a good part of this country, and had many more experiences than I ever could have, just staying in one place. Even though my smithing business is doing well, I can see that it will be obsolete some day. Ford is selling more and more of those Tin Lizzies, and the price has been lowered to less than three hundred dollars. So, you see . . . with my being so shifty . . . I just might take off again."

How come he used the word "shifty?" thought Meghan, with a look of puzzlement. *Oh no, wait 'til I get Tommy alone. I'll bet he listened in on our mother-daughter conversation and told Oliver.* Her face reddened with embarrassment.

"I hope that you meet someone deserving of yourself, someone to make you happy. Thank your mother for the great dinners. I'll catch an early train. Good-bye Meg O My heart. Cest la vie. That's life, I guess."

"Good luck, Oliver, I'll always remember you." She tried to hide the tears in her eyes as she opened the screen door.

Thirteen

Instead of taking an early train, he walked to the next street parallel to E. Mark: Columbia Street, where his friend Dom still lived. Dom, Uncle Nickie and Aunt Molly were just about to have dessert, and with their usual cordiality, insisted on setting another place for Oliver.

"Hey Ollie, you look pretty glum, pal, what's up?" asked Dom, knitting his brows.

"Momma's pie and coffee is a gonna fixa you up, boy," said Uncle Nickie.

"Does Momma's pie fix a broken heart?"

"Maybe no, but I giva you a strong drink of brandy. Thata will fixa you heart, yes?'

"That might help. Thank you."

Being with these fun loving people did cheer Oliver, and after the dessert and a couple of drinks, they had a sing fest while Uncle Nickie strummed his guitar.

Oliver took the late train after all; he felt much better after having been with friends.

*   *   *

It was another busy week at the blacksmith shop, though Oliver's heart wasn't in his work. He worked later than usual and by Friday evening, he was pleasantly surprised by a visit from Dom.

"I didn't expect to find you working at this late hour, Oliver."

"It's a way to keep my mind occupied . . . what's up, Dom?"

"Well, the showboat is on the lake this weekend and I thought you might like some fun entertainment."

"Showboat? I've never heard of it."

"It's an eighty-foot barge that has been converted into a showboat . . . its pulled by a steam tug. They put on a lot of different kinds of entertainment. It would do you good to have a few laughs . . . how about it? Uncle Nickie suggested that you stay over at our place tonight, and Aunt Molly agrees. After dinner tomorrow, we could all go to the show in his wagon . . . the theater boat is tied up right near Silver Creek."

"That sounds swell, Dom . . . let me get a few things from my room and we'll be on our way."

These are true friends, thought Oliver; *how will I ever repay them for their kindness?*

After Chicken Cacciatore with peppers and mushrooms, salad, Italian bread, and fruit with biscotti, the well-sated group helped Aunt Molly clear the table. Dom and Oliver insisted on doing the dishes.

Uncle Nickie tied up his horse and wagon by Silver Creek, after which they spotted the gaily garbed entertainers, just returning to the boat from their shore duty of drumming up business.

The toot of the calliope was the signal that the show would soon begin. The show began with lively comic songs. The clever magic tricks, some with audience participation, were almost as funny as the comic songs.

"Wow, how did he do that?" was frequently heard from the viewers.

One woman skillfully walked a tightrope. That same woman sang romantic songs while playing the dulcimer.

There were acrobatics, plus a comedy farce . . . all good family entertainment that drew large groups of people who rarely saw such fun-filled shows.

On the way back to Uncle Nickie's place, everyone was in agreement that the show would be worth seeing again.

"It's just what the doctor ordered" joked Oliver, "and so was that delicious meal, Aunt Molly. Thank you so much!"

"We lika you company, Oliver; with you greata sense a humor, you coulda be entertainer ona da showboat."

"Don't give him any kind of encouragement . . . he'll be taking off again for who knows where!" exclaimed Dom.

"No, Dom, now that I have a business, I'll have to stick around longer than you think. I'll always be grateful to you and your aunt and uncle for all the kindnesses you've shown me."

"What you need now, Oliver, is a new female companion . . . I know just the girl for you."

"Oh yeah? How about yourself, Dom . . . who's just the girl for you?"

"I've already met her . . . the girl for me . . . and she has a very nice friend. Okay if we arrange a double date . . . a blind date for you? What do you say, Ollie?"

"You're twisting my wrist . . . I won't say uncle . . . so I guess I'll just say okay. When is this meeting supposed to take place? And where are we taking the girls?"

"St. Anthony's parish members are rehearsing a talent show that's going to be held in the church hall next Saturday at 6:30 P.M. After the show, we could take the girls out for dinner. How does that sound?"

"It's a date. Tell me about the girls . . . or, I should say . . . tell me about the girls first . . . *before* I say it's a date."

"My girl is Amalia . . . pretty Italian with big black eyes, sparkling smile, and olive complexion. I hope to marry her."

"Hey, wait a minute . . . I want a description of her friend . . . what makes you think that she's the girl for me?"

"She's a funny kid . . . good sense of humor . . . a clown . . . like you, Oliver."

"But what does she look like? And what's her name? Minnie Ha Ha?"

"Wouldn't you like to be pleasantly surprised? . . . like . . . wait and see?

"What if I'm *unpleasantly* surprised? I'd have a bone to pick with you, Dom!"

"Okay, okay . . . . .I won't take that chance. Her name is Hedda, and she's German-American, and I'd say she could be a Gibson girl, as graceful as a swan with long blonde hair, blue eyes, nice features . . . you'll like her, . . . I'm pretty sure. Her last name is Kreisig."

"What in heck is a Gibson girl?"

"Haven't you ever seen the stories in magazines? This guy named Charlie Gibson did engravings and lithographs of beautiful All-American girls of his imagination. His creations supposedly helped parents realize that their daughters were every bit as lovely as European girls."

"You mean he had to imagine these gals? Don't you kinda feel sorry for him? I don't know any European females, but I've known of a few very pretty girls right in my home town, and I don't have to imagine their good looks. I'll take your word about Hedda, the Gibson girl . . . sounds like a date."

"See ya at Uncle Nickie's place no later than five P.M. next Saturday."

"Yup, so long."

A new riding school started up in Fredonia: The Fredonia Riding Academy. That was a source of encouragement for the smithy business. The academy boasted of sixteen high bred animals. Four of the horses were brought to Oliver's shop by the groom, that very first week. Oliver's favorite was a beautiful bay, with its brown coat shining with shades of red; its mane, tail, and stockings were of jet black.

Oliver had loved horses since he was introduced to them at a very early age by his father. The chestnut horse, he shoed that same day, had hairs almost the same colors as the bay, but his mane, tail, and stockings were much lighter . . . another beautiful animal. Oliver was in his glory.

The groom asked Oliver if he knew of any young boys who would be willing to work at the stable, helping to groom the horses, as well as the less pleasant task of keeping the stalls clean.

"Yes, there are two young brothers who recently asked me for jobs here. I'm sure they'd be interested. Next time they come around, I'll tell them about that job opening. I only know them as Matt and Jim. I don't know their last names and I don't know where they live. I think that they are about fifteen and sixteen years old."

"Thanks, we'll be needing at least three boys."

With the extra activity at the shop, the week seemed to take wing . . . a blind date . . . hmm; Oliver was feeling slightly uneasy.

However, he had a very able helper at his shop; he had found the new man, Burt Nettle, through the Roy Croft Company, where Burt had apprenticed in smithing.

Burt agreed to hold the fort on Saturday, and Oliver put on his new shirt and tie with his neat, but slightly worn brown suit. He just about made the train to Buffalo and got to Uncle Nickie's house only ten minutes late.

"I was getting edgy, Oliver; I thought you might have gotten cold feet!" Dom exclaimed.

"I do get cold feet . . . especially since the *Larchmont* episode, but I didn't get cold feet about the date. So, where are the girls?"

"Well, since we don't have one of those new Studebakers, it seems that we'll have to hoof it. They'll be waiting for us at Amalia's house, about a twenty minute walk from here, and the church hall is just around the corner from there. Mrs. Saperato is friendly, so don't worry about meeting Amalia's mother."

"I'm more concerned about meeting Hedda."

*　　*　　*

Dom was right, Mrs. Saperato answered the door knock in a most cordial manner. She seemed to greet Dom with such an approving delighted expression.

"Ah, it's a nice to see you; who dis nice a boy?"

"Mrs. Saperato, this is Oliver Janvier. Oliver, meet Mrs. Saperato."

"Pleased to meet you, Mrs. Saperato."

"It's a nice to meet a you, too. The girls are in a da parlor. Come."

Oliver was relieved when all the formalities were over with, and he was delighted to greet his "blind date." Dom was right again, reflected Oliver . . . Hedda looks like a movie star. She seemed equally pleased with her "blind date."

Wow, these two seem right for each other . . . look at those sparkling eyes, mused Dom.

The two couples happily headed for the church hall.

The show was purely amateurish. Some of the jokes didn't go over too well, but the overall presentation was rather entertaining. Some of the singers and dancers almost reached professional status. When it was time to leave, the four of them agreed on the Italian Restaurante.

The conversations at the table were mostly about the show; they repeated some of the funnier jokes, Oliver adding some of his own. They ended the evening in a most mirthful mood.

"This has really been a fun evening; we should do it again," exclaimed Oliver, looking toward Hedda for a sign of approval.

"I'd like that," she said.

"Do you like horseback riding? We have a new riding academy in Fredonia."

"I've never ridden . . . but I'd like to try."

"How about next Sunday afternoon? I'll call for you around one o'clock."

"Oh Oliver, I wouldn't mind taking the train to Fredonia, if you would meet me. You would have too much extra traveling to do if you come to Buffalo . . . but, I would appreciate it if you would take me home on the return trip . . . then you could meet my mother. Okay?"

Dom and Amalia said that they had other plans and had to decline Oliver's invitation, but agreed that it sounded like a fun time.

80

It was another busy week at the shop, so time fled. It was Sunday and Oliver met Hedda at the specified station. He was surprised to see her wearing jodhpurs.

"You look well prepared to ride, Hedda."

"These things belong to my cousin . . . she says that she used to ride . . . well, at least her pants will be riding today." They were off to a laughing start again. *As Dom says, this gal is funny*, thought Oliver.

They were in luck . . . Oliver's two favorite horses were available, the Bay named Buff, and the Chestnut named Velocity.

"The name Velocity sounds kind of feisty," Oliver reasoned. "This one here might be more subdued. Here Buff, meet your rider, Hedda."

"Oh, I'm sure he understands," laughed Hedda as she patted the horse's nose.

"Since you're new at this, you need to learn about the horse's equipment, called the tack. That includes the saddle, bridle, halter, and shank. When I rode horses in Montana we used the Western tack . . . the tack here is English."

The head groom, nearby, overheard Oliver's instructions.

"We could use such a knowledgeable fellow here. Want to join us?"

"I have a job . . . remember me? How did you make out with the two boys, Matt and Jim, that I sent over?"

"Oh, I thought you looked familiar . . . those boys are working out just fine. Thanks for sending them here."

"Glad to be of help."

"Ready to mount, Hedda?"

"As ready as I'll ever be."

"Okay now, keep just a light contact on the horse's mouth with the reins. If you increase the tension, the horse will take that as a direction signal. The reins give him direction to turn, go forward, or back. If you apply pressure with your left leg he'll move to the right. With pressure from both legs, he'll move forward."

"Gee, Oliver, I envisioned myself just getting up on the horse and trotting off into the wilderness. I had no idea that I'd have to be schooled in procedures."

"I don't mean to get too technical about it . . . but, you'll feel more secure as you learn more about the animal . . . he does need your direction, you know. We'll start off with a walking gait. Be sure to center yourself . . . don't move from side to side; he'll take that as direction and become confused."

They took a scenic bridle path through the woods, leading to Lake Erie. Hedda caught on quickly, and found this new activity to her liking. As the path widened, they were able to ride side by side, telling their life stories.

Oliver learned that Hedda worked as a teller in a bank.

"It's not fair, the men tellers are paid more than the girls, the reasoning being that the men are breadwinners for their families . . . but I am the breadwinner in our house. I support my widowed mother . . . that doesn't seem to count."

"I agree, Hedda, that's not fair at all."

When they got near the water's edge they dismounted, tethered the horses to a tree and sat in the grass by the water. It was late October and the weather was having a last warm fling, known as Indian summer.

"We won't be doing this much more . . . possibly until next spring. If this weather lasts, would you want to ride again next Sunday?"

"I'd like that, Oliver."

✻   ✻   ✻

Oliver rode the train back to Buffalo with Hedda and was introduced to Mrs. Kreisig, a frail woman in her early fifties. Oliver learned that Mrs. Kreisig was a small child when her parents came to America, and he also learned that her father had been disenchanted with the German government. There were constant clashes between Germany and France, and Germany and Russia, Germany trying to expand its borders.

The next Sunday proved to be a repeat performance, but with more familiarity. They were more relaxed, joking more and having fun. This time Hedda learned how to post as they trotted their horses through the same paths. The weather turned much cooler, but with no trace of early snows. The harsh winters of the Lake Erie area were traditional.

They hitched their horses to the same tree and strolled by the lake.

"I should have dressed more warmly. Brrr." Hedda shivered.

Oliver put his arm over her shoulder, enjoying the opportunity to become chummier.

"Ooh I like that, Oliver."

"How would you feel if I kissed you?"

"Warmer," Hedda replied with a twinkle in her eyes.

They both thrilled to their first embrace, first kiss . . . and there were more kisses and sighs. They reluctantly returned to their horses, and trotted back to the stable.

Oliver and Hedda held hands in the train, all the way to Buffalo. Hedda broke the spell by asking Oliver a question.

"Would you be willing to play Santa Claus at our church fair?"

"Gee, I was anticipating a much more romantic question. Skinny me, a Santa Claus?"

"They have a wonderfully realistic red suit . . . we could fatten you up with pillows."

"You really want to put me through that embarrassment?"

"Oliver, you would be a lot of fun for the kids; they'll love you. Think of the joy you'll bring to them."

"Ouch, you've twisted my wrist enough . . . I'll do it," he said with a shrug of his shoulders.

"The fair is being held next Saturday at one o'clock. Can you be at my house around noon time?"

"I'll get my helper to watch the shop . . . see you then, Hedda."

The ride back to Fredonia seemed long and lonesome. I wish she lived closer, lamented Oliver.

Burt agreed to take the responsibility of working alone at the shop. The thought of Oliver playing Santa, struck him as a hilarious joke. Oliver agreed that the concept was laughable . . . but he had committed himself to the task and wasn't about to back out.

The Santa Claus suit was very large, but Hedda enjoyed filling it with a number of soft pillows, some of which she had brought from home.

"Hey fatty . . . here's your beard . . . kiss me, I want to see if it tickles," she teased.

He grabbed her quickly, but fell backwards as he kissed her. She landed on his fat pillowed body, laughing hilariously.

"*Well* this is hardly the place for such activity!" bellowed Father Riccio, upon entering the dressing room.

The embarrassed twosome apologized, but then realized that the priest was amused, not shocked.

"The children are anxiously awaiting your entrance to the hall, Santa," the priest announced.

There the children were, all in a single line, reminding Oliver of his grammar school days, when the nuns prepared the children for entrance to the church, guiding them down the aisle, and filing into the pews in exact order. He almost expected the children to genuflect.

Santa was directed to his "throne" and the fun began.

"HO, HO, HO, little fellow, what do you want for Christmas?"

"Well, last year, I sent you my list . . . I guess you didn't receive it . . . so this year, I'm delivering it myself." He handed Oliver his long list.

"Young man, I thought your list was too long last year. Let's not be selfish . . . let's leave enough toys for other children. Take this list back, shorten it and mail it back to me at the North Pole . . . I'll see what I can do . . . *next.*"

Oliver was having a wonderful time. He felt happy that he had accepted the challenge. Things moved along well and it was nearing the end of the long line of youngsters. One little fellow sat shyly on Santa's lap and sadly asked for toys, not for himself, but for a poor friend who didn't get anything last Christmas. Oliver, feeling compassion for poor kids, (he was in those shoes once) was determined to donate a few toys to the church for the needy.

After this sobering experience, his next little guy asked for a big slingshot "with a thick, heavy elastic."

"What would you do with it?" asked Santa.

"I'd shoot squirrels out of the trees."

"Oh sonny! I wouldn't want you to hurt little animals. The only reason I would consider giving you a slingshot would be if you promise not to hurt a living thing. A slingshot is fun to use if you line up empty soup cans on a fence and see how many you can knock down. Will you promise me you won't use it for living creatures?"

"Okay, Santa Claus, I promise."

Most little girls wanted dolls and carriages, but one little girl asked for a "big, big truck, because my brother won't let me play with his."

Elated parents shook Santa's hand and said he was the best they had ever had at their annual fair.

Oliver went home with humble satisfaction.

❋ ❋ ❋

Dom, Amalia, Hedda, and Oliver celebrated New Year's Eve with Aunt Molly and Uncle Nickie. A wonderful Italian dinner of lasagna, salad, garlic bread was prepared by the expert cook, Aunt Molly. The girls helped Molly by serving the wine and setting the table. After the dinner Oliver played his ukulele, Nickie strummed his guitar, and they all sang "Ol Sole Mio," "My Gal Sal," "Sweet Adeline," "Bicycle Built for Two," "Auld Lang Syne," and many other familiar tunes.

"Itsa gooda time we have, no? We do dis again a soon. Itsa fun."

Everyone agreed that it was a happy celebration of the new year, 1910.

1909 had been an eventful year and having a new love interest gave Oliver a feeling of satisfaction. However, not all the news that year was comforting. There was always news of wars, and the civil war in Honduras was frequently covered by the newspapers.

Turkey and Serbia finally recognized the Austrian annexation of Bosnia and Herzegovina. That news made Oliver wonder how long the specious peace would last.

News of the inauguration of the 27th president, W. H. Taft, was welcomed.

On the lighter side, it was announced that the first permanent waves were given by London hairdressers. *Hedda's beautiful hair wouldn't need that treatment*, thought Oliver.

Oliver and Hedda had their usual Sunday dates, occasionally double dating with Dom and Amalia.

Dom was able to get Oliver aside to tell him that his old sweetheart Meghan, married Jake Ronan's son, Sean.

"Well, as she once said to me . . . 'La De Dah' . . . However, I do wish them well."

It had taken Oliver a while to get over Meghan's rejection, but since meeting Hedda, he looked upon the situation with no regrets. It's just past history, he concluded.

Both Oliver and Hedda were attendants at Dom and Amalia's wedding April 26, 1910. Hedda was bridesmaid, and Oliver, Dom's best man. After the ceremony, a small reception was held in the church hall. The bride and groom went off on their honeymoon to nearby Niagara Falls.

Fourteen

It was Wednesday in May when Hedda phoned and was sobbing so uncontrollably that she had difficulty telling Oliver that her mother had passed away.

"Burt, I've got to help her out and give her some comfort."

"You go ahead, I'll hold the fort."

When Oliver arrived at Hedda's house, he was hesitant about entering, especially when he saw the customary crepe wreath hanging on the front door, signifying a death in the family. Mrs. Kreisig's body was laid out in an oak casket, and there were many flowers displayed all around the parlor and the open coffin. Several people were seated along the walls of the room, mournfully wiping away tears. Hedda was comforted by Oliver's presence.

"The funeral is set for Friday . . . I don't know what to do . . . it will be so lonely without my mother. She was my best friend and confidante. Oh, Oliver I'll need help in making decisions. Will you come to the funeral? Will you be here for me? This is the worst thing that has ever happened in my whole life."

"I've heard that one should never make *major* decisions while in an aggrieved state. Yes, I'll be with you at the funeral. Do you need a pall-bearer?"

"That's been taken care of . . . but, I need you by my side. Please, Oliver?"

"That's for sure, Hedda."

The funeral Mass was to be at nine o'clock, Friday. Oliver was at the house by eight. Everything was done in fine order. Father Riccio and attendees recited the rosary before the undertaker directed guests to the three horse-drawn carriages waiting to transport them to the church. The horse-drawn hearse followed.

It was a High-Mass sung with complete rites, with Deacon and Sub-Deacon chanting while swinging the incense crucible.

Oliver felt that the music should reflect promise of the person's soul ascending into Heaven, instead of being so drab . . . pulling one's spirit to a lower ebb. Maybe some day the church will change, he pondered.

It was after ten o'clock when the procession of mourners lined each side of the casket at the cemetery. Many more prayers were offered before the coffin was lowered into the grave, and the mourners dispersed. Oliver held Hedda's hand, heading for the carriage that was to bring them back to an empty house.

Once inside, Hedda threw herself into Oliver's arms, sighing and sobbing uncontrollably. He was at a loss for words, but held her tightly, feeling so much compassion for the grieving girl. They moved to the sofa in the parlor where they sat enveloped in each other's arms, too emotionally drained to speak. Oliver, kissing her tears away, then found her lips quivering with want and need. They both were consumed with desire, and the compassion he had felt for her turned into flaming passion for both of them.

"Oliver, on the day we buried my mother! . . . Oh, Oliver, this is so against my beliefs. I have always been steadfast in believing that I would save myself for marriage. I can't believe that I got so carried away." She felt too exhausted to shed any more tears.

"We were both carried away, Hedda; don't blame yourself. Now, you'll have to think about the future. You shouldn't stay here alone, Hedda . . . what will you do?"

"Will you stay with me here tonight to help me to decide what I should do?"

"That won't set too well with my new helper; he's been minding shop a few extra times for me lately. I'll come back in the morning, and we can go out to eat dinner . . . how does that sound?"

"I'd rather cook dinner for you here . . . please come early."

He kissed her tenderly, and promised he'd be back the next morning.

＊　　＊　　＊

"I thought that you'd understand, Burt; she's been through a trying time, and I want to help her out."

"We had a lot of customers here yesterday. Why in hell were you gone so long? I don't appreciate filling in so much without some extra help! If you can't work again today, then close the damn shop. I'm out of here." Burt slammed the door, as he exited the building. Oliver was dumbfounded and wondered if he should contact Roy Croft for a new man.

I can't bring myself to disappoint Hedda, thought Oliver, as he scrawled a message on a piece of cardboard and nailed it to the door: CLOSED THIS SATURDAY ONLY.

He arrived at Hedda's by ten-thirty Saturday morning. They had coffee together, went to the park, holding hands while walking, breathing in the fresh air, but hardly knowing what to say. Finally the silence was broken.

"I don't like wearing black, Oliver, but I can't break the custom . . . I'll have to dress like this for a solid year . . . It's a long time to mourn."

"Custom, be damn . . . oops, sorry, Hedda . . . what you wear has nothing to do with how you feel inside. I honestly believe it's a stupid custom, and your loving mother wouldn't want you to experience any unhappiness."

"But when Daddy died, Momma wore black for a whole year, and cried almost every day."

"If you wore other colors, it would brighten up your spirit, and you'd continue to live with the living . . . not with the dead.

"I don't mean any disrespect for the dead . . . but, sometimes people shorten their lives through such drab customs."

"But Oliver, what would people say?"

"What people?"

"Neighbors . . . relatives . . . friends."

"Who are these people to sit in judgment? Hey, I believe that God is our only judge . . . you know . . . judge not, lest ye be judged. I don't give a hoot about what anyone thinks . . . as long as I know that I'm sincere. Its what is in *your* heart that counts."

"You make it sound so simple, Oliver; maybe I'll instigate a slight change in custom."

"This walk is making me hungry, Hedda. Lets go to that new restaurant on Main Street."

"Remember I said that I'd cook dinner today? I planned on making Sauerbraten mit Spatzie."

"You'll have to translate that one for me."

"It's beef pot roast with German dumplings . . . and I'm going to serve it with Bavarian Red Cabbage."

"It sounds like a lot of work . . . I thought it might brighten your day if we went out."

"I want just the two of us at the dinner table . . . nobody else around . . . please?"

"It's a tempting invitation. I accept."

Many weekends were spent . . . just the two of them . . . eating home prepared meals by Hedda, many German dishes she had learned from her mother:

Rhein Lachs Vom Grill (Marinated broiled salmon topped with sauteed onions.)

Gerostete Kalbslebe (Calf's liver sauteed with onions, and topped with bacon.)

*   *   *

It was October when Hedda told Oliver that someone offered the generous sum of twenty-five hundred dollars for her home.

"That's a lot of money, Hedda . . . you should sell!"

"But where would I go?"

"Put that dough in your bank account and leave it there to accumulate interest . . . and live with me in Fredonia."

"You've got to be kidding, Oliver . . . I can't live with you . . . we're not married!"

"Lots of people live together without getting hitched. Let's look for a flat . . . we can tell the landlord that we're married."

"We could be arrested; there are fornication laws on the books."

"Maybe we're not married according to law . . . but, we're really married to each other. You know what I mean . . . it's happened many times . . . hasn't it?" Oliver showed Hedda a copy of a John Keats poem that he wanted to share with her. He read her the second and third verses of "Sharing Eve's Apple."

There's a blush for won't, and a blush for shan't,
and a blush for having done it,
There's a blush for thought and a blush for naught,
and a blush for just begun it.
O sigh not so!   O sigh not so!
For it sounds of Eve's sweet pippin;
By those loosen'd lips you have tasted the pips
and fought in an amorous nipping.

"I've never made a commitment that lasted this long . . . come on . . . life is a gamble, anyhow."

"What you're saying is that if I live with you . . . it's a gamble? It sounds pretty risky to me. But I feel that I don't have much of a choice . . . okay . . . when do we go tenement hunting?"

"Next Saturday?"

"Meet me at the station by ten A.M."

Last Christmas, Oliver had given Hedda a friendship ring. When he met her at the train station at ten, he advised her to wear it on her left hand fourth finger, and turn the ring around.

"It will look like a wedding ring," he said.

"It seems so deceitful."

"I'll get you a real wedding ring, later."

*　　*　　*

There were three FOR RENT addresses that he had clipped out of the newspaper. They rejected the one on the third floor. The second flat had possibilities, but was in much need of repairs. The third flat was worse. They walked through many neighborhoods until they spotted a sign in the window of a two-story tenement: FOR RENT. The contract was signed, and they were told that they could move in November first.

Hedda sold her house. Oliver would not consider using one red cent of her money for their new tenement.

"Some day you may need that money . . . it's yours . . . none of it is mine."

"We'll share expenses . . . since I was able to secure a transfer to a local bank, here in Fredonia."

Oliver agreed to that arrangement.

They were like honeymooners in their new home. Since Hedda was working, too, Oliver helped with household chores. Dom and Amalia accepted their invitation for Thanksgiving dinner. Amalia and Hedda worked on the dinner together, while the men talked about current events . . . however, after a while loud exchanges were overheard from the parlor. The girls froze in disbelief of what was being said, but stayed in the kitchen and couldn't help but overhear.

"Hedda is too nice a girl to be used this way . . . make an honest man of yourself and marry her."

"Butt out, Dom, this is none of your business."

"It is my business! You wouldn't have met her if it hadn't been for us!"

"It is a mutual agreement . . . mutual arrangement . . . it's between Hedda and me . . . no one else . . . do you understand? We're committed to each other."

"I don't call that commitment! You know it's unlawful . . . you could be arrested."

"Are you thinking of turning us in?"

"I couldn't do that to Amalia's best friend."

"Oh, but you could do it to me . . . eh, *friend?*"

Their voices grew louder and sharper, and it sounded, to the girls, as if things might come to blows. Finally, Dom stormed out to the kitchen and forcefully took Amalia by her arm and said: "We're getting out of here . . . get your coat."

"The day is ruined," sobbed Hedda.

Indeed it was ruined, ruined for several days. Oliver and Hedda hardly spoke to each other.

They finally made up in time for Christmas. It was a lonesome holiday. Oliver thought about his family in Lawrence. He hadn't been home for some time, not even for his sister Eva's wedding; she had gotten married a few months before the holidays.

The New Year 1911, rang in without much hoopla.

They read the recap of news headlines of 1910 without much gusto.

"Do you think that our style of living would be regarded as immoral, Oliver? Look at this headline!"

U.S. CONGRESS PASSES MANN ACT: PROHIBITS TRANSPORTATION OF WOMEN ACROSS STATE LINES FOR IMMORAL PURPOSES.

"Hedda, those are different circumstances; those women are often used as prostitutes for hire. I believe that we are decent moral people. Don't worry your pretty little head about it." Oliver drew her close as they continued to scan the news of the passing year . . . news they had read as it had happened; this issue was somewhat of a recap.

MARK TWAIN DEAD.

"Oh yeah, I felt badly when I read about his dying. I've read several of his books. I'll bet that his writings will live on," Hedda said.

"Hey kid, let's dance . . . da, dit da da."

THE SOUTH AMERICAN TANGO GAINS POPULARITY IN EUROPE AND U.S.

Attitudes were lightening up and the lithesome couple danced around their tiny parlor like a couple of pros. They laughed happily, then Hedda plopped herself on the sofa in exhaustion but still maintained her festive mood.

"Let's see what other merry news we can have fun with," she said.

HALLEY'S COMET OBSERVED.

"I read that way back in the 1600's that superstitious people believed that a comet foretold evil things to come . . . oooh, does that scare you?"

"It might have been an omen about that pinch you just gave me," and she pinched him in retaliation.

"Ouch, you little vixen . . . I'll take you to this new bridge and toss you over."

NEW YORK MANHATTAN BRIDGE, BEGUN IN 1901 IS COMPLETED.

"I give up, Oliver . . . you've teased me enough for one day."

"One more headline, my sweet."

REVOLUTION BEGINS IN MEXICO.

"Come with me, and we'll start our own revolution," said Oliver as he directed Hedda to the bedroom. They had, for a few moments, forgotten about the encounter with Dom, but still things weren't quite the same. Oliver became a little irritable at times. They didn't have much of a social life . . . except for a few snowy evenings when they played cards with the tenants downstairs from them. The winter proved to be a drag with snowstorm after snowstorm.

It was May when life took on a livelier and less grim tone; horseback riding was the remedy. Oliver and Hedda relived their courting days, *and* nights to the fullest.

Amalia and Hedda had kept in touch, but felt alienated from best friends.

"I get the feeling that Dom is sorry about confronting Oliver. They've been friends for so many years. He's been feeling kinda blue," said Amalia.

"Well, Oliver hasn't been the same since that happened. Is there something we could do to reconcile them?"

"Dom is too stubborn to apologize."

"It must be a male trait . . . I doubt that Oliver could find it in his heart to excuse the flare-up . . . remember the fun we used to have riding? Oliver and I have been a few times lately . . . we even seem to be recapturing a little romance."

"Could we *accidentally* bump into you two at the stable . . . say . . . next Sunday afternoon?" It was a sneaky trick—but it worked.

Oliver and Hedda were just about to mount Buff and Velocity when Amalia and Dom walked into the stable to choose riding horses.

"What a surprise, Oliver . . . look who's here!" Hedda ran over to Amalia, and they hugged.

Oliver waited, said a soft "hi," to Dom.

Finally, Dom said, "How've ya been, Ollie?"

"Okay, and you?"

After a long hesitation Dom said, "The truth is . . . we've missed you two."

"Yeah, we have too, Dom."

This tender exchange brought tears to the girls' eyes.

"Is it okay for us to disagree . . . without being disagreeable?"

"We've disagreed about politics and a few other things . . . because of our differing viewpoints, it shouldn't spoil a long friendship. Bury the hatchet, Dom?"

"Sure thing, Oliver . . . let's shake on that, and then forget the whole episode."

The girls were relieved that all was patched up. They would forever keep their little secret.

Later, the men had formulated a little secret, also. They planned a surprise weekend trip to New York City, a stay in a grand hotel, and tickets to a Broadway show.

It was the first time the two couples had been to the "Big Apple." The adventure was a marvelous change from their everyday routine, and they lived every moment, eagerly tasting this new kind of excitement.

Dom, Amalia, and Hedda had heard so many stories about their ancestors' happiness upon entering the New York Bay harbor, and seeing the Statue of Liberty, the symbol of freedom. Their delight sparked more enthusiasm in Oliver, as he envisioned immigrants reaching this country for the very first time. How moving it all must have been . . . and here are their children and grandchildren, enjoying the fruits of this land.

After having dinner at the hotel restaurant, the girls were treated to George M. Cohan's *The Little Millionaire*, which was premiering on Broadway . . . the men had sent for tickets, unbeknownst to Amalia and Hedda. This occasion was like a mystery holiday . . . full of delightful surprises. The weekend adventure ended all too soon, but the men promised that there would be a repeat in the not too distant future.

Home again and happily experiencing weekend pleasures, the two couples cemented their relationships with picnics, horseback riding when the weather permitted. When it rained, they viewed enjoyable one- and two-reel silent movies at the local Nickelodeon where they preferred the comedies to the melodramas.

Amalia and Dom became parents in October, naming their son Nicholas, after Uncle Nickie. With the new parents came new responsibilities. Oliver and Hedda didn't see as much of their friends. It was Christmas again, and they eagerly accepted a dinner invitation from Aunt Molly and Uncle Nickie. Hedda enjoyed holding and cuddling baby Nicholas.

"Don't get any ideas," warned Oliver.

He wasn't sure that he meant that, because he thoroughly enjoyed having his turn, holding the little tyke. It brought back recollections of holding his little brother, Joseph, when Oliver was only ten years old, way back in his life when his family was whole.

Oliver drew himself back to the present at this wonderful Christmas celebration, typically in the Italian manner, all the emotions riding high. They vowed to celebrate the New Year, 1912, together. They did, with good food, champagne, music, . . . hugging, kissing, and good wishes abounding.

*   *   *

Oliver and Hedda again read the edition of recapped headlines for 1911:

ARMISTICE ENDS MEXICAN CIVIL WAR.

"Hey, Hedda, remember our little revolution celebration when we read about the Mexican war last year? Let's practice our armistice."
"Be serious, Oliver, let's read on."

MARIE CURIE WINS NOBEL PRIZE FOR CHEMISTRY.

"Hedda, sweetheart, chemistry is working on me right now!"

CHARLES F. KETTERING DEVELOPS FIRST ELECTRIC SELF-STARTER FOR AUTOMOBILES.

"Do you have a built-in self-starter?"
"Now who's the clown in this family?"

PHILADELPHIA, (AMER. LEAGUE), DEFEATS NEW YORK, (NAT. LEAGUE), 4–2 IN WORLD SERIES.

"This is Oliver versus Hedda . . . and I will not be defeated." Oliver gave Hedda a long passionate kiss, and he won.
Dorothy Dix's column had this advice for men:
"Find out what is inside a girl's head instead of being content just to admire the outside scenery."
Wow, how can a man tell what's inside a woman's scheming head? wondered Oliver. Though, I do think that Hedda is intelligent . . . but she sure has a nice body, too. That's what gets my engine going.

＊　　＊　　＊

1912, and snow, snow, snow. "At least I've had a few sleigh runners to repair, and a few horses to shoe, but not enough business to stay open on Saturdays," Oliver complained.
"So, let's make use of the Christmas presents to each other, and go skiing . . . eh, my love?" mused Hedda.
The heavily waxed skis glided easily over the soft snow. The brisk clear winter air brought roses to their cheeks, and rosiness to their play-

fulness. Oliver and Hedda had a few falls and made the best of being down in the snow by rollicking in it like two little bear cubs. Happy laughter filled the air.

"Oh, Oliver, this is the most fun we've had this winter . . . we should be out every day."

"There's another blizzard on the way . . . and something tells me that you and I will be house bound . . . how does that grab you?"

"I guess that means that we'll be spending evenings with our downstairs neighbors, Anita and Jerry, playing cards."

"Whist is all right, but, my pumpkin, I have better ideas than that!"

"I don't doubt that at all!" she said, as she playfully washed his face with a handful of snow.

"Ooh . . . you little vixen!" he said, as he tried to reciprocate the gesture.

They returned to their flat exuberantly energized, their playfulness not ending until well after midnight.

Fifteen

It was March when Hedda announced the happy news, but her elation was short-lived by Oliver's reaction.

"I don't know why . . . but somehow, . . . I assumed this wouldn't happen . . . after all this time!" Frustration was written all over his face.

"How could you *not* expect it to happen, Oliver?" Hedda began sobbing. "Every woman *wants* to be a mother . . . *I* want to be a mother . . . why don't *you* want to be a father?"

"Please don't cry, Hedda . . . we'll make the best of it."

"*Oh nice, Oliver* . . . does that mean you'll just tolerate your own child . . . you don't want your very own child . . . he or she is in the making right now, and probably feeling the distress that I'm feeling right here and now!" She flung herself on the bed in tears.

Oliver wanted to comfort her . . . but he couldn't think of anything to say. He left her to her sorrow . . . and sat at the kitchen table with a beer. Soon he returned to the bedroom.

"Hey, mon 'tse chou . . . I love you, you know, . . . we never stay mad at each other . . . do we? Will you forgive me?"

"Maybe I will, if you tell me what 'mon 'tse chou' means," she said with a half sob and half sigh.

"It's a term of endearment that my mother would use, tenderly . . . interpreted, it might lose the softness and affection intended."

"Tell me . . . you funny guy."

"Well, you asked for it . . . it means 'my little cabbage.'"

Oliver put his arms around Hedda, and they both laughed.

"There now . . . mon 'tse chou . . . we'll have to think of names for our little one."

"If it's a girl, let's name her Heidi or Gretel."

"Let's not . . . Shirley would be better."

"I can see where we'll have to put names in a hat, and draw . . . we don't agree on a girl's name . . . how about boys' names?"

"I suppose you'll want Hans, or Felix . . . William, that's my middle name, you know."

"I've heard of some men named Shirley . . . what do you think of that name?"

"Hedda, we have until October to think about names . . . let's wait before we decide."

They both agreed to delay the decision about baby names.

*　　*　　*

Frank, Oliver's brother, mailed this clipping to Oliver:

JANVIER WINS THE NEW ENGLAND CHAMPIONSHIP AT MECHANIC'S HALL, BOSTON.

Oliver phoned home, spoke with his mother, and when Frank came on the line, Oliver let him know that he was miffed about not being notified of the wrestling match beforehand.

"I was so busy working out . . . sorry, brother . . . I'll let you know about the next match."

"I'll be there next time . . . did Joe attend?"

"Yeah, so did Eva's husband, Joe. The arena was mobbed. It felt great to get such recognition."

"You deserve it, Frank. Say, I could use your help in the shop, here in Fredonia . . . want to be a blacksmith, like your old man, and big brother."

"That might work out pretty well . . . Ma would have one less guy to cook for. When should I be there?"

"Any time you can make it."

"I'll give it a lot of thought, and let you know."

*　　*　　*

Oliver was concerned and very protective of Hedda; she wasn't one to curtail any physical activities. He thought it best to cut back on skiing, but she was confident that there was no danger to herself or the baby. The snows kept coming right through March. In April, they were back riding Buff and Velocity, oftentimes riding with Dom and Amalia while little Nicholas was being cared for by Aunt Molly.

Hedda still looked as slender as ever; no one would have guessed

98

that she was pregnant.

"Should I tell them, Oliver?"

"Let's wait a while longer," he answered.

The two couples continued to meet for riding, dinners, and shows, and it was only in June when Amalia asked, "Hedda, have you been binging on chocolates and ice cream, or did you swallow a watermelon seed?"

"You noticed!... it must be a seed... it's growing and growing... isn't it wonderful, Amalia?

It would be more wonderful if they would marry, thought Amalia. Outwardly, she expressed happiness for the parents to be. Dom shook Oliver's hand and congratulated him in a subdued manner.

By September, Hedda had become large and restricted.

"I feel as if I'm in my own way... I'll be happier when I can carry my baby in my arms, instead of in this stretched out belly of mine."

"Just three more weeks, Hedda, and you'll have your wish." Oliver was beginning to feel impatient, too.

Hedda began labor in just two weeks, and Oliver was able to call on the services of a midwife, who refused to have him present during the delivery. A healthy eight-pound, six-ounce boy was born October 5, 1912. This little robust child was named Theodore... to be nicknamed "Teddy."

Oliver was most helpful, cooking meals, and tending baby and mother. Within two weeks, Hedda took over with the household duties, and proved to be skilled at child care.

In early December, Oliver built a sleigh with a carriage-like handle, and nailed it to old sled runners. They bundled Teddy warmly and set off for the park, where the new mother and father delighted in pushing the sleigh while skating around the rink.

Again, Uncle Nickie and Aunt Molly hosted the Christmas dinner, including Dom, Amalia, Nicholas, Oliver, Hedda, and Teddy.

"You kids a so lucky a hava bambinos... we not a so lucky as you," said Molly.

"You want us to give you Teddy?" Oliver offered jokingly.

Hedda didn't appreciate that kind of joke... she kept quiet, but her leer towards Oliver spoke chillingly.

"*Oops*," he said "I wouldn't take a million dollars for this little guy. Sorry, you can't have him."

Hedda seemed placated, for the moment. However, Oliver had noticed that she was a bit touchy of late.

After dinner, the girls were in the kitchen with Aunt Molly . . . the men in the parlor.

"Women are a little unsettled for a while after having a child . . . believe me, it will pass," Dom whispered to Oliver.

Dom was right. It did pass and by the New Year, 1913, life was as pleasant as it could be with fewer downs than ups.

❖   ❖   ❖

Oliver still enjoyed reading newspapers. The highlights of the events of 1912 had his full attention, until he decided that he wanted to share the interesting headlines with Hedda.

"Can you hear me from the baby's room, Hedda? The good ole US of A has expanded with two more states. ARIZONA AND NEW MEXICO HAVE BECOME U.S. STATES."

"I'll be out in a minute, Oliver, Teddy's eyes are getting a bit weighty. He's almost out like a light."

Hedda sat next to Oliver to review the headlines.

"This is old stale news. We've read this stuff during the year. We already know that Woodrow Wilson Won the Election. What's the point in rehashing the old headlines?"

"Maybe so, but I find it interesting, like the headline about the Lawrence textile workers' strike. It was bad news for my home town. A lot of businesses depend on the mill people to buy their products."

"Aren't you glad that you didn't stay in Lawrence. Gee, I wouldn't even know you if you had."

"You bet, kid." He gave her a peck on the cheek and a light pinch on her rump.

"Ouch," she said as she pressed her nose against his, peering into wide open eyes. They both laughed, then continued reading.

"Hedda, I saw pictures of the *S.S. Titanic* after it had been launched. Wow, what a rich boat! A lot of wealthy people must have lost their lives, and who would have believed such a tragic thing could have happened on the maiden voyage, of all things! Look at this . . . 1,513 people were drowned. Wealth can't buy everything!"

"Yeah, their money couldn't save them. Being not so rich, like us, isn't all that bad."

They read on about sports. Boston defeated New York four to three.

"Now Hedda, did you root for the New York team? I've always

100

rooted for Boston. Well, no matter what team would have won, I'd be a winner either way."

"Aw come on Oliver, where are your loyalties? You've been in New York a good part of your life!"

"You know that my family is still in Massachusetts . . . can't I have two loyalties?

"Sure, as long as you remain loyal to *our* family," again peering into his eyes, creating pleasurable feelings of playfulness for both . . . which Teddy's cry interrupted.

*   *   *

Frank wrote to Oliver that he had met someone special and decided not to go to Fredonia . . . not just yet. He was also continuing his active wrestling career, but would seriously consider working with Oliver, "maybe in a year of two."

Who knows, thought Oliver, *by that time, things could change a great deal.*

Sometimes, the coincidental thoughts that enter one's head can have a smidgen of prophesy.

*   *   *

Dom and Amalia bought a Model T Ford, and the two couples saw more of each other. The girls were always comparing baby development, while the men talked about baseball and current events. Oliver told Dom about the fancy iron fence work he was doing for a wealthy customer. They both went to the shop while the girls prattled on.

"Amalia, have you ever looked at other men and wondered if you could be happier with someone else?"

"I could never imagine myself with anyone else but Dom . . . what are you trying to say?"

"I feel guilty . . . ,but, I'm not really married . . . I don't know how to tell you this . . . if I do, promise not to tell Dom?"

"Whatever it is . . . maybe I shouldn't hear it!" Amalia couldn't imagine what Hedda would be telling her. She hoped that nothing would happen to change a friendship that she cherished.

"But I need to tell somebody . . . you're my best friend . . . at least hear me out."

101

"Okay, and it won't go any further than these walls."

"Well, each day after Oliver goes to work, I bundle up Teddy and put him in the sleigh, and we go over to the stable. The man who owns the riding academy and I have been talking . . . just casually. Oh Amalia . . . he is *so* nice! . . . handsome, too."

"Does Oliver know about this?"

"I only told him that I take Teddy out for fresh air each day. Mark Anker is his name. We've conversed just about every weekday afternoon for about two weeks. He knows my situation . . . hey, if Oliver won't marry me . . . I'm free . . . right? He is *so-oo* nice!"

"This disturbs me, Hedda . . . after all these years . . . you and Oliver seemed so in love."

"He's not the same since Teddy came. Oh, he's good to me I guess, and good to the baby . . . I just can't quite put my finger on what ever is bugging him. Sometimes, I think that he is itching to make changes . . . changes for himself, not including me and Teddy. You know about all the wandering he did in the past. This is the longest he has ever stayed in any one place. Do you blame me for thinking of other possibilities?"

"I don't know what to say. I won't tell Dom, but I know that this news would hurt Dom terribly. He and Oliver have been so close for so many years."

They heard footsteps and voices from the hall, and as the men entered the flat, Dom said, "Amalia, you should see the wonderful fence Oliver is making . . . some day, honey, when we get a bigger house, we'll have Ollie make us an iron fence just like that one!"

Yeah, thought Amalia, *Oliver might be long gone by then.*

＊　　＊　　＊

When spring came, and buds were on the trees, and young couples were full of romantic ideas, the men made plans for a "mystery" ride. Oliver, Hedda and Teddy took the train to Buffalo where Dom picked them up at the station. Teddy and Nicholas were left in the care of Aunt Molly for the afternoon . . . then the mystery ride began.

"Come on fellows, let us in on your plans," said Amalia.

"Where are we going?" Hedda asked.

"Be patient, girls, isn't it more fun to try to guess? You'll see . . . it's not far . . . only about seventeen miles," said Dom.

"Let's see, at 25 miles an hour, that should take us less than an hour to get there—is that right?" asked Amalia.

"See how brainy my wife is! Now, let's see if she can figure out our destination."

"I think I know," chimed in Hedda. "I've never been there, but I know two people in this automobile who *have* been . . . am I right, Dom?"

"It's about time that you and Ollie see this place. You two should spend a romantic weekend there . . . just the two of you. We'll take care of little Teddy. Right, Amalia?"

"Oh, you clowns . . . we're going to Niagara Falls!" exclaimed Amalia. "Sure, we'll take care of Teddy. Just let us know when."

"Sure thing, friends."

The two couples didn't seem to notice the jostling on the rough road. They sang and laughed, and ate lots of popcorn-like treats.

"Are these Cracker Jacks new to you? We love them and have been munching on these treats since they first came out," exclaimed Dom.

"It's all new to me," mumbled Oliver with a mouthful.

"Hey, look at this little whistle that was in my box," said Hedda.

"Yeah, each box has a prize in it. Amalia got a little watch the other day . . . they're fun little treasures for the kids. We save them for our little guy."

"That piggy bank was in yours, Oliver?"

"That's a laugh. It's just big enough to fit in five pennies . . . just enough to buy another box of Cracker Jacks. That's their ploy to get people to buy more. I will admit, it's a tasty treat though!"

"If you want to keep your little guy happy, buy some of those biscuits in the shape of animals. They're called Barnum's Animal Crackers. Kids love them," Amilia said.

"I prefer the new cookie sandwiches that are called 'Oreos,'" said Oliver, the chocolate lover.

"I've never seen so much new junk in the stores these days!"

"Good junk, though."

In less than an hour, they entered the Niagara Reservation State Park. It was a wonderful day. They went into the observation tower, took an elevator down into the gorge, at the base of the American falls. The part they all enjoyed the most was the boat trip into the waters at the base of the Horseshoe Falls, Oliver and Hedda laughing and holding on to each other, shielding their faces in the mist.

"It's been a long time since you've held me like this," Hedda whispered into Oliver's ear.

"I had the same thought; what's happened to us, Hedda?" He held her tighter.

"Are you unhappy, Oliver? Things have changed since our son was born."

"No, Hedda . . . I love Teddy, but I just don't want it to happen again."

"It won't. Amalia told me about a method to prevent pregnancy. I'll tell you about it when we get home . . . but now, let's just enjoy the here and now."

"To think that this is so close to home . . . why don't we come here more often?" asked Dom, unaware of the other couple's preoccupation with each other.

Finally Oliver said, "Well, why did you wait so long to get an automobile?"

"What's taking *you* so long to get an automobile?" Dom answered.

"Who knows? I might surprise you." Looking at Hedda, "Would you like that?"

"Oh yes, yes, yes."

The ride home was almost as much fun as the whole affair. They exhausted the list of just about all the tunes they ever knew, singing boisterously. It seemed that *Happy Days* were here again.

Aunt Molly assured the couples that their babies were little angels, and she would gladly take care of them again. During the train ride home to Fredonia, Oliver and Hedda exchanged loving glances, though she did wonder if the outing of the day was a secret ploy concocted by Amalia.

Summer weather was conducive to lots of outdoor activities. Teddy was a nine-month-old active, toothless baby boy, who delighted everyone he encountered. The two couples and the children often picnicked in the park. Occasionally, when Aunt Molly took care of the boys, the two couples went horseback riding, or attended musical shows, presented by the local talents of Buffalo.

October 5, 1913. Teddy's first birthday. Hedda made him a cake, and they celebrated by giving him a Lionel train set. The child was happy watching the trains move, but his Daddy was still happier *playing* with the trains. Here was a toy that he would like to have owned, as a child, but poor children just dreamed about owning such an expensive toy. Oliver finally looked up and noticed Teddy's unusual suit.

"Hey Hedda, what's our son doing in a sailor suit?"

"Don't you think he looks adorable? Nautical attire is a big thing for little boys' clothes since pictures of the Prince of Wales in similar outfits have been in magazines. I'm just keeping up with the times."

"And if the Queen wore a sailor suit, I suppose you'd get one for yourself, too."

"Now you're being ridiculous."

"If you want my opinion, I think our kid looks ridiculous."

"Well, that's just one opinion out of many. Amalia bought a little suit for her son, too."

"I don't mind if you occasionally try to keep up with the Joneses, but I find it ludicrous for an American to try to keep up with foreign royalty!"

"I still think that Teddy looks pretty spiffy."

"I'm just teasing you, baby."

"I know," she said as she pushed him back from his sitting position on the floor.

Oliver pulled Hedda down to him, but was distracted by the little tyke who had crawled over to them with a wide smile, wanting to take part in their playfulness.

Sixteen

The snows came early that year, which precipitated another spell of the doldrums for Hedda. She again yielded to the temptation of visiting the stable, purportedly out for an afternoon walk, pushing little bundled up Teddy in his sleigh.

"Hello stranger! Where have you been keeping yourself?" asked Mark Anker.

"We came here a few months ago. We were glad to see that you still have Buff and Velocity. You never seem to be around when we come to ride. So, I might ask you, where have *you* been keeping yourself?" asked Hedda.

"Would you believe I've opened up another riding academy; this one's in Dunkirk, so I'm just *here* . . . then, *there*! Would you like to come inside and say 'Hi' to Buff?"

"Sure, if I can sit Teddy on him."

"Better still, Teddy can sit on our new pony, Max. We'll give him a ride around the track. It's all cleared of snow. We plow it out for exercising the horses in the winter."

Hedda held Teddy on Max, while Mark led the pony around the track. She and Mark were elated to see the mirthful expression on Teddy's face; his eyes were lit up with joy, and his mouth, wide open with baby laughs.

The time passed all too quickly. The sun was setting, and Hedda would have just about enough time to get home to prepare the evening meal.

"I hope you'll come again soon," Mark said, as he took her hand in his.

"I'd like to . . . now, I'd better get going," she said shyly as she exited the barn.

"Gosh Hedda, I've been worried about you. It's almost dark out. Where have you been?" asked Oliver.

"Just pushing the sleigh in the snow. It pushes much more easily since you've waxed the runners. I lost track of the time, I guess."

"Well, in the future, please make it a point to be back home before dusk."

"Yes, my master," she said, bowing low to Oliver.

Not suspecting anything, he took her gesture good naturedly and gave her a loving bear hug, which made her feel somewhat sheepish.

The winter didn't seem quite so long because of her clandestine meetings with Mark; they talked more, laughed more, and he seemed to enjoy the little guy, who had begun calling all men, 'Daddy'.

"That could be very embarrassing," noted Hedda.

"Are all women, 'Mama'?" asked Mark, with a grin on his face.

"No, not really, but he does know who Max is. Have you heard him say 'Max'? Teddy, you want to ride Max?"

"Wide Max, wide Max," he said excitedly. So, Hedda and Mark took Teddy around the track again . . . and again . . . and again.

"Daddy, Teddy wide Max," he told Oliver when they arrived home.

"What is he trying to say?" asked Oliver.

"I went by the stable to pat Buff today, and they have a new pony named Max. The groom let Teddy ride him around the track. Of course, I held on to him. He loved it, Oliver; he'll be a rider like his Daddy some day!"

"Oh, well . . . when Teddy gets a little older he can go riding with us."

Whew, thought Hedda, *that went right over his head.*

*　　*　　*

Another New Year. Another celebration with friends at the home of Aunt Moll, and Uncle Nickie. It was 1914.

All the newspapers had special editions, recapping many events of 1913. Hedda didn't show much interest, but Oliver sat in the parlor contemplating the happenings of the past year.

16TH AMENDMENT INTRODUCES U.S. FEDERAL INCOME TAX.

"You know, Hedda, I don't think that we'll be earning enough to pay taxes this year. Business has fallen off considerably. We'll have to watch our pennies."

"Are you saying that I'm not careful with our budget?" she shot back hastily.

"Why do you take things so personally? I meant that we'll both have to be careful about *how* we spend and *how much* we spend. Gee Hedda, why are you so touchy? Remember when the Foxtrot first came out and we practiced it with Dom and Amalia? Here's the headline."

NEW DANCE CRAZE, THE FOXTROT, IS FASHIONABLE.

"Let's try it . . . ta ta ta ta . . ." Oliver danced toward Hedda and tried to put his arms about her, but she pulled away. He dejectedly went back to the news highlights.

HENRY FORD INTRODUCES NEW ASSEMBLY LINE TECHNIQUES IN HIS CAR FACTORY.

That means more cars on the road, less work for smithies, mulled Oliver.

U.S. TEAM WINS DAVIS CUP TENNIS TROPHY 3–2.

Only rich people play tennis. Who else can learn the sport?

NEW YORK GRAND CENTRAL TERMINAL, COMPLETED.

It took them long enough. Oliver had his own views concerning these headlines.

PHILADELPHIA DEFEATS NEW YORK IN WORLD SERIES 4–1.

"Hey Hedda, maybe you're out of sorts because New York didn't win the World Series!"
"Don't say such dumb things, Oliver. You know that I couldn't care less about baseball."
"I wish I could figure out what you do care about. Maybe you could clue me in." There was dead silence after that remark.

28TH PRESIDENT, WOODROW WILSON, INAUGURATED.

Let's see if this guy can improve Washington politics.

BALKANS AT WAR AGAIN.

"Wars and rumors of war...just like the Bible says," shrugged Oliver with a sigh, after reading news highlights.

"Are we having a war of our own, Hedda? I'm willing to negotiate."

"You seem to blame me for this impasse. Aren't you ever aware of how often you've just ignored me and Teddy?"

"I'm sorry. I just have a lot weighing on my mind these days. Forgive me mon tse chou. Will you let me put my arms around you now? Honey, we both need comforting."

There was nothing like an apology, and the little French phrase to soften Hedda's mood. A truce was made.

* * *

"I don't want to think about what it might be like if war came to this country," said Dom, who was visiting Oliver at his shop.

"My biggest concern right now, is the fact that Ford will be producing more and more cars...and where will that leave me?" lamented Oliver. "My brother, Frank, is on his way here with his new bride. I promised him a job. I don't know if there will be enough business for two families!"

"I've heard that the owner of the Fredonia Riding Academy has opened another riding school in Dunkirk. There's not another blacksmith around. Business from him might hold you for awhile," said Dom.

"I certainly hope so," sighed Oliver. "But I doubt that he would transport his horses all the way from Dunkirk to be shod."

* * *

Current newspaper headlines read: ARCHDUKE FRANCIS FERDINAND OF AUSTRIA-HUNGARY ASSASSINATED

It was June 29, 1914 when Oliver read about the Archduke being murdered the day before at Sarajevo, capital of the Austrian domain of Bosnia. A Serbian terrorist, Gavrilo Princip, was the assassin.

There were many speculative theories of how this would affect America. Oliver viewed it as a tragedy that might precipitate untold burdens on the U.S. of A.

Too many personal concerns were going on in the lives of the Wilson family during the unfolding of the European conflicts. Two of Wilson's daughters married in the White House. Mrs. Wilson died in August of 1914.

"President Wilson speaks about remaining neutral and wanting peace, but I wonder if we can retain neutrality if our way of life is threatened in any way," commented Oliver, adding to the many discussions going on with concerned customers.

"I see this as a long drawn-out stalemate, and we will eventually have to put in our efforts to save democracy," said Phil, a regular shop customer, who was always eager to express his opinions.

Later headlines reported: AUSTRIA DECLARES WAR WITH SERBIA. Austria-Hungary were on unfriendly terms because the Serbs were determined to unite into a single state. Backed by Germany, the murder was used as an excuse to resolve the Austrian dispute with Serbia. Within one week of the declaration of war, *all* of the nations of Europe were at war.

On August first, 1914, Germany and Russia were already in conflict. On August third, Germany declared war on France; they had been at odds in previous wars. On August fourth, Britain declared war on Germany.

Germany began her submarine campaign.

"That's the last straw. Germany's use of unrestricted submarines to sink all vessels, even neutrals, if found in a zone off the Allied coasts. How can the merchant ships get through?" Oliver remarked to his friend, Dom.

"It looks bad, Oliver, I understand that it's a violation of international law."

"I wonder if we'll have to go to war. So far, we're a neutral country, but so was France until it got hooked into the war. Here's a thought, Dom, if America gets into the conflict maybe you and I will be too old by then."

"How old is too old, Oliver?"

"Wouldn't they want nineteen-year-olds, in preference to twenty-eight-year-old guys like us?"

"I won't worry about it right now . . . we'll have to settle world affairs another time. At this moment my wife is expecting me home. See you later, Oliver."

Oliver was caught up in all the talk about world events.

"It's hard to keep up with all the news . . . it's so mind-boggling!" he exclaimed to Phil, who was at the shop again.

Phil showed Oliver the latest news about Italy remaining neutral. "How long can that last?" he asked.

The Allies consisted of Russia, France, England—even the Balkan States sided with Serbia and the Allies. The Germans defeated the Russians at Tannenberg in August, 1914. On August 23, Japan joined the Allies.

The American public was on edge and abuzz with uncertainty; was there the possibility of American involvement?

"Well, in spite of the Germans going through neutral Belgium, they didn't make the headway that they thought they would." Phil was spending more and more time at the shop, solving world problems. At times, the anvil rang out perplexing strikes as Oliver was working on projects—and at the same time, working off frustrations.

"Yeah, the French and British troops surprised the Germans at the Belgian Frontier."

"Hey, look at this advertisement!" pointed out Oliver. "It seems that because of the threat of war, some of the American Germans are under suspicion. I guess they're afraid that their beer gardens might lose customers, so here's an ad for the Schlitz Palm Garden in Milwaukee. Hey, I'd like to go there, wouldn't you, Phil?"

"Maybe we could go sometime. People who blame *all* German's for the world's troubles are knuckleheads," said Phil.

"I live with a German. Wow, I should have the OSS check her out. Maybe she's a spy," joked Oliver.

Both men had a good laugh . . . for a change.

*   *   *

Hedda felt that Oliver was so engrossed in thoughts of war, that it affected their home life.

"Listen Oliver, nothing you *say or do* will be of any consequence. The outcome won't be one iota different. Let's just calm down, and live a little! I'm tired of all your ranting about things you can't change."

"Sorry kid, I guess it takes just the guys to understand."

"Well, I'll give you credit for one thing, Oliver, no matter how excited you get, I've never heard you use foul language like some other men do."

"My mother used to say, 'Children, we don't eat swill like pigs, and we don't speak swill either.' And I also learned even more important lessons from my eighth grade teacher, Brother Emile. I guess those lessons stuck with me."

"I'll have to remember that one if Teddy ever comes home spewing out bad words."

*   *   *

It was time for another birthday celebration. On October 5, Teddy had reached the "terrible two" stage. He was a precocious child, much like his father had been.

"Our Teddy is two years old, Hedda. Did you know that when my brother Joe was two, our father had long before left the scene."

"That's a terrible thing to do. What kind of man must he be?"

"Well, I can't understand it myself, but he treated me decently while teaching me forging in his blacksmith shop."

"That seems to me like too little too late. He wasn't there for you in your childhood. Sometimes I wonder if that affected your ability to make the ultimate commitment, *marriage*."

"Let's not get on that trolley again. I refuse to go on any guilt trips."

"It seems to me that you want to have the option to bow out of this relationship with no strings attached. Is that your reason for not wanting to marry me?"

"If you keep on harping like this, for the sake of *peace*, I just might take you up on that idea."

"I don't think that it's *my* idea . . . haven't you entertained the thought of being free of your son and me?"

"Hedda, let's not create these conflicts. I am not planning on leaving you, if that's what you worry about, then it's *your* problem."

Nothing was resolved by these altercations, and each held in his and her mind a building resentment. The battles went on becoming more and more conflicting.

November and December were snowy months, and there were moments of reconciliation. They rollicked in the snow, skied, skated, and had snowball fights. Their relationship seemed mended, and Hedda asked herself, what was I so edgy about?

The rest of the year took wing, with the usual celebrations. Thanksgiving at Oliver and Hedda's flat, Christmas at Dom and Amalia's place, and New Year's with Aunt Molly and Uncle Nick.

A great surprise treat was furnished by Uncle Nick. He had arranged for a sleigh ride for eight people including the two little boys. They had to meet the fancy "barge" at the bridge. Several other families and couples had reservations for the ride, also. The huge carriage with its many riders was pulled by ten horses. When they settled into their seats, their knees were covered with the warm blankets that Aunt Molly thoughtfully brought along. This was a new experience for the "Uncle Nick clan."

"The weather couldn't be better—and just look at that full bright moon!" exclaimed Dom.

Oliver couldn't resist adding: "You know what they say about more crazies being out during a full moon!"

"Let's just enjoy, Oliver. The 'crazies' are all home getting drunk."

"That's right, Hedda. We'll just have our own sane fun."

And the carriage jerked forward until the horses were directed down the snow-covered road, trotting in a rhythmic pace with bells clanging to warn people to step aside from the path. The uniformed driver suggested that they all sing, "Jingle-bells."

Everyone aboard sang loudly and happily, even the little ones knew the words.

"What a happy way to begin the new year. Thank you so much Uncle Nick—or better yet, we should call you Saint Nick," said Dom.

All applauded and expressed gratitude.

The singing resumed with joyous song after joyous song, until the driver directed the horses to speed up near a sharp turn in the road. The carriage was thrown to its left two wheels. Oliver yelled to the riders: "Move to this side of the carriage, quickly!" Their weight stabilized the vehicle so that all four wheels were finally on the ground.

"Sir, I saw you taking swig after swig from your whiskey bottle. You are drunk! Move over, I'm driving this carriage."

There was a struggle, but the glassy-eyed intoxicant relinquished the reins and slumped back as if made of rubber.

Oliver received many kudos from the occupants and when they parted at the bridge, all applauded his bravery.

Back at Uncle Nick's house Oliver stated: "I told you that all the crazies are out when the moon is full." They all laughed, maybe not about the crazies, but they laughed because they felt relief in their safety.

Seventeen

"Here we are, leaving another year behind us, Hedda. Let's review the recapped news together."

Teddy was having a nap while his parents reviewed the news highlights of 1914.

PANAMA CANAL OPENED.

"A neighbor of ours in Buffalo was killed working on that project," said Hedda.

"Yeah, it was hazardous work. I'll bet the engineers are relieved that it's over with."

AUSTRALIA WINS DAVIS CUP FROM U.S.A.

"Well, the cup didn't stay with us very long."

CAPE COD CANAL OPENED BETWEEN CAPE COD AND BUZZARD'S BAY.

"Hedda, someday if we make enough money, we should visit Cape Cod. I've seen pictures of some of the resorts . . . but, maybe they only cater to rich people."

PEACE TREATY BETWEEN SERBIA AND TURKEY.

"Oliver, when you see articles like this, doesn't it make you wonder just how long the peace can last? Hey, here's a bit of info that will tug at your loyal heart, you diehard Boston fan."

BOSTON DEFEATS PHILADELPHIA 4–0

"Yeah, wish I could have seen that game."

The couple did have some time together. Life went on.

Business had dropped significantly. Oliver had sent for his brother Frank to work with him, but now he was afraid that there weren't enough customers to keep both men busy. One of Oliver's neighbors was the proud owner of a new Chevrolet, another one owned a Buick.

Now, worried Oliver, *Dodge is coming out with its introductory model. However*, he reasoned, *there are still businesses using the old horse and buggy—but how long will that last?* There were still repairs to make on plows and fences. Mrs. Watkins wanted specifically made baking tins for her bakery. The owner of the riding academy still availed himself of the services of Oliver's shop. Phil was still a frequent contributor to the bull sessions Oliver reveled in these conversations, in spite of the guff Hedda had given him about his obsession with war news.

"I read where the British Navy is blockading Germany, but German submarines almost cut off the supplies to Britain," added Phil.

"Had you heard that the Germans defeated the Russians at Tannenberg? And now with Turkey joining the enemies, Russia's sea communications are cut off from the Allies. The Allies are forced to keep troops near the eastern end of the Mediterranean Sea to prevent the fall of the Suez Canal."

"You know, these conversations are going to grow, and grow, once my brother Frank arrives in Fredonia. He's a great talker. One might say, 'he's got the gift of gab.' You'll find out once you meet him," said Oliver.

Frank and his bride, Eva, were grateful for the flat that Oliver and Hedda were able to secure for the newly married couple. They were able to pick up some secondhand furniture, which was adequate for the time being. Frank didn't waste time in helping Oliver with duties at the shop, but Oliver found that his brother had much to learn about blacksmithing. In fact, Frank became Oliver's apprentice, though he did prove to be a fast learner, and wanted to take on some of the heavier duties.

"It helps to strengthen my muscles. Besides, I do work out on my own. I'm still interested in wrestling, you know," he told his brother.

It wasn't long before Frank was asked to wrestle in Buffalo. He spoke excitedly about the Buffalo tournament:

"I guess I made a hit in Buffalo...the crowd carried me out of the ring. I was held high on their shoulders!"

"Is that the love of your life, Frank?" Dom asked.

"Well truthfully, it was the first love of my life, until I met Eva Latourneau, the gal that I married, now she comes first . . . *then* wrestling."

*   *   *

Hedda prepared a welcoming dinner for Frank and Eva; also at the table were Dom and Amalia. Nicholas and Teddy had their evening meal earlier, and were playing with wooden blocks on the kitchen floor.

"Do they always play this amicably?" asked Eva.

"Once in a while, they display a little greediness. They're just beginning to learn to share," responded Amalia.

When the hostess was seated, Oliver raised his wine glass and toasted Frank and Eva.

"Here's to the newlyweds. May all their troubles be little ones."

"We'll work on that," said Frank, looking lovingly at Eva. Then he said, "Here's to the smithing business. May I develop the necessary skills to please my boss, my big brother."

"Frank, don't consider me your boss, consider me your partner," retorted Oliver.

"You'd better watch out. Don't boss Frank around too much. He knows too many wrestling holds!" said Dom, jokingly. It was a most gregarious evening, ending up with a songfest, Oliver accompanying with his ukulele.

*   *   *

Frank did prove to be *the* talker, often monopolizing conversations.

"The war is getting nastier with the Germans using poisonous gas against the French; the French retaliated with gas-filled shells. Ypres, in western Belgium, is being bombarded by the Germans." He didn't just contribute to conversations, he just went on and on.

"The Germans proclaimed the waters around Great Britain, including the English Channel, a war zone, and that merchant ships found in that zone would be destroyed— even those ships of neutral countries. This trouble is getting closer and closer to us. We have merchant ships supplying the allies!" Frank continued.

"The British are fearful now . . . millions of tons of their shipping

116

have been sunk. Can't you just see the implications of the *Lusitania* being torpedoed? There were 124 Americans drowned."

"We're not going to stand for that!" Oliver was able to interject.

"I wondered how long it would take Italy to get into the conflict. In May, at long last, they declared war against Austria-Hungary."

All Phil was able to say was, "They're all getting into the act, I heard . . . " He gave up on the last interruption, and went home thinking, Frank's a nice guy—but no one else can express his own views.

* * *

The brothers got along affably. Frank, realizing that he had a lot to learn from his older brother, took it all in stride. Besides their work together, their social life fitted in comfortably—birthday celebrations, parties—just about any reason for the three couples to get together for a day, or an evening of fun. Happy times were had for all during the holidays: Thanksgiving, Christmas, and the New Year 1916.

"I like your brother and his wife," said Hedda.

"Yeah, I like having them near. He was just a little kid when I left home. Since then, he had attended a seminary. We thought that he might become a priest, which would have pleased Mama to no end. I don't know what made him change his mind, but here he is a married man!"

"Eva is a lucky woman."

"You mean because she's married?"

"I'd like *that* situation. Do you know that kids who are born out of wedlock are called 'bastards' by righteous people? Would you mind having your child called bastard?"

"I've heard *that* word before, but used in a different sense. I'd say that any so-called righteous person who would address an innocent child with *that* word, is one himself! Society needs to change its cruel ways."

"I hope that society never changes, because I believe that the binding of family life through marriage is important. It's a state of dignity where a man and woman vow to each other, in the presence of God, to stay together until death parts them. Why can't *you* make that commitment?"

"Here goes that trolley again. OOPS, I didn't buy my ticket!" Oliver spoke sarcastically as he exited the kitchen.

"*That's a hateful thing to say,*" Hedda yelled after him as she ran to the bedroom sobbing.

Oliver felt depressed. He didn't want to hurt Hedda. He kept asking himself, should we do it? His answer to himself was always . . . look at Mama and Papa; where did it get them? He had been fighting these thoughts for about a year and often reasoned that the only way to avoid these confrontations would be to leave. She's still pretty. She'll find someone else.

To change his mood, Oliver picked up the special Sunday newspaper feature which had the 1915 news recap.

PRESIDENT WILSON REMARRIES, DECEMBER 1915.

Married a second time, eh? It must have been right the first time around, that's bravery. Oliver was feeling a tinge of resentfulness for anyone plugging the lifestyle he had always shunned.

FIRST TRANSCONTINENTAL PHONE CALL BETWEEN ALEXANDER GRAHAM BELL IN NEW YORK, AND DR. THOMAS A. WATSON IN SAN FRANCISCO.

Ah communication! New ways to communicate. Hedda harps on communication.

WIRELESS SERVICE ESTABLISHED BETWEEN U.S.A. AND JAPAN.

More communication. We're communicating with Japan . . . and I can't even communicate with that good woman, crying in the next room! I want to go to her and try to comfort her. God help me!

FORD PRODUCES ONE MILLIONTH CAR.

Yeah, God help me, all right . . . I'll be going out of business!

MOTORIZED TAXIS APPEAR.

Another new form of transportation. I wonder if Teddy will ever witness so many changes in his lifetime.

BOSTON DEFEATS PHILADELPHIA 4–1.

This must have been a great game.

118

"Hedda, are you okay? I feel sorry and depressed and in need of a hug."

Hedda came out of the bedroom with red puffy eyelids and shoulders lifting up and down with each sad sigh.

"What can I do to make it up to you?"

She didn't dare to bring up the M word, but just spoke softly.

"I guess I'll be all right."

Though they could ill afford it, they went out for a romantic dinner, while Teddy was placed in the care of a neighbor. Each wondered, are fences mended?

        ✻   ✻   ✻

More fodder for the blacksmith shop debaters:

GERMANY INTENSIFIES BLOCKADE OF BRITAIN.

"Turkey, a threat to the Suez Canal, was thwarted by British and Arab forces. It's good that the allies have the power to protect the canal." All were in agreement with Oliver.

Wise discourses took place during business hours, and after business hours; they all seemed obsessed. Their nervous systems worked overtime, feeling apprehensive of what the future held for this country and for them.

BRITISH WIN BATTLE OF JUTLAND, May 31, 1916.

"Wow, that battle makes it possible for Britain to continue the blockade of Germany. It seems that the British forces are recovering. They went to the aid of the French in the battle near the Somme River; they went deep into the German lines . . . nine miles," said Frank, who was a bit more laid back, and doing a little more listening.

"The new British armored vehicle, with caterpillar treads certainly helped! And how about the new airplanes, outfitted with machine guns. Boy, what power! The air must be full of fighter pilots on both sides. If we have to serve our country, Phil, would you want to be a fighter pilot?"

"Maybe they'd take younger guys than us, Oliver."

"Things are happening at a quicker pace—look at this! Italy declared war against Germany this month. It's August. They've welshed on their neutrality. Who knows when we'll do likewise!"

"When we do, you and I are bound to be called, not just the young guys."

"That zeppelin raid on Paris is awfully scary. The Germans are using every new tactic at their disposal."

"Phil, on the lighter side, I know that you're all out for the New York baseball teams. How do you feel about Boston defeating Brooklyn four to one?"

"Brooklyn will get the bums one of these days."

"Hey fella, you're talking to a Boston fan."

"Yeah, sure. By the way, baseball fans won't like those votes against alcoholic beverages. Twenty-four states cast negative votes."

"That's bad news for most men in this country. Lots of us like our beer, and a bit of the hard stuff occasionally. I doubt whether they can put a stop to our few bad habits."

"A little drink, our little women, and the new dance craze, jazz, makes for a fun evening once in a while."

"Jazz is certainly catching on in this country, and I'll have to agree with you that our gals could use a social night out. Let's do it before the booze is banned."

Jake's Cabaret in Fredonia was where Phil and Oliver took their girls. It was a much needed break, especially for Hedda. They not only danced to jazz, but they also did the polka and the tango. Dancing was one of Hedda's delights, but the opportunity came about less frequently as she and Oliver began drifting apart. She was happy on the dance floor, happy to feel the closeness, which she thought they had lost. Hedda enjoyed meeting Phil's wife, Doris. The two girls were engrossed in conversation, not noticing how much their men had been drinking until it was time to leave.

"Two men with rubber legs aren't fit to drive," said Doris as she and Hedda pushed their soused men into the back seat of the car.

"Thanks for the lift home, Doris . . . It's a good thing that you can drive. Our men are in no condition to steer your Buick."

*　　*　　*

"You know, Oliver, prohibition will be a good thing for our family."

"You don't know what you're talking about. I'm not an alcoholic!"

"Well, tonight you certainly showed symptoms of it!"

120

"Knock it off, gal . . . come here and give your man the lovin' he needs."

"You'd have to sober up first. I'm not sleeping with you tonight," Hedda announced as she took her pillow and blanket to the parlor sofa. She was overcome with deep disappointment in what might have been the climax of a joyous night out.

Oliver awakened with an agonizing headache, but received little sympathy from Hedda. He slunk off to work with nary a glance toward her. She prayed that he would be over his ugly mood before returning home.

Oliver and Phil talked about their over imbibing the previous night. The only positive accomplishment between them was the purchasing of a few long stemmed roses for their women, and a few encouraging words like:

"Good luck, let's hope this will make it all right with the gals."

"Yeah, they'll forgive . . . maybe not forget, but they will forgive."

Talk about a change of mood, thought Hedda. *What can I say?*

"Sure, I forgive you. Thank you. The roses are beautiful."

Well that worked. Oliver was relieved that she didn't mention the drinking.

"The dancing was fun, and we should do it again. I'll have just one drink—no more. I promise."

"I'll hold you to that, Oliver."

✻   ✻   ✻

The holidays were upon them again. 1916 was an eventful year, a year of tensions, anxieties about what the future had in store not only for them, but for the country.

Thanksgiving was celebrated at Oliver and Hedda's flat. Hedda's new Fanny Farmer cookbook with all its exact measurements took some of the guesswork out of cooking. She had bought several tin measuring utensils, and followed the tried and proven recipes to the letter. No longer did she cook with a pinch of this, a handful of that. Fannie Farmer was the first woman to write such a book with level measurements. Everyone enjoyed the way Hedda was able to add a touch of German cooking to the feast, though Oliver wished that once in a while she would learn to cook some of his favorite French dishes. All their guests were impressed by Hedda's cooking skills.

The Christmas feast was prepared by Aunt Molly and the girls, Hedda, Eva, and Amalia. This was a change from the usual New Year celebration at Uncle Nicky's home.

"Happy 1917, everyone!"

A different kind of New Year celebration was held at Frank and Eva's home. Eva was the one to prepare Oliver's favorite New Year pie.

"Oh Eva, you don't know how I've craved Tourtieres! You're a gal after my own heart."

"Eva got the recipe from Ma. Don't they taste just as wonderful?" asked Frank.

"It's a heavenly treat!" exclaimed Oliver.

Even Aunt Molly, Amalia, and Hedda requested the recipe. It was a festive celebration with lots of music making, lots of laughs. It was a wonderfully happy holiday, and to the surprise of Oliver, it was topped off by a phone call to Mama, who was now living with Eva Gagne and her family at their new residence, 506 Haverhill Street, Lawrence.

Mama liked the place, but said it was a little tiresome climbing the stairway to their third-floor tenement. The telephone connection was not too clear, too much static, so their conversation had to be cut short.

January second was another work day. That evening, Oliver read the newspaper including the Dorothy Dix advice column. At about halfway down the column, he read a letter that hit home. It read:

Dear Dorothy,

A few years ago, I was charmed by a very persuasive young man, and I made a decision that I now regret. We have lived together for almost seven years and have a son. Every time I bring up the subject of marriage, he becomes resentful and neglectful.

I have recently met a very kind and understanding man who shows an interest in me and my son. Please advise me as to what steps I should take, if any.

On Edge

Dear On Edge,

You didn't tell me whether you love the man you are living with or not. However, if marriage to this man is what you really want, and he doesn't want, you're barking up the wrong tree. Can't you see that he will never agree? Let this dog go. I gather that he will never learn the meaning of responsibility.

Mr. Kind and Understanding may be your ticket to a more fulfilling life. I wish you the best.

"Hedda, did you write this letter to Dorothy Dix?"

"Oh, I read that . . . it has a familiar ring to it, don't you agree?"

"You didn't answer my question. Did you write that letter?"

"What if I did?"

"Well, for your information, the trolley is leaving for real this time!"

"What's that supposed to mean?"

"You'll see."

Oliver hardly slept a wink that night, and the following day, his distraught mood was heightened by a disturbing conversation with his brother, Frank.

"Say, Oliver, how come you didn't let the family know about your marriage to Hedda, and then the birth of your son?" asked Frank.

"Who said I'm married?" Oliver shot back.

"You mean to tell me that you are not married?" Frank was stunned. "I never thought that my brother would pull such a lousy trick on a woman. You've been living in sin all these years. Gosh, man, I thought you were someone I could look up to and respect. I'm, I'm just shocked!"

"Listen, little brother, just because you attended the seminary, doesn't give you the right to preach and sit in judgment of me. At least I'm not leaving five kids like our old man did. Did you know that Ma received a document that declared them divorced? Pa told me about it when I was in Providence. See, if you don't tie yourself down to anyone, you can go on with your life—and she can go on with hers. That was his theory."

"Oh, so you're going to adopt *his* theory, ay? Just because he's our father, that doesn't make him right. Oliver, do the decent thing—marry the girl."

"Frank, *butt out*. Just because we're the product of the same parentage, doesn't mean that we have to think alike. We're all individuals, and as far as I'm concerned I'm getting out of this damn business. You can have the building, everything in it. It's yours, brother. Good luck. I'm joining the army."

"You mean that you're leaving? Leaving Hedda and Teddy? How can you be so insensitive and cruel?"

"Hey, call me what you want. I have no strings attached. Hedda will find someone else. She'll be better off. Who knows, maybe she's found someone already!" Oliver felt sure of that after reading the Dorothy Dix column.

Oliver had mulled over his situation. He decided that he wanted no part of the domestic life. He had a feeling of entrapment, a feeling that he just had to change the course of his life. He wondered if he could ever find "la joie de vivre." (The joy of living.)

Oliver did stay on at the shop for a while longer, though the brothers were indifferent toward each other. It was upsetting to Frank when Oliver chose to come and go in irregular work patterns. Oliver spent his time fishing or gambling with old acquaintances.

Eighteen

On April 6, 1917, war was declared by President Wilson.

Soon after, it seemed obvious that man's duty would be to his country. It came as no surprise when on May 18, 1917, it was announced the selective service act had passed.

Oliver phoned Phil.

"Hey, buddy, remember that ad about the Schlitz Palm Garden?"

"I sure do, Oliver. Say, Doris has gone to visit her mother in Albany. Now would be the time for us guys to go have some Schlitz beer at the Palm Garden. How about it?"

"This has got to be some kind of coincidence—that's why I called you!"

"Well what are we waiting for. When's the next train?"

They got the necessary information and left the following day. They were able to take a train from Buffalo to Chicago, then from Chicago to Milwaukee. They each pitched in for a taxi cab to the famous Schlitz Palm Garden.

"I never dreamed that this place would be so huge," exclaimed Phil.

"Wow, this must be how the rich live! Just look at those beautiful stained-glass windows!"

"Did you ever see such carvings on these archways? And look at all those palm trees . . . are we in Florida?"

The two men just marveled at the magnificent building.

"Am I seeing things? That sign says meat sandwiches for five cents!"

"Yeah, Oliver, they must make their money on all the Schlitz beer they sell. Let's get a couple of sandwiches and a big pitcher of beer."

The atmosphere, the peppy polkas, played by a live band, and the German dancers in costume, gave Phil and Oliver a feeling of extravagant exuberance.

Phil exclaimed with much enthusiasm, 'We should take our gals here—give them a fun time. Let's do that Oliver. This is great!"

"Maybe I didn't make myself clear, Phil. I've had it with the domestic life. I'm bowing out. See, no divorce . . . don't need it . . . no commit-

125

ments. I'm free, free, free!"

"No, you're not, my friend, wherever *you* go, you have *you* with you. You'll never get away from your selfish self. 'ME, ME, ME' is what you think about. What about your son Teddy and the woman who has stood by you over the years? Come on, Oliver, do the right thing. I had no idea that this trip was your exit from responsibility, or I wouldn't have come."

"I'm just a self-reliant guy," Oliver said in flippant manner. "Emerson said: '*What I must do is all that concerns me, not what people think.*'"

"You have it back-side to. I believe he was referring to *duty*—not to just your wants. Does Hedda know how far away from home you are?"

"She doesn't have to know my every move."

"If you don't phone her right now, I will! She must be worried sick!"

"You might be right. I'll call her now but it's not going to change how I feel."

Oliver found the public telephone and put in his call to Fredonia.

"Hi, Hedda, I'm in Milwaukee, Wisconsin with Phil. I thought you might be worried."

"Oh, I knew where you and Phil went . . . Doris phoned me. She thought it would be a nice change for Phil since she had been in Albany caring for her mother. Are you having a good time?"

"Yeah, I guess so."

"When will you be coming home?"

"A couple of days, I guess. Then, you know what we discussed . . . so don't expect me to stay. I'll be leaving for Camp Yaphack in August."

There was a long pause.

"Are you still there, Hedda?"

"Yes.

"Well, I'll see you in a couple of days. So long." And he hung up.

"Are you satisfied, Phil? She already knew our whereabouts. Now let's have some fun in this place, unless you want to go home to Doris's apron strings."

"That remark was uncalled for, Oliver."

"Sorry, I've been as edgy as an untamed bronco."

"If you still want to stay another day, it should give you time to unwind and get your head on straight. We'd better not have too many beers, or neither of us will have our heads on straight!" proclaimed Phil.

*   *   *

126

One part of the varied entertainments consisted of the costumed performers going into the audience and choosing dancing partners from the clientele. Phil and Oliver were chosen by two rather attractive dancers. They both felt somewhat embarrassed, knowing that these women were professional dancers. However, they quickly got into the spirit of the polka music, losing inhibitions as the beer that they had consumed took effect.

"Yahoo," yelled Oliver as he swung his partner, leading her swiftly across the dance floor. He almost moved like an 'untamed bronco,' but his edginess had subsided. When the music stopped, the two men returned to their table breathless and exuberant.

"The girl I danced with introduced herself as Gretchen. She said that we should have been here last week to hear John Philip Sousa's touring band. We can't seem to connect with that band. A few years ago, I missed Sousa by one week at the Buffalo World Fair. One of these days, I hope to hear his outfit in person," said Oliver.

"I've heard him on radio; this was after he had left the Marine band," said Phil as he reached for the pitcher for a refill.

"Let's have a couple more sandwiches, Phil. We're less apt to get tipsy if we eat more."

The entertainment went on and on after the orchestra returned from a short break. A colorful gazebo was lowered from the ceiling to the dance floor. A group of about twenty singers boarded it as they sang merry German songs. Then the gazebo was raised halfway to the ceiling, where all the audience had a better view of the performers.

"I've never been so impressed with so much going on," remarked Phil.

"It makes us forget about the world troubles and our impending part in the war."

"Ah Oliver, let's not talk about that . . . let's just enjoy ourselves."

Enjoy themselves, they did, with more dancing and lots of varied performances.

Heading home, Oliver's regained spirit made the trip back to Fredonia unexpectedly pleasant; he told Phil that he looked forward to being able to serve the country in the war effort.

"Gretchen, one of the dancers at the Schlitz Palm Garden, told me that two things will soon close the Palm Garden. One: Some patrons' ill feelings toward people of German extraction, and two: The new prohibition laws which are pending."

"So that means we've experienced a dying trend of entertainment. That's disappointing. I had hoped to take Doris there some day."

"I really don't think that prohibition will catch on too long. I can't see the harm in having an occasional relaxing beer."

They both agreed.

*   *   *

Oliver greeted Hedda with civility. At her request, he told her all about Palm Garden.

"Daddy! Mommy and I were sad when you were away. Don't go away again," fussed Teddy, with his mouth quivering.

"Daddy loves you, Teddy, but sometimes people have to leave for grownup reasons. Some day you will understand." Oliver kissed his son.

Did I understand on that terrifying day when I discovered that my father was going far away? pondered Oliver. My poor little son is so much younger than I was. He'll forget in due time . . . more quickly than I did.

*   *   *

On May 26, 1917, Major General John J. Pershing was made Commander-in-Chief of American Expeditionary Forces. He advised that millions of men would be needed.

Oliver had made up his mind; he wouldn't wait to be drafted. He told Hedda that he would not return after the end of the conflict.

"You'll find someone who can commit to the vows of marriage. It's not for me." Hedda replied: "The rolling stone must roll once again, and God forbid, it must not gather moss."

"What's that supposed to mean?" muttered Oliver with a confused look on his anxious face.

"It means move on, move on, but make no commitments that will interfere with the rolling or roaming."

"Yeah, I get your drift. I'll live my life as I choose. We're both free, free, free!" Neither spoke after his tirade of heartbreaking words.

*   *   *

Oliver said good-bye to Fredonia, and everyone there.

His army stint began August 20, 1917. He served in Battery B, 11th

128

Field Artillery. It didn't take long for Oliver to write a long letter to Eva and family.

Well, I'm in the army! We got our G.I. issue clothing and the only things that fitted well were the belt and necktie.

We were so lucky to have a brand new barracks. However, with a new building, the small paned windows had about a quarter inch of putty securing the glass and each pane still had factory stickers on them. Since we're new here, they put us to work cleaning them. After two days our First Sergeant said, "We have good news and bad news. The good news is that you men did a good job on all seventy-five windows, and the bad news is that we are in the wrong barracks." We had the same window assignment in our new quarters.

After two weeks, it was time for our familiarization of firearms. We gathered for our first session in one big room where a Sergeant demonstrated care of a rifle, assembling and disassembling. We each were given a white cloth about a yard square upon which to place the rifle parts. We practiced assembling and disassembling our rifles. After several failing attempts by some of the guys, we had to practice more. When we thought that we were finished, we were ordered to start all over again. Finally, when all accomplished the reassembly correctly, that phase was ended.

The next session was at the firing range. This is where we had to shoot well in three positions, standing, kneeling, and prone. Our safety record was perfect. We put down our unloaded guns at our firing position. Then we went out to hang our targets about fifty yards from the firing line. We returned to our firing lines, loaded our rifles, and each took three practice shots to adjust the sight of the gun. We then fired ten shots in each position. Upon completion of the thirty shots, we stood up to indicate that we were finished. When all enlistees were standing, we proceeded to retrieve our targets to check on our scoring. Back in the orientation again, we disassembled, cleaned, oiled, and reassembled our arms, At last it was time for chow which wasn't all that bad, especially being so hungry . . . most of it tasted better than it looked. At least we survived until the following meal.

We learned about scoring. Bulls eye—5 points, next outer ring—4, etc. I was named the "BIG SHOT" of our platoon because I scored 190. Anyone in the 190's range is considered the elite of the firing range. So what do you think of your big brother now?

Oliver

At Camp Yaphack, on Long Island, Oliver became known as a great marksman. He was soon upgraded to Corporal, and felt sure that because of his skill on the shooting range he would be sent overseas;

that's what he wanted. When he was made Sergeant, he was informed that his expertise would be needed at Camp Yaphack for training younger men for the infantry. He was greatly disappointed, though he did feel that he *was* helping in the war effort.

Oliver reveled in army life. He was well liked by his peers, and even those under his status. He took part in camp shows, comedy skits, and formed a band, which pleased his superiors. He was instrumental in keeping up military morale.

His kid brother, Joe, tried so hard to get into the army, then the navy, but failed because of his flat feet. Then, when this letter arrived, Oliver was almost envious of Joe.

Dear Brother Oliver,

So, you joined the army, thinking that you would see the world . . . and there you are, still in the states. Well Sergeant, your kid brother is *the* one seeing the world! Because of my flat feet, they didn't want me in the army, or the navy, so, the Merchant Marines took me in . . . Ha, Ha, I'm in Marseilles, France. Would you believe??

I was working down below, shoveling coal to keep the ship's engines going, when a crewman came down and said, "Hey Frenchy, go get cleaned up . . . the Captain wants to see you!" None of the crew is allowed to leave ship . . . but, your petit brother Joe, was taken ashore to act as interpreter for the bigwigs . . . How do you like that? . . . my fellow crewmen didn't! They didn't hesitate to show their jealousy . . . especially since I am a low grade worker in the hole of the ship. They don't stop to realize that if we didn't do our job down below, the ship couldn't move. I figure, we're pretty important guys . . . don't you think so?

While ashore, the officers said that I may as well enjoy a little sightseeing. In the short time allowed me, I watched as a carver made me two pairs of wooden Dutch shoes, one small pair and one large. I'm bringing them home . . . my souvenir from my World War experience in France!

My guess is that we are delivering some pretty important stuff here to aid the allies, fighting the war.

Have fun in the army . . . train your men well . . . then, maybe *they'll* come over here to "see the world."

Your kid brother, Joe

That was not the only letter that Oliver received while at Camp Yaphack. He had mixed emotions about the letter from Hedda:

Oliver,

When you left me, I was very upset and lonely. Teddy cried for daddy. However, now that we have the possibility of a more stable life, I'm feeling more confident about our future.

Mark Anker, who owns both the Fredonia and Dunkirk Riding Academies, has asked me to marry him. Teddy loves Mark . . . and so do I. That will end your responsibilities with Teddy and me, and you'll be free to roam as you wish. We had a good life for a while, Oliver. We *were* happy, weren't we? I sensed that you tired of our routine lives together and wished to move on. Well move on, Oliver, I hope you will be happy in all your endeavors.

Hedda

Oliver agreed that it would be best for both Hedda, Teddy, and also Mark Anker to become family. He wrote and told them, "no strings attached." He vowed that when his service stint was over, his very next move would be to continue his quest to set foot in all forty-eight states.

*   *   *

Woodrow Wilson was inaugurated to his second term as President. Oliver thought that Wilson was in error when he vetoed the literacy requirements for U.S. Citizenship. He felt that Congress did the right thing to override the veto. He felt that more stringent requirements might have forced his mother to learn the language of her adopted country. She never made that effort.

Oliver felt angered by the fact that the four women who picketed the White House in behalf of women's suffrage, were sentenced to six months in jail and then, the U.S. Senate rejected President Wilson's suffrage bill. Some day, Oliver pondered, those politicians will wake up and realize that women have just as much right to vote as men do. Some of his cronies didn't share his views:

"Ah, the dumb broads wouldn't understand politics. They'd just vote for the best looking guy, not for what the better man stands for."

"I can't agree with you," countered Oliver, "I've met some pretty damn smart broads in my day, and I know some men who are so detached from what's going on in the world that they don't make such wise choices of candidates themselves."

When Oliver learned that the first U.S. division had arrived in France, he lamented the fact that he wasn't with them. I may be a little older than some of those guys, but I could handle the weapons as well, if not better than they can.

News headlines read: U.S. declares war on Hungary and Austria. The Allies execute Mata Hari as a spy. U.S. purchases Dutch West Indies. What do we need that land for, he wondered.

Oliver always made an effort to read as much as possible, and when the new Sinclair Lewis novels, *The Job*, and *The Innocents* were published, he lost no time in buying copies. He also kept up with the baseball news, and that year Chicago won the world series, playing against New York, four to two.

Oh, he thought, Hedda wasn't that disinterested in baseball . . . she must be disappointed. I guess I can't help thinking about her . . . she was once part of my life . . . and then there is our Teddy. Gosh, I long to see my little boy. Oh God, did I do the right thing? When Oliver wasn't occupied with teaching marksmanship, and performing with the band, his thoughts reverted to his former love partner and their son.

Nineteen

The holiday celebrations didn't offer much to celebrate about. Oliver was finally granted a leave for the New Year, 1918. With some of his service pay, he bought himself a large diamond ring.

"That's quite a rock, Oliver," Frank said, but was really thinking: *This guy has rocks in his head...he must think that he's Diamond Jim Brady.*

Eva made Tourtieres special for Oliver. The holiday was not as festive as in other years, but he did get to see some of his old buddies, play some poker and do a little cross-country skiing. Dom was still around, and hadn't been called in the draft, which pleased Amalia to no end.

The armistice was signed November 11, 1918 and Oliver was discharged from the Army on January 16, 1919. He, like numerous other veterans, looked for employment. He found that jobs were not that easy to come by. He had read about several glass factories in Philadelphia, Pennsylvania, where he thought he might learn the glass-making business in one of the smaller plants.

Earlier in the century, factories were located west of the Alleghenies because of the proximity of coal fields and rivers. However at this time, most factories had switched to gas-fired tank furnaces, which modernized their systems of glass-making. Sand was still the main ingredient, but the salts, extracted from marine plants, were replaced with synthetic alkaline. The smaller plant put out mainly utilitarian products, so Oliver didn't feel that he would learn much about glass-making, especially since he found out that he would have to study about the processes from the ground up, and would also have to learn chemistry. With little education, that was out of the question. He was not a candidate for apprenticeship.

He became an operator of a Michael Owen's rotary bottle-making machine, which proved to be an automated, low-skill job. Oliver also learned to work other Owen's machinery for blowing light bulbs, tumblers, and lamp chimneys. He never did learn the chemistry of the business, but at least he had a job. Many of the returning servicemen weren't that fortunate. He wrote to his youngest brother Joseph about openings at the factory. Joseph visited Oliver, but was not that interested in the boring repetitiveness. Joe seemed more interested in the fact that Oliver knew how to play the drums and had formed a group of servicemen musicians while at Yaphack; that's what inspired Joe to go home to take drumming lessons.

Oliver stayed with the company for a year and a half, saving all he could for further wanderings; regardless, his gambling addiction set him back a few months' worth of funds.

He recalled a quote from Kin Hubbard: "Why they call a feller that keeps losin' all the time a good sport gits me." Speaking about gamblers, Mark Twain once said: "If there were two birds sitting on a fence, he would bet you which one would fly first."

Oliver thought, *I'm not that kind of gambler, I just like an occasional poker game.*

What George Washington had written made sense to Oliver: "It (gambling) is the child of avarice, the brother of iniquity, and the father of mischief." Even so, Oliver, being true to his somewhat mischievous self, thought of a little mischief as being fun. That "fun" didn't intrude on his becoming a little more open-eyed in his gambling ways.

* * *

Travel is the thing for me, he pondered. The weather became a factor in his choices of states he wished to visit, so he decided that winter time would suit him well in the southern states.

In the winter of 1922 (the year that Warren G. Harding was inaugurated as the twenty-ninth president), Oliver journeyed to Florida, the first stop being historic Saint Augustine where he found the history of this old city intriguing, especially the fact that in 1513 Juan Ponce de Leon searched for the fountain of youth at that site. Oliver visited the Spanish fortress Castillo de San Marcos, on the bay. He learned that the national monument is the oldest masonry fort in the United States, and that the construction began in 1672. He enjoyed the many remaining features of Spanish buildings, examining the wrought-Iron grilles and balconies lining the narrow streets. Thinking back on his blacksmithing experiences he reasoned, I could make these things. He recalled making similar wrought-iron fences in Fredonia.

When he returned to his small living quarters, he dumped the contents of his money belt on the bed, and counted his financial reserves to determine how long he could stay in this historic city, or how far the meager savings would get him to another state before he would have to find employment. *I'm going to keep this rock,* he thought, as he looked with admiration at his diamond ring. The last thing he would want to do is part with his only valuable asset. He wasn't exactly broke, but it seemed imperative for him to become a bit more frugal. The determining factor was the price of train fare to Alabama. He had to leave St. Augustine, or get a job.

Oliver's arrival at Mobile, Alabama found him so low on funds that that night he slept on a bench in the train station. In the morning, he was able to find his way to Mobile Bay where he found work in a ship-repair building, working on the most menial tasks for the professional craftsmen. He was more of a gopher: "go for this," and "go for that." The job was demanding, and the work heavy, plus long hours. *It's better than nothing*, he thought, and stayed long enough to stash away sufficient funds to finally become the tourist he set out to be.

He visited historic Montgomery, "the Cradle of the Confederacy." Oliver enjoyed learning the history of this large city, where he visited the first White House of the confederacy. Jefferson Davis had lived there until 1861, when the confederacy was moved to Virginia. He learned that the city was named for a Revolutionary war general, Richard Montgomery. The architecture, Oliver discovered, was mainly Georgian, characteristic of British influence of the eighteenth and nineteenth centuries.

His funds were sufficient to get him to Biloxi, Mississippi, where immediately upon arrival, he sought employment. The boat building industry would have interested Oliver, but he was told, "Sorry, young man, no openings." The only thing he found available was a job as a short order cook, by the shore of the Gulf of Mexico. He picked up the jargon rather quickly, and added his own witticism to it.

"I'll have a coffee," a customer ordered.

"Draw one," Oliver yelled.

Another customer ordered two coffees: "A pair of drawers."

Two poached eggs on toast: "Adam and Eve on a raft!"

An order of corned beef and cabbage: "Irish Turkey."

Hot dog on a bun: "Coney Island chicken."

Oliver was happy when he could clown around, and the customers expressed their appreciation by laughter—also, by paying him a little extra. He didn't make much money on the job, but it afforded him some amusement such as treating himself to the Charlie Chaplin movie, *The Kid*.

Weeks passed, and he gloated over the fact that he was comfortably warm in the south, while the north was deluged with freezing weather and snowstorm after snowstorm.

Oliver succeeded in getting to the Dixie National Rodeo which was held in Jackson, the state capital. He would have loved to have gotten on one of those broncos to show off what he could do. After all, he had been a cowboy once. He did meet some of the riders, met them later for poker, lost a good portion of his earnings and ended up with just enough money to get him back to Biloxi. It was like starting over again, but he finally had enough money to move on.

Once settled in the French Quarter of New Orleans, Louisiana, Oliver wrote to his brother Frank:

Hey Brother,
. . . this is the place to be! You know that an important part of my travel gear is my drum sticks and leather practice pad . . . well I was in my room practicing all kinds of rhythmic patterns, including jazz. All at once this loud annoying knock startled me out of my concentration. I thought . . . oh, oh, my landlord is here to complain that I was disturbing the peace . . . but no, it was a guy named Pete Amirault. It seems that he heard me from his room across the hall, and thought that I might be the solution to a problem they've been having with their jazz band; the drummer is often out on binges and doesn't show up for performances at the Monique Cafe, and would I be interested in the job? Would I? You bet! I'm proud to be a part of such a professional group. Norm Cartier plays trumpet, and Pete plays piano. We had a couple of jam sessions before playing at the club, and everything is just clicking . . . boy, you should hear us . . . and we're drawing the crowds. We'll have at least a month of this before Mardi Gras, then they tell me, that things will quiet down somewhat as the tourists leave.
I met a few Cajun trappers who get around prohibition . . . in illegal ways. Boy, its good to get a drink once in a while. I went with them one morning in their hand carved pirogue, they had trapped several beaver and a few other fur bearing animals. They earn their livelihood by selling the pelts. Their French is sometimes difficult to understand. It's like . . . what we used to call, P. I. French.
Have you heard anything about the "ladies" down here? They're quite

the gals. We're having a swell time, dancing . . . and etc., etc., etc.!

I'm eating well, too. The guys in the band have wives who are very good cooks! We get along great . . . but I don't put up with their women making a play for me.

The drummer was back. He had been jailed while in a drunken state, and was released only after he had disclosed the source of the booze. Oliver at least had earned enough money to be on his way again. Frank's letter arrived in the nick of time as Oliver was packing to leave for Arkansas. It gave him extra reading material while traveling on the train.

Hi Oliver,

Got your letter, brother, it sounds like you are fitting in anywhere you go . . . that's our Oliver!

A lot of things have been happening here in Fredonia. Our brother, Joe, loaned me money to buy a couple of washing machines to start a laundry business. Eva and I have been working hard, building up our business. We are advertising it as "THE STAR LAUNDRY. GETTING YOUR WHITES WHITER, AND YOUR COLORS BRIGHTER." We could never again make a go of the smithing business . . . too much competition with all the new automobiles coming out! We almost landed in the poor house before the idea of switching to the laundry business. We're working on getting the local hospital to use our services . . . who knows, maybe we could expand services to Dunkirk and Buffalo.

Have you gotten one of those new things called "radio" yet? We get a station called KDKA, transmitted from Pittsburgh, with up to date news: our former president, William Howard Taft, was named Chief Justice of the Supreme Court . . . also, radio station WJZ from Newark, broadcasted a play-by-play description of the world series in which NY, National league, defeated the NY, American league, 5–3. If you want to know what's going on in the world, pronto, you'd better get yourself one of these new gizmos.

Our little brother, Joe, seems flush these days since he came out of the Merchant Marines. He spent $900 on a Steinert grand piano and is taking lessons from Helen Hamel . . . remember her? She's that cute little blonde, blue eyed gal who lives on Butler St. in Lawrence. We were glad to hear from you. Write again when you can, but watch out for those "ladies."

Frank

Oliver was happy to read that his brother was making a success in a business other than smithing. *What a transition*, he considered, *what a switch from horse-shoeing to laundry bags.* He chuckled to himself when he thought, *I hope they clean up.*

I'll have to get myself one of those radios, that is, if I ever settle down long enough in one place. I'd certainly look silly carrying such a bulky thing under my arm while lugging my bags, mused Oliver.

*   *   *

Oliver's main objective of his visit to Arkansas was to find relaxation in fishing and hunting. He had read so much about the state's well-stocked lakes, rivers and streams, and of all the scenic splendor. His finances would keep him in the vacation mode for a not too prolonged visit—as long as he didn't encounter any card sharks. He hoped *that* temptation would not relieve him of his holiday funds.

Well, he thought, *maybe this place called, "The Land of Opportunity" might prove to have just the right kinds of opportunities I'm looking for.* The Hot Springs, in the Ouachita mountains, was advertised as having curative waters and the ad told about how Indians first sought out the thermal waters which they found to have curative powers. The "Quapaw" bath houses were built in the twenties. The water is heated by contact with hot rocks beneath the building and the springs have been piped to the row of bath houses. When Oliver arrived at the health spa, he was impressed with the unique character of the main white building with its fancy designed east and west walls, and domed top, complete with cupola. He luxuriated in a two-day restful stay that energized him for his next escapade.

Oliver found his way to the area east of the Ozark Mountains. Needing ammo for his rifle, he arrived at a trading post where he met a few small time fur traders who turned out to be small time hunters, gathered around a pot-bellied stove. They were not the type of businessmen who were out to make big bucks in the fur trading business. They were Choctaw Indians eeking out a living for their tribal people. One young man asked Oliver what his business was in the area.

"I'm just a tourist out to enjoy a little fishing and hunting."

"And, what do you plan on doing with your catch?"

I hadn't thought much about that . . . maybe do a little outdoor cooking."

"Our Choctaw people frown on hunting as a sport. That kind of

138

hunting is wasteful. We hunt only when food is needed, and kill no more than we can eat. Much of our food source has disappeared because of hunters like you."

That bit of information found Oliver a little chagrined. He pondered his response and asked, "If I hunt and give my kill to your people, would that make things right?"

"Do you wish to come on a hunt with us? Come to our village and we will make arrangements with our chief."

Oliver agreed, and spent time with his new friends, hunting and fishing, but never wasting any of the kill. He gained approval and respect of the men after displaying such accurate marksmanship. Choctaw Indians were not usually so trustful of white men, but Oliver turned out to be an exception.

After these expeditions, it was the custom for the women to skin carcasses, cut up the meat and prepare it for cooking, or drying it for future use.

Oliver learned of the Choctaw customs and some words of their Muskogean language. The Choctaw claimed no political or religious system, though they were peace loving people. That didn't mean that they wouldn't defend their territory with tenacity if the need did arise. There were other districts, each headed by a chief, but no head chief over all the Choctaw.

Oliver witnessed their elaborate burial customs. They helped the deceased find their way to the land of their ancestors; they believed in the immortality of the soul. Their numerous deities included the sun and fire.

The Chief's sons taught Oliver their methods of farming. He was surprised to see that the harvest of corn, beans, pumpkin, and melon was so abundant that they sold much of it to their neighbors. *These people know how to live by hard work, and still find ways of themselves socially,* thought Oliver.

Oliver always loved games of chance such as the Indian hand game. Two bones were used, one marked, the other unmarked. As a player held them in his hands, his opponents tried to guess which hand held the plain piece. Oliver won a brave's horse in one game, but soon lost it in another game. The men also played ball games.

Women were held in great esteem and were allowed to participate in their own ball games after the main events...which were the male games. These games were often used to settle disputes.

Both men and women were fond of these social events and Oliver's participation gave him a sense of belonging. *Who knows,* he thought, *maybe I'm part Indian. After all, it is known fact that many French Canadians had wed Indians. That doesn't seem so far-fetched to me.* With this thought, he let out a whoop that made his new friends direct a questioning glance his way. He had endeared himself to these people by his willingness to learn their ways and to labor readily, but some wondered about his strange "white man ways."

Sometimes as women worked at their skilled basket weaving, Oliver watched in amazement as the colorful designs unfolded. The basket making wasn't all that had interested him. There was one particular young maiden whom he watched with curiosity. He was thinking, I noticed that she shyly bowed her head, but her eyes still met mine. Was that a little sweet smile I detected on that pretty face? I've heard her called "Little White Feather."

*　　*　　*

It was springtime and the air was still cool and brisk, but Oliver enjoyed the sport and camaraderie so much, that he stayed on longer than anticipated—that is until he had gotten too involved with "Little White Feather." The fact is, the beautiful Indian maiden lured him into a most enticing trap. She knew of hideouts for their clandestine meetings, that no one else knew about, and if he had never before made love, she would have been the experienced master of instructors. How could he leave such an alluring paradise? Months passed, and he was shown the way to leave.

It was after one of their trysts that Oliver was encircled by Little White Feathers father and four brothers. There he stood in the center of threatening glares.

"You marry my daughter, Little White Feather, yes?"

"Ooh . . . a . . . no . . . no . . . please . . . no!"

"Man of honor should say, 'yes.' Because you have worked and helped our people with food, we will let you leave our village in safety, but we warn you, if you ever come back, you will not be safe! Now leave!"

Oliver was escorted out of the village by Little White Feather's four brothers. He promised never to return, but when they were out of sight of the village, Oliver suffered the worst beating of his lifetime; each brother took a turn at this human punching bag. They left him on the ground panting for breath and painfully trying to lift his bruised body from the blood-stained dirt. He pondered a phrase that he had heard Hedda say and at last understood her meaning about gathering no moss.

Twenty

In the summer of 1922, he visited Frank, Eva, and family in Fredonia. Frank showed Oliver a poster he had kept, which announced a championship welterweight bout on Monday night, February 3, 1922. Eugene Tremblay vs. Frank Janvier. Frank was proudly victorious.

"I'm so sorry to have missed another victory, Frank. Any more matches coming up?"

"Yeah, I'll be wrestling for the World Championship December 10, 1923. My opponent is the European champ, Jim Scott. I suppose you'll be in Florida, or some warmer spot on the globe."

"Heck no, Frank, that bout is only four months away. I want to be here to watch my kid brother become the world champ!"

Frank's Star Laundry had become a flourishing business and Oliver took advantage of earning money, working as a helper in the wet wash department.

In his spare time, Oliver hung around with old buddies, playing poker, and taking fishing trips. Dom Abati joined him on one of his fishing ventures.

"You're looking well, Oliver. Have you found a special place where you might settle down—or am I being too presumptuous? Maybe nosy, eh?"

"You mean where I can gather a little moss?"

Dom looked puzzled, but Oliver continued.

"Who knows, I'll probably resume stepping foot in all the rest of the forty-eight states. I've been to all the New England states, plus eight others. I only have thirty-four more to go."

They both laughed.

"Do you think you'll ever find your Shangri-la?" Dom asked.

"I wonder if there is such a utopian place on earth. Have you found it, Dom?"

"Settling down with the right person is darn near it; we have our ups and downs like anyone else, but it makes us feel that we are on solid ground."

"I thought that I was on solid ground with the Choctaw Indians in Arkansas, but I blew it . . . like a white feather in the wind. Gathering moss doesn't seem to be my forte."

"What's this business about 'gathering moss?'"

"Well, I keep thinking about what Hedda said. She said I was like a rolling stone. She meant that I'm afraid of commitments. Maybe she's right."

"I think that I know what she means. Now that you've mentioned Hedda, wouldn't you like to hear more about her and Ted?"

Dom looked anxious and wondered if he had overstepped his bounds. He had hoped that Oliver would broach the subject of Hedda and their son, Teddy.

After a restrained moment, Dom ventured to tell Oliver that he and Amalia often saw Hedda and her husband, Mark.

"I really expected you to bring up that touchy subject. I'm not objecting, because I'd like to know how things are going for them. I'm not so cold that I haven't thought about Hedda, especially my son Teddy. You're a down to earth person, and I do wish that I had your patience and fortitude . . . plus perseverance. I was once told that I'm flighty. That's me—flighty Oliver. It doesn't mean that I'm happy . . . or not happy. Happiness to me, seems like gems you find, that pick up your spirits and make you feel good. Other times, you might pick up rocks. Is that what you mean by ups and downs?"

"I will admit that happiness is somewhat illusive, but life is what you make of it. Hedda made a good choice when she hitched up with Mark Anker; she's happy, Oliver. A strong commitment is what she needed. She's a wonderful girl, and he's a good man. A good father, too, for Ted and their new son, Billy. Ted is eleven, now, and doesn't like to be called 'Teddy', just Ted. You'd be proud of him Oliver. His school marks are tops."

Oliver had a lump in his throat, and didn't speak again until he could contain his emotions. After the lull, he spoke softly, clearing his throat, and looking pensive.

"Yes, I will admit that she is better off."

Dom could see that their conversation was hurtful for Oliver, so a quick change of subjects was in order.

"Hey buddy, Aunt Molly and Uncle Nickie want to attend your brother's wrestling match in December. Are the tickets sold out yet?"

"Not that I know of. I'll get them for you. My treat . . . and don't argue about that. I owe those great people a lot of gratitude."

*　　*　　*

Oliver was happy to sit along next to his dear friends. All their cheers blended with the huge crowd of Janvier fans. It was the most exciting match anyone had ever attended. The professionalism was first class. Jim Scott was a formidable wrestler, who finally was defeated by his challenger, Frank Janvier.

One newspaper reported: "'At 145 pounds, Janvier is considered one of the fastest and most scientific professional wrestlers of his time. The New York State Athletic Commission has declared him the welterweight champion of the world after he defeated European champ, Jim Scott, December 10, 1923, in Fredonia, New York."

*　　*　　*

There were twelve inches of snow on the ground when Oliver ventured to continue his quest to "hit the forty-eight." He visited a former buddy and comrade of the World War One days, who was at the Veteran's Hospital in Dayton, Ohio. He kidded Leo about the cute nurses, played and sang some raunchy songs for him. He cheered up a bunch of guys, who needed his kind of humor. Oliver felt good about himself that day—he told them that he'd be back. (Could this be prophesy?)

It was 1924, the year that Calvin Coolidge won the presidential election. Oliver was on his way south again. He took trains through Indiana, Illinois, and stopped in Missouri where he took a paddle-wheel riverboat ride on the Missouri River, headed west, then disembarked at Kansas City, where the Kaw and Missouri Rivers meet. From there, it was a short distance to get to the other Kansas City in Kansas.

Now I can add four more states to my list, he thought. Kansas had employment opportunities, and since Oliver's cash reservoir had diminished, he soon found work in wheat fields, running a combine machine which harvested and threshed the crop. It was different from anything he had done before; the bonus—all that fresh air! Also, the replenishing of his holdings. However, his gambling with the farmhands was not all that lucrative.

As his money belt flattened, Oliver consulted his map and decided on Tulsa, Oklahoma, where there were jobs available in the petroleum

144

business. He ended up driving a tank truck to transport petroleum from the stock tanks to a pipeline. Oliver's first preference would have been a visit to Cimarron City on the Panhandle.

He wanted to see the ancient carvings on the canyon walls, along the Cimarron River, but the area could only be accessed by wagon, a long arduous, dusty trek. He had hopes of getting to a Will Rogers's show, but at that time Will was touring elsewhere, telling his audiences about his growing up days in Oklahoma.

By December of 1924, Oliver's money belt had fattened again, and he set off to visit his cooking buddy, Jose, in San Antonio, Texas.

The winter of 1925 was more comfortable in San Antonio, than Tulsa, and he had more companionship, too. Jose and Oliver renewed their acquaintanceship, went hunting together, and visited Pedro's, and now that Oliver was no longer the little naive boy, Jose took him to Señora Dondero's bordello. He half expected to see the scam artist, Lorie, but Jose told him that Señora Dondero had a different crop of girls; some had married their customers, and others, after having been found by their parents, were promptly returned home.

*   *   *

"I go visit my family . . . you come with me?" Jose asked.

"Where is your family?"

"You come to Mexico with me . . . you meet them. O.K."

"What part of Mexico?"

"Oh, not far . . . it's CHIHUAHUA . . . you come?"

"That sounds more like a dog . . . not a city!"

"It is beautiful place in the valley. We surrounded by Sierra Madre Mountains. Beautiful, beautiful!"

"What would I do there?"

"My friend . . . Jose have beautiful cousins . . . nice, nice senoritas. You want work? You help on the farm."

"I wanted to do the forty-eight states. I guess I could add Mexico to my plans. Okay, Jose, I'll join you."

It wasn't the short distance that Jose had implied. The first part of the journey was by train, then to the surprise of Oliver, they had to ride donkeys for many restive hours, through dusty valleys, and up mountainous terrain. Oliver progressively regretted his acceptance of Jose's invitation. After sleeping under the stars, they continued their expedition, sometimes walking, sometimes riding the animals. Their destination was at last in sight. As they walked the donkeys down into the valley, groups of Mexican natives rushed to them with excited Spanish greetings.

Oliver felt like an awkward goose, unable to spread its wings and flee from the unfamiliar flock. He wished that he had not come to this country where fast spoken Spanish was the only language, but what was he to do? He would have to make the best of living with these peasants for just two weeks, after which Jose had to be back at his job in San Antonio. At this point, the thought of a day and a half trudge by donkey, back to the train, discouraged him from turning back alone.

Oliver's disparaging attitude was allayed after a shower, shave, and a change of clothes. He was no longer blinded to the pristine beauty of the valley, and majesty of the surrounding Sierra Madre Mountains. He breathed the pure air while viewing the gorgeous scenery which held him in awe. That evening, a special meal was prepared in honor of their much loved relative, Jose.

Dressed in their colorful native attire, sisters, brothers, girlfriends, boyfriends, and cousins, danced to spirited Mexican music. One couple danced what Jose called "El Jarabe Tapatio," an old courtship dance, known in America as "The Hat Dance." Jose explained to Oliver: "The boy tosses his sombrero at the girl's feet, as a proposal. The girl steps onto the brim and dances around it with quick dainty steps. She then holds her skirt out as she dances, and she bends lower and lower. She dances off of the hat brim and puts the hat on her head, which means that she says 'Yes.' The boy and girl then dance together faster and faster with his large colorful serape thrown around both of them."

Oliver was favorably impressed with both the dancing and the guitar performance. His enthusiastic applause pleased his Mexican hosts and encouraged them to play and sing many Spanish folk songs.

Two of Jose's attractive cousins danced around Oliver, singing their native songs, and by their seductive movements, he assumed that they were singing love songs. Oliver seemed more fascinated with the Spanish rhythms and harmonies, and asked the guitarist if he could try out the instrument. It took some interpreting from Jose before the musician relinquished his guitar to Oliver.

He became slightly chagrined while he strummed a cowboy-type song on this classical instrument, in no way doing the instrument justice.

Oliver's effort brought chuckles to the Mexicans, which embarrassed him further. He thought, *I want out of here. I can't fathom a word that's said.* The owner of the guitar, red with rage, yelled at Jose in what Oliver construed as Spanish swear words. Jose tried to placate the irate musician, but the tirade continued further. Once it ceased, the guitarist sent a cold glare in the direction of the classical offender. The look sent icy chills down Oliver's back, though it was a hot humid night.

*   *   *

Each day, Oliver helped with the farming chores, and each evening, the Mexicans demonstrated extreme talent for folk dancing and intricate rhythmic guitar music. He smiled a lot, out of politeness, but was relieved when the time came to say "adios."

Jose went back to his job in Texas. Oliver headed for Los Angeles, California.

Hi Brother Frank,

Here I am in famous Hollywood where they make the movies. I was hoping to be selected as an extra . . . no such luck. Did you see the Buster Keaton movie, *The Navigator?* I got a glimpse of Buster, dressed in costume, working on a new picture. It's amazing how he does all his own stunts. I also saw Charlie Chaplin, where they were filming *The Gold Rush.* It's an exciting place, but I'm running low on cash.

Here I am in Arizona . . . I move fast, eh? I started this letter three weeks ago, traveled to Phoenix . . . got a job at a riding corral . . . nice horses . . . I'd enjoy them more if I didn't have to clean the stalls . . . as I told you, I needed the mazooma.

I sent our sister, Eva, the new song, "Show Me The Way To Go Home." Should I heed the lyrics of this song and head for Massachusetts? Not yet! I'll be leaving for New Mexico this week . . . I'll add to this epistle when I get there.

Ah . . . Tis the "Land of Enchantment." I visited the ancient Pueblo ruins, the cliff dwellings rise three-hundred-fifty-seven feet, and they were once occupied by the Acoma Indians.

I learned that my friend, Jose, played a dirty trick on me, making me travel by donkey to his home in Chihuahua, Mexico! All that time, he knew about "The King's Highway." We could have gone from El Paso, Texas . . . It also goes to Santa Fe, New Mexico, from El Paso.

Now that the weather is getting warmer, I'll take train after train, heading for home, I just might stop over in Kentucky and look around.

147

Any more wrestling matches? If you write in a few weeks, I might be home by then.

Oliver

The summer of 1926 was approaching, and Oliver was on his way home again, but decided to visit the Mammoth Caves which he had heard so much about. It was his first experience, visiting a cave. The guide led the tourists down into a section of the cavern where he explained that remains of a body were found. Unbeknown to the victim, there was an opening above the cave, where the person was seemingly swallowed up, and never found until many years later when a group of archeologists located a more accessible opening, and discovered the victim's bones many feet below the opening through which he had fallen. All present marveled at the awesome shapes of the stalagmites, and stalactites.

To demonstrate the darkness of the cave, the guide shut down the lantern which had illuminated the dank room. He said, "Just imagine yourselves, here alone, finding your way through the many rooms . . . then suddenly your lantern dies. How could you ever find your way out again? Am I scaring you people?" Many groans and ooohs were heard before the lantern was relit. This had an effect on Oliver which left him questioning whether he was the intrepid traveler he thought himself to be.

That night, as he reviewed his reactions, he was reliving his most frightening experience: the *Larchmont* disaster. He didn't like to admit to himself that being in the pitch black cave with no light had frightened him into thinking about his life, thinking, who am I? where am I going?

He further reflected: I prayed to God to save my life. My prayers were answered. Have I prayed since . . . at least said a thank you? What am I trying to accomplish? Oh God, am I failing whatever mission I have in this life? What is my mission? My father doesn't seem to have a care in the world. Is he my mentor? My mother is so saintly . . . I don't take after her . . . At the very moment in which he was pondering, his mother, Azilda, was having a conversation with brother Joseph's wife, Rita.

Translated from the French language, it went like this:

Azilda to her daughter-in-law:

"If a mother and son and his wife were in a boat and there was a mishap and he could only save one person, whom should he save?"

Rita, after much contemplation:

"According to the Bible, people who are wed should cling to one another; I believe that he should save his wife."

"That is where you are wrong; he should save his mother, because he can never get another mother, but he could get another wife."

Then and there, Rita knew how she fitted with her mother-in-law, and she also realized the hold the mother had on her sons—all except Oliver, the free soul.

However, that free soul didn't feel so free at this time. He prayed: "Help me to know what I should do."

*　　*　　*

As Oliver traveled by train through Ohio, Pennsylvania, and New York, he watched the fast moving scenery without seeing it; he was too engrossed in thought. He wondered if his parents' broken marriage had affected his choices in life. He had never been able to make a lifetime commitment . . . "til death do us part." I've never gathered moss . . . just like Hedda said to me . . . her words are haunting me . . . he wrestled with these thoughts. Did I do wrong by Hedda, and Teddy? Ah, they're better off without me. I would just like to get a glimpse of them without being seen. I'll go to Fredonia before going to Lawrence.

Frank welcomed his brother with open arms and Oliver got to know his two little nieces, Helen and Lorraine Janvier. Things had changed for Frank and his family since he was no longer interested in the wrestling sport.

"Wrestling, as a sport, is finished, Oliver. It has turned into show business; they're all actors. I was asked to throw a match and become an actor in the ring. I'll have no part of that game. Where's the integrity of it all?" lamented Frank.

Oliver agreed that the true honest sportsmanship no longer existed.

"I'm proud of you, Frank! You won the world championship with honor! Just don't dwell on the adverse changes that have been made. You're rich in other ways, Frank. You have a beautiful family and a thriving laundry business."

And what have I got, thought Oliver, *a few mementos from my wanderings.*

Oliver had to get over the depressing thoughts that had been plaguing him of late. Dom and his family were instrumental in uplifting his spirits.

"Oliver, you remember our boy Nicholas? Well, here are three more

149

Abatis; meet Maria, Anthony, and Paula. Nicholas is going on fifteen."

Amalia prepared a wonderful Italian dinner . . . just like Aunt Molly did, years ago.

Oliver found it difficult to broach the subject of his son, Ted, but it was on his mind as he watched Nicholas. He couldn't hide his feelings. Finally, he said, "My son Ted is fourteen. It's hard to believe, so many years ago. Do you have any news for me?" he asked hesitantly.

"Hedda and I are still best of friends and keep in touch. They're living in Dunkirk and Ted helps out at his dad's . . . I mean his step-dad's riding academy," Amalia offered.

"Is Hedda happy?"

"Oh yes. They have two other children, and you'll be glad to know that Mark treats Ted as his own. I don't think Ted remembers any other father; he was so young when you left."

"I'm glad that it worked out so well for them."

"And how are things working out for you, Ollie?" chimed in Dom.

"Can't complain. I did my own thing, so there's nobody else to blame if I've faltered at the game of life."

"You've changed, Oliver. Where's that ole funny clown I used to know?"

"Maybe I'm turning into a Pagliacci. You know, laugh, clown, laugh. Lately, I don't feel much like laughing . . . but, I'll get over it."

"Still searching, my friend, eh?"

"But there's no pot of gold. I'll have to find the rainbow first!"

"Let's see if we can luck out, and win a pot of gold. I'll phone Harvey, and a few of our friends for poker tonight. Okay with you?"

"Sounds good to me, Dom."

Good friends, good poker hands, and beer perked up Oliver's spirits.

He still wanted to get just a glimpse of his son, without Ted knowing who he was. Oliver went to Dunkirk the following day. It was after school hours when Oliver walked into the barn where Ted was grooming Velocity.

"Isn't that the horse that once was housed at the Fredonia Riding School?"

"Yeah, my dad sold that outfit and kept the best horses."

"Do you work here every day?"

"When I'm not studying for a test. Hey, who are you anyway? Did you come to rent a horse for riding?"

"Can I ride Velocity, son?"

"Okay, I guess. Hey, how do you know his name?"

"I used to ride him in Fredonia. Just call me Bill."

The next afternoon, Oliver went back to the stables. Two men were cleaning stalls while Ted was grooming a bay horse.

"Hey Bill, I thought you looked familiar yesterday. When I went home I asked Mom if I could look at her photo album again. I pointed you out and said, 'That's the guy who rode Velocity.' Mom got all flustered and said, 'Oh God! that's Oliver.' I tried to tell her that your name is Bill, but my dad had his arms around her, calming her. So, what's the big deal if an old friend shows up? Were you just an old friend? Is your name really Oliver?"

"An old, old friend. Some people know me as Bill, my middle name, but my name is really Oliver. Is Velocity available, son?"

Oliver rode out of the barn, down the bridle path, in a state of anxiety. He thought it best to leave Dunkirk and never return. He wasn't on the path long when he heard hooves approaching from the rear.

"Oliver, wait up." It was Hedda.

They slowed the horses' gait, rode side by side, not saying a word until they reached the river, where they tethered their horses to a tree and sat on a nearby rock.

"It's not exactly like old times, Hedda, but I am glad to see you."

"Why did you come . . . after all these years?"

"I've thought about you and the boy so many times. I just wanted to be reassured that you and Ted are happy. That's all I want. Just to make sure that I didn't leave you in a bad situation."

"I *am* happy . . . and Mark is the best thing that could have happened in our lives. At first I hated you for leaving so in haste. Then I sort of felt sorry for you . . . unable to bond, even to your own son. It seems to me that if you were that concerned, you wouldn't have waited all these years to come back."

"I'm sorry Hedda. Have you told the boy who I am?"

"He knows no other father but Mark. I'd hate to spoil it for him. Maybe I should tell him. But it kind of puts *me* on the spot. Do you think that I should tell him?"

"It would be selfish of me to want to hear him call me 'Dad.' So let's leave well enough alone. I won't come back to Dunkirk again. I don't want to disrupt anybody's life. This will have to be good-bye . . . again. Thank you for giving me a chance to see you once more. I understand that you have two other children."

151

"Yes, Andy is twelve and Heidi is nine . . . they're wonderful kids."

"I'm sure they are, considering who their mother is. You're doing a good job of raising your kids. So, I'll be on my way, knowing that all is fine. Now I can be at peace with myself, that is if you can forgive me."

"Of course, I forgive you. Take care of yourself, Oliver."

Hedda stayed seated on the rock while Oliver mounted Velocity and rode off toward the barn. Halfway there, he looked back and waved. She watched him until he was out of sight. Both were left with aching hearts. Both knew that the clock could never be turned back, and for Oliver, it was too late to gather moss.

Oliver stayed in Fredonia for the rest of 1926, working and earning a little money for his next venture. He still was not all that reliable and steady with his work schedule, which provoked his brother, Frank. A buddy would say, "It's a good fishing day," and Oliver would reply, "Oh, why not," and off they would go. Or, "There's a poker game down at Kelly's Cafe." "Let's go." There were ways to procure beer, in spite of pro-hibition.

Frank had given up on the idea of Oliver ever changing.

"He's just an entity unto himself," he would tell his wife, Eva.

Nobody was surprised when Oliver left . . . not to go home to Lawrence. "It's getting too damn cold around here." Before he left, he bought and sent his sister Eva two of the popular songs of the day: "I Found a Million Dollar Baby in the Five-and-Ten-Cent Store," and "Bye, Bye, Blackbird."

Twenty-one

It was January, 1927 when Oliver traveled through New Jersey, Delaware, and Maryland, where it was somewhat warmer. Because of a gut feeling that something was amiss, he decided to phone his mother before visiting Fort McHenry in Baltimore.

Oliver felt a deep concern while waiting for the call to go through. Eva answered the first ring. "You have a call from Baltimore, Maryland. One moment please," said the operator. The connection was poor, full of static, but most of the important parts of their conversation were understood with much repetition.

"Yes, Ma is fine. She's at church right now," informed Eva.

"That figures. She probably feels that she's making up for her wayward son. Is there anything happening that I should know about? I don't know why, but I've had this gnawing feeling that there's something wrong," he said without his usual gaiety.

"Well, our brother Joe got a call from Providence. He was told that Pa is very sick."

"Is Joe going to Providence?"

"I think so. Did you know that last year he took little Claire and Russell to meet their grandfather?"

"Wow, Joe became an adult before meeting his own father!"

"Yeah, and here I am with kids of my own and I haven't seen Pa since he left home! Pa took Joe's kids around the race track in his sulky. They're so young . . . they'll never remember him. I hardly remember him myself," she said in a sad tone.

"I got to know him pretty well when he taught me blacksmithing. I'll leave early tomorrow and head for Providence. Maybe I can be of help . . . we'll see. I'll phone you when I get there, which will be in a couple of days."

                     ✳   ✳   ✳

When Oliver finally reached his father's residence, a woman in her mid-fifties opened the door. He recognized her from the times he had seen his father out with a woman, but he had no idea that this woman called Anita was his father's common-law wife of many years. She led Oliver to the ailing man's bedside, where Oliver viewed a man who was just a shadow of the man he knew as his father.

"Pa?"

"My son. Oh, how I longed to see you once more." Isaiah stretched out a weakened hand to greet his eldest son.

Oliver thought of a John Greenleaf Whittier quote he had read "For all sad words of tongue or pen, the saddest are these: It might have been."

Yes, thought Oliver, *how different things might have been had my father not left our family. When Pa wanted those thick red steaks, Ma warned him—though she must have known only by instinct that they would do him in. Now, look at him, dying of stomach cancer and suffering a hell on earth.*

"Is there anything I can do for you, Pa?"

"Stay with me a while. But when I tell you to go, get out of my room for about fifteen minutes."

Oliver said, "Okay," but didn't understand the strange request.

They began conversing but suddenly Isaiah let out a strong yelp and said, "*Go.*"

When Oliver left his father's room, Anita met him to explain the situation.

"Your father doesn't want anyone to see him suffer, and when he feels the strong pains coming, he insists on being alone."

"Can't the doctor do anything for him?"

"He has a prescription for morphine tablets but will only take them at night to help him sleep. He claims that he is offering up his suffering to God for all his sins. Your father is a good man and does not deserve all that pain."

* * *

Oliver phoned Eva and gave her the sad news that their father was dying.

"Joe won't be going . . . he can't get off from work. When we told Ma, she said nothing, but has been looking pretty grim. Let us know when it happens, Oliver."

When the fifteen minutes were up, Oliver went back to his father's bedside.

"Is there anything you'd like to talk about, Pa?"

"Yes, son, I have many regrets and I want to clear my conscience of them. I want you to know that I did love your mother, but after Joseph was born, she cut me off completely . . . you know what I mean? I was still a young man and had needs that she refused to take care of . . . that was the end of married life for me. I left my family, my church and led a sinful life. All I can ask for is forgiveness. Please find a Catholic church in Providence and send a priest to hear my last confession. Anita is a good woman, but I didn't do right by her. She is so good to care for me." His voice gradually weakened, but then he mustered up the strength to yell "Go."

Oliver again had to leave the room abruptly. He told Anita about his father's request to see a priest and she agreed to receive the cleric into their home.

Father Simone administered the last rites of the church after hearing Isaiah's confession. After the priest left, Oliver returned to the bedroom where he found his father looking so peaceful and serene. Oliver spoke but there was no response. Isaiah had died.

After the funeral, Anita told Oliver that Isaiah had made a will, naming her as sole beneficiary. He told her that she deserved it, and that he didn't think that anyone in his family would contest it. He was ready to see his family again.

Oliver was comforted by the attention bestowed upon him while back in Lawrence. He visited his mentor, Brother Emile, whom he found aged considerably.

"Brother Emile, I want to thank you for the good influence you had on my life. I've thought of you often and only wished that I was endowed with even half your wisdom. I've made a number of mistakes in spite of your good examples. I am what you would call, 'a fallen away Catholic.' Maybe I shouldn't be telling you this. I don't know what possesses me to reveal this to you!" Oliver bowed his head as if in shame.

"Oliver, you're a grown man now . . . I do remember a troubled young fellow, whom I was sure, would find his place in the world. What are you doing with your life?"

"I'm what you might call a vagabond . . . flitting from one place to another. Aimlessly, I might add. Ya know . . . no roots."

"Do you know that when I was young, I had often entertained the thought of seeing the world, but my parents saw a different life for me—one of conformity to their fervent religious beliefs. I can't say that they were wrong, but I wonder what my life might have been like if I hadn't been led by the nose to the religious life. My sister, Estelle, was less of a conformist than I was. She became a nun, and after about six years she left. Our parents were heartbroken. Sometimes it is hard to recognize that we are all individuals with differing feelings and differing ideas from all other individuals. God didn't mean for all of us to be cut from the same pattern, but we must remember to respect all the different patterns we encounter. It is my belief that a person must follow his leanings. Are you happy with your life, Oliver? Do you ask God for guidance?"

"Maybe not enough, Brother Emile."

"Pray for help, Oliver . . . I'll pray for you, too."

Oliver left Brother Emile and was struck in awe that the good man had not said one word of condemnation of his neglected Catholic heritage. That made him think . . . *well, maybe I'm not so bad after all.*

Back with his family, Eva accompanied the usual songfests with all the songs from Oliver's travels. Azilda was once again happy to hear her children joined together singing so merrily. Two weeks of these festivities were enough for Oliver, who itched to move on.

On the trains, he read newspapers that told of the plans to build the George Washington Bridge, which was to span the Hudson River. I'll see that on my next return to New York, he mused.

Charles Lindbergh flew solo on the monoplane, "Spirit of St. Louis."

Oliver had rooted for the heavyweight boxing champion, Jack Dempsey, but to his disappointment, Gene Tunney won the title.

He had so much travel time that besides newspapers, he was able to finish reading the new Sinclair Lewis book, *Elmer Gantry*.

Oliver had always enjoyed deep sea fishing, and opted to travel to Morehead City, in North Carolina, where large fishing boats and trawlers docked in Bogue Sound, the inland waterway; he was able to pay fare on a fishing boat which advertised: "DAILY SIX HOUR DEEP SEA FISHING TRIPS, leaving at nine a.m." There were at least twenty-seven fishermen on board, willing to ante up a buck each for the man who could catch the largest fish.

It took the craft almost an hour to get far enough out into the Atlantic Ocean before anchoring at a preferred spot. It didn't take long for the men to bait their hooks and lower their drop lines. Ernie caught the first red snapper, weighing only three pounds. Oliver's first catch was a tad smaller. The fishing grounds seem to be lucrative; fish upon fish were hauled in great numbers, but none weighing beyond five to ten pounds. It was after noontime lunch, consisting of sandwiches, and the men still had high hopes of pulling in the big one. A group of men joked: "What would our women say about handling bait and then eating without washing our hands?"

They feigned what they thought a woman would say. Ralph lifted his shoulders, scrunched his face and mocked, "Ooooh, ugh, how can you eat like that!" Sid answered, 'Well, honey, it adds flavor." All laughed mirthfully.

Oliver felt a jolting pull on his line. He jerked the line toward himself, and felt that the fighting fish was really hooked; it jumped up out of the water in a great struggle to free itself.

Oliver was hearing all kinds of advice: "Play with him for a while." "Give 'im more line," and "Don't be too quick to bring 'im in . . . you might lose 'im!"

He finally pulled in the fighting twenty-pound sea bass. Oliver imagined that he could see himself putting that twenty-seven dollar reward into his money belt, but Chuck was almost jerked over the edge of the boat by a "whopper." That one weighed thirty-two pounds. Just one more hour of fishing before heading back to the dock; the men were getting anxious—all but Chuck, who felt assured of the prize. Then, the unexpected happened.

Oliver's line was pulling out further and further; he couldn't seem to stop the momentum. He wrapped some of the line, twisted it around his fist, and leaned back with all his might to stop the fish from going out much further. The fish put up a tremendous struggle, and at one point Oliver thought he had lost him. It was just a moment of rest before resuming the battle. It seemed like a long wait before the fish tired enough to be hauled in. "What a huge son of a gun!" one guy exclaimed. The sea bass weighed in at thirty-three pounds and fourteen ounces. Oliver did put the twenty-seven dollars into his money belt, besides selling all his catch to the fishery market men, his finances had greatly improved.

"That was better than getting a temporary job to add to my travel money. Maybe I'll do that again tomorrow!" he told Chuck.

Chuck was a little disappointed about the pot, but he did well with the sale of his catch.

"I doubt that the weather will hold out for a repeat of today's trip, they're expecting pretty rough seas for tomorrow, in which case, the boats will be staying in the sound."

Oliver, upon hearing the weather forecast, decided to see what the town of New Bern was like. He was able to secure lodging at the Gaston House, a hotel on South Front Street. Oliver learned that the Gaston House was reserved for Union officers during the Civil War. Many of the Union soldiers were so impressed with the town that they returned to New Bern after the war and established permanent residences. Oliver was also surprised to learn that a great number of them were from his home state, Massachusetts.

After paying a week's rent for his room and settling in, Oliver took a walk near the picturesque Trent River waterfront, where he saw the bustling market docks. Ships were unloading farm produce of all kinds, and there were many small sailing crafts delivering fish and oysters harvested from Pamlico Sound, which he later found out to be along the lower parts of the Neuse River, nearer the sea. He was intrigued with what he saw, and could understand how his fellow Massachusetts neighbors could leave their fair state for this.

He hung around the docks for some time before wending his way back to East Front Street and across to a large field, which jutted out into the broad Neuse River. Several locals had cast their fishing rods from shore, reeling in good size flounders. Others were on rickety wharfs, dropping lines baited with chicken wings to catch crabs. Oliver sat on a tree stump to watch.

"Y'all from around here, fella?" asked an interesting looking man wearing a straw hat, tiny sun glasses, and a pipe hanging from the corner of his thin-lipped mouth. He sat next to Oliver on a large rock.

"Just passing through. Interesting town you have here."

"Yep, been in this here town all mah life, seen it growed more 'n more. They's even talk about making this here piece of land into a park with benches 'n all."

"That would be pretty nice, wouldn't it?"

"S'pose so if they put in some fishin' piers. See that fella jist pullin' up a big crab? How much will ya bet that the next fella will haul in a bigger or smaller critter? Watta ya say, wanna bet?"

"I'd say you're a gambling man."

"Why not . . . ya like to take chances now 'n agin?"

"I don't bet high stakes, but you're on, buddy. Fifty cents says the guy in the blue sweater pulls in the next crab, big or small."

"Make it seventy-five, and I'm bettin' on the one with the dirty white shirt with the sleeves rolled up."

Oliver lost the first bet, but won the next three, coming ahead by a dollar and a half.

"Y'all seem to be on a streak . . . wanna do some real gamblin'?"

"What kind of gambling?"

There's a place on Spencer Street, a bachelor pad, a guy by the name of Floyd . . . but, ya need a password and four dollars to get in."

"You mean that it's illegal?"

"Well, ya know, he's gotta take precautions. What's ya name?"

"Just call me Bill," said Oliver.

"Well if ya go tonight, just tell 'em that Les sent ya."

Oliver thought, *What the heck . . . it's something to do.*

The directions took him on a long walk going south on Pollock Street. He took a left on Eighth, and a right on Spencer. The house was as Les had described it: full front porch, the width of the house, four windows, separated by the front door, facing the porch, three little windows on the upstairs dormer. Yeah, this looks like it.

Oliver climbed the many steps to the piazza and rang the door bell. A bald man with thick rimless glasses magnifying his round dark eyes, opened the door.

"What can I do for you?"

"Les sent me."

"And who are you?"

"Bill."

"Okay, Les informed me that a man named Bill just might show up. Come in."

Oliver was surprised to see that the adjacent rooms of the foyer were lavishly furnished, but no one was about. He was then led to a back room, filled with men and smoke you could cut with a knife. There were two tables of poker, and one green felt top table where five men were engaged in the game of craps.

"Seven come eleven," chanted a ghostly thin man while shaking the dice in his bony hands. Oliver watched as the rolled dice settled on a five and a three. The other men who had bet against him, picked the money up from the table and divided it.

"Baby needs a new pair of shoes," called a new dice roller. Baby could get new shoes with the five and six showing up on the green felt.

Oliver wasn't interested in craps, and chose to take the place of a losing poker player who had to leave broke.

The men introduced themselves, first names only.

The cut for the deal went to Al, to the left of "Bill" as Oliver chose to be called. After five cards were dealt each player, Al said, "Bye me." Next, Dave opened with a quarter. Gordon, Bob, and Bill anted up in turn. Al stayed and dealt out the limit, three cards to Dave. Gordon took two; Bob, the limit; Bill said, "I'll keep these"; and Al dealt himself the limit.

At that point, the tension began. Dave bet fifty cents, Gordon raised him another quarter, Bob said, "I fold," and Bill put in the seventy-five and raised another fifty cents. "I'll see ya," said Al, contributing to the pot. Dave raised another quarter. Gordon fattened the pot. "Here's your quarter and fifty more," said Bill confidently raising the ante. Al folded. Dave and Gordon "called." That left just three people in the game. Bill showed his five card royal flush. Dave and Gordon dejectedly placed their hands over their cards without showing them. "Bill" picked up the pot and thought, *I feel lucky tonight!*

And luck was surely with him. The games went on until the deadline of two in the morning. Oliver had never been so lucky at poker. He shook hands with the men and they asked when he'd be back so that they could recover their losses.

"Yeah, I think I'll be back," he said, not really promising.

*   *   *

Oliver slept until eleven o'clock the next morning, and had a late breakfast at The Busy Bee Cafe on Middle Street. He speculated that the orange juice, grits, bacon and eggs, toast, and coffee would hold him for the rest of the day. Feeling chipper after his meal, he began to explore the area.

He walked with the pride of an Astor or J. P. Morgan, feeling his oats and feeling rich after his winnings at the Floyd house the night before. Oliver meandered down Middle Street looking in store windows.

Ah, music . . . he heard. Inside, near the entrance of S. H. Kress and Company, the five and dime store, was a counter with stacks of sheet music, and a nice looking piano player who played songs that were requested by customers. *She not only plays well, but she's darn nice looking*, thought Oliver. Emma Dodson was playing, "My Heart Stood Still." She played so beautifully that *his* heart almost stood still.

"You do a good job at the keyboard, Ma'am," exclaimed Oliver after the last customer had left.

"Thank you, sir. Is there a song you would like to hear?"

"How about 'Blue Skies'?"

"Sure thing," she said, as she sat at the piano again and played the requested song with a few flourishes that weren't written on the music sheet.

"I'll buy that one and send it home to my sister."

"Thank you. Are you musical, too?" she asked as she wrapped the song.

"Oh, I just pluck the uke, and play drums . . . not at the same time, though." They both laughed shyly.

Oliver reluctantly left the store, determined to return the following day.

Emma hoped that she would see him again.

The next morning, Oliver found his way to Middle Street again and entered the Busy Bee Cafe, for breakfast. Eating grits was a new experience for him. The closest thing to it would be Cream of Wheat, which is more of a northern breakfast cereal, he mused.

He enjoyed a long walk after breakfast, and wanted to discover places of interest along the way. Bradham's Drug Store, at the corner of Middle and Pollock Streets, advertised the soft drink that the local pharmacist, Caleb D. Bradham, had formulated in 1898: Pepsi-Cola . . . and proud of this they were. He also admired the structure of the Episcopal church, just across the street from Bradham's. He remembered having seen Flemish-bond brick buildings before, but the tall Gothic revival steeple interested him most. Oliver's curiosity led him toward the sound of fire engines clanging. Turning left from Middle Street on to Broad Street, he found the engine house, and pondered: That is a different style building than I've ever seen before! It has a Spanish look to it. Then, he followed the railroad tracks down Metcalf Street, looking at historic homes as he doffed his hat at passersby.

Most Newbernians were generous with their "Southern Hospitality," but Oliver found that after detecting a Yankee accent, not all were that friendly, especially members of "The United Daughters of the Confederacy"! Many of the southerners were still in the war posture.

I wonder if that pretty piano player is one of them. I'll soon find out, he thought as he ventured back down Middle Street to the five and dime store.

She was playing tunes from Irving Berlin's "Music Box Revues," for a potential customer. Oliver enjoyed listening, and when he was next in line, he requested another song of Berlin's: "April Showers." They talked more this time, exchanging information. Now he knew her name was Emma, and found out that she was a young widow with a six-year-old daughter Patty, and lived on Johnson Street.

Maybe next time, I can get a date, he mused. Maybe next time, he'll ask me out, she wished.

Oliver had never sent Eva so many songs from any one city before, but it gave him an excuse to see and hear Emma playing the popular songs of the day.

Dear Eva,

Surprised? Here are more songs from North Carolina. "Nothing Could Be Finer In The State of Carolina In The Morning." Isn't that song great? I've been seeing the piano player who plays such tunes in an especially talented way! You would like her, Eva. She's a pretty blonde gal with expressive blue eyes, and is about five foot two . . . that sounds like another song! "Five Foot Two, With Eyes Of Blue . . . Has Anybody Seen My Gal?" More lyrics by Gus Kahn, eh?

It took me three days of picking out music before I gathered up courage to ask her for a date. We went to the Athens Theatre, and saw a Laurel and Hardy movie . . . it wasn't romantic, but we had a few laughs. We needed some laughs after Emma's six-year-old daughter carried on about my taking her mother out. Boy, that kid wants all the attention she demands. She screamed and kicked so, that her grandmother had to drag her up to bed. I hope she gets used to the idea that her mother needs a life of her own. She said that this is the first time she has dated since the death of her husband, almost two years ago. This week, we are going to rent a canoe and paddle around on the twin rivers, the Trent and the Neuse.

Give everyone hugs and kisses from me.

Oliver

"You're invited to dinner this Sunday, Oliver," said Emma.

"Thank you, I haven't had a home cooked meal since I've been here. I'll be looking forward to it. Do you suppose that Patty will allow me to sit next to you?"

"Oliver, I'm so embarrassed about the way she acted Wednesday night. I'm sure that this time, she'll be her usual sweet self. She can be a sweet child."

Dinner was at five in the evening. Oliver arrived a half hour earlier and asked if he could be of help.

162

"My mother and I are preparing the meal together . . . as a matter of fact, you could help by getting acquainted with Patty. She understands that you are my friend, and promised to be her better self."

Patty entered the parlor attired in her pretty pink organdy dress with a matching ribbon in her long blonde tresses.

"Hello, Mr. Oliver," she said in a very sweet voice that assured her mother that it would be okay for Patty to get acquainted with him.

"I'll be in the kitchen. I'll leave you two here to get to know each other."

"It's nice to see you again, Patty, I hope we can be friends."

With Emma gone from the room, Patty took on a different personality, walked over to where Oliver was sitting and gave him a painful kick in the shins.

"That should tell you something, Mr. Oliver."

He winced as he held his ankle and said, "Your message is very clear, young lady, but tell me, what does it accomplish?"

Oliver was trying hard to hold back his feelings for this little brat. He felt that he wanted to take her across his knee and wallop her behind firmly.

"Well, doesn't it tell you that you're not wanted around here?"

"Your mother wants me around . . . and if that makes *her* happy, then *you* should be happy too. Your mother keeps telling me what a sweet child you are. I would like to see that side of you."

"Well you won't," she pouted.

"Dinner is ready, Patty and Oliver," Emma announced. "And as long as you two have become friends, you may sit together, next to me."

"Oh that will be nice," said Oliver, feigning a smile.

"What did you two talk about in the living room?" asked Emma.

"Well, it seems that Patty has a way of sending secret codes with strong messages in them."

"Patty, you never told *me* about secret codes. Mr. Oliver must be pretty special for you to reveal secrets to him."

"Well, if he can't read my special codes, I'll give him a lot more . . . so that he'll get my message," said Patty with a pretty little fake smile.

There were pleasantries exchanged during the superb meal of roasted chicken, mashed potatoes, a wonderful assortment of vegetables, and a salad. The dessert was a large serving of the most delicious lemon meringue pie Oliver had ever tasted. Patty behaved rather smugly, thinking that Oliver's good-bye would be his last.

"Oliver, would you be interested in going to Patty's dance recital Wednesday night?"

"Oh, I'd like to see her up on stage. She's gifted with great talents and she'll have the whole audience giving her all that attention. You'll like that, won't you, Patty?"

"Why does he have to come? I don't want him to come!"

"Well I like him, and I want him to be with me. It would be nice for Mr. Oliver to see how beautifully you dance." Emma was trying to persuade her daughter to be more civil.

"If he comes, I won't dance . . . so there."

"I'll have to decline your offer, Emma. I wouldn't want to make her so unhappy that she would refuse to dance. I find it quite evident that what *you* want doesn't mean anything to her. The important thing is what *she* wants."

"Oh, Oliver, that statement sounds rather sarcastic and cruel. She's my child and I love her, and it is important that I give her what she wants."

"Well, Emma, maybe it takes an outsider to see that Patty is running your life. If you don't see it that way, then I feel sorry for you. She has made it clear to me that she does not want me in your life—and she rules. Doesn't she?"

Emma stood there at a loss for words, tears welling up in her eyes.

"It was nice while it lasted. I felt that we could have been more than just friends. Keep up the great piano playing. I wish you well, and I wish you a life you can call your own. Good-bye, Emma."

She choked on her parting good-bye.

The very next day Oliver reached the Union Train Station at the corner of Queen and Hancock Streets, via foot, He embarked the train headed for the historic seaport of Charleston, South Carolina. He had read that Charleston was the site of the beginning of the Civil War, and since he was somewhat of a history buff, he wanted to see the famous Fort Sumter National Monument in the Charleston Harbor, where the first battle of that war was fought.

Oliver was lost in deep thought, mainly about his experience with Emma. I felt so attracted to that woman, but I wonder if it would have amounted to anything. Patty would never accept me. It probably happened for the best. If we did marry, I would be forever battling that child. Oliver was jolted out of his contemplation when the train jerked to a stop in Wilmington where many other new passengers boarded. The seat next to Oliver was the last one to be filled.

"Hi, my name is Ralph Dixon. Where y'all goin?" The portly young man introducing himself was undeniably a southerner.

"Oh, hi, my name is Oliver Janvier. I'm going to Charleston."

"Oh, I can tell by that accent that you're a yankee, eh! I think of you Northerners as *damn* yankees! Ya know, ya ain't really welcome down here. Why don't you stay up there where you belong?"

"Wow, I've heard of people *still* fighting the Civil War. I take it you're one of them, the very first one I've ever met in all my travels."

"Yeah, yankee, if we had won the war, you'd need a passport to visit our country."

"Well, for your information you *didn't* win the war, and *you* are an American and *I* am an American. *Hello fellow American!* Let's be civil to one another. Neither of us was living when the war was fought. Why should you resent someone who had no part in it? What's your gripe?"

"Two of my mother's uncles were killed in the battle of Chancellorsville. Robert E. Lee, our great general, won that battle against the Union troops. Mom says that we had your guys over a barrel, then things went downhill after that."

"I can't believe that after more than fifty years, people like you are still lamenting the outcome of that war. Just think of the progress in later years. The Federal government has sponsored so many improvements like railroads, roads and canals."

"Yeah, but they took away a lot of our states' rights. The tariffs were too high which hindered our trading cotton for cheaper foreign goods."

"You know, Ralph, this is a new experience for me. I know that this is unsolicited advice, but to go on with your life, it's more important to look to the future. Sure, it's good to know history . . . but let go and find new avenues."

It took a few moments of silence and reflection before Ralph finally said, "Maybe you're right. I've seen so much bitterness in my family for so many years that we've lost sight of the here and now. It's the first time that I've ever met a challenger to the thoughts that plague so many of us southerners. Yeah, you *are* right. The older folks do find it harder to acknowledge the truth though."

"Are you going to Charleston, Ralph?" Oliver spoke calmly as if the earlier conversation had never taken place.

"Yep, that old place was once hailed as the 'Holy City,' but that wasn't because people were pious . . . it just happened that the many church steeples appear to be jutting high above other buildings."

"From what I've heard and read, it's an interesting place. Can you tell me anything else about it?"

Well, a couple of centuries ago, English settlers—some of my ancestors—had difficulty with the Spaniards, who considered Carolina their land. They had Indian problems, slave problems, and problems with pirates . . . all that before the 1812 war and the Civil war. The early colonists had named the city 'Charles Towne,' after the English King."

"I read that the Confederates fired upon the Union garrison, holed up in Fort Sumter, but Union boats sealed off the Port."

"Yeah, there was the 54th African-American unit from your state, Massachusetts. They had the audacity to try to take Fort Wagner, which was further south of Charleston, but the Confederates were successful in defending that fort, We had the very first submarine, the CSS *Hunley,* which sank the USS *Housatonic.* Unfortunately, the sub also sank, along with its crew. The Charleston people were shocked when the 55th Massachusetts unit marched through the streets emancipating the slaves. So, what I'm telling you is just a quickie historic synopsis."

"It sounds as if the early citizens of Charleston had witnessed a terrible amount of hardships. I'm glad that those days are far behind us. Do you admit that slavery was a bad thing?"

"We finally came around to believing that. Now that things have settled down and the economy has improved, Charleston is advertising for tourist interest. How did you find out about it?"

"A friend in New Bern told me about it."

"I'll give you a guided tour of Charleston if you'd like, Oliver."

"I'd appreciate that, Ralph."

They alit from the train as buddies, and Ralph told Oliver that all that was worth seeing was within walking distance.

"Can you imagine that these stones which pave the streets came all the way from England? They were used as ballast on the English ships," said Ralph.

"We had some cobblestone streets where I come from. I wonder if those also came from England. Before we had automobiles, a horse and buggy ride was pretty rough on those roads. It was less jostling riding on the dirt roads," offered Oliver.

"Some of the streets are being improved by macadamized pavement . . . I understand that the new highways are a lot smoother with the new paving materials. Things are improving steadily. Since the dredging of this port and the construction of a jetty system, bigger trading ships can come in, which certainly gives a boost to the Charleston economy. There's the Sumter Fort over there," Ralph pointed out.

"Can we take a boat over to see it?" asked Oliver.

"Not yet, Oliver; I found out recently that there are plans to renovate the Fort, and then there will be tour boats for visitors . . . that's in the future . . . you'll have to come back. Will you be staying over tonight? There's the Fort Sumter Hotel . . . want to register now?"

"I think that since the weather looks a little threatening, I'll go back to the train station and continue on from here. Thank you so much, Ralph, for all your historic information and your friendliness. I really do appreciate it."

"I'm glad we met, and I'm sorry that I needed the chip on my shoulder to be knocked off. Thanks to you, Oliver."

The men shook hands as they parted.

Twenty-two

Traveling further south through South Carolina, Oliver could barely make out the scenery; the fierce torrential rains obscured his view through the train windows. It would have been a little wet out on the streets of Charleston to visit more of the historic spots. It looks as if I left just in the nick of time, reasoned Oliver.

Atlanta, Georgia, was his next destination. He had read a history book about General William T. Sherman who, in 1864, led a campaign to Atlanta, where Confederate weapons were made and stored; the siege lasted for over a hundred days. After the surrender, Sherman ordered the city evacuated and burned; out of thousands of buildings, only 400 remained.

How young our country is, thought Oliver, *this happened just twenty-two years before I was born.*

History intrigued him. He found his way to Stone Mountain to see the huge face carvings of Confederate war heroes, Robert E. Lee, Stonewall Jackson, and Jefferson Davis. Oliver thought about the statement attributed to General Sherman, "War is Hell!" and he prayed that peace would be lasting.

Oliver, "the free soul," Oliver, "an entity unto himself," Oliver, "the clown," Oliver, unknown to most people, had a serious side to himself. *Am I gathering moss?* he asked himself.

Travel is knowledge, contemplated Oliver. I feel somewhat fulfilled in all the knowledge I've gained about so many new places. I plan to see much more . . . but then what? There's an emptiness that gnaws inside of me. I have trouble understanding what I am all about. What am I accomplishing, I've yet to reach self-satisfaction. What am I seeking? God help me to know.

Music always had the potential to lift Oliver's spirits. He fantasized about going to The Grand Ole Opry. *That's what I want to hear.* He felt compelled to head for Nashville, Tennessee, the city of country music.

He found a music store where he could purchase song sheets for his sister Eva. This time, a letter accompanied the music.

168

Dear Eva,

I hope you will enjoy these songs: "Blue Skies" sounds pretty happy . . . I hope you and your family are. One of the latest songs is, "Let Your Smile Be Your Umbrella." Once in a while I try to imagine seeing . smiling faces back home. I hope you have a lot to smile about.

Have you heard "My Blue Heaven"? Here are all these songs just for you, and I'm wishing that the next time I visit home, we'll have the fun of singing them together.

I'm in the land of country music. The lilt of the music is enjoyable, but the lyrics, which tell many tales of country life, are compelling. I feel happy here, especially after meeting Lily-Mae, a cute little country singer. She can play a guitar like I've never heard a female play. If you couldn't see her plucking away, you'd swear that it was a man. This gal is not only a wonderful country singer, she is bright and fun to be with. I'll write more later.

Oliver

Lily-Mae told Oliver that Nashville was known as the Athens of the South. Together, they visited Centennial Park where they viewed the full-scale replica of the Parthenon, erected in 1897. She pointed out the classical Greek design of the Capitol building. They were like two kids on a holiday; both took to one another and visited historic places hand in hand, as if they had grown up together in this town.

They strolled in the park along the Cumberland River, sat on a park bench and learned more about each other's life. She had no idea of Oliver's age. He was a young looking forty-one-year- old man. Oliver thought she might be in her early thirties. Neither mentioned age until things seemed to become a little more serious; this was after they had visited historic places, such as Belle Meade Mansion, built in 1853. It was a plantation home on one of the first thoroughbred horse farms in the USA.

Oliver was thrilled with this visit, and told Lily-Mae all about his cowboy and smithing days. They also visited the historic building, Travelers' Rest, which was built by Andrew Jackson's law partner in 1792. She also showed Oliver where the eleventh President of the United States, James K. Polk, was interred.

"Oliver, you've told me so many things about your life . . . It all sounds sort of compacted into the life of such a young man. You don't look much over thirty."

"Well, a bit over thirty. How about yourself?"

"I'm a little past my twenty fifth birthday . . . a lady doesn't tell all."

169

"I'll respect that." But he thought. *Maybe she's too young for me. Ah, what the heck, I don't intend to marry anyone...and we do have lots of laughs together.*

He asked, "Are you tied down to your job here? If you want adventure, tag along with me for a while. What do you say, kid?"

"I often thought that I would like to see places other than Nashville. Where do we go from here?" she intoned with no hesitation.

Is she impulsive? thought Oliver. *Wow, she sounds more than willing.*

"Have you ever been to Colorado?"

"No, never been there . . . kinda far away isn't it?"

"Let's look at train schedules and then decide."

"I'll have to tell my aunt that I'm leaving." They agreed to leave the following day.

This, to me, seems like the recklessness of the young—am I beyond that? She'll probably think it over tonight and decide against it. I'm a little uncertain about this myself, Oliver considered.

✳   ✳   ✳

"Lily-Mae! are you crazy or something; you're not going with this man; I won't allow it!"

"You met him, Aunt Pearl, you said that you thought he was nice. Anyhow, what counts is that I like him and I want to go with him."

"Foolish, foolish girl; why I bet he's a good ten years older than you are. He probably picks up young girls, and then dumps them."

"I'm twenty-six, and I'll bet he's no older than thirty-four."

"I'll make a deal with you, Lily-May. If he is as young as you say . . . who knows . . . he is a likable man. Well, what I mean is, if he is older than thirty-four you'll agree not to go, right? A deal?"

Lily-Mae was so sure about Oliver's age that she shook hands with Aunt Pearl and agreed with the "deal."

Oliver brought train schedules with him when he went to see Lily-Mae that night.

"Young man," said Aunt Pearl, "tell me how old you are."

He was taken aback by the aunt's terseness, but didn't want to appear rude, and couldn't bring himself to lie.

"If you must know, I'm forty-one."

"There now Lily-Mae, he is *fifteen* years older than you are . . . and you know our agreement."

170

"What agreement is that?" Oliver asked.

Lily-Mae was so shocked and embarrassed that she flew upstairs sobbing.

Oliver told Pearl that he didn't realize that there was such a disparity in their ages. He left a little downhearted—but almost relieved that he wasn't "robbing the cradle."

*   *   *

It didn't take him long to decide to be on his way; the very next day, he boarded an early morning train to Kansas City, and from there, he took the Santa Fe to Pueblo, Colorado. Oliver had read about the Gold Rush of 1859; Pikes Peak was the fortune hunters' landmark. He had seen old pictures of canvas covered wagons with crude lettering, "Pikes Peak or Bust."

He was also eager to visit many of the scenic wonders, such as the red granite cliffs, the Garden of the Gods, and the ancient cliff dwellings of Mesa Verde. He did get to see the well-preserved prehistoric cliff dwellings where prehistoric Indians built no less than 600 cliff houses. He learned that the more developed Pueblo Indians later lived in these earth lodges until about the year of 1300.

Oliver took tour after tour to visit these wonders, and wished that he could have shared the excitement with a companion. There was one man, on the many tours, who seemed to be a loner, like himself. Ron Moore was also a rover, and they became acquainted when boarding one of the first trains to travel through the Moffat Tunnel, which had just opened to transcontinental railroad traffic.

"Did I see you at the cliff lodges?" asked Ron.

"Yeah, I thought you looked familiar . . . where are you headed for?"

"I thought I'd see what might be interesting in Utah . . . then maybe Nevada. I'm trying to hit the forty-eight states."

"I thought I was the only inveterate roamer who aimed at *that* goal! We'll have something to write home about . . . being on the first train through the hole in the Rocky Mountains!" exclaimed Oliver.

"Isn't it an amazing feat?"

The new acquaintances were glad to have someone to converse with while going through the dimly lit tunnel, it would not have been possible to read.

They talked about baseball mainly about Babe Ruth who had hit his sixtieth home run for the New York Yankees.

Ron told Oliver about Al Jolson's new movie, the first talkie, *The Jazz Singer*. Oliver told Ron about some of the gigs he had done in theaters, playing drums with other musicians, for silent movies. They wondered just when the talkies would make the silent films obsolete.

The transcontinental railroad brought them near the northeastern shore of the Great Salt Lake. Ron said that the lake was just a remnant of the prehistoric freshwater Lake Bonneville, which originated a million years ago. *He did his homework on this place*, thought Oliver.

"There are three rivers that feed into this lake—the Bear, Jordan, and Weber Rivers—but, the lake has no outlet, so the salts keep building up, saltier than the oceans. The evaporation is faster than the water coming in from the rivers."

"Hey, Ron, you're a living encyclopedia. I'm glad I've met you. Let's travel together—you can educate me."

"If we can share expense, that might work out well. What might be even better is, if we could each ante up half the cost of an automobile, travel over some of the trails, if they're not too rough, and we'd be able to stop whenever we wanted, and see whatever we wanted."

"It sounds good to me, but there's one hitch. I don't have that kind of money right now. I need to get a job, though I do have a couple of hundred bucks on my person."

"I happen to have a little more than that. We might be able to get wheels for about six hundred. We'll both get jobs to make up the money we'll be needing."

The two men found their way to Ogden, Utah, a railroad, industrial, and canning center. They were both employed by the same processing company, working with sealing machines; one end of a can was left open until it was filled and the sealing machine did the rest. It was just a tedious job that did require some alertness to keep the automated system flowing. The earning rate was thirty-five cents an hour. They worked nine hours a day, so they earned three dollars and fifteen cents each day. Working six days a week earned them eighteen dollars and ninety cents, minus living costs—they were left with about thirteen dollars to save each week.

"You know, Oliver, if we work just about twenty weeks, we'll have saved two-hundred and sixty-three bucks. That should do for a pretty darn nice automobile."

It was spring of 1928 when the two men visited one of the few automobile showrooms.

"I tell ya fellas," said the spiffily attired salesman, "you've come to the right place for the best buys. We have this 1927, three-pedaled Model T for only five hundred dollars. But, you look like men who would be more satisfied with a later model, say, this here Ford Model A. It has a conventional gear shift, lots easier to handle than the T model. This new 1928 open roadster has safety glass, balloon tires, and the Kettering electric self-starter. No more cranking the engine like you do with the Model T's. This is a steal at only eight hundred dollars. Whata ya say, pals?"

"Give us a few minutes to talk this over," said Oliver.

"Sure, come into my office and have a cup of coffee. I'll leave you two gentlemen to make your decision. But remember, there's no better buy around."

After the salesman left them, Oliver said that he thought that eight hundred dollars was a little steep, and would leave them with too little money for further travel.

"You're right, Oliver, but that guy is too anxious to make a sale, and I think we could get a better price by threatening to look elsewhere."

"Try if you want, but I doubt that he would lower the price."

"Hey, he'd rather have a smaller commission than none at all."

The salesman was back. "Have you fellas made your decision yet?"

"I've heard that there are better buys in Salt Lake City. Guess we'll look around there."

"Okay fellas. Suit yourselves."

When the salesman saw that the potential buyers were really about to leave, he called them back with, "What would be your highest offer? Maybe we can compromise a bit."

"We were thinking about seven hundred," Ron responded.

"You have got to be joking, pal. I tell you what I'll do, I'll let you have the Model A for seven sixty."

"Seven fifty and you've got a deal,," said Ron.

"You guys are hard to bargain with." The salesman reluctantly agreed.

For three hundred seventy-five dollars each, Oliver and Ron were proud owners of a Ford Model A automobile. They were ready and eager to travel the new highways. Of course, this meant that it was necessary to study the booklet they had received with their new vehicle, especially printed for cross-country travelers like them; they were soon learning to read the maps with new route numbers.

They planned their itinerary through Nevada, into California, trav eling along the Pacific coast, up into Oregon and Washington. It would be well into the summer months of 1928 when they would finally reach Washington.

Ron took the wheel on the first leg of the journey.

"My Grandad had a Stanley Steamer, and allowed me to steer it when I was a kid, but the fastest the darn thing would go was about four miles an hour—you could walk faster! Later, my dad had a Tin Lizzy, and he let me take the wheel. Boy, would dad enjoy this. Wow, these buggies can travel over sixty miles an hour. Of course, if we did that speed on the dirt roads, we just might break an axle. I'm not planning on testing the speed limit of this beauty."

"I have a buddy in Buffalo who bought an early Ford Model. He took us to Niagara Falls, and it took us almost an hour to travel just seventeen miles. In those days, it was necessary to follow color coded posts. My buddy had a road guide with pictures of landmarks; there might be a picture of a big oak tree, and the guide would say something like, "Take a right at the big old oak." Well, what if the tree had been struck by lightning—there goes your landmark," laughed Oliver.

"Those guides were not as efficient as the maps with route numbers that we have today, and the automobiles are also more dependable. We'll make far better time than your Buffalo friend did! I figure that at the speed around forty to fifty, we should reach Carson City, Nevada in a day and a half. I understand that the Overland Trail leads all the way to Sacramento, California. Did you know that that trail was traveled by stagecoaches and the Pony Express in the old days when frontiersmen were headed for the gold rush?"

"We'll be needing to gas up at the next station. Ah, here's a Shell Oil station. These guys will do anything to please a traveler—check the oil, clean your windshield, and even give you a coffee mug for filling your tank. Let's get out and stretch a bit, and ask about motel accommodations."

The men slept in a rather seedy roadside motel that had a small cafe attached to it. They eagerly arose from the creaky beds at five the next morning, anxious to be on their way again. Lake Tahoe was just fourteen miles west of Carson City.

"To think that we could have found a motel here by the lake, instead of that rat hole we stayed in," Ron exclaimed.

"Would you agree to a relaxing day off from traveling to enjoy this place? We could go fishing, and cook our catch right by the lake."

"Sure thing, Oliver."

With no time-clock to punch, they enjoyed their leisure hours in a rented rowboat, with rented fishing gear. They sometimes trolled with their lines in the water, other times, just drifting over the clear blue waters, slumped in the bottom of the boat, catching up on lost sleep.

"Ah, c'est beau d'être riche," Oliver mumbled as he closed his eyes and rested in the warmth of the midday sun.

"What the heck does that mean, Frenchy?"

"It means that it's great to be rich. I know that we're not rich money-wise, but could you ask for more?"

"Yeah, I could ask for more. Money may not buy happiness, but it sure could buy a lot of things that would make me happy."

"Like what?"

"Some day, I'd like to buy a home . . . have a wife and a family . . . that takes money."

"I know what you mean. I had a wife once. Well, you might have called her a common-law wife. We were happy for a while, but, I just couldn't stand the sameness. I like spice in my life. Different people, different places. I could take *this* life for a while, but, tomorrow, I'd want to be moving on."

"Have you ever thought about old age? Wouldn't it be nice to have people nearby who really cared about you?"

"I don't like to cross bridges before I get to them. Sure we're all getting older, but living in the present, not in the past . . . not in the future. I'll take things as they come."

"That's where you and I differ, Oliver. I'll be looking for roots pretty darn soon."

✻   ✻   ✻

The person who rented them the boat loaned them a frying pan and showed them an outdoor fireplace, where they fried their fish with a few potatoes.

Funds were quickly becoming in need of replenishing. The weather was conducive to sleeping outdoors; that would save them a few bucks. The automobile proved to be comfortable that night, Oliver in the back seat of their roadster, and Ron in the front. By six o'clock the next morning, they were on their way again. They traveled the distance of about a hundred miles in good time and arrived in Sacramento, California in time to look for employment. Picking peaches and plums wasn't exactly what they had in mind—but, the only jobs available were in the fruit industry.

"There's not much choice, Oliver, but that's life . . . we'll take it as it comes."

It took a few weeks for their wages to amount to travel money. Actually, they did enjoy the fresh air, and exercise. In looking over their map, it was decided to travel to the east of the coastal range, where they were told that the roads would be better; that meant giving up the idea of viewing the coastal scenery.

Their next stop was Redding, about a hundred sixty miles from Sacramento, but filling the gas tank was a must.

"Ah, there's a Shell Oil . . . look at that huge treasure chest on top of the building!"

"What's that all about?" asked Oliver.

"Well, I've read about their promotions. They attract customers with tempting treasure hunts. They deck their stations with skulls and crossbones and their attendants wear high boots and eye patches. These pirates check your oil, fill your tank, and hand you a 'clue slip.' There are designated digging fields and on a chosen day, contestants with their spades, dig up treasures. You'd laugh at the so called prizes. All they dig up are little plaster-of-paris shells, stuffed with coupons to redeem for cheap merchandise at local stores. We'll just get gas and oil, if needed."

The road to Redding was surprisingly well-paved, a great improvement over some of the rough dirt roads over which they had traveled.

"Now that the car has fuel, what do ya say we tank up ourselves?"

Ron and Oliver stopped at a roadside eatery, which bragged about "The best home cookin' east of the ranges." It did prove to be like *some* home cooking: burnt toast, greasy home fries, and not so hot coffee. It was a lunch—disappointing, but enough sustenance to last while they forged ahead to the border of Oregon, just a hundred miles. In a little over three hours, they were at the border.

"I'll bet we could make Eugene in no more than four more hours. Are you game, Oliver?"

They found roadside lodgings in Eugene by eight o'clock that evening. Two starving travelers ate in the adjoining eatery, where the food owned up to its publicity, delicious lamb chops, mashed potatoes, vegetables, and mint jelly . . . with apple pie and coffee to top it off.

176

Posters around the small lobby bragged of "The Best County Fair This Side of the Columbia!"

Oliver asked Ron if he would be interested in staying tomorrow for the fair.

"Sure, I've heard that the best county fairs are in Oregon."

The fair was all that was expected, and more. The opening included a parading brass band and several yoke of oxen. Local farmers competed for best of everything, livestock and vegetables, while their wives competed for best quilting or pie making. The county fair was where rural folks gathered each year for the happy festivities. Their hard work paid off in great dividend, including colorful ribbons for the fattest pig, the biggest pumpkin, the prettiest quilt, not to mention the many entertaining attractions. Besides the auctioneer, calling out the weight of animals on the block and getting the best price per pound from the highest bidder, there were magicians performing unusual feats, a sword swallower, a fire eater and many other entertainers. The chance booths were where most of the young folks gathered, testing their skills at ringing a prize with a small hoop, or shooting at a bull's eye to win a stuffed animal. Booth after booth tempted the families with a myriad of ethnic foods. They even had a Ferris wheel and other carnival attractions.

Oliver shot the bull's eye several times and gave his winnings to the many children who were drawn to the booth by his generosity. Finally he was told that because of his skilled aiming they might have to go out of business. Oliver didn't want that to happen, but as he and Ron left that booth, they were trailed by a group of hopefuls.

"Sorry kids . . . that's all for today."

And it *was* all . . . they had had their fill of the carnival atmosphere.

*   *   *

"Have you heard of Crater Lake?" Ron asked.

"Is it on our way to Washington?"

After consulting their map, they found that they would have to backtrack about a hundred thirty-five miles—on a different route—not knowing what kind of roads they would encounter.

"We're not on a schedule, Ron. If it's worth seeing, I say let's go!"

So, they did . . . and confronted a number of rough dirt roads. Their fears were allayed when they came upon a one pump gas station by a small eatery. The thought of being stranded in the middle of nowhere had hounded them as they watched the gas gauge register almost on empty.

"Fill 'er up," Ron told the attendant.

"Sorry fella, we ain't had a delivery for some time. I could give you a couple of gallons to hold you over 'til you get to Diamond Lake Junction. I'll bet you guys are tourists, going to Crater Lake. You ain't the first ones to stop here today."

"Is your restaurant low on grub, too?" asked Oliver.

"Oh, I think the little woman could whip up something for you guys to eat."

The "little woman" was not so little but pleasant enough, and willing to stir up a cheese omelet with toast and coffee that satisfied the travelers.

The road was well-paved at the junction, and the area was more populated. They found a motel after filling the gas tank, and were ready to turn in for the night. Crater Lake National Park was only about fifteen miles from the motel.

After a hearty breakfast the next morning, they followed the signs that led them to Sinnott Memorial Overlook, where a naturalist talked about how the horrendous fire and devastation of the crater, thousands of years ago, gave birth to what is now this blue lake that is incredibly symmetrical. He told them that the lake water is so pure that it supports very little life, and because of inadequate spawning grounds and lack of food, there are no fish.

Ron and Oliver found their way to Cleetwood trail and walked over a mile to the Cove, where they were just in time to catch the launch boat which took them to view Wizard Island, the small volcano near the western shore.

From the boat, they saw eagles and falcons soaring over the lake. Some of the tourists squealed with excitement when they spotted a cougar on the shore, across from the island. The guide told them that there were deer, bears, red foxes, and other animals that had been occasionally spotted in the park.

"This excursion was certainly worth backtracking the roads of Oregon. Now, where do we go from here?" Oliver asked.

"What about our maps?"

"There are lots of scenic sights along the Columbia River. If we take this route up to Redmond, a hundred thirty-five miles, stay overnight, and then in the morning we would only have about a hundred miles to get to Dalles—right on the Columbia. How does that grab you?"

"I hope your figures jibe, Oliver."

Oliver's calculations proved to be accurate, and they arrived in Dalles, two famished travelers looking for a good eatery. They found a rustic-looking cafe which served customers out in the open with a fantastic view of the Columbia River. The two men lingered over their superb meal, enjoying both the food and the scenery. Their triumphant attitudes quickly changed when they exited the cafe and saw their automobile speeding off, heading eastward.

✳   ✳   ✳

"Sheriff, I'm calling from the Dalles Cafe . . . someone just drove off with our Ford Model A . . . yes, the plate number? . . . hold on . . . Oliver, what's our plate number?"

"I think it's 77885 . . . yeah, that's it."

"Yes sir . . . it's 77885. Thank you sir; we'll wait here until we hear from you."

Ron and Oliver were left with just the clothes on their backs, but luckily they still had an ample supply of cash stashed away in their money belts. They anxiously awaited news from the Sheriff's office, and when none was forthcoming they notified the office of their whereabouts at a nearby motel.

Two days later, information came to them that their auto had been found in an isolated area, where the Snake River meets the great Columbia, near Kenniwick, Washington. The rabble rousers who had run out of fuel, abandoned the vehicle and after ransacking the valises, and leaving all the contents widely strewn on the ground, fled on foot. One of the deputies drove the two men as far as the Washington border, where the Kenniwick Sheriff met and transported them to the site. The men appreciated the thoughtfulness of the Sheriff who emptied a gas can into the automobile tank—just enough to get them to a filling station near Pasco, Washington.

After consulting their maps, they opted to continue their trek to Spokane, just about a hundred fifty miles from Pasco.

"I have relatives in Spokane, Oliver; would you mind if we paid them a quick visit?"

"That's fine with me, Ron, I'm not in a hurry to go any place."

"After our visit, we'll have only about twenty miles to get to the border of Idaho."

"What is there to see in this part of Washington? I take it you've been here before?"

"Sure, I'll show you a few places. There's Deep Creek Canyon, a spectacular view! There's Manito Park, where we can see the outstanding sunken gardens.

"Right in the middle of town you'll see the Spokane Falls. We could visit museums. I know of one that has lots of Indian artifacts. In fact the name Spokane is Indian, meaning 'Children of the Sun.'"

"It sounds like an interesting place. There's only one little consideration, Ron, I can't stand real cold weather, and it's a little late to be in the northern part of our country."

"Yeah, it's hard to believe that we've been on the road for so many months. I was hoping that we could spend the holidays with my Aunt Harriet and Uncle Todd, then we could head south again."

Oliver reluctantly gave in to the idea of spending Christmas with Ron's relatives, he would have felt selfish to insist that they head for a warmer climate, since it was not just *his* car, but *theirs*.

Aunt Harriet and Uncle Todd were a congenial couple, who made the "fellas" feel most welcome.

Oliver had written home to wish his family happy holidays, using Ron's relatives' address. He was elated to receive two letters, one from Eva and the other from Joe, his kid brother.

Dear Oliver,

We couldn't believe that you bought an automobile! You must be rolling in dough! Ron sounds like a nice fellow and his aunt and uncle must be even nicer to take you in for the holidays.

My youngest kid, Margret, just turned three and is so active that she's wearing us all out.

Ma takes care of the kids when cousin Clara and I practice our duets. Ma does a lot for her age. It's hard to believe that she is seventy-two years old! She still goes to daily Mass.

Rita and Joe visited with their two little kids, Claire and Russell. Joe will always be 'Tse Boy to me, Everyone sends love to you. Don't eat too much.

Eva

Hi Brother,

Wow, you're on the other side of the country. Washington looks so far away on the map! Frank told me all about your Jamming sessions with a jazz group in Louisiana, I'd like to hear you guys, You must have learned a lot of new rhythmic patterns suited to jazz. I'm a drummer with a different beat . . . no jazz, but some pretty complicated stuff. I've joined the American Legion band of Lawrence. We play for May processions, parades, and last fourth of July, we did a band concert at a park in Ballardvale. We played Phillip Sousa marches, Strauss Polkas, and some show tunes . . . directed by Billy Russell. I also play with Charlie Pierce's orchestra. We do weddings and dances.

If I start my own orchestra, I'm thinking of naming it "The Builtmore Dance Band." We'll play a couple of tunes that I wrote and Charlie orchestrated for me.

When we perform in an open bandstand at a park with the Legion band, my two kids run all over the place, eating junk and sometimes standing next to the bandstand watching their daddy drum. They clap hands to the rhythm . . . maybe they'll be musicians, too!

Where will you go after the holidays? Let's hear from you, eh? Have a happy time.

Joe

Joe's life seems all cut out for him, thought Oliver, almost envious. *He has a pretty wife, two nice kids, and he's into the music field, even composing! Lucky guy, my brother. I'll find my niche some day.*

✳   ✳   ✳

Aunt Harriet and Uncle Todd treated Oliver as one of the family. Their Christmas celebration was far more elaborate than any he had experienced at home.

"Wow, what a cook your aunt is! I feel like a stuffed turkey."

This was after the Christmas feast. It was a white Christmas, which Oliver hadn't seen for some years. He did admit that the snow was picturesque but felt reluctant to partake any of the winter sports, and his host and hostess understood after Oliver related his experience with the *Larchmont* disaster. He had stayed in Fredonia during several winter months, but as he aged, the circulatory problem became less bearable.

After the New Year celebration, Ron, not minding the cold weather, had decided that he didn't care for the idea of a long trek south. He had been there, seen all he wanted to see, and since Uncle Todd offered him a job in his hardware store, he thought that to stay put for a while was an attractive idea. The problem—what to do about the jointly owned automobile? He would have to consult with Oliver.

* * *

"Oliver, there are all kinds of trains, heading in any direction from Spokane. What do you think of the idea of my buying your half of our vehicle—then you'd be free to travel in comfort by rail?"

"I was wondering how long our tour of the country would last. I'll miss your companionship, but if that's what you want, it's okay by me."

"What would you consider a fair price? Of course, considering that the car was in use for a year, I'm sure you wouldn't expect the amount you put into it—or would you?"

"Come on, Ron, you know me. Haven't I been fair? What's your offer?"

"How about two hundred?"

"Sold!"

Twenty-three

Oliver boarded train after train, catching up on his reading. He usually enjoyed train travel which gave him an opportunity to meet new people, and yet have lots of time to read. He had purchased the Ernest Hemingway book of short stories. *The Short Happy Life of Francis Macomber* was a favorite for Oliver. He could relate to the story of hunters, though he had never been on an African safari. He lived the story of big game hunting as it unfolded. The ending was surprising, but that Macomber guy lived the thrill of a lifetime.

Travel time seemed short for Oliver since he busied himself throughout most of the trip. He hadn't traveled to Oklahoma, as yet. I'll get off this train to at least put a foot in Oklahoma, so that I can say, "Yeah, I've been there." But, before he had disembarked, he had spoken with a traveling Cherokee Indian who told him a few interesting things about the land. Looks like I'll put both feet in Oklahoma for a more meaningful stay. After a three day stay, he wrote to his sister Eva.

Hi again, Eva,

I'm visiting the "Sooner State." Know why Oklahoma is called that? Well I found out that settlers staked their claims on land SOONER than when it became legal! This is a state much different than any that I have visited. One area called Little Sahara is all sand dunes! It reminded me of desert scenes in cowboy movies, only I half expected to see approaching camels over the wavy windblown hills.

Wow, what a spectacular scene at Turner Falls! A beautiful cascade falls over seventy feet and forms a great swimming pool below . . . You guessed it, I did have a swim.

I hope that the pot I sent Ma did not break in transit. It was made by a Cherokee Indian where I visited a village named TSA-LA-GI. These Indians were settled in Tahlequah after being driven from their native habitats in the East. I witnessed the drama called the "Trail of Tears." It depicts their sad exodus, the long trek from their homeland. Our early government certainly treated the earliest Americans poorly!

I'm off again where the trains will take me through Arkansas, down to

Louisiana to visit some old buddies. Stay healthy and keep warm up North. Give my love to all.

Oliver was happy to be back in Louisiana, where he recaptured his musical experiences with the group he had filled in with a couple of years before.

He stayed at the same boarding house, filled in with the same fellows, Norm Cartier, and Pete Amirault, at the Monique Cafe. It was near Mardi Gras time, 1929, the best time of the year to be in New Orleans. He stayed there for months, even in the humid months of July and August. He gained introductions to some "fun ladies," and was still there when the shock of the October 24 collapse of the stock market occurred.

Many businesses closed—work was hard to come by. Banks failed, tax revenues decreased so much that the hands of government were tied and unable to respond to the economic crises. Newspapers were replete with suicide notices of people who had lost their life's savings; men jumping out of skyscraper buildings.

"Sorry, Oliver, the Monique Cafe is closing down. l don't know what will become of us!" lamented his friends.

The only thing for Oliver to do was to go home to Lawrence—but where is home? he pondered. Ma is living with my sister Eva, and her family of four children. Is there room for me? Wow, what a predicament!

Eva's husband, Joe Gagne, was still working for a baking company, delivering bread to neighborhood stores. At least he had a job, though his wages were lowered. The value of money had increased in proportion to the lowered salaries, which made things slightly more bearable. Oliver joined the Gagne family; they had space for him in a small shed-like room to the left of the top stairway to their third floor flat on Haverhill Street.

Brother Joe visited the family frequently, and on one occasion Oliver and he were able to converse privately.

"I understand that Ma was living with you and your family, Joe. That arrangement didn't work out?"

"I didn't mind having Ma living with us, but Rita was unhappy because Ma insisted on handling the household finances. They had words . . . so now, you can see why Ma doesn't care for my wife, and my wife doesn't accompany me here very often. Rita doesn't know that I slip Ma a few bucks to help out now and then."

"Well, Joe, can you see your wife's side? Ma does have the knack for leading other people's lives."

"Oliver, how can you say that? Did she ever lead your life?"

"I think that I'm the only one who had the guts to get away from that possibility."

"You're the mama's boy . . . especially if you feel that you have to fork over a few bucks. Hey, you have a family to support—don't your wife and kids come first?"

"Sure, but when I have an orchestra job, I don't tell Rita about the extra money; then I can help Eva and her family. You know that little Robert Goulet kid downstairs? I played in an orchestra for his folks' wedding a couple of years ago. Yeah, it was Charlie Pierce's group, and we still get jobs with his outfit."

"Do you know of a group of musicians that I could fill in with? I'll have to find some kind of work."

"You could ask the Gibeau brothers. They sometimes play at the movie theaters. I don't think they have a drummer."

The kitchen door opened, and Azilda entered breathing heavily from climbing the three flights of stairs.

"Oh, bon jour, Mama. Vous retournez d'eglise?" (You're returning from church?)

"Oui, Il fait beau temps pour faire une promenade." (Yes, the weather is beautiful for a walk.)

Oliver sat in the old rocking chair and pulled his mother into his lap. It was a rare occasion to see and hear her laugh. There were more laughs to come because Oliver was the family clown . . . and they were glad to have him back home, especially his mother and Eva's children, Germaine, Marcelle, Russell, and little Margaret. Oliver entertained the children with card tricks, games, and comical songs.

It didn't take long for Oliver to find employment playing the drums at a local movie theater, featuring silent films. The live music for the films was performed by pianist, Fred Gibeau; violinist, George Gibeau; and drummer, Oliver Janvier—a most versatile trio. Oliver worked at any job he could find, including being a clown in the Winter Gardens, an amateur theatre on Essex Street, where there were plays presented weekly and which were surprisingly well-attended.

Oliver found that since he was living back with Mama, he had to curtail some of his acquired habits—and to be the good little boy his mother expected him to be. That included going to church on Sundays, and holy days of obligation. However, through some of his newfound friends, he was able to obtain the prohibited beverages he had enjoyed

185

during all his travels.

In fact, one provider solicited Oliver's help in building a false brick wall in his cellar. They figured out a way of installing a brick-covered door, with seams that were undetectable from the outside; just a slight push on a certain brick, and the door would open slowly, exhibiting the wares on shelves inside the long narrow compartment. This paid project assured Oliver of his fair share of the hidden inventory. He enjoyed drinking, but the habit never did become extreme; in other words, he could hold his drink.

Mama Azilda was none the wiser about Oliver's outside activities, though at times she did wonder what he was up to. She still worked at her dressmaking business, but was experiencing a reduction of her clientele because of the Depression.

Brother Joe found ways to eke out a living. He had become known in the music circles as an accomplished percussionist, and was able to perform with well-known bands in the area. He even had a student who was sent to him by Frankie Frazelle, Rudy Vallee's drummer, who was originally from Lawrence.

Joe's versatility outranked Oliver's level, but it never caused jealousy or friction between the brothers because Oliver was proud of his kid brother's accomplishments and that his kid brother had met and married the pretty, blue-eyed, blonde Couture girl, Rita. Now there were two more little Janviers, Russell and Claire. Joe and his family lived in the upstairs flat at the corner of Hudson Avenue and Ames Street: a home built by John B. Couture, his father-in-law.

*   *   *

The Depression years were felt keenly by the majority of citizens. There wasn't as much buying power; all Americans were surrounded by poverty. Though times were unpredictable, the Gagnes and Janviers were thankful for roofs over their heads.

People who were less fortunate were sleeping on park benches, covering themselves with newspapers at night. Some of the formerly wealthy people resorted to selling apples on street corners for five cents each. Tax revenues had fallen so that the government was powerless to lend a hand to so many needy citizens.

Agriculture was almost eradicated, compounding the problems. The terrible drought of the 1930s made matters worse. Each nation imposed higher tariffs on their industrial goods, which did not protect their industrial base, as they had expected; it only created more problems.

Buying power began to improve slightly in 1931, after the collapse of the gold standard. Nations found markets for their goods by devaluating their currency. Oliver, who never had money to spare, found no difference in *his* financial situation than when he had been on the road. It was 1932 when he began checking maps for his next venture.

✳   ✳   ✳

"Mr. Independence!" Eva exclaimed. "Mr. Itchy Feet—can't you ever stay put? You're not a kid anymore!"

"Mon fils, tu vas encore! Mon Dieu . . . peut-etre je ne tu jamais verrai encore." (My son, you are leaving again! My God . . . perhaps I will never see you again.) Mama sobbed.

Oliver kissed them all adieu, and left without a forwarding address. "I'll write you when I get to the Dakotas."

Oliver kept his promise:

Dear Folks,

Mount Rushmore in Keystone, South Dakota is really something! The sculptures of presidents Washington, Jefferson, Lincoln, and Teddy Roosevelt are huge! 60 feet high! What a feat that Borglum guy accomplished!

Another mountain carving in the town of Custer is of the Sioux warrior, "Crazy Horse." That one is taller than the Washington Monument, it's the world's largest statue.

I'd like to have a chance to get in on the reenactment of mountain men in the early fur trading business at the old Fort Union trading post in Williston, North Dakota. It would be fun to dress up as a trapper with buckskins on . . . but maybe they accept just locals. Who knows . . . I'll write more later.

The summer reenactment crew at the Fort Union trading post had already been filled, much to the disappointment of the showman, Oliver. He traveled through Idaho and on to revisit his buddy, Ron Moore, in Spokane.

"It looks like you've planted your roots, Ron. Wow, a married man with a kid!"

"Yeah, Oliver, it's a good life . . . just what I wanted. My uncle made me manager of his hardware store. We haven't done too badly with the Depression and all. Yeah, it was the right decision to remain in Spokane. Are you still the wandering minstrel?"

"That's me. This old dog hasn't learned any new tricks. My sister Eva calls me Mr. Independent, and Mr. Itchy Feet. My family doesn't understand me. I'm living my life the way I want. No nuzzling up to what other people think I should be or do. I'm just Mr. Rolling Stone, gathering no moss."

"You're one in a million Oliver. I like a little independence too, but I like to depend on loved ones for lots of things. I guess some plants can be uprooted, and transplanted, where others would just wither and die. You and I are not at all made of the same fiber. I had had my fill of roaming. Now, I'm more content to stay put."

"I'm glad for you, Ron. Well, I'll probably see you in the next life."

They both laughed, shook hands and wished each other well. After Oliver departed, Ron's wife Natalie declared, "What kind of man would seek travel on his own for the sake of setting foot in all forty-eight states?"

"Gee honey, I was almost like him at one time. I think that I understand him, but I wouldn't want to be in his shoes. He's looking for something, but doesn't know what it is."

"Well I'm glad you changed your goals. The poor guy. I wonder what the future holds for him. Maybe he'll meet some woman and get married."

"That would surprise me. He's just a whimsical, free-spirited individual with a healthy curiosity. I got to know him pretty well when we traveled together. I found him to be outwardly a fun loving person, but paradoxically he is introspective and, at times, self-deprecating. Yeah, I'll have to agree with you when you say, 'the poor guy.'"

✳   ✳   ✳

After exploring part of the state of Idaho, Oliver wrote home.

Hello Family,
    This gypsy wanderer had visited an old friend in Spokane, Washington when off I went to Idaho and found Lake Coeur d'Alene, just about fifty miles from Spokane. The beauty just captured me in awe. Idaho claims that most of its two thousand lakes are in the northern part where this special lake was carved out by ice age glaciers. I took a day-long cruise, a forty-eight mile trip down the lake and up the St. Joe River to St. Maries.

St. Joe River is said to be deep and wide enough for ship passage and besides, it's the highest river in the world.

At St. Maries, our tour boat picked up other passengers for the ride back through Lake Coeur d'Alene. That was a new and very enjoyable experience for me. The scenery and the amazingly beautiful animals sighted along the route excited everyone aboard.

I met a man and wife who are visiting from Methuen, Massachusetts. They have an automobile and suggested that I join them traveling to Yellow Stone Park. All I have to do is share travel expenses. I've decided to take them up on that. I probably shouldn't tell you how I got to Lake Coeur d'Arlene . . . it might cause some worry about me. But, believe me, there are lots of good and honest people in this world . . . Oh well, I may as well tell you . . . I thumbed rides to get to the lumber-jack town north of the lake . . . so now, how can I refuse the great offer from fellow Massachusetts people, Chuck and Hazel Nolet, to go to Yellowstone in Wyoming?

I'll write you all about it later.

"What a great experience this is! If it weren't for you two kind people, I don't know how I would ever get to come to this park," exclaimed Oliver, expressing his gratitude to his newfound friends, the Nolets.

"Can you see why all three of us have to sit in the front seat to travel? We have all our tenting gear packed in our small trunk and in the back seat. Our son was going to come with us and when he backed out, we didn't bother unpacking his sleeping bag. You're welcome to use it," Chuck offered.

They had entered the park through the west entrance, then drove about seven miles, passing the Madison River. They took the first right along the Firehole River, passing the Lower Geyser and Midway Geyser Basins, because they all agreed to make their first stop at the most famous Geyser, Old Faithful, which was just sixteen miles from the turn off. Visitors were ooing and aahing at the gushing of Old Faithful. The park guide told them that there are two hundred active geysers in the park. Old Faithful, the one that most visitors opted to see, spews out nine thousand gallons of boiling water over seventy feet high.

Hazel remarked, "We arrived here just in time. There's a seventy-three minute wait between spewings. I want to see the limestone terraces I read about. We can't see everything in one day. We'll look for a suitable place to pitch our tent."

They drove further into the park, stopping occasionally to watch the bison. They read the signs warning visitors that these two-thousand

189

pound animals are subject to unpredictable behavior.

"Who would be nuts enough to challenge a huge buffalo? I wonder if they get used to seeing humans around. They're no longer hunted. Maybe they're tamer. Want to get out of the automobile to see how close we can get to them?"

Oliver opened the door, then quickly closed it and said, "Just joking!"

"I've read that the Shoshone Indians hunted big horn sheep and bison. They made tools and weapons from the horns and bones. Nothing was ever wasted."

Chuck drove on and stopped again when they saw an antelope running lickety split . . . chased by a cougar.

"That cougar will be outrun by that antelope. They're the fastest animals in the park. He'll tire and have to quit. No dinner tonight, *Cougie,* unless you find a rabbit or two," said Oliver in an upswing mood.

"I wonder if there is a safe place to pitch a tent!" exclaimed Hazel.

"Aah," said Chuck as he pulled over to the side of the road where he spotted other campers set up for the night. "This looks pretty safe with other people around. Look at these huge pole pines. Get a whiff of them!"

Oliver was in a gregarious frame of mind while helping Chuck set up camp. They had a good supply of food, bought by Oliver before entering the park. The Nolets had a metal chest of ice for perishables. That night they were allowed to build a fire in a pit especially made for campers. They ate fried ground chuck mixed with a can of beans. After appetites were satisfied, they sat on stones surrounding the fire and sang cowboy and other tunes such as: "Tiptoe Through the Tulips," "Singin' in the Rain," and "Walkin' My Baby Back Home," accompanied by Oliver's uke. Though Oliver was invited to sleep in their tent, he thought about being an extra cog in the wheel of friendship, so he opted to sleep out in the open.

No one was up and about when Oliver awakened at five in the morning. He recalled the Shoshone Indian saying: "May *the Great Spirit make sunlight in your heart."* And sunlight was truly in Oliver's heart, in his face too. He again thought about his friends, the Choctaw Indians and recalled how attuned to nature he had been at that time in his life. If there is such a thing as reincarnation, I most definitely was an Indian, he told himself. I had to be to feel so much peace with myself. He took out his note paper and pencil to scratch out another letter to his family.

I slept under the starry sky last night, breathing in the appealing scent of pines. I didn't mind when it got a little chilly during the night, I was snugly wrapped in a warm sleeping bag. This is a good time of year to be here; it's a short summer season. We're told that the winters are long and hard. We arrived yesterday traveling through the Western entrance, and now we are camping near the Eastern section, not very far from the Yellowstone River. Today, we'll visit the river side geyser which spews boiling water every six hours, lasting a full twenty minutes! Then we're off to the Mammoth hot springs where calcium terraces are being constantly formed. Ah, the Nolets are up, and I smell bacon, eggs, and coffee! I'll add to this later.

Yeah, there's nothing like eating out in the open. We did get to see the terraces, which were formed probably thousands of years ago and still changing. What a sight! They were formed by the evaporation of hot water oozing through rocks of calcium carbonate which creates a variety of interesting earthen colors.

We'll be leaving this place of wonder tomorrow. The Nolets want to visit Minnesota. This is a great deal for me . . . I furnish the food and contribute to the cost of gasoline.

To be continued.

Here we are in Minnesota . . . It took us ages to get to Leech Lake which is the third largest in this state. We rented an old rowboat and caught dinners for two days. The "Walleyed Pike" proved to be a tasty fish. We also hiked the "Stony Point Trail" for an hour each way. It wasn't too easy going . . . it was stony, but what can one expect of an area hewn out by glaciers thousands of years ago? We're off again. I'll try to get this mailed when we get to Duluth.

Chuck and Hazel changed their plans and decided against going to Wisconsin.

"Hazel and I have decided to head north from Duluth to Ontario, Canada. We have cousins there whom we haven't seen for many years. You're welcome to come with us if you want," Chuck said, hoping to make further travel—just for the two of them.

Oliver sensed the hint and also felt it was time to part ways.

"Thanks anyway. I'll just hop a train in a different direction. There are a few places I'd like to see in Wisconsin. Thank you so much for hauling me this far. Maybe we'll get to see each other in Lawrence some time."

They all shook hands and went their separate ways.

Oliver boarded the train from Duluth, heading southward through

191

western Wisconsin. He especially enjoyed train travel because it afforded him reading time and also he liked meeting fellow travelers. One young man he met was a descendant of a Chippewa Indian chief. He told Oliver that the name "Ouisconsin" could be translated as meaning, "Gathering of waters."

"Giant glaciers carved out this part of the country during the Ice Age. That's why there are thousands of lakes and streams in this state. If you want to see an interesting sight, you should visit Devils Lake," insisted the young man.

"What's to see at Devils Lake?" asked Oliver.

"Well, from the Cliffs, which are as high as six-hundred feet, you can see Balance Rock—which seems to defy gravity. Its narrowest end rests on a ledge, and the rock gets wider and much bigger at the top which seems sort of weird. It gives me an eerie feeling—as if it's unreal. The small lake itself has the clearest blue water I've ever seen; at least it looks that way from up on top of the quartzite cliffs."

"That sounds interesting. Can you tell my why Wisconsin is called the badger state?"

"Yeah, well you know how a badger digs into its burrow and lives underground. The term was applied to lead miners because they dug into the side of hills and created mines. It could be called the copper state, too. There are copper mines in the northern part of our state."

Oliver was happy to converse with the young man, and was disappointed when it was time for his new friend to get off at his stop.

*   *   *

1932 was the year that F.D.R. won the presidential election with 472 electoral votes. His opponent, Herbert Hoover, gained a mere fifty-nine electoral votes. Oliver was proud that he had voted for the winner. Other news that he got caught up on during his travels: Amelia Earhart became the first woman to fly solo across the Atlantic Ocean. Lindbergh's baby was kidnapped. The March King, John Philip Sousa, died. *I always wanted to hear Sousa's Orchestra, I traveled a different route. Unfortunately, his tour of concerts never connected with my meanderings,* thought Oliver.

Now they're putting the many years of planning into motion, he thought as he read that work had begun on San Francisco's Golden Gate Bridge. He was pleased to learn that the World Series was won by New

192

York, over Chicago 4-0. That brought him back to the many years he had spent with Hedda, and the many times they had teasingly argued about the New York versus the Boston teams.

Then he read about the list of popular songs of 1932: "I'm Looking Over a Four Leaf Clover," "When the Moon Comes Over the Mountain," "Try a Little Tenderness." I'll have to buy Eva some of those new songs, mused Oliver as his train approached Manitowoc.

As he browsed the ads in the *Manitowoc Herald*, he found one which seemed to suit his needs for housing. A Mrs. Koski advertised: *Room available for single man or woman. Breakfast and dinner served daily. Phone 22049.*

Oliver had much difficulty understanding the woman with a strong Finnish accent. He was able to make out the River View Drive address and he presented himself in person. He found Mrs. Koski to be likable, and he was able to discern her faltering English, when the chubby little woman used her hand motions to help reach an understanding about the rental. Once settled in his neat comfortable room, he searched for job openings.

The Manitowoc Speedcrane Company, a subsidiary of the Manitowoc Shipbuilding Company, was manufacturing cranes for a Chicago Company. Though salaries had been cut during the Depression, the crane work kept the company sound. Oliver applied for work at the relatively new factory. A most charming secretary interviewed him. I wonder if all these questions that she's asking is part of the job, or if she's prying into my life considering me as a heartthrob contender. I like those bright blue eyes and that pretty light and shining hair with the traces of a little gray. She's a very dignified looking gal . . . pretty white teeth, too.

"Mr. Janvier, you didn't answer my last question."

"Ah, oh . . . what was it?" He was paying attention to her appearance, instead of her interview.

"I was inquiring about your last place of employment and the reason for leaving."

"The only thing that I can tell you is that after being discharged from the Army, I chose to be a traveler, and while on the road, I worked at a number of jobs. It would take me several lunch dates—I mean lunch breaks—for me to enumerate all the things I've done. I did at one time own my own smithing business, but the proliferation of the automobile industry just about wiped me out. I'm a good worker and capable of learning just about any kind of work."

"Mr. Janvier, are you flirting with me? It's not just your slip up on the word dates and breaks, but that wry grin and twinkle in your eyes did suggest that you are a man of winsome ways." After a spell of hesitation, she continued, "However, back to your application. You must complete this form, and after doing so, please leave it with this office and I will see if Mr. Worth will accept it. Please be here tomorrow at about nine in the morning. Good day."

Mr. Worth interviewed Oliver. He found that this new man was not qualified to fill positions, such as engineering, rigging assembling, or machining, which ultimately left the jobs of welding, grinding, riveting, or painting.

The fact that Oliver had once owned a smithing business qualified him for a welding position, which he began the following Monday.

Mrs. Hilja Koski's home had a most pleasant atmosphere. She had been allowed to remain in the home, especially built for workers of the former boat building industry; her deceased husband had been an assembly worker at the crane factory, and the board of directors didn't have the heart to evict the saddened widow. The small rooms were immaculately kept and the Finnish cooking was a pleasurable new experience for Oliver. He especially enjoyed the saffron raisin scones for breakfast with her uniquely flavored coffee, but her Finnish buttermilk crepes were superior to any he had ever eaten.

After a day's work at the factory he enjoyed dinner consisting of beef stew, filled with root vegetables. It went so well with the dark sour rye bread which Mrs. Koski called "reika laipa." Peach tarts, or blueberry bars often topped off the nourishing meals.

One day, Mrs. Koski called Oliver to the phone which was in her spacious living room. *Who could be phoning me?* he asked himself. *How did the person get this number?*

"Oliver Janvier here," he spoke so businesslike.

"Oliver, this is Gretel Kuntz. How are you, and how do you like your job?"

"I'm sorry, but I don't recall meeting a Gretel Kuntz. Are you sure that you have the right number?"

"Oh yes, I got it from the personal file at the office . . . remember me? I did the preliminary interview for Mr. Worth."

"Now I know—you had me pegged as some kind of flirt."

"I really enjoyed that little episode and was hoping to hear from you not for a break, but for that other word . . . "

"Oh, you mean date?"

"I guess I'm being forward, but I'm a lonely widow who hasn't had a male companion since my husband passed on three years ago. Would you consider coming to dinner at my home next Sunday?"

"Now how could a lonely guy refuse an invitation from a lovely lonely widow. It sounds good to me. Tell me how to get there and at what time."

This was the start of an unusually unexpected relationship with the pretty widow Kuntz.

"You've got to be kidding, Oliver. You mean to tell me that the widow Kuntz asked you to dinner at her place!"

At lunch time, the men sat outside eating, with their lunch pails on the bench beside them.

"Yeah, she said that she's been a lonely widow since her husband died three years ago."

"And you fell for that line?"

"She seems sincere enough . . . why? What do you know about the woman?"

"She went out with this guy I know and all she wanted from him was: 'Bert, my sink is blocked. Could you fix it? Bert, I can't put up my storm windows by myself. Will you do it? Bert this and Bert that.' And no recompense," he poked Oliver in the ribs with his elbow as he winked and said, "Ya know what I mean? You can be sure . . . she'll use you as her handyman . . . wanna bet?"

"I'm not betting on anything. I'll just see what she has in mind. You never know what lurks in the minds of women."

"Sounds like you've had a few experiences yourself."

"By the way, fellow worker, what's your name?"

The fellow worker, with raised eyebrows and a glint in his eyes exclaimed, "Bert."

That revelation made Oliver feel that he wanted to cancel the "date" with widow Kuntz.

The next Sunday, he reluctantly climbed the steps to the widow's unpretentious home on Pine Street.

Her cordial greeting had the effect of changing his hesitant demeanor. Bert's mistaken about this lady, I'm sure, he reasoned. After a glass of sherry and a tour of her home, Oliver felt relaxed and assured that her intentions were proper and that only a platonic relationship was expected.

"This meal is excellent. You're a good cook!"

"Not everybody appreciates German cuisine."

"Well, it's cooking that I am familiar with. To tell the truth, I lived with a German girl many years ago . . . back in my youth."

Gretel appeared somewhat shocked that he should live with a woman without being married.

"I'm sorry if that disappoints you . . . but that's the way it was in those days."

"I've never known that to be . . . I . . . I just can't imagine a woman allowing that situation!"

"It was an arrangement that we both agreed to, and as it turned out, we might have divorced had we married . . . which is probably just as reprehensible in your eyes. You see, I like my freedom."

"I never felt that I had ever infringed on my husband's freedom. Our marriage was a partnership from the start. He was free to pursue his golfing interest . . . though I was lonely at times. But then, I had my freedom to go out with my lady friends and participate in church functions, which didn't hold his interest. But we still had a good life together in spite of our little differences."

Oliver did appreciate the fine home cooked meal and some of the conversation, but still felt a little embarrassed about what Bert had told him. *When is she going to ask me to wash her windows or something?* he couldn't help thinking. *Maybe another time he reasoned.* They said their good-byes with no mention of chores. *Maybe Bert was pulling my leg,* he thought.

"Hey, Oliver, tell me about your date." Bert was curious about Oliver's meeting with the widow Kuntz.

"There's nothing to tell, Bert." Oliver was determined not to share any information with the man who seemed to have wanted a close relationship with the woman, but was turned off by her demands for chores—"Without recompense," as his fellow worker had put it. It seems that Bert expected some payment . . . other than cash for his labors.

"Did she ask you to empty the garbage, or paint her porch?"

"She's a very nice lady and made no demands on me."

"What did you two do after dinner?"

"Come on, Bert, save your grilling for your dinner tonight. What are you having? Grilled pork chops? Grilled beef?"

You're no friend if we can't share a few tidbits about females. You should enjoy the game of pursuit and tell. I could tell you a few things about some of the wives of some of the guys who work here."

"Bert, I don't care to hear about any of your exploits. Knock it off, will ya."

"I've known a few killjoys in my life—you top the list."

After their exchange, Bert avoided Oliver, which made the lunch time more agreeable for the new worker.

Oliver was not one to kiss and tell. Oh, he and Gretel did kiss after a few dates, going further and further each time, until finally, they became lovers.

Gretel became possessive of "her man," and wanted a full account of his day, each time they dated.

"You know that I'm fond of you, Gretel, but don't hold on to me so tightly that I can't breathe. I can't give you an account of all my thoughts and doings. If it makes you any happier, I'm not seeing any other woman."

"I'm sorry if I seem so grasping, but my losing you worries me. I feel that at last I've found someone I could spend the rest of my life with."

Oh God, what have I gotten myself into? he asked himself.

His lack of a reply and look of bewilderment frightened Gretel.

"I would never allow a man to make love to me if I thought he didn't have honorable intentions," she exclaimed with tears in her eyes.

"Gretel, we can go on loving each other without feeling that we own each other. I'm my own person . . . have been all my life. I just cannot be owned. Can we come to an understanding about this relationship? I don't want to have to give an account of myself to anyone . . . don't take it personally," he announced as he lovingly patted her cheek and wiped away a tear.

His tenderness consoled her.

"I'm sorry. I didn't realize that I had given the impression of wanting ownership—like a piece of furniture. But I'd like our relationship to be open by confiding in each other. That way we'd get to know each other wholly. Do you get what I mean?"

"I'm more the kind who likes a little mystery. Don't tell me so much about yourself that there's no intrigue left. It's more exciting that way, don't you think? You pretty young blue-eyed princess." He had a way with women, kissing her tenderly and repeating his last six words softly and luringly.

Oliver succeeded in convincing her that they could express their love for each other without feeling possessive or being possessed. She did tell him about a certain man, without naming him.

"One of the workers at the plant approached me and asked if he could do a few handyman jobs for me. I agreed. After helping me with the storm windows, he made it clear that he wasn't here for the money. He wanted . . . well, how can I put it? He wanted to be paid in another way . . . you know what I mean? Well, I furiously told him he could go fly a kite and never come back!"

"Is he still flying his kite?" laughed Oliver.

"Well, I'm thankful that he never came back."

"So am I. Hey, does that Victrola work?" asked Oliver walking over to the tall mahogany phonograph.

"Sure, wanna dance? I have a few records. Just crank the handle so that the record will play at the right speed."

"This reminds me of cranking up a friend's ole tin lizzie. I guess cars don't need to be cranked any more. Maybe some day they'll figure out how to put a self-starter on a record player, too."

Gretel placed the black disc on the turntable, moved the arm containing a needle to the edge of the record, slid a lever that began the rotating table . . . then they heard, "I'm Getting Sentimental Over You."

As Oliver held his partner and they danced, his thoughts became sentimental. This closeness is so warm and enticing, he contemplated. *She's so light on her feet. Those blue eyes. Oh how those blue eyes sparkle...like sapphires. They send a message of love. I want so much to return that message. Am I in love? Is this for keeps?*

"You're awfully pensive, Oliver. What are you thinking about?"

"Oh, lots of warm, comforting things about you. I must really be 'getting sentimental over you.'" He sang with the music.

That night, Oliver remained at Gretel's home.

"Oliver, please move in with me?"

"That's an invitation that is difficult to refuse, but I'll have to think about it."

*   *   *

The next day when he got to his own residence, Mrs. Koski acted like a mother hen.

"You not come home last night. You all right?"

"Yes I'm fine."

"Tank Got, I vorried."

198

Wow, I'm caught between someone who wants to mother me...and another woman who wants to smother me.

"I'm sorry, Mrs. Koski, I had no idea that you would notice when I come or go. I stayed over at a friend's house for the night . . . I should have phoned you."

"Dat's goot. Tank you."

To move in with Gretel, or not—what should I do? he pondered with knitted brows.

"Hey Oliver, did you have a fight with your girl?" called Bert with a know-it-all smirk on his face.

"No Bert, and if I did I wouldn't tell you." Oliver tried moving away from this obnoxious, nosy fellow worker, but Bert pressed on with his questioning.

"You ain't looking too happy today . . . got a lot on your mind, eh? The widow Kuntz workin' ya too hard?" Bert chuckled as he kept jabbing Oliver's ribs with his elbow.

"Cut it out, Bert . . . just stay away from me." Oliver moved quickly to join some other workmen on lunch break.

"Not many men would put up with the crap you're taking from Bert. Does he have something on you?" exclaimed Arty.

Oliver didn't want to disclose the fact that he's involved with the pretty office worker. All he offered was, "Bert's just a harmless pest. I don't like to encourage him by acknowledging his foolish cross-examinations."

"Is it true that you're dating Mrs. Kuntz?"

"Where did you got that notion."

"Rumors travel fast in this place . . . ya might say it's spread like butter on hot toast." Ed spread the last few words slowly with assertion and deliberation. "There's been talk for some time," he added.

"You guys are like a bunch of old ladies who have nothing else to do but gossip. Let's see . . . where's the back fence . . . let's spread all kinds of rumors," Oliver added with fake laughter.

He didn't want to be on unfriendly terms with his fellow workers and offered a handshake with the men, saying: "No offense, guys, I promise not to butt into any of your affairs."

"That's fair enough, Oliver. We just do a little teasing now and then. Hope you won't take it too seriously." They all joined in with handshakes and pats on the backs. Oliver felt that they were sincere and he reverted to his jolly self, laughing with them.

His relationship with the guys was improved greatly and from then on he enjoyed his lunch hour with Arty, Ed, and a number of other employees . . . all but Bert.

"Gretel, I had a slight confrontation with a few men at the plant today. Do you have any idea how they found out that you and I are dating? I've never confided in anyone about us."

"Mr. Worth sort of drew the information out of me. He seemed interested in asking me for a date, but I discouraged him by saying that I'm seeing someone special. Why do you ask?"

"Rumor at the plant has it that we're very close. I told the guys that I wouldn't butt into their affairs if they stay out of my personal life. I feel that the situation is in hand—at least I hope it is."

"Just ignore it, Oliver. Consider the source."

"That's good advice, Gretel. I never thought of it that way."

"Let's you and I do something different this weekend, Oliver."

"What did you have in mind?"

"How about a getaway. We could take the ferry to Ludington, Michigan, and stay at a beachfront hotel on the lake. Crossing the lake takes about four hours. It could be our love cruise." Gretel seductively swept her lips across his mouth.

"You're a hard one to resist . . . you know my weaknesses," he said as he gently held her in his arms, kissed her passionately . . . that was the beginning of their love weekend.

Oliver did phone his landlady to inform her that he would be away for the weekend.

"Now see, you wouldn't have to phone that woman if you moved in with me."

"I'm still considering that idea. But, with our combined work hours, there would be little time for making the evening meals. Believe me, Mrs. Koski has such wonderful meals prepared when I get home from work. Well, you know she has the time, but you don't. I know that you're a good cook and all that, but the preparation of meals would be a big thing. What's so pressing that we need to change the present arrangement?"

"I'd just like to have you always with me 'cause I love you."

"You don't feel that you need to have what I call 'me' time? You know, time to read and think about things? That there is the big contradiction between us. I need my space." After a pause he exclaimed with reflection, "Don't crowd me, woman."

Gretel recalled other conversations with Oliver where he expressed the importance of being "his own man." I can't argue with him, she reasoned. Therefore, she said no more in fear that he might decide to leave her.

"What time does the ferry leave in the morning?" he asked, ignoring the timid looking expression on her face.

"It leaves at eight-thirty A.M. We'll have to be there by eight in order to buy our tickets."

After purchasing their tickets for *The City of Flint 32,* one of the ships of the Pere Marquette fleet, Oliver couldn't believe what he was seeing.

"How on earth did they get those freight trains into that boat? and look at all the automobiles being driven in . . . this is not at all what I expected!"

"Well, it's a shorter distance for the freight to travel over the waters rather than by rail. Did you notice the tracks leading to the ferry? This is a common sight on the Great Lakes, even more so since the world war."

"So, this is not like a cruise ship," he said as they climbed the ramp leading into the upper deck of the ferry.

"The first ship to be constructed with a steel hull, was the *Pere Marquette.* It was 350 feet long. The design was so readily admired, that it began to set the standard for railroad ferries on the Great Lakes. It was also confirmed to be a great ice-breaker."

"Boy, am I glad to be here," exclaimed Oliver. "I remember learning about the Great Lakes at St. Anne's School. Let's see if I remember correctly . . . Lake Michigan is over three hundred miles long, and over a hundred miles wide . . . is that right?"

"Close enough. Did you learn that it is from 400 to 600 feet deep?"

"I'll add that to the information between my ears." They both laughed.

At eight-thirty, they watched over the rail while men released the heavy ropes from the pier, and they were off on a new adventure . . . for Oliver, maybe not for Gretel.

"Have you done this before?" he asked.

"Anyone who has lived most of his or her life in Manitowoc has gone this route. Sure, some people just like to take the round trip without stopping off at Ludington. They like being on the water."

They walked arm in arm around the deck a few laps, and then went inside, had a lunch, and walked some more.

"The weather is ideal . . . of course, it's not like traveling on an ocean steamship. I traveled on a ship called the *Larchmont*, and almost lost my life." After relating his experience of the disaster, he added, "The ocean holds much more danger than a lake."

"You have got to be kidding, Oliver. Haven't you ever heard about lost ships on the Great Lakes? They call Lake Erie 'The graveyard of ships.' Lake Michigan is even bigger than Erie. There must be tons of ships under these waters. Storms can whip up waves as high as any ocean waves."

"I'd have to see that."

"Well, if you live in Manitowoc for a few years, you're apt to see it happen."

"A few years . . . a few years," he repeated, not realizing that his head was nodding—not favorably. The idea of staying anywhere for years never appealed to him.

They arrived at the *Ludington* dock at twelve-thirty, and took a taxi to the Lamplighter Inn. There was just one room available, overlooking the lake and small sandy beach.

"Oh Oliver, I feel so hypocritical checking in as man and wife."

"Would you have felt better if we had announced that we're sharing a room as friends?"

"You know that that wouldn't be allowed."

"Some day there'll be no questions asked. We're consenting adults."

"Would you ever consent to tie the knot?"

Oliver ignored her question and tried to speak calmly as he pulled the curtain back to admire the landscape.

"Look at this for an inviting view of the lake. Let's take a swim."

He seems like a hopeless cause, thought Gretel. *I'll give him a little more time, and then he'll have to make a choice...marriage or nothing. I can't take this uncertainly much longer.*

The swim was exhilarating, working up their appetites for the romantic dinner in the dining room of the Inn. The menu offered a complete New England dinner, which puzzled Oliver.

"Here we are in the midwest . . . how can they claim to serve an authentic New England meal?" They agreed to give it a try.

The chowder had tomatoes added to it.

"That's not New England! The chowder back home is made with cream, lots of fish, onions, and potatoes. I'll bet the chef has never been there."

202

The next dish consisted of some kind of fish unlike any from the Atlantic Ocean.

"This is a popular fish in this area, caught in the Great Lakes. It's called walleye, though, Maybe it's trout. I don't know, but it's good, isn't it?"

"All I detect is that it isn't cod or haddock. In other words, this menu is a false representation of a New England dinner . . . but, I will admit, it tastes darn good."

The wine, which was the specialty of the house, was smooth and delightful.

The two lovers walked in the colorful Inn gardens holding hands, expecting the rest of the evening to be a continuation and a strengthening of their loving mood. It was.

On the return trip, their loving attention toward each other did not diminish.

I wonder what he's thinking, mused Gretel. Will he agree to a permanent commitment?

"This weekend away was a great idea, Gretel. I guess I would never have thought of it. Of course, being born in this area, you know of places of interest. I really had a fine time." He hugged her closely.

*   *   *

She didn't care for the idea of their going separate ways when they got back to Manitowoc. He just won't give me an answer to the question of moving in with me. If he really loves me, we would spend the rest of our lives together, she reflected.

We had a fine time, he mused, but I think that she pushes too much, expects too much. She's an alluring gal with lots of vim and vigor . . . and raring to go . . . and eager to marry. I'm not willing to tie myself down to anyone, or . . . am I just fooling myself? When I'm with her, I'm happy. But when I'm off by myself, fishing and contemplating about my life and thinking of what I could possibly be looking for . . . oh . . . sigh . . . what am I looking for? *What am I all about?* It will take me a few days to hash these thoughts over in my head . . . and heart.

*   *   *

After Monday's workday, Arty and Oliver went out on the lake in

203

Arty's small craft. They anchored a short distance from shore, cast their lines and leaned back in old pillowed chairs.

"Thanks for inviting me to fish with you, Arty. Does your wife mind your being out on your boat without her?"

"Nah, she's into William Faulkner's new book called *Light in August*. I get bored when she hangs around reading, so she doesn't mind if I leave to fish or play poker with the fellows."

"When people marry, I think it's important for the spouses to each foster his and her own interests. I couldn't stand to live with a person who wants me all to herself."

"Is that the way it is with the widow Kuntz? Are you serious about her?"

"I've had thoughts . . . maybe I need to straighten out my thoughts. Could I use you as a sounding board?"

"Why not. I'm not one to let the sounding board echo out to other parties, if you know what I mean."

"Thanks Arty. I need to go back a ways in my life so that you understand where I'm coming from."

Oliver almost sounded as if he were reading from a long saga as he unfolded his life story to Arty.

"Here's what I gather from what you've told me. You are afraid to make any kind of a commitment . . . and you seem to think that it's because of your father's abandonment. How old are you, Oliver?"

"I'm forty-six, why?"

"When you left home, you were on your own. You made your own decisions—some good, some not so good. But they were your own; they had nothing to do with what your father did or said. You are fully responsible for your life! To look back and say, 'my parents were like this or that, and they did this or that, or they said this or that,' and then transfer the blame to them for anything you've done or not done . . . it's kinda childish . . . don't you think?"

"Wow, what are you? A priest or something? I will admit I have been transferring blame. I guess it's time to grow up! But I still don't know what to do about Gretel. I am fond of her, but she's a little pushy and possessive."

"I would find that a bit difficult to put up with myself. Why don't you join the guys and me each Friday night for poker . . . and maybe one evening of fishing. That will give Mrs. Kuntz time to think about loosening the strings a little. You'll have your time away from the female influence for just a couple of evenings. Think of it as a test of what might be and you'll find out the results soon enough, and then make a decision about your future together."

"Arty, I can't thank you enough for your advice. We didn't catch any fish, but you caught this fish and set him free," Oliver said pointing to himself.

*　　*　　*

"Oliver, I phoned Mrs. Koski last night. She said you went out. Why didn't you call me?"

He responded with a sly grin, "Why, to get your permission to go out on my own?"

"You're being sarcastic. Are you going to tell me where you went?"

"Ooh," he said, pinching her cheek, "mother hen needs a report, does she? If you must know, I went fishing with Arty." Oliver advised her further, "I'm invited to the Friday night poker games with the guys. Do I have your permission, Mrs. Kuntz?'

"I thought that Friday nights were special for the two of us," she said dolefully.

"Don't take it so seriously, love. A guy needs his time out with other guys. Besides, we have Saturday and Sunday together, possibly Tuesday and Thursday."

"What happened to Wednesday?"

"Ah come on, Gretel, be reasonable. Don't you have other things to do in your life?"

"But I want us to be together like . . . like married people. Move in with me?" she pleaded.

"Do I feel those apron strings tying around my waist . . . or my *neck?*"

Her face reddened with anger.

"You make me feel like I'm a rotten person, Oliver. You want to make love to me without any commitment whatsoever! What can I do?"

"Well, to begin with, don't be self-deprecating. You're a very lovely woman and I am very fond of you. Can we leave it like that for now . . . then . . . who knows."

On Thursday evening Oliver brought Gretel a new record, which he placed on the turntable, took her in his arms and sang lovingly in her ear, "Night and Day, You Are The One." That night, she felt really special.

205

Friday night was a different story. Gretel felt abandoned. *Is he really out with the men playing poker? He seemed sincere—why do I suspect that he's just kidding me?*

The game was at Arty's house. Oliver recognized some of the fellows from work, all but Max. There was Ed, Jack, Bill, six players.

"We kinda limit ourselves to twenty-five bucks an evening. The white chips represent fifty cents, the blue, one dollar, and the red two dollars," Arty informed Oliver, the new member of the group.

Oliver acknowledged the announcement with a slight grin, but felt that the outlay was a little steeper than he had expected. The men all began with ten white chips, ten blues, and five reds. *Well at least it puts a cap on anyone's losses,* considered Oliver.

"This is quite the table, Arty. Made for professional gamblers, I'd say." Oliver was impressed with the large round green felt covered table with six depressed sections in which to fit each person's chips.

"Yeah, my wife Marge, picked it up at a secondhand store, but after each use, she insists that I store it in the garage.'

The men cut the cards, high card began the deal. Max announced, "Draw poker." Arty looked at Oliver and said, "Dealer's choice."

The order of the men around the table was: Max, Ed, Oliver, Arty, Bill, and Jack.

The serious business began after Max dealt out five cards each.

Bill opened with a pair of jacks. Each man anted up a white chip. Ed discarded three cards; Oliver, taking his chances on a straight, discarded one. Arty took three, Bill, the opener, looked as if he might have three of a kind. He took just two cards. Jack took three. Ed said, "Check." Oliver bet one, Arty dropped out, Bill called, Jack raised one, Max folded. Ed said, "I'll call and raise you another." After pondering what he should do, Oliver raised one more. The remaining players called. Bill showed his three aces, Ed had two pairs, kings and tens, Jack had three nines. Oliver took the pot with a straight. He added $5.50 to his stack.

"Nice going. Oliver, but it's just beginner's luck," called Ed and they all laughed.

Ed said, "Stud," as he dealt the cards, one at a time, the first face down. The next three face up, showing Max with two kings. They all anted up except Jack. "I fold." The last card faced down, then the serious betting began. With the three cards showing, Max still had two kings and a ten. Ed had three hearts, eight, Jack, Queen. *Hm, possible flush, or a royal flush,* they all were thinking. Oliver had a pair of threes and an ace.

Arty showed a possible straight with ace of clubs, king of diamonds, and jack of spades. Bill had two sevens and a jack showing. Oliver bet with a white chip. Arty raised with a blue chip. Bill threw in a blue and raised it with another blue. Max called with two blue chips. Ed said, "I fold." Oliver called. Arty called. Bill showed his hand . . . full house three sevens and two jacks. Max threw in his hand without showing it. Oliver had a full house, three aces, two threes.

"Hey where did you pick up this guy, Arty? In Las Vegas?"

Oliver felt slightly embarrassed, though elated to have won both games. The men had a lunch break of ham sandwiches and beer, served by Marge. Oliver's luck took a turn after that, losing most of his winnings, but he ended the evening with an overall gain of $3.50.

"Next Friday at my house," announced Bill.

"I'll swing over before then with the table," called Arty as the men left.

Oliver stayed behind for a few moments to thank Arty for including him in with such congenial cronies.

"How did Mrs. Kuntz take the news of your nights out with the boys?"

"I'll really find out the next time I see her. I haven't met any of her lady friends. She should get together with some . . . go out to a show or something . . . or have a tea party. Whatever women do when their men aren't around. I'll let you know how things work out."

On his way home, Oliver began to think about how he could entertain the men at Mrs. Koski's home. Would she agree to that arrangement? *I could prepare a lunch before our poker night. What if she would not hear of it. Maybe, just maybe, Gretel might let me use her dining room for just one night every six weeks. First, I'll ask Mrs. Koski.*

"Dos men gamplink in mine house!" she nervously blurted out. "Nyet, never! Shame ont you, Mista Yanvier!"

Oliver's face reddened as he said, "I'm sorry, Mrs. Koski, I had no idea that you would object to a little card game."

"Gamplink vit money ist no small cart game. Is evil it is."

Oliver didn't try to win her over. *She's steadfast in her belief,* he reflected. *I won't upset her further.* He left the house to speak to Gretel.

"Sure, Oliver. If Arty wants to bring his poker table, you can set it up in the parlor."

That was easier than I thought, he mused. She even agreed to serve the men sandwiches and beer.

"Thanks for bringing your table, Arty. Isn't it kind of a nuisance lugging it to every one else's house?"

"Nah, it works out better to use the same system with the chips and all. See ya later tonight." Then he said in a whisper, "Your gal is using you right, eh?"

"Seems that way."

All the guys showed up at "the widow Kuntz's house." After introductions, she went to the kitchen to make up the sandwiches with the ham, cheese, and rye bread that Oliver had brought.

She was happy to learn that Friday night was really Oliver's poker night; it allayed all her suspicions. With a tray of refreshments all set to go, she decided to sit next to Oliver to see how the game was going. The men looked uncomfortable as she pulled up a chair to watch them play.

It was draw poker, and each fellow drew two or three cards, as needed to replace their discards. The betting had started, but when Gretel looked at Oliver's hand, she startled the players by exclaiming, "WOW!" Each player in turn folded, except Oliver. He pulled in the small pot and glared at Gretel. He couldn't drum up the nerve to exclaim, "Woman, leave us to our game . . . get out!" It was Arty's strong rebuke. She left sheepishly. No one had called . . . so Oliver was too ashamed to show his paltry two pair hand—threes and eights.

The games continued without interruptions. When it was time for a break, Oliver went to the kitchen to see why Gretel wasn't serving the guys.

"If you think that I would go in there to bring them stuff to eat, think again."

"That's okay, honey, I'll take care of it," and he pecked her on her damp cheek.

Oliver was embarrassed about the little sandwiches. Gretel had cut the crust off, and sectioned each sandwich into four diamond shapes. Ed picked up a piece so daintily, raised his voice to an unnatural pitch and said, "Oh aren't these lov-e-ly!" Max followed with a high pitched, "Oooh my." Bill also mocked with, "How sweet." Then they went into a fit of laughter. They wondered if the "widow Kuntz" could learn to make he-man sandwiches.

"Knock it off guys, this is her first experience. Let's not embarrass her further," Oliver came to Gretel's defense. But Gretel had eavesdropped on their comments and was deeply hurt.

"Do you like those hooligans, Oliver?"

"They're just a bunch of regular fellows, Gretel."

"They didn't impress me that way. I see them as crude, crusty . . . I'll think of other words suitable to describe them. I never want them in my house ever . . . ever again!"

"I can see that you're hurt, and I can understand how you feel, but please don't lash out at my friends!"

"You can still call them friends after they've humiliated me so cruelly?"

"You're overreacting, Gretel. You'll see the funny side of this in a couple of days."

"Funny side! Funny side! What was so funny?"

"Well to begin with, women don't act as kibitzers at a men's poker party, and it is not a woman's tea party where little itty bitty sandwiches are served. Men like to sink their teeth into something substantial. I should have made that clear before the guys came over. I'm sorry, honey. I feel that I'm the one who goofed."

"I'm sorry if I spoiled it for you . . . forgive me?"

"There's nothing to forgive," he said as he kissed her gently, "but I don't understand why you said wow."

"Well when I saw all the low numbers and no face cards, it surprised me that you would stay in the game."

"Let's just forget it all and decide what you might like to do this weekend."

"We could just relax on the little beach at the end of Lake Side Boulevard. How about a picnic lunch? I promise that I will make real he-man sandwiches!"

It was August, and the lake water was about as warm as it would ever get. It was still too cold for Oliver, and he began thinking about the winter storms of the upper midwestern states.

"I don't know how much longer I'll be able to stay in Manitowoc. I'm already beginning to feel a chill in the air," Oliver exclaimed as he wrapped his towel around his shivering body.

"You'll get used to it, Oliver. The winters aren't all that bad," answered Gretel as she pressed her body against him, her arms enfolding him while she briskly rubbed his back.

"Hey, I don't want to be on public display here. Save the chummi-
ness for later."

They ate their "he-man" lunch with ravenous appetites and played a
game of catch with the ball Gretel had brought. It was a relaxing, happy
day.

"I like this little beach, but it can't begin to be compared to the Salis-
bury, and Hampton beaches in New England. Although, I must confess,
the ocean water is every bit as cold as this lake water. Some summers the
temperature does reach all of seventy-three degrees. It's nowhere near the
warmth of the Gulf of Mexico. Now that's where to be when winter
approaches."

"Move in with me and I'll keep you warm all winter long," she said
with a hopeful sparkle in her eyes.

Oliver ignored her invitation as he began gathering up the lunch
basket and beach blanket, and before heading for home, they had their
desserts at Beernsten's ice cream parlor. That night he phoned Mrs. Koski
to tell her that he was staying with a friend and would return sometime
Sunday.

* * *

After work hours on Monday, Arty and Oliver went fishing
again.

"The fellows felt sorry that they reacted to Mrs. Kuntz unfavorably
the other night. Was she hurt?"

"She's over it by now. I led her to understand that the wives or girlfriends don't participate in the poker game. They either serve or go out
for the evening. Her husband was a golfer, not a poker player."

"That's what she told you? Ha, I knew the guy. He had his nights
out . . . and not just with the guys."

"I wish you hadn't told me that! Now I understand why she's so possessive and distrustful."

"I honestly believe that the guy is still living. She told everybody that
he died while visiting his mother in Chicago. She took a couple of days off
from work, purportedly to attend his funeral in Chicago . . . rather
strange, don't you think?"

Oliver puzzled over that bit of news, but made no reply.

"Hey I've got one! He's fighting hard . . . hope it's big enough to
bring to Mrs. Koski for tomorrow's dinner."

Oliver caught four trout. Arty caught a six-pound salmon and several trout.

Mrs. Koski was pleased to receive the fresh fish which Oliver had so skillfully cleaned.

Oliver phoned Gretel to tell her of his fishing luck.

"Oliver, I can't talk to you right now," she seemed to whisper into the phone.

"Are you all right? Want me to go over tonight?"

"No, no, please don't even phone again . . . I can't explain, I'll probably call you in a couple of days," and she hung up abruptly.

Oliver was sincerely concerned. He had decided that she was the one for him, and he wanted to set a date for their marriage. *At last I feel confident enough to make the ultimate commitment*, he told himself. He was anxious to speak with her.

He inquired at the office and was told that she had called in sick. *She must really be ill if she doesn't even want me to phone. I've got to go to her. I'll break the door down if necessary. I'll take care of my loving Gretel.* He was beside himself with worry.

Oliver knocked on the back door calling "Gretel, Gretel . . . let me in." When there was no answer, he went to the front of the house and almost leaned on the door bell. The door suddenly sprung open, and there stood a tall muscular man wearing a sleeveless undershirt and boxer shorts.

"Who the hell are you?" he bellowed.

"I might ask the same of you," Oliver answered, confused and threatened.

"This happens to be my home . . . the home of my wife and me. Are you selling something?"

"No. Is Gretel all right?"

"Of course she's all right. Hey, are you the guy who's been foolin' around with my wife?"

Without giving Oliver a chance to respond, he grabbed the front of Oliver's shirt and swung his strong fist, aimed at Oliver's left eye, sending him whirling down the steps, landing at the bottom sprawled out in a stunned state.

"Just tell all your fellow workers that Gretel and her husband are celebrating the resurrection of the dead," and with boisterous laughter, he slammed the door.

Oliver's heart felt as if it were slamming against his chest . . . breaking into a million pieces. He had never felt so hurt, physically and emotionally. But when he got up, he brushed his clothes vigorously as if he were not only brushing off the dirt but subconsciously brushing off any trace of moss that might have clung to him.

At the factory, he tendered his resignation with a week's notice. Arty sympathized with Oliver, but repeated his suspicion that that rat of a husband was thought to be still alive. His words did not comfort Oliver's aching heart.

"How could she have lied to me—saying that she loved me and wanted to marry me?"

"I honestly believe that she meant what she said . . . never believing that he would ever return," said Arty.

"She once told me that Indians called Manitowoc 'Mundeowk', meant 'home of the good spirit.' Now, I've lost any 'good spirit' I might have felt for this place, and I can't leave it soon enough!"

Mrs. Koski was sad to lose her favorite roomer, and made him sandwiches with some of her homemade "reika laipa" to eat on his journey.

Twenty-four

This time, the "FIint" car ferry didn't hold the excitement Oliver had enjoyed with Gretel. He felt lonely and despondent. *The one time that I was willing to give up my bachelor status for a woman I honestly cherished . . . and where did it get me? It now seems to be payback time for what I did to Hedda . . . now, though it's too late, I fully understand the heartache I must have caused her. It seems that life is so full of lessons, and this is about the hardest one I've ever had to endure.*

Friendly passengers, strolling the deck, smiled and said "Good morning" to Oliver as he sat on one of the long benches, but he was too engrossed in self-pity to notice anyone. Even Mrs. Koski's wonderful sandwiches did not placate his feelings. It was a long four hours of self-deprecating thoughts before he had awakened to the fact that the ship had arrived at the Ludington port.

With both heavy luggage and a heavy heart, Oliver took a trolley to the train station and bought a ticket to Grand Rapids, Michigan. He could not bear to remain in Ludington, where the memories of his past love affair were too painful.

"Grand Rapids," called the conductor, and Oliver followed the many travelers disembarking the train. After passing several shops, he bought a newspaper to search for a place to stay . . . just for one night, he reasoned. He found a small Dutch hotel which boasted of the neatest rooms, and the greatest home cooked food, served in an adjoining restaurant. It was at about three o'clock in the afternoon, and he was beginning to feel pangs of hunger. *I'll see whether these Dutch claims are for real.*

"Sorry, we are not opened until four-thirty," exclaimed a petite blonde girl, with pigtails, a little Dutch cap, and colorful apron.

"I hope it's worth waiting for," he told the young maiden.

She closed the door of the eatery, and this time the click of the lock was heard.

I'll take a look at the "Grand" river that I've heard so much about, he thought as he walked a distance before getting to the water.

"Any luck?" he asked an elderly man who was fishing from the river bank.

The man picked up a pail to show Oliver what he had caught.

"They've been biting pretty well today . . . look at these critters. Got enough walleyes to feed a family of eight."

"That must be some family you have."

"Yeah, got my daughter, her husband, and their five young ones. My son-in-law lost his job at the furniture factory—things are pretty tough these days. Are you looking for work?"

"No, I'm just traveling through. Thought I'd go to Detroit to see if I could get myself an automobile real cheap."

"People are leaving Detroit in droves . . . lots of jobs gone. Bad times, bad times," the old man shook his head with a worrisome look on his wrinkled face.

"Do those logs, floating down the river, get in your way for fishing?"

"Well, there aren't as many logs headed for the mills these days. You know, Grand Rapids is known as 'The Furniture City' and logging was once important because of the furniture production . . . but we've got bad times, bad times," and he shook his sad head once more.

Oliver patted the man's back as he said, "Well, when things get to the bottom, there's just one direction in which they can head . . . up, up, up. Believe me, and take courage, sir, things will get better."

Oliver's words amused the older man, and he showed his toothy grin."

Why can't I practice what I preach? thought Oliver as he wended his way back to the restaurant. I told that old guy to take courage . . . no more moping around like a lovesick kid. I'm going to enjoy my freedom and do more traveling.

The Dutch meal was a whole new experience for Oliver. He sat at a long table with benches on each side. He didn't know any of his fellow diners at his table, but found the experience as pleasant as sitting with family and being served as family. It didn't take long before all the friendly diners were conversing with each other, some with strong German and Dutch accents. *Wow*, thought Oliver, *I feel as if I'm in a different country!*

The pretty waitresses, in their costumes, unique to Holland, brought huge bowls of mashed potatoes, squash, green beans, carrots, gravy, and platters of freshly cooked pot roast, and chicken. All the diners were kindredly, passing bowls to the neighboring patron. They seemed like immediate friends. The spread of desserts was a tempting sight to behold. Too much to choose from, mused Oliver, as he reached for a slice of the Bavarian chocolate cake.

With boosted spirits, Oliver slept well and was happily on his way to Detroit the very next day.

"Are you headin' for Detroit to git a job?" asked the man who sat next to Oliver on the train.

"I'm going there to try to get a good buy on a Ford."

"Did you know that they're havin' big layoffs and there ain't many people left on the assembly lines?"

"I heard something to that effect. Is the Ford Company still in operation?"

"Barely. I'm goin' back to try to git my old job back . . . ain't much hope, though."

"Sorry to hear that. What will you do in Detroit if you don't get rehired?"

"I got friends who'll take me in for a while. Some of them fellas meet at one of the 'blind pigs' hideouts. Ya heard of 'em?"

"I've no idea what you are talking about." Oliver looked confused.

"The police 'pigs' turn a blind eye to the hideouts serving liquor. Ya like a drink now 'n agin?"

"I could live with that . . . you must know of some hideouts?"

"Sure do. I'll point some out to you if you're interested. I'll even help you find the factory where they might have some autos to sell. Ya should be able to pick up a buggy for around two-hundred bucks."

"Sounds pretty good to me."

"If you wuz a man of color, I could direct ya to the 'Black and Tan Club' fer people of all races."

"I don't have any prejudices . . . people are people."

"Hey, I like ya fella . . . you're a regular guy."

The men talked about a number of subjects and Oliver felt that he was learning a lot of new things about Michigan, and Detroit in particular.

He learned that when Detroit was first founded it was considered "One huge uninhabitable swamp," later becoming "Motor City." Between those two monikers, there was lots of history. That all happened in the 1700's when Antoine de la Mothe Cadillac founded Detroit for Louis XIV of France.

"Then the British cums along, so the war chief of Ottawa . . . his name was Pontiac. Well, he tries ta drive the British people outa here so's to help the French git it back.

"Pontiac didn't succeed though, but the Brits signed a treaty in Paris, givin' the area to the United States. How d'ya like them for facts of our state?"

"You certainly learned your history well!"

"I ain't no scholar, but I am interested in our beginnins. My parents cum over frum Ireland. We've had a ruff time . . . jist when we thought the things wuz gettin' better, then the market crash dun us in. We still eat our 'taters and 'av a little change for a whiskey now and then."

"I'll buy you a drink when we get to one of the 'Blind Pig' hideouts," offered Oliver.

When they left the train station, they walked toward the Detroit river, slunk down a side alleyway, passing a policeman on the way.

"Did you notice how that cop just passed us like he didn't see us?"

"Is that a good sign?"

"Yeah, well it just means that he ain't gonna see us go inta the hideout 'cause he's playin' blind . . . he probably jist cum frum gittin' a drink himself."

The two men entered a shabby looking store which purportedly sold tobacco, but the door behind the back counter led to the bar.

"Hi ya, Jake . . . brought a new customer fer ya. What'll ya have, Oliver?"

"Scotch on the rocks . . . and you?"

"Git me a double scotch."

"Wow, I hope you can hold your liquor. You told me that you'd lead me to the Ford Company . . . you might lead me on the wrong path, Pat."

"Ya ain't got nothin' ta worry about. If one of me eyes meets t'uther, then I'll know that I've 'ad too much." After just two refills, Pat and Oliver left arm in arm like two old buddies, singing happily. "The old grey mare ain't . . . (Hic) what she used to be . . . (Hic) what she used to be, many long years ago. Many loooong years agooooooo." People walking by turned around to take another look at these two kooks.

Pat put his stretched out left hand in front of Oliver's face and said, "See here my friend, this is a map of Mich-hic-igan, hic. You and me is right at the bottom of the thumb, right here, see?" and as Pat pointed to the base of his thumb he continued, "an did ya know that the Detroit river links all the Great Lakes, that it does, hic."

"Okay, just get your hand out of my face, pal, and lead me to where

I can buy an automobile."

When they arrived at the building, all was closed for the day. Oliver left Pat and walked back to the train station, where he had placed his bags in a locker.

He found a room in a sleazy old hotel, where doors seemed to be slamming all night long. He arose at eight o'clock the next day, as if in a stupor from lack of sleep. On second thought, he attributed his condition to the boozing. He felt better after his second cup of coffee at the little breakfast cafe, down the street from the hotel.

At least I know how to find my way to the Ford Company. I'll go there with a clearer head today, he reasoned. Oliver needed a clear head to haggle with the Ford salesman.

"I'm looking for the best buy in an automobile," announced Oliver.

"You've come to the right place. My name is Bud, and I'll be happy to help you." The agent extended his hand to greet Oliver. *There aren't many buyers these days,* he thought.

I'll begin with my highest price and hope this guy won't barter too much . . . need that commission.

"Let's start with the '32 models, because your '33's will be coming out soon . . . right?" said Oliver.

"I see that you are a man who wants to keep up to date. Okay, walk this way, please." And Bud lead Oliver to some of the latest Fords on the market.

"Over here, we have our '32 Ford V-8 with horse power of 65, a great buy for only $460.00."

"Too much . . . what else do you have?"

"Well, if you want an older model, here's a '31 Ford. It's a model A DeLuxe coupe. It's got five windows . . . also has a built-in trunk. Last year, this sold for $525. We could sacrifice about $150 off that price."

"Give me a break! In another couple of months, this car will be *two* years old. You'd have to discount it more than that!"

"This is a tremendous buy for only $375. Now mind you, it's never been on the road. It's a year old, not two. It's really brand new. Of course, if you want an earlier model, we have that also."

"I'll give you $275 for the two-year-old coupe. If it stays on your lot another year, you won't get half that."

"I can't do that. That doesn't even cover the cost of making the damn machine," the salesman was becoming impatient.

"Keep your machine, sir . . . there are other auto makers in this area." Oliver exited the building before the man could lure him back.

The GM company had a 1930 AD Universal Sport Coupe for sale, marked down from $615.

"This is a great number," exclaimed the salesman. "We sold more than forty-five thousand of these when they first came out. Look at all these unique features: The rear window lowers for ventilation . . . or for talking with your buddies in the rumble seat. It has six cylinders and fifty bhp. It's a fantastic buy at only $415."

"Looks pretty good," said Oliver, admiring the vehicle. "But I don't have that kind of money. Besides, in another couple of months, this machine will be three years old!"

"Make an offer, fella."

"Two-hundred-fifty dollars."

"Two-hundred-seventy-five and it's yours."

Oliver didn't want to appear too eager. "Well, maybe I can scrape up that much."

"We do want to make room for the '33 models. Two-hundred-sixty is the lowest we can go."

Oliver had renewed his license each year in the event that he might own his own vehicle. Securing a tag and insurance was no problem.

*　　*　　*

His plans were to visit his brother Frank, and his old buddies in Fredonia, then off to Lawrence to see the rest of his family.

It was September, getting a bit cooler, especially traveling the road near Port cities of Lake Erie. It took most of one day to travel over a hundred-sixty miles to get to Cleveland, Ohio. I can make it to the Pennsylvania border before it gets dark, he told himself, just seventy-five more miles to go. These roads are pretty well paved, so far.

*　　*　　*

"Hi Frank, your big brother is on his way to Fredonia, that is if you can put up with his visit for a few days," Oliver phoned from the lobby of a small, but neat hotel in West Springfield, Pennsylvania.

"It's about time we hear from you, Oliver. Where have you been hiding?"

"Maybe I'll tell you that long story when I get there. I figure that if I

218

leave this town by nine in the morning, I should arrive at your place by one o'clock, the latest. Tell Eva not to prepare a noon time meal. I'll grab a bite on the way."

"Are you catching a train at nine?"

"No, got myself a little Chevy Coupe . . . so far, so good . . . no troubles."

"What did you do? Turn in your diamond ring?"

"Heck no, that stays with me."

"I'll take tomorrow off from work to greet my big brother. It'll be good to see you."

Oliver's visit was a little longer than anticipated. He was able to see Dom, Amalia, and his family, and some of his old fishing and card playing pals. Frank let him work at his place of business, which helped Oliver replenish his money belt. When Oliver told his story of his Manitowoc experiences, Frank couldn't believe that his brother was finally thinking of taking the "plunge."

"The one time you were willing to give up your freedom, you were caught up in a scam. That was a close call, Oliver. You could have been indicted for adultery."

"I really was taken in by Gretel. It was a narrow escape and it won't happen again."

"Don't let that scare you into not tying the knot some day. You could still meet Miss Right, but don't wait too long—your forty.-seventh birthday is coming up soon."

"You don't have to remind me."

The threat of the predictable midwest snowstorms sent Oliver on his way by mid-October.

"Hi Eva. I'm on my way to your place—if you'll have me. I thought that I would like to spend the holidays with Ma, you and your family. Ma is getting up there in age and I feel that I should spend some time with her."

"We've all been worried about you. Where have you been? We haven't had news for so long!"

"I should have phoned you from Frank's. Sorry."

"You were in Fredonia all this time, and you didn't let us know?" Eva sounded irate.

"I know that I have a lot of explaining to do. I arrived in Fredonia in September. Maybe I should write a book, and then let you read it."

"Where are you now?"

"I just got into Connecticut this afternoon. It will take me another four hours to get to your place. You'll see my new wheels when I get there at about eight o'clock tonight."

"Wheels! You got yourself a car? Did you come into some big money or something?"

"Nothing like that . . . I . . .

"Your three minutes are up. Please deposit twenty-five cents more," interrupted the telephone operator. Oliver and Eva said a quick "bye" and both hung up.

✻   ✻   ✻

"The prodigal son has returned," cried Eva as she hugged and kissed her brother. Mama came out of her room with arms outstretched and a look that only a mother could express after finding a long lost child.

"Mon fils! Ça fait trop longtemps que je ne t'ai pas vu!" (My son! It's been too long that I've not seen you!)

Oliver was too emotional to speak. All these family members' excited attention filled him with consternation. Eva's children awakened from their sleep, ran from their bedrooms screaming in joy, "Uncle Bill, Uncle Bill!"

(Oliver had requested that they call him by his middle name, which he liked better.) A more euphoric greeting he had never experienced. It was way past midnight when all calmed down and decided to hit the hay. He was awakened by the children's cheerful laughter, and also by the inviting aromas of a special breakfast. Mama sat next to him at the table and held his hand as they said grace.

Oliver noticed that Mama's tall, frail frame was slightly bent. But her mannerisms were still quick and spry for a woman in her late sixties. She was happy to have her eldest son home again, and she smiled contentedly.

Mama disappeared quietly while Oliver helped Eva with the dishes.

"Where did she go?"

"The usual place . . . every single day. St. Anne's Church wouldn't be the same without her. Of course, she had to go to thank God for your return."

Oliver was happy to spend the holidays with family members. The Thanksgiving feast was as he remembered it from his early childhood when Papa was with them; the meals were less festive after Papa had left his family.

At the dinner table, the family members expressed their thanks for their health and the ability to make ends meet during hard times . . . and of course, for having, "Uncle Bill" home for the holidays. After helping to clear the table, they all went into the parlor for a songfest. By this time, Eva had a stack of sheet music that had been sent by Oliver, mailed from many of the states he had visited. Mama listened contentedly as her children and grandchildren filled the air with cheerful sounds.

A few days before Christmas, one of the biggest blizzards of the season occurred. The snow was so deep that Oliver could barely make out the shape of the roof of his Chevrolet Coupe. He had parked the machine on Hampton Court, in the back of the Gagne residence.

"It looks as if we're snowed in for a long haul," he said ruefully.

The children were happy about the situation. "Maybe you'll stay longer and go sledding with us," said seven-year-old Margaret with glee.

It was then that Oliver decided to give them their Christmas present early.

"Follow me, guys," he said as he led them to the front hall closet where the toboggan he had purchased was hidden.

All four Gagne kids teased him until he agreed to go tobogganing at the Tower Hill Reservoir that very day.

Russell, who was now fifteen, found extra longjohns, woolen trousers, sweaters, scarves, and handmade mittens that just about fitted Oliver, and off they went pulling the toboggan up Haverhill Street, with the youngest child, Margaret, getting a free ride.

There weren't many people on the reservoir hills and when they arrived at the top of the biggest hill near the Tower, they looked down at all that pristine snow with anxious anticipation. The screams were the same as they would be on a roller coaster ride at Canobie Lake Amusement Park. After arriving at the bottom of the hill, one look at Russell and they rolled in the snow with laughter; he was the lead man and got the brunt of the spray; only his dark brown eyes were visible.

"I want to ride in front next time," squealed Germaine.

"Now it's my turn," yelled Marcelle.

Each had a turn at being "front man," even Uncle Bill.

"Ma Mère, nous avons eu beaucoup de plaisir!" (Grandma, we had lots of fun!), shouted the girls, after hanging their wet clothes over the top stair railing in the back hallway. "Je me semblais comme un homme de neige!" (I looked like a snowman!) added Russell.

They all had ravenous appetites at the evening meal.

"It looks as if you haven't eaten for a week," exclaimed Eva as she dished out third helpings.

That evening after supper, Tse boy showed up with an unusual tale.

"Eva, how about just calling me Joe. I'm no longer a Tse boy, your baby brother."

Joe Janvier, Oliver and Eva's youngest brother, related a rather disturbing experience.

"My kid Russell and I were in my truck at a railroad crossing in South Lawrence, and just as I got halfway across the tracks Russell shouted, 'Dad, a train is coming.' Luckily there was no car behind us. I was able to back up quickly enough before the engine appeared within inches of my truck. The rear bumper of the car that was in front of us got peeled off like a banana skin. I'm telling you, it scared the stuffin' out of me and my kid. The gate tender has been fired for sleeping on the job."

Mama and Eva both made the sign of the cross in thanksgiving.

"Uncle Joe," said little Margaret, "we went sliding in the snow today."

"Is that why all those wet clothes are hanging in the back hall?"

She nodded and was excited to tell about the whole tobogganing experience.

"Daddy, daddy," she yelled as her father Joe Gagne entered the kitchen. After hugging his little daughter, the two Joes shook hands.

"How's the bread delivery business, Joe?"

"Keeping us in the dough, Joe. How's the laundry business, Joe?"

"Cleaning up, picking up."

The silly banter of the two Joes was an expected exchange, but the amusement was wearing a little thin with family members.

"Looks like your hair could use a little trim . . . get my clippers, Russell."

Joe G. became the family barber since the Depression began, and Joe J. was happy to exchange services by doing the Gagne laundry.

"I'll bring my boy over next week . . . his hair's getting a little long."

✳   ✳   ✳

Christmas and New Year's were spent enjoying usual Canadian traditions.

"My friend Jerry agreed to travel with me and share auto expenses," announced Oliver after the excitement of the holidays was over. Though all showed disappointment at this notice of departure, the Gagne kids lent him a hand in shoveling out his motor car from under the mountain of snow, left by the street plows. Jerry and Oliver bid their respective families adieu and were off to a surprisingly good start, headed southward.

"Hey Ollie, would Newport, Rhode Island be far out of our way? I've heard a lot about it and would like to go there."

"Well, the January thaw is showing up at a convenient time—let's give it a go."

There was just a slight residue of slush when they got to the famous forty steps which lead down a perpendicular cliff. From there, they walked near the shoreline onto a rugged path called "Cliff Walk." They were able to get a rear view of the rich mansions built in the nineteenth century by the most wealthy Americans.

"This is where the famous yachting events have been held . . . right off this harbor. The winners take what is called the 'American Cup.' It's open to European yachters, too."

"So you knew about this place, ay Jerry. I'm glad we came."

"Yeah, our New England coast holds lots of treasures. Wanta see an old whaling ship that was built in 1841 ? It's docked at Mystic Seaport in Connecticut."

"Come on, Jerry. I want to hit a warmer climate. We can go there another time."

"Oh hell, I hope we'll have some mutual interests."

"You wanted to come here and we came . . . what more do you want?"

The two men caught the car ferry from Brenton Point to Narragansett Pier. Both liked the scenery.

"You'll never be a seaman, Jerry. Ya look kinda green around the gills."

"I was hoping that it wouldn't be noticeable," said Jerry as he made it to the boat railing just in the nick of time.

When they drove off the ferry, they were soon on to Connecticut roads.

At dusk, Oliver told Jerry about the difficulties he previously had trying to find lodging when going through Connecticut. So, they had no alternative but to continue on until they were able to get to White Plains, New York.

"Boy, that's a long haul from Lawrence . . . my back is killing me!"

"When you've done all the traveling that I've done, you'll take your little aches and pains in stride."

I suppose ya think that I'm just a complainer, Ollie."

"I'd appreciate it if you keep your gripes to yourself . . . it kinda gets to me!"

Oliver wondered if he had made a mistake inviting Jerry on this sojourn.

They did find lodgings in White Plains where they rested their bags of bones from eleven that night until six-thirty the next morning. After a nourishing breakfast, they crossed the Hudson river into New Jersey.

"Ya know that song about the 'Boardwalk of Atlantic City?' I've always wanted to see it. What about you, Jerry?"

"It's not summer yet, Ollie!"

"Yeah, I know, but there's no snow and I'd like to walk on that four mile boardwalk to breathe in the delicious sea air. If you think you'll get seasick . . . you could sit and wait for me."

"Quit ribbin' me about being seasick. I'll be glad to walk and get the kinks out of my bones."

Both men enjoyed the cold stroll on the famous boardwalk.

"Hey, on the way back home, the weather will be warm enough to come here again and maybe we could pick up a couple of chicks."

"Now we're in agreement, Jerry. You're beginning to talk my language. I heard that in the summer, all the piers are like show places. Sousa's band has played here, also Bob Hope and lots of other famous performers. Around the fourth of July would be the best time."

After filling their lungs with cold fresh air, they were jubilantly ready to move on, cruising toward Cape May, singing "By The Sea, By The Sea!"

They came to a narrow strip between Delaware Bay and the Atlantic Ocean.

"See that sign? We must be in Cape May."

Before driving on to the car ferry, they got an eyeful of the Victorian homes, trimmed like Gingerbread houses.

"Kinda feminine, lacy . . . don't ya think, Ollie?"

"I'm thinking about all the hours, days, weeks, months and maybe years consumed in the building of them! Poor carpenters! The trimmings do look like lace . . . just imagine painting all that fancy work!"

They drove on to the ferry.

"I've made up my head that I won't get sick on this ferry."

"Good for you, Jerry, sometimes it is just a matter of preparing yourself mentally."

They arrived at Cape Lewis, Delaware without incident. They cruised along on Route 9 toward Georgetown.

"Say, why don't we go to Dover, the capitol of this state."

"Heck Jerry, that would mean turning toward the north . . . too far out of our way. Besides, we want nice warm southern weather. Pretty soon, we'll be in Maryland."

"Sorry, I didn't realize that Dover was that far from this route. Let's see, what should we talk about? I know. Don't you think that it's ironic that of all the guys in Brother Emile's class, you and I are the only bachelors?"

"Is that good or bad, Jerry?"

"Well, I kinda wish I had met the right girl . . . I'd like to have a little wife and a couple of kids. Wouldn't you?"

"I'm not looking for a ball and chain. I like being unattached . . . ya know . . . free . . . free to be . . . well, . . . just free!"

"Gee Ollie, I never knew that you were so anti-commitment. What ever shaped you to be that way?"

"I don't know. Maybe it's family history. You know . . . my father . . . you know."

"That doesn't mean that it would be the same for you. You're a nice easy goin' guy . . . not too hard to get along with."

"Maybe for a short time, Jerry. I get tired of sameness. I need changes, not sameness."

"Ya know, I read a book last year called *Babbit* by that guy who won a Pulitzer Prize for literature."

"I read that book last spring. His name was Lewis . . . Sinclair Lewis. The character, George Babbit, should never have married. He wasn't satisfied with family life . . . sibling arguments, and arguments with his kids made him . . . as he said, 'So darn tired.'"

"Aside from the fact that Babbit is just a fictional character. Little family tiffs are inevitable. Things that pass, and when all is finally smooth, family life can be most rewarding. I'm thinking about the togetherness of my mom and dad and all us kids."

"Your family is an exception. Your mom and dad weren't like mine. Ya know what I mean. Maybe my dad could be compared to Babbit. He had a roving eye, too. And was also a businessman. Babbit's main interest was making money, money, money."

"That character was in the real estate business and was in cahoots with an unsavory politician who fixed some of the shoddy inspections of properties, which proved that Babbit wasn't all that virtuous."

"Yeah, but if he didn't have family to think about, maybe he wouldn't be always plotting to make more and more money. Say, talking about money, it's your turn to pay for the gas. Here's a station . . . thirty-one cents a gallon."

Jerry most willingly filled the gas tank, and then they stopped to fill their stomachs; it was at a small cafe in Jimtown, which boasted of home-cooked meals. The fare was becoming more southern and the two buddies experienced their first taste of fried okra.

"Have you ever heard of this stuff, okra, Oliver?"

"Sure, but this is the first time I've been brave enough to try it . . . it's not bad. I'm told that southerners are brought up on okra and collards. Up north, people have never heard of that stuff."

"They must have lots of pigs down south. We see lots of advertisements for barbecued pork. Flavorful, don't ya think?"

"Yeah, but I like seafood once in a while. Let's look for an eating place to get red snapper or grouper. Don't expect to get haddock where the waters are warmer than New England. I kinda like the fish down here, there's more to choose from. Do you like catfish?"

"Ach, I wouldn't eat catfish if you paid me! I remember when my dad got back from a fishing trip and brought home two big live black fish with horns. He put them in the bathtub and boy was my mom mad! I'll never forget the ugliness of those things swimming around in our tub. Right then and there, I vowed never to eat such a scary creature. Mom said she wouldn't cook them if no one wanted to eat them. They finally died and Dad buried them in our garden. Poor Mom had a devil of a time cleaning out the slimy tub and every time I took a bath, I imagined those weird things swimming around in there!"

"They're really not all that bad fried in batter . . . just put lots of catsup on them."

"No thanks."

"What do ya know . . . it says Maryland on that sign. I'd like to stop in Baltimore."

"Hey wait a minute! I know it's your car, but remember when we were in Cape Lewes, Delaware and I thought it would be great to visit Dover. You said it was further north and didn't want to head north?"

"Yeah, what are you trying to tell me, Jerry?"

"If you look at this here map, where is Baltimore? Even further north than Dover would have been."

"Okay, maybe we can hit those places on our return trip. I can see where it would be wiser to go through Washington, D.C. before the rush traffic, then stay over in Alexandria, Virginia tonight."

"Good idea."

✻   ✻   ✻

It was dusk by the time the men checked into the small inn in the historic city of Alexandria. After getting settled, a walk through the city took the kinks out of their legs after the long drive.

"Ya know, Jerry, this place reminds me of Charleston, South Carolina. There are so many historic homes. Look at this one! It's Robert E. Lee's childhood home. Remember all the things we learned about Lee in Brother Emile's class?"

"Gosh Oliver, how far back can one's memory go? I kinda remember about Lee graduating from West Point and he served as an engineer officer in the Mexican War."

"I didn't remember that part of it, but I do remember learning that he came from a line of servicemen, and that his father, a friend of George Washington, was a hero in the Revolutionary War. It must have been a tough decision for Robert E. Lee to make when Virginia considered secession. He fought with the options of either staying with the Union and he even led the army to coerce his state back into the Union. But he chose to resign from the Union army and serve the Confederacy. He was a hero to southerners, but in the end, he found that he had made a losing choice. Rah to Brother Emile—the best teacher we had at St. Anne's School!"

"He really was a swell teacher."

"I've never heard of Ramsay, the town's first postmaster. Guess the town is proud to name any of these old brick buildings after their well-known townspeople."

"Look at this! Gadsby's Tavern . . . too bad . . . no booze. Let's get a lemonade here so that we can brag that we drank in the same tavern George Washington patronized. Only I'll bet he had a bit of gin or scotch. It was allowed in those days."

On the next morning, they ate breakfast at a small coffee shop and then left for Williamsburg, a four-hour drive. A hearty lunch was enjoyed at the Raleigh Tavern on Duke of Gloucester Street in Williamsburg.

"Washington certainly got around . . . he ate here."

"So did Jefferson and Lafayette . . . so this restaurant brags."

227

Oliver and Jerry continued down the Duke of Gloucester Street which is full of historic interests.

"I can't believe what I'm seeing! William and Mary College! Remember the Croteau kids on Forest Street?" exclaimed Oliver.

"Sure I do. I've had my eye on Yvette. I don't think she ever married. So what's so exciting about this college?"

"One of the Croteau boys graduated from here . . . I don't understand why he would go to a college so far from home. He's teaching in a public school in Manchester."

"Yeah, we have good schools nearer home. I would have chosen Lowell Tech. That sister of his is a swell kid—good looker, too!"

"If she's such a knockout, how come some guy hasn't latched on to her by now? She was younger than us, but heck, she must be all of forty . . . an old maid!"

"Old maid? Don't ya hate that term? Like we're old baches. How does that grab you?"

"It grabs me and keeps me more and more determined to stay as such. Does it bother you?"

"Truthfully, I'd rather be a married man with a family. I don't like the sound of the word bachelor! Doesn't it have a lonesome ring to it? But it's not just that. Being part of a family seems more normal to me."

"Not for this guy!"

"I'll try dating Yvette again. Last time I asked her out, she was going steady with Ray Poulin. I just might stand a chance now that they've broken up."

"Good luck!" Oliver changed the subject. "Back to the present. do ya know that Jamestown is just six miles from here?"

"So-ooo."

"Well, that was the first English settlement in America. Take a look at this, Jerry. This old courthouse was still in use until just two years ago! Built in 1770!"

"Let's take a look at the Governor's Palace on that boulevard. There it is. This sign says that it was built in 1720, and the governors, appointed by the British Crown, lived there."

"Wow! Patrick Henry and Tom Jefferson were once governors of Virginia."

"I read that the Palace burnt down in 1781 and was rebuilt only four years ago. I'm glad that we didn't come a few years before this."

"Say Ollie, I'd like to visit Norfolk where there were many battles fought. I want to see that St. Paul's church that still has a cannonball in its wall."

"Sorry to disappoint you, Jerry. A snowstorm is due . . . even in Virginia. I hope we can make it to North Carolina before that happens."

They drove on . . . each in his own thoughts.

Jerry, who still made his home with his aging parents, wondered: is there any place Oliver can call home? At least, after work, I can go home to Ma's great cooking and then listen to *Amos and Andy, Fibber Magee and Molly*, or any other radio program. I wouldn't want to live like a gypsy. I'm just lucky . . . That's it! I'm a lucky guy.

At the same time, Oliver pondered Jerry's lifestyle: poor Jerry. I can't understand how a guy like him could still be living with Mommy and Daddy in dullsville. I couldn't stand to live like that. I'm lucky, I'm not caught up in that trap. It's swell to be free to do as I please.

It took them another four hours before crossing the North Carolina border. Conversation kicked in between their deep thoughts.

"I've been thinking, Ollie. Here we are, on the go for almost a month, and we haven't found a place to anchor down for a while!"

"Anchor down!" Oliver responded vociferously. "Don't ya like to see new places? Learn some history?"

"I kinda like staying put for a while—it's more relaxing!"

"Me thinks that you are homesick." Oliver pronounced each word in staccato fashion and continued, "That's where you anchor . . . it must be on a permanent mooring! Poor fellow misses his mommy and daddy?"

"Now you're becoming sarcastic. I thought we were friends!"

"And I thought that I had an adventurous fellow traveler!"

"You sold me on an idea that sounded swell. And at first it was. Now I want out. Don't be combative toward me, Oliver. I do want to go home. Do you understand?"

"Okay! Okay! We'll find a train station in Raleigh, North Carolina. You'll have to get information as to how to make connections back to Lawrence."

*   *   *

On the road again, Jerry and Oliver rehashed the Babbit story, each with a differing view.

"I'll say it again. Babbit should not have married. He would have been free of all his guilt feelings, and free to enjoy those parties and little

229

flirtations with various women. His naughty behavior troubled him . . . well, not all the time."

Jerry countered, "He started out as a decent man and fell into a trap of non-conformity. He lowered his moral standards in a rebellious way. He rebelled against the status quo, but he hadn't lost his soul completely. The jolt of his wife's sickness brought him down to earth and he finally realized how important she was in his life. A reformed man is a saved soul."

"Well, I still see it all in a different light. I don't conform to certain molds. Does that make me a lost soul?"

"Let's drop it, Ollie. I'll not judge, lest I be judged. Say, are we almost there yet?"

"We still have a way to go. Let's stop for a bite."

"Good idea!"

They stopped at a nondescript eatery in Rocky Mount. Having nourishment put them both in an improved frame of mind, in spite of the fact that they saw newspaper headlines: HITLER PROMOTES BLOOD BATH. JAPAN RENOUNCES WASHINGTON TREATIES OF 1922 AND 1930.

"Good God!" exclaimed Oliver. "I hope there won't be another World War. Remember what was said about World War One—The war to end all wars!"

"Look at this article, Ollie. Public Enemy No. 1, John Dillinger shot by the FBI."

"Yeah, one less crackpot in the world. Now someone should shoot that Hitler!"

"Let's change the subject . . . news is too depressing. How about singing some of the new hits," and Jerry began singing "Blue Moon." Oliver joined in, and they both wailed out the popular tunes during the remainder of their journey, until they arrived at the Wilmington and Raleigh Railroad Station.

"So long, Jerry. Have a good trip back home and marry that swell gal, Yvette."

"That's what I hope to do, Ollie. Enjoy your ventures, and let's hear from you." They shook hands, and Jerry disappeared into the second car behind the locomotive.

*   *   *

"Oliver! Oliver!"

Who the heck do I know in this neck of the woods . . . someone else must be named Oliver, he mulled as he continued walking away through the train station.

She grabbed his arm and only spoke after trying to regain her breath.

"Are you trying to get away from me?" she panted.

"Oh my gosh, it's Emma! What are you doing in Raleigh? Is Patty with you?"

"No, she's with my mom back in New Bern. I'm just here for a few days . . . just got off the train. Then I couldn't believe my eyes when I spotted you! I plan to hear a lecture concert tomorrow at the art museum at three o'clock. Madame Michelle Chateauneuf will be lecturing about famous Impressionism art work, and playing impressionistic piano pieces, complementing the paintings. What are you doing here, Oliver?"

"I just said good-bye to a traveling buddy who is returning home by rail. Do you know of a good hotel where I can bunk down for tonight?"

"We could take a taxi together to my hotel . . . you might be able to get a room."

"No need for a cab. I've got my own wheels. Know the way?"

"I should. This is a popular getaway for me—from time to time."

"What are you getting away from? Ah, this is my automobile here. Say, how about dinner tonight? We could get caught up on the happenings of the last seven years."

Emma didn't say why she needed a getaway, but she did agree to go out to dinner.

Oliver was able to secure a room in the same hotel, and after they were both settled in, he purchased a bottle of champagne at the store adjacent to the hotel. When he knocked on the door of room 312, he presented the bottle to Emma saying, "To old times!"

"Yes," she responded. "To old times!" There were two glasses on the oak dresser.

They gently touched glasses and sipped the bubbling liquid . . . with sparkling eyes locked in admiration of each other.

After awkward moments of reminiscing, and affectionately hugging and kissing, they both agreed that it was time to go to the restaurant. They were within walking distance to the eatery near Capitol Square. They ordered the specialty of the house: mignon with potatoes au gratin, salad, coffee, and lemon meringue pie.

"After that splendid meal, I feel the need to walk off the calories. How about you, Oliver?"

"So that's how you stay so trim. Sure, let's take a look at these old buildings."

"The architecture of this state government building is Greek Revival. It was completed in 1840."

"Wow, it's stood up pretty well. Looks like it can last another ninety-four years, eh?"

"Oh I'm sure it will. In the earlier years, Raleigh had an Experimental Railroad which carried stone to help build the Capitol."

Emma was knowledgable in many aspects of governmental buildings.

"You could serve as a tour guide," commented Oliver.

And she went on and on, serving as his private tour guide until Oliver suggested going to a movie.

They had a choice between *Little Women,* starring Katharine Hepburn, and *She Done Him Wrong,* starring Mae West. Oliver tossed a coin—Mae West won out.

Back at the hotel, Oliver was about to leave Emma at her door to go down to his room, when she turned on a sultry voice saying, "Come up an see me some time."

They both laughed, and after she unlocked her door, Oliver left with, "I'll pick you up for breakfast at about nine in the morning." He would like to have stayed—but didn't dare make the suggestion.

Over the breakfast table, she pleaded with him to attend the afternoon lecture concert.

"It's not exactly my cup of tea, but if you insist, I'll go."

The seats were uncomfortable folding chairs, set up in a special, almost bare room, bare hardwood floors, bare walls, but there were two easels placed beside a Steinway grand piano.

When the portly French woman, Madame Chateauneuf, entered the room, the audience gave her a rousing greeting. She immediately got down to the business of the lecture by quoting the Harvard Dictionary of Music which, she said, states that Impressionistic music is "a music that hints rather than states, a music that is vague and intangible as the changing light of day."

She went on to say that she felt that description suits both painting and music in the impressionistic style. Two paintings were placed on the easels and Madame Chateauneuf proceeded to compare the art works of

Renoir's *The Garden of the Rue Cortot,* 1876, and Monet's *Garden at Vetheuil,* 1881.

"Notice here, Renoir's garden has dense greenery with a mix of white dahlias in the foreground. Dahlias in shades of reds, yellow and orange are in tangles of possibly weed growth; it appears that this garden had been unattended for some time. To the right of this painting, notice a small knotted tree base with three branches, but no leaves . . . this could indicate the changing of seasons. Notice, the two men in the background are having a discussion; this man is gesturing with his right hand in the air as if expressing his point of view. The trees behind them display traces of fall coloring."

Oliver whispered to Emma, "I never would have noticed all that. A picture is a picture."

"It's educational, Oliver . . . shush."

Madame Chateauneuf moved to the next display. "Now, we'll compare Monet's garden. See the flowery hill with a stairway descending from a house. The sunlight is illuminating the edges of the stairway as an adult figure and a small child descend. See this other child, at the landing, is dwarfed by the tall growth of sunflowers and greenery. This pathway is lined with ornate pottery, holding long stemmed flowers. The small wagon on the path is partially in the sunlight. Here, the shadows are streaking across the path. And notice the puffy clouds in the azure blue sky.

"While you enjoy these lovely scenes, I shall perform Debussy's 'Jardins Sous La Pluie,' even though there's no rain," she chuckled. The enrapturing music proved apropos, giving more meaning to the art works, and also painting mental images through Madame's interpretation.

Oliver shifted uncomfortably on the hard chair.

The next paintings set on the easels were Renoir's *Dance at Bouqaval,* 1883, and *Moulin de la Gaette.* Madame Chateauneuf pointed out the grace in the figure of the woman. The same dancing couple is seen in both paintings. After her full description, she sat at the keyboard and played more Debussy: "La Fille Aux Cheveux de Lin," and the waltz, "La Plus Que Lente."

One could imagine this couple waltzing gracefully. Madame noted that "Whether a picture is painted on canvas or painted with sound, the viewer or listener can enjoy the beauty, style, color, and texture in either medium."

Two more paintings were placed on the easels: Monet's *Regatta at Argenteuill*, and Renoir's *Sailboats at Argenteuill*, 1874.

Madame compared the paintings in every detail, and said, "The reflection of the sails are shimmering in the water . . . and Debussy's 'Voiles,' (sails) shimmer in the breeze." She then performed "Voiles."

Madame went on to critique Renoir's *A Road In Louveciennes*.

Oliver's throat felt dry and scratchy. He quickly exited the building before causing a distraction with a coughing spell. The wait outside seemed forever while Emma remained until the completion of Madame's performance.

"Oliver, what made you dash out like that?"

He explained about his fear of creating a disturbance with his coughing. "Ya know, Emma, you're far too intellectual for me. I can't stomach so much of this hoity-toity stuff. I'd much rather sit and listen to you play the up to date songs."

"But Oliver, classics live on forever! Pop tunes soon die and are forgotten."

"See, you're intellectual. I'm just an uneducated man."

"No you are not," she countered vehemently. "You're more well-read and traveled than a lot of college grads!"

"Ya think so?"

"I know so!"

"I've got to get the kinks out of my old bones after sitting on that uncomfortable wooden chair. Lets walk a while," he suggested.

They strolled along Pullen Park where a bunch of boys were playing baseball. A young batter hit so hard and high, none of the players could get to it fast enough. Oliver jumped the fence and caught it, bare-handed. The young umpire yelled, "Out!" and the batter and his team mates argued that, "That man is not on either team—that doesn't count!" But they had to learn that the umpire is always right.

"That's impressive, Oliver. You must have played ball as a kid."

"I've had some experience, and as kids, we used to watch semi-pro teams play in a ball park on Water Street in Lawrence."

"When I was in grammar school, we girls had a softball team. A bunch of boys used to perch in the tree that was near home plate. One day when we didn't have our gym suits on, I hit a home run—but when I slid onto the home plate, my dress flew up over my head, and the fresh boys cheered at seeing my bloomers. I was so embarrassed that I quit the team."

"Gosh Emma, I wish I could have witnessed that scene," Oliver said in a burst of laughter.

"Now I wish I hadn't told that story. Your imagination is too vivid."

"You're a sensitive gal, but bygones are bygones, and you still tell of your embarrassments. You'll have to admit, it paints a comical picture which might suit a Laurel and Hardy film."

Emma elbowed him sharply in the rib cage.

"Ouch!" but he continued to find the scene humorous.

After dinner, they returned to the hotel with another bottle of champagne.

"Your room or mine?" asked Oliver.

"Mine will be fine," she replied.

Oliver and Emma each described school day incidents, she laughing hilariously over the pranks he had played on the nuns and brothers of St. Anne's parochial school. They became more relaxed and playful as their champagne party progressed.

After their lovemaking, she pleaded with Oliver to return to New Bern with her the next day. His thoughts returned of his experiences with her daughter, Patty. He reasoned: *Patty was six at that time and WOW! what a bruising kick in the shins she had administered! Now, she's thirteen years old—much bigger feet. I like her mother, but that monster could ruin any relationship. Also, I don't want to let on to Emma that my money is running low. Maybe I could get a job as a smithey at Churchill Downs in Kentucky.*

"My darling," she whispered while brushing her lips against his cheek. "What is taking you so long to answer me?"

"You just might not like my answer. You see, I'll be moving on—in a different direction."

"After what has just happened? You just love me and leave me?!!!"

"You might say that's so. It's the story of my life. I don't see longterm commitments for me, in the present or in the future."

Emma arose from the bed in a disturbed state.

"Get out! Get out! You are a scoundrel, a dirty rotten scoundrel!"

Upon exiting the room, with a sly grin, he asked: "Want me to drive you to the train station in the morning?"

There were no more words from her—just a pillow flung from across the room, striking her target plumb into his smirking face.

Twenty-five

Oliver checked out of the hotel at seven in the morning, and was happy to escape a chance meeting with Emma.

He tanked up his auto and was on his way, hoping that his vehicle was capable of the trek across the Great Smoky mountains into Tennessee. Two days after leaving Raleigh, and crossing the high, winding mountain roads he arrived on the outskirts of Johnson City. He approached a weather-beaten, derelict-looking service station, in much need of paint. The old roof, minus a few shingles, lent an eerie appearance to a forgotten business. The antique sign across the front read Pop Sidley's. There were discarded tires and inner tubes on the side of the ramshackle building.

Oliver wondered, *Are those pumps in use? I'm running low on fuel—and that front tire looks pretty deflated. I'll pull in here and check out the place.* He saw that in the shade of the overhang, an old man rose from his wooden rocking chair and was approaching Oliver's automobile.

He was a skinny old gent, wearing torn overalls, several sizes too large. The old man's knees must have bent, but his pants didn't. The poor old guy was bent over like a broken twig hanging from a tree. When he spoke, his dentures seemingly danced in his mouth.

"What can I do fer ya, sonny?"

"My right front tire is low. I might need a new inner tube."

Pop kicked the tires and said, "By gees, Sonny, ittle cost ya less if I can patch it up. Jist help me git that dawgone fella off the rim, en I'll fix the thing with a patch an ittle be good as new."

"Thank you, sir. I'd appreciate that."

"Now, folks from this here town all calls me Pop, not sir, sonny. Sounds kinda formal."

"Okay, Pop. Do you know where I might get a job around here?"

"Ya come jist in time, sonny. I've been needin' some help. Tain't no young uns around willin' to help an old fella like me!"

"Okay with me, Pop. What will you have me do?"

"Well, ya could work the pumps an when ya ain't busy, ya could help paint the place."

"And where can I bunk down, Pop?"

"I ain't got nothin' fancy, but there's an extra bunk in the back room. Got me an ole cookin' stove. We ain't got runnin' water, but we got us a well out back, an theys an outhouse, too. Will that do ya?"

"Sounds kinda rustic, but I'll manage."

"Got one of them newfangled radios near ma chair. If ya like, theys good dancing music on between them ball games. Like baseball, Sonny?"

"Doesn't everyone?"

There weren't many customers at the pumps on Oliver's first day of work. Pop showed him to the cans of paint and brushes he could use to brighten up the building.

"But Pop, you have too many colors here. Wouldn't you rather have a nice clean looking white station?"

"The color ain't no mind ta me. Why, I got those cans frum people jist gettin' rid of paint they ain't had no use fer."

"There isn't any one color that will go far. Most of those cans are half empty, some even more."

Pop scratched his balding head and exclaimed with a bit of a chuckle: "Sonny, we'll have a colorful place that will have customers comin' jist to see sumthin' like theys never seen before."

"Is that what you really want?"

"Shor'nuf. Start with this here yella . . . up near the roof. When yas run out of that, hows about the green, then thers sum white . . . "

"Gee, Pop, you'll have a striped station with all these colors . . . and if we run out, what then?"

The old man, with the dancing teeth, just laughed and laughed until they almost fell out of his mouth.

Curious townspeople did buy more gas, as Pop had hoped. The mayor exclaimed: "Ya got a mighty impressive place here, Pop. We can see it from a mile down the road."

"It's bringin' me more customers. Thanks to ma helper here. He ain't no slouch . . . hard workin' kid. Jist what ah needed."

How long does the old guy think I'm going to stay here? Oliver asked himself. I've been here for over four months and haven't had a decent bath or shower. After another week on the job, Oliver gave Pop a week's notice . . . said that he had to leave.

"Ya becommin' like a son ta me. Yep, ma son abandoned me too. He ain't never come back. Dunno what I'm gonna do." Pop put on a most pitiful face which *almost* made Oliver feel too guilty to leave . . . *almost* . . . but he did leave the following week.

✳   ✳   ✳

It took him three days to get to Louisville, Kentucky. Showering and shaving in hotel rooms for two nights proved to be a reprieve from his former accommodations. He wasted no time in presenting himself to stable managers of Churchill Downs.

Mr. Feeney told Oliver: "The only work available is for ostlers. You do know what that entails, Mr. Janvier?"

"Yes, I do, Mr. Feeney. If an opening happens in the smithing field, would you consider me as an applicant? I'm professionally experienced in that line."

"You will probably have a long wait to prove your skills. Are you willing to begin as an ostler?"

"Yes sir."

"We have bunkhouses where most of our men stay—or do you have your own place near here?"

"The bunkhouse will do fine."

Oliver was fifty years old, the oldest of the ostlers. He feared that maybe the young workers might begin calling him Pop, but that never happened because he worked with more zest than most of them.

"Hey, new fella,, whatever ya name is. Don't try to show us up by scrambling around, trying to overwork yourself. Tomorrow is another day and there'll be more and more manure to clean out of the stalls. No end to it, ya know."

"I'm just doing what I get paid for, pal. Besides, my muscles can use a little extra workout. Energy begets energy, you know."

"Energy begets energy!" the young whippersnapper mocked. "That's a laugh . . . ya spend too much energy an . . . ya done for . . . especially an older guy like you."

"Cut it out, kid. We're not in competition. You do your work as you see fit. I'll do mine."

Oliver wasn't too sure that things would work out smoothly for him, what with younger men carrying chips on their shoulders, and ready for someone to challenge them.

The beautiful thoroughbred horses were with their trainers when their stalls were being prepared for their return—and Oliver did a thorough job of cleaning and applying fresh hay.

When a horse was returned to the stable, Oliver enjoyed the most rewarding job of all: he felt elated to take part in grooming the splendid animals, preparing them for the "Sport of Kings."

Oliver learned that thoroughbreds were once solely the property of the privileged few of aristocracy; modern racing began with King Charles II. The Kentucky Derby at Churchill Downs began in 1875.

He was happy with his job but looked forward to being elevated to a smithy position, which meant more money in his pockets. He wrote to Eva and included up to date pop songs.

Dear Eva and family,

Here are three more songs for you . . . go tickle the ivories with: "Pennies From Heaven." (I'm getting more 'pennies' on this new job.) "I'm An Old Cow Hand. " (I'm not from the 'Rio Grande,' but I'd rather be working with beautiful horses than cows.) "On Your Toes." (Yeah, I have to be on my toes working with a bunch of young guys, ready for confrontations.)

You know how I've loved horses, especially Dad's Morgan horses . . . well, thoroughbreds are something else! The breed was developed in England . . . trained for racing and jumping.

They're shaped differently than Morgans, their bodies are slim, and they have refined heads . . . sort of delicate like . . . their backs are kind of short. I love grooming them! They seem so intelligent . . . I find myself talking to them.

The oval shaped track here is three quarters of a mile. I haven't bet on any of the races yet, but the young guys think they know it all by advising betters on certain "winners." Did you know that bookie betting is illegal in America, but legal in England? The only acceptable betting here is pari-mutuel; the betting takes place at the tracks.

Before a race, the horses are saddled at the paddock, that is also where the jockeys go after being weighed in . . . the trainers then give the men instructions. A jockey can't weigh any more than 126 pounds if he rides a male horse. The guys riding a filly can't weigh more than 121 pounds.

When the horses are identified by a tattoo on the inside of the upper lip, then the jockeys mount to parade past the stewards for inspection. This gives the fans a chance to see the horses close up before the race begins.

"My Old Kentucky Home" is played as they head to the track. Did you ever think that there would be so much to the racing business? I had no idea. If I don't get a smithy job, I just might leave for elsewhere, but I just might give in to Charlie's nagging request about wanting to buy my automobile. (He's one of the young ostlers.) If I make that decision, I'll go back to train travel which isn't all that bad.

Most of the guys here are OK kids. One kid carries the new Dale Carnegie book, called, *How To Win Friends and Influence People*. Some of the other guys could use a few lessons in friendliness. Have you read the new book, *Gone With The Wind*? It's by Margaret Mitchell . . . read it. Its great!

> I love you all,
> "Itchy feet." (or rolling stone)
> (no moss, no moss)

"You've been at this track for a few months now, ain't ya ever gonna place a bet? All us guys take chances now and then," exclaimed Tod, a young worker.

"Maybe I'll try a small wager—any recommendations?"

"Ya know how to bet pari-mutuel? Or do ya use bookies? Illegal, ya know."

"Yeah, I know. Explain what you know."

"Well, if ya bet two bucks on a special horse to *win*, and he comes in, you'll probably git about forty bucks or more.

"If ya bet *place* and ya horse comes in first or second, ya still win something . . . maybe ten bucks. If you bet to *show*, and ya horse comes in third, ya might win about four bucks."

"What horse will you bet on?"

"I like the looks of Indian Broom . . . might bet 'em ta win."

Oliver had overheard Joe Widener, the owner of Brevity, talking to Mr. Coyne, the trainer. Hmm, thought Oliver, *sounds like a winner*. He paid his bet on Brevity to place. He felt his need to be a bit cautious, but put up five dollars on his very first wager. While he cleaned stalls, the race was broadcast on the radio. Indian Broom wasn't in the lead very long before Brevity overtook him. Oliver's heart pounded with excitement as he visualized himself a winner.

Along came Bold Venture. After beginning at a slow pace, he picked up momentum and rounded the outside at the final half mile, and upon entering the stretch, had an easy win.

Bold Venture, ridden by jockey, Ira Hanford, came in first; Brevity, with jockey, Wayne Wright, came in second. Oliver collected his winnings of twelve dollars.

Many months passed before a smithy job was available, but only on a temporary basis, as one of the horseshoe men was out on sick leave. Oliver proved to be an expert in the field in which he had excelled many years before. The job was not as short-lived, as expected; the former smithy did not return, and Oliver was secure in his regained profession.

Oliver reread what Benjamin Franklin had written in *Poor Richard, 1758.*

For the want of a nail the shoe was lost,
For the want of a shoe the horse was lost,
For the want of a horse the rider was lost,
For the want of a rider the battle was lost,
For the want of a battle the kingdom was lost—
And all for want of a horseshoe-nail.

How important it is to do an expert job, reflected Oliver . . . and he proved to be most reliable.

Charlie still wanted to buy Oliver's Chevrolet, so at last, Oliver agreed to sell it, asking three-hundred dollars for it.

"You're asking three-hundred for a seven-year-old car!. Come on, be fair," Charlie frowned.

"This auto is in excellent shape and is well worth the asking price," Oliver offered, as he imagined himself sounding like some of the automobile salesmen he had encountered. He had soon decided that to travel alone would be more comfortable and less lonely doing it by rail. I'll barter a little with this guy, decided Oliver.

"Well, what do you say, Charlie?"

"I'll take it off your hands for two-hundred-fifty."

"Okay, it's yours, providing I get cash."

"No problem. I've been saving for wheels long enough."

They shook hands on the deal and Charlie made good his agreement to pay cash.

*   *   *

Christmas and New Year of 1936–37 were lonesome, uneventful holidays. Spring was a welcome improvement after a chilly winter.

Oliver had a difficult time deciding on which horse to bet on. There was Melodis Reaping Reward looks good, he reflected. Then there's War Admiral, and Pompoon. Gosh, it's a hard decision. This time he decided to go whole hog for the big win. It's like war. Yeah, I've got it! I'll bet on War Admiral to win!

War Admiral ridden by jockey, C. Kurtsinger, came in first. Oliver's biggest bet yet, brought him a win of over three-hundred dollars.

In 1938, the year Eddie Arcaro rode the horse, Lawrin, Oliver's big win amounted to over four-hundred dollars. The guys claimed that he had the Midas touch. But, that didn't change his mind about moving on.

I'll quit while I'm ahead. This rolling stone is all set to roll some more, Oliver decided, and he again set off on another journey with his finances greatly enhanced by the money from the car sale, his winnings, plus two or more years of stashing away most of his earnings.

After changing trains several times on his trek to New York, Oliver began to regret having sold his automobile. His brother Frank met him in Buffalo with his shiny new Pontiac. Enroute to Fredonia, Frank informed Oliver that the family would soon be leaving for a reunion in Lawrence, Massachusetts.

"We'll have plenty of room in this car for you to come along with us. What do you say?"

"Why not? I don't have any long-term plans."

"Good," said Frank, "it will give us all a chance to see Ma and the rest of our clan. Even Blanche will be allowed time off to be with us. Maybe I should call her Sister Marie Gerard? I could never figure out why she chose those names for the nunnery. I'll bet that some day the nuns will be able to keep their own names, then she'd be Sister Blanche Janvier. What's so bad about that?"

"They choose names of saints. It seems strange, though. She chose two saints, one female and the other male. Eva says that Blanche is teaching piano and violin. Can you figure that one out?"

"Wow! When did she ever study those instruments?" exclaimed Frank.

"Changing the subject, Frank; do you recall all the banter at my smithy place before the World War broke out? What do you make of what is happening these days?"

"Things don't look too promising, what with Roosevelt asking Congress for more than five-hundred-million dollars for defense. And how do you take this, Roosevelt asks Hitler and Mussolini not to attack us. If they conquer Europe, what's to stop them!"

"I believe that it is Hitler's goal to conquer the world. He's been renouncing nonagression pacts. The agressive nations are leaving the League of Nations like escaping rats. I see it as the start of another world war."

"It's another political mess, which I hope won't escalate."

"By the way, Oliver, we'll leave for Lawrence in just two weeks."

"Good, it'll give me a chance to regain my equilibrium after this long trip from Kentucky."

The trip to Lawrence proved to be enjoyable enough, with Oliver and his two nieces in the backseat of Frank's Pontiac singing "Roll Out The Barrel," "The Last Time I Saw Paris," and many more old and new tunes.

"Uncle, do you know the new song, 'God Bless America?' asked Helen, the older of the two girls.

"No, but I know 'Three Little Fishes,' and 'Over the Rainbow.'"

And again, the chorus of voices sang out the newer tunes with Frank and his wife, Eva, joining in. Then, the girls taught everyone the words to, "God Bless America."

Oliver couldn't believe that this trip went on and on without a night's stay over.

"Do you always do this in only one day, Frank?

"Why not? We left at six this morning and we'll be in Lawrence by six tonight." Frank added, "You can stay at our sister's house. Eva and my family will stay with Mattie Latourneau. Eva's sister always has room for our family."

The family reunion included seventeen people, Mama, husbands, wives, eight kids, the nun, and Oliver. The big festivities were held at the Gagne residence, still in the mode of Canadian customs.

In deference to Ma, all spoke in French, except the young ones. Most of the children couldn't fathom the conversations because of learning only English. Sister Marie Gerard whispered to brother Joe: "This will, no doubt, be our last reunion with Mama. Look how frail she has gotten."

"At our ages, we're still lucky to have her around," answered Joe.

"Mama has always been willowy, and she is still abounding with energy. Look at how quickly she waits on people—even if you can't fit another thing into your stomach, she'll make you feel guilty not to accept more. She's still about the same, but maybe a little paler and maybe just a little more bent over." Oliver had eavesdropped.

243

When everyone had retired to the parlor, Eva Gagne was in her glory accompanying the song fest; it afforded her an opportunity to play songs from the stack of music sent to her by Oliver.

Joe Janvier's boy, Russell, was asked to play the piano; he was Eva's favorite nephew. All listeners marveled at how well he performed a Chopin waltz.

Joe proudly announced: "When my kid was seven, Doctor Lee asked our permission to take Russell to Symphony Hall in Boston to hear the famous Polish pianist, Paderewski. The hall was so crowded that some of the patrons had to sit on the stage. Russell said that he sat so close to Paderewski that he could have touched him. What an experience for such a young kid."

Everyone clapped and young Russell played more.

There were two more days of celebrating, and then the Fredonia entourage were heading for home.

"Thanks for this opportunity to be with all our family, Frank."

"We're happy that you could come along. Now, what are your plans?"

"I'll need a little rest after this trip . . . okay if I stay with you for a couple more days?"

"Sure thing. You do look a little peaked. Aren't you feeling well?"

"I don't seem to have the stamina I used to have."

"Well, you're not getting any younger, you know."

"I don't want to hear any more about age. I'll be all right after a couple of day's rest."

"Sure." All was quiet, each in his or her own thought chamber.

After two days of lazing around, Oliver got in touch with his old pal, Dom.

"Hi, old man," said Dom as he and Oliver shook hands.

"What's this 'old man' stuff? We're only as old as we feel—you feeling old?"

"Heck no, but when a guy becomes a grandfather, he's no kid."

"You mean to tell me that you are a grandfather?"

"Heck no . . . but you are!"

Oliver stood in shock, dumbfounded. *It can't be so*, he thought.

"Ted got married two years ago, and the ironic thing is that he married your old girlfriend's daughter."

"Meghan's kid? They're too young! Much too young!" he exclaimed in disbelief.

"Do your math, Oliver. Your kid was born in 1912, and here it is 1939. He was every bit a man years ago. Now, he's the proud father of a year-old boy. His wife, Cathy, is as pretty as her auburn-haired mother, Meghan Kelleher Ronan. How does that grab you, Oliver?"

Oliver's distressful facial expression warned Dom to say no more about his being a grandfather.

Finally Oliver broke the silence. "I'll be leaving tomorrow," he spoke in an almost inaudible tone of voice.

"Where are you going?"

"My first stop will be Hammondsport. There are some small plane pilots giving airborne tours. Sounds interesting to me."

"I'd like to do that some day. Good luck, friend."

Dear Eva, Ma and family,

I feel so excited! I've had the best experience of all my travels: my first plane ride! I met a guy who pilots a Curtiss Jenny Biplane from Hammondsport, New York, and he gave me the most fantastic aerial views of many interesting sights in New York—for a slight fee, of course. We saw Fort Ticonderoga, which sits on a promontory where Lake George flows into Lake Champlain. I'd like to visit the fort on the ground some day, but it was a great sight from way up in the sky!

The dairy farms were interesting to see, the cows looked almost like ants from where we were. There were red barns and towering silos . . . pastoral fields of corn, alfalfa, oats and hay.

In Glens Falls, they were preparing for their annual Hot Balloon Festival and even from high up we could see all the colorfully decorated airships in a huge field below.

We also flew over many vineyards . . . acres and acres of grapes!

I've decided to go to Pennsylvania for a while . . . by then it will be 1940 . . . and Ohio will be next, where I'll visit some of my old war buddies at the Dayton Veterans Hospital. Hope you all have good holidays.

Love to all the family.

Oliver

Upon examining his attire, Oliver decided that he was in much need of improving his wardrobe. He was enroute to Philadelphia, Pennsylvania.

Two things I'll do in Philly, planned Oliver; one . . . I'll get myself a new suit . . . two, I'll visit Independence Hall where our founding fathers met to sign the Declaration of Independence in 1776 . . . and, I want to see the Liberty Bell. He did all of that and felt like a new man in his grey tweed suit and bold green tie.

He found an eating place not far from the location of the Liberty Bell. The restaurant was so crowded that one gentleman, sitting alone at a table, beckoned to Oliver to join him. This chance meeting proved to be ironic in the fact that Ray Nolet was a relative of the Methuen couple who had taken Oliver to Yellowstone Park, some years ago.

"Hey, if you want a real swell meal, we'll drive to Lancaster where the Amish people live. There are Dutch restaurants that serve food in abundance, family style, bowls of mashed potatoes, bowls of all kinds of vegetables, platters of meats and a swell array of desserts, like pies, cakes, and apple strudel. It's hard to know what to choose . . . all you can eat for a reasonable price."

"You're telling me that you have wheels—right? I got here by rail," Oliver informed his new friend.

"Sure, I've got wheels and I'm aiming to go to Lancaster . . . want to come?"

"Let's be fair about this. You drive us in your car and I'll pay for our meals."

"That's a swell deal. Mind traveling a little over one-hundred miles to get there?"

"That's not a problem with me."

"Good. We can stop at places of interest. Valley Forge is only about twenty miles from here."

"Wow, lots of history there! I'm itching to go, Ray."

In a little more than a half hour, they arrived at Valley Forge where a tour guide explained that, "General George Washington and his Continental Army were encamped here in the winter of 1777 and 1778, at the time of the American Revolution."

"How many men did he have?" asked Oliver.

"There were at least eleven thousand. They had a rough time with too little provisions. Many of the soldiers died in the bitter cold, horses also died from lack of food. Because of the miserable conditions, some of the men deserted. The more hearty ones emerged as a strengthened force."

"That was a great visit, Ray. I had read about that fort and never thought I'd be privileged to see Washington's headquarters, and all the other buildings, even though they look in tough shape."

"I'm sure that they'll be restored for future posterity."

"Let's hope so."

"Now we'll head for Lancaster."

It wasn't a long drive, though it felt that way to Oliver. Ray was pouring out a litany of woes, a tale of epic proportion, that had a depressing effect on the listener.

In a shortened version, the tale was thus: Four years ago, his wife of eleven years needed to "find herself," a divorce ended the marriage. He had visitor's rights with their two children, ages seven and nine, but she moved to Indiana— he hadn't seen the kids for three years.

"That's where I'm going after the big feed in Lancaster."

"I think that I can get a train out of Lancaster, though I haven't decided where I'll go from there."

"You can ride with me to Indiana if you want."

"I'll decide that in Lancaster."

"I don't know why she chose the 'Hoosier State.' She didn't need to go so far away to find herself."

"Maybe she found herself by losing people she didn't want to be near." Oliver's head stayed straight forward, but from the corners of his eyes, he glimpsed the driver's face for some reaction to this comment. Ray was too engrossed in his personal travails for him to notice any disparaging remarks.

"I have her address right here." He placed his right hand over his jacket pocket, and continued, "She's in Lawrence . . . Indiana, that is. She claims that she wanted to be near more culture and that's what she has found in Indianapolis. Just a few miles from her home. What's wrong with Lawrence, Mass, near cultural Boston? I asked her. 'Too close to you,' she says."

Oliver didn't want to touch that comment and remained reticent.

If I decide to go along with him to Indiana, I'll have to suffer through his rantings, he mulled.

The Dutch restaurant served all that was described by Ray; a sumptuous repast.

Ray couldn't understand why Oliver refused his offer to join him on to Indiana.

They shook hands, taking leave at the railroad station in Lancaster, parting as pals and wishing each other, "Good luck."

Oliver sat on an old wooden bench in the train station feeling so alone . . . thinking, thinking, thinking. Where to now, old man? Where do I go from here? I've always been able to move in any direction that pleased me. I feel apart from everyone and everything. I'm a grandfather

. . . grandfather! That thought shakes me up; it sort of jolts my theory of a peaceful freedom.

He leaned forward with his elbows on his knees, and his face hidden in his hands.

"Are you feeling ill, sir?" queried a uniformed train conductor who was about to leave the station.

"Huh?" Oliver was jostled from his absorption.

"I can get help for you . . . you do look a bit whitish," said the concerned man.

"Thank you, sir, but I'll . . . I'll be just fine. Any trains leaving for New York soon?"

"Here's some information." The conductor pulled a train schedule from his side pocket, handed it to the pale man, and headed for the exit as if he had just remembered that he might be late for a dinner date.

Oliver scanned the schedule and found that he would have to return to Philadelphia for a direct line to Albany, then transfer at Albany for Buffalo.

It's as if a magnet is drawing me to that place . . . the start of my wanderings. My first experience away from home. Boy, did I feel so independently self-reliant! I recall what Henry Thoreau said about freedom: "What other liberty is there worth having, if we have not freedom and peace in our minds . . . "

I do have freedom, but peace in my mind is another story.

Oliver phoned Dom Abati from a hotel in Albany.

"What can I do for you, Oliver?"

"Could you pick me up at the railroad station at eleven in the morning'?"

"You mean that you're coming back here? You're usually gone much longer than this!"

"Yeah, that's true. I guess Buffalo holds some kind of a magnetic field that keeps drawing me back."

Dom wondered what was up with his old pal, but he agreed to be there at eleven.

*   *   *

"Our son, Anthony is away at school, Oliver. We'd be glad to have you stay with us for a while. You can have his room."

"That's swell, Dom. Thanks a lot!"

248

"The girls, Maria and Paula, are still home, and share a bedroom. Our eldest son, Nicholas, is in the Marines at Fort Bragg, Fayetteville, North Carolina. It seems that our kids grew up so fast. Here we are . . . like my house? Just finished painting it last week."

"Looks pretty nice, Dom.

Amalia had an excellent meal prepared.

"This reminds me of Aunt Molly's cooking," complimented Oliver.

"Thanks. We often reminisce about Aunt Molly and Uncle Nick. God rest their souls."

"Yeah, we had swell times back in those days . . . back when we were young," spoke Oliver, remembering and rueing the fact that he was no longer a kid.

Oliver and Dom went out for a walk after dinner. Oliver had indicated that he wanted a private conversation with his friend.

"What's going on, Oliver?" asked Dom as they walked the tree-lined sidewalk.

"Dom, I've made lots of mistakes in my life. I'm thinking, freedom doesn't mean stepping on people's toes. I've hurt a few people in my day, and I could never seem to say, 'I'm sorry.' I am sorry in my heart. I'm sorry that I never got to know my son, Ted. I'm sorry that I'll never get to know my grandson. What's his name?"

"They named him William, and call him 'Billy,' a cute little guy!"

"I wonder if Hedda ever told Ted the real story about us."

"She finally had to disclose the fact that he was adopted by Mark Anker."

"Do you know how Ted took the news?"

"Well, Hedda and Amelia talked about it. It seems that Ted considers Mark his 'real' dad because he's the one who brought him up, but he did say that some day he would like to get to know you."

"He really said that?" Oliver asked with an uncontrolled tremor in his voice and tears escaping down his cheeks.

"Yep, he really did."

"Do you think that if I showed up at his door, he and his wife would let me in?"

"If you really want to try that, I can get the address from Amalia."

At eleven that night, Dom and Amalia bid Oliver and their daughters "good night," and had a hushed conversation in their bedroom.

"Why on earth did you ever tell him that I'd give out Ted's address? Hedda wouldn't approve of it!"

249

"Honey, Ted is just as much Oliver's kid as Hedda's."

"How can you say that when he abandoned him more than twenty years ago?" her voice rose in crescendo.

"Shhh. Let's stay calm, honey. This is nothing to be upset about." Dom tried to placate her.

Amalia lowered her voice to almost a whisper, but pounced on each word in staccato.

"I refuse to give him the address—he doesn't deserve it!" In a softer, nervous tone, she continued, "And anyhow, if I cave in to that demand, I might lose my best friend, Hedda."

Dom remained placid. "I don't think you need to fear that, honey . . . and by the way, aren't I your best friend?" He put on his puppy dog eyes as he patted her cheek tenderly, looking longingly at her attractive face.

That act never failed, and they both couldn't help laughing . . . they kissed and made up.

*   *   *

It was Sunday morning and all readied for Mass, including Oliver.

Dom couldn't believe his eyes when he saw his friend all decked out in new duds.

"That's a pretty snazzy suit, Oliver," Dom exclaimed.

"Thanks, Dom. I splurged for it when I was in Philadelphia."

"Just one thing though . . . that Irish green tie is a little loud . . . I'll lend you this more subdued one in different shades of blue."

"Yeah, it is more conservative, and it does coordinate well with this tweed suit. Thanks."

The church service went by rather quickly. The priest seemed in good humor as he lectured on making marriages work. Oliver noticed that Dom and Amalia touched each other's hands—that love affair has lived on, he mused. It's too late for Hedda and me. Could it have worked if I had stayed on? He still felt that a gold band on the fourth finger left hand would feel like a ball and chain. Hedda was right—no ball and chain, no moss. I'll roll on after I get to see Ted and baby Billy.

Dom drove his family home after the church services, and explained to Amalia that he wanted to show Oliver the new building projects of Buffalo.

"It's a lame excuse I've given my family. It's really a ploy to get you to

250

Ted's house without Amalia phoning Hedda."

The drive took only a little more than a half hour. Dom stopped in front of a small, unpretentious, attractively landscaped home. Oliver began to have second thoughts about ringing the door bell. He felt a slight tremor in his hands and tightening of his stomach muscles.

"I don't know," he said, "do you think that this is the right thing to do?"

You want to see your son—don't you?"

"But I feel too chicken right now."

"Look, I'm going to visit a friend near here. You get out, make your visit, and I'll be back for you in about an hour. Relax pal, everything will be fine."

Oliver felt that Dom all but pushed him out of the car and there he stood, in front of the shrub-lined walkway. *Should I, or shouldn't I?*, he asked himself. He finally strolled to the porch steps, rambled up to the door, rang the bell, and almost hoped that no one would answer . . . but after a few moments, somebody did.

She was holding a small child in her arms as she opened the door, looked at Oliver and said, "Yes?"

He was speechless for a moment, then slowly said, "Is it really you, Meghan?"

"Oh my God, Oliver! What are you doing here?"

"Is this where Ted Anker lives?"

"Why yes, do you know him?" She looked puzzled. "Come in, come in." She stepped aside to allow Oliver entry into the hallway. After closing the door, she led him to the small parlor, where they sat, too astounded to speak. Finally she asked, "How do you know my son-in-law?"

"This may come as a shock to you, but I'm Ted's biological father."

She hesitated, trying to recover from this overwhelming news.

"My daughter, Kate, told me that Ted had been adopted, but I assumed that he had been orphaned."

"Oh no, Hedda is his real mother. I met her shortly after you and I had broken up. We lived together for a few years before the war. I went into the service, and after the war, I resumed meandering. You know what I mean."

"And you're still at it, Oliver? So you never did settle down for keeps?"

"I guess that I shouldn't be proud of my state in life, but I've seen a lot, done a lot, and learned a lot."

Meg felt that it would be unwise to comment.

"I can't believe that you and I share a grandson. Want to hold him?"

"Yes, I'd like to . . . Thank you."

Billy looked up at Oliver as if to say, "I've never seen you before." As Oliver held him, the baby began to whimper a bit before letting out a frightened scream.

"Don't worry about that, Oliver, it's past his nap time. I'll change him, give him a bottle and he'll be off to dreamland in no time at all. Don't leave, I'll be right back."

Meghan returned to the parlor saying, "Our little grandson is fast asleep. This is only the second time that Ted and Kate have asked me to baby-sit for two days; they went to Niagara Falls for the weekend and should be back at about six this evening."

Just then the door bell sounded. Oliver stood up ready to leave, assuming that it was Dom here to pick him up, but he heard Meg as she opened the front door.

"Darling. I'm glad you're back. How was the game?"

"It was great. You'd be so proud. I'll be surprised if your brother Tom isn't picked up by the major leagues; his pitching saved the day, and there was news buzzing around about scouts at the game looking for new talent. Any problems with Billy?"

"None whatsoever. Sean, there's someone I'd like you to meet."

Oliver was seated again, wishing it had been Dom at the door.

The Ronans entered the room.

"This is my husband, Sean. Sean, meet Oliver Janvier."

The two men shook hands and automatically said, "How do you do."

Sean recalled having heard that name before, but where? Is he my wife's old beau?

"Oliver came to see Ted. The kids should be home around six." Then looking toward Oliver she said, "I hope you will stay long enough to see them."

He just nodded shyly, feeling more anxious for Dom to arrive. Dom did say in about an hour. It seems that I've been here far more than that.

The telephone rang and jarred him from his anxious thoughts.

"Yes dear, Billy is napping. No problems at all. Tell Ted that Oliver Janvier is here.

"Well, I think Ted will know who he is . . . I'll let him tell *you* that. You're leaving Niagara at seven!? Oh . . . I see . . . you haven't had dinner

252

yet . . . yes, Dad just came in before your call. We'll manage with a sandwich or something. No hurry, Kate . . . everything is under control. Bye sweetie. Love you, too."

Both men had listened to Meg's conversation, and after she had hung up, the doorbell rang. This time, it was Dom . . . *at last!*, thought Oliver.

"This is a busy place," noted Sean.

"Dom! What are you doing here?" Meg exclaimed, as she let Dom in.

"I'm calling for Oliver."

"Oh . . . he's in the living room with Sean."

Oliver was glad to be rescued from an awkward situation. He had never felt so relieved when Dom and he were at last heading back to the Abati home.

"Too bad you didn't get to see Ted." Dom shook his head, feeling sad for his friend.

"Yeah, I wish I had known beforehand that he wouldn't be there."

"We'll try again another day . . . and phone first."

"I don't know, Dom. I'm uncomfortable about the whole thing. Maybe I should have let well enough alone."

"Don't say that, Oliver! Your kid has every right to get to know you."

That night, Oliver had an uncanny, disturbing dream. Of all places to be! He found himself at the Tower Hill reservoir, in his home town of Lawrence, Massachusetts. In his school days, his friends and he rolled down the steep grassy hills to see who could reach the bottom first.

He was no longer a child in his dream, but he rolled and rolled all alone. Part way down, he saw an ethereal image of Meg. He held out a hand to her—but she just looked at him and said "La de dah," and grasped her husband's hand as they faded away.

He seemed to be rolling faster and faster down this never ending slope. "Hedda, Hedda," he called as he tried to reach for her. The tenuous figure regarded him, but only saw a rolling stone. He rolled on and on at a more dizzying speed. Then, Emma Dodson appeared to him, willing to be with him, looking at him lovingly, but her image faded as her daughter, Patty, kicked him relentlessly.

Lily-May appeared with her guitar and began serenading him with celestrial harmonies. *Peace...heavenly peace*, he thought . . . until Aunt Pearl abruptly seized Lily-May by the ear and pulled her away saying, "too old, too old."

As Oliver's body twisted down and down, he could feel himself aging his hair turning snow white. Then he saw Gretel Kuntz's image, seeming to be more real. She rolled with him, laughing happily. Ah, this is better, he thought, until that brute of a husband pounded Oliver to the bottom of the hill.

Where is everyone, he wondered as he rose to his feet. A beautiful little white feather floated by in the warming breeze. I'm floating, floating—or so it seemed to him. He followed the feather as it buoyantly picked up speed . . . out of reach . . . suddenly disappearing.

The air stilled, and Oliver dropped with a thud to the ground. There, he saw little Billy, playing peacefully on the grass. Upon seeing Oliver, the little fellow screamed, screwing up his face in terror.

At that point, Oliver awoke with a start, thinking that it would be senseless to try to fit in where he wasn't needed or wanted.

"I can't do it," he told Dom at the breakfast table.

Dom and Amalia felt at a loss to understand why Oliver appeared to be so gaunt and fatigued. Without wanting to upset him further by offering unsolicited advice, they said nothing . . . until Dom asked, "What will you do?"

"I'll take a bus to Frank's place for a while."

Twenty-six

Oliver was so self-absorbed during the bus ride to Fredonia that he missed the bus stop to Frank's house. When he realized the mistake, he got off at the next stop and walked back almost two miles, feeling a bit revived. He felt lucky that the welcome mat was always out for Frank's eldest brother.

"You'll stay for the holidays...another New Year coming up!" Frank would be happy to bend his brother's ear about the disconcerting current events.

Congress had passed the Selective Service Act. Oliver expressed his opinions and said, "I'm glad that my son, Ted, is beyond the age to be called."

"You never showed that much concern for Ted before."

"I know. I've made my mistakes."

They turned their conversations toward FDR's re-election. "Wow, a third term. I wonder if that will be allowed in later years," commented Frank.

"The English are getting slaughtered in the London Blitz. It won't take long before Roosevelt feels we should help."

With holidays gone by, things settled down and family routine was just routine. It was 1941. Oliver stayed on and worked at Frank's Star Laundry, still being the Oliver his brother expected—taking time off for fishing outings, poker games with friends and practicing drum rhythms with his sticks and pad. Frank no longer argued the fact that Oliver "was and still is an entity unto himself."

"Oliver is Oliver," he reiterated to Eva.

"I'm surprised that he has stayed in Fredonia this long," she added.

*   *   *

"Our ambassador to Japan has sent some negative reports to Roosevelt," Oliver told Frank.

"Yeah, I read where he expects a possible attack by the Japanese."

The tragic news came on radio that day . . . December seventh. "The Japanese have bombed Pearl Harbor."

On December eighth, United States and Britain declared war on Germany and Italy.

"What can we expect to do about it?" exclaimed Eva, not wanting to listen to the men discussing the unnerving events.

"We can buy war bonds," countered Frank as Eva left the room.

"To think that we fought the 'War to end all wars,'—so it was said in our day—back during the First World War. I have a feeling that each successive war will be more and more devastating. I fear that for young people," commented Oliver. He didn't mention that he was itching to take leave on another expedition, but he waited patiently for another year of fishing, gambling, practicing, and working for Frank.

The holidays were still celebrated in the Canadian fashion. "Tradition is hard to break," commented Eva as she served everyone's favorite Tourtieres, Gorton, and Boudin.

1942 and after the holidays, Oliver began to assess his feelings toward his accomplishments. There must be something I should be doing, he told himself after reading a poem by John Greenleaf Whittier:

Let the thick curtain fall;
I better know than all
How little I have gained,
How vast the unattained.

I don't want the curtain to fall on my life just yet . . . I must have something to attain, he pondered, but I'd rather make new decisions in a warmer climate. I wonder how the guys in Louisiana are doing. I could recapture my youth down there—I'm not all that old! I'll go! He remembered to pack his drum pad and sticks.

He arrived at the French Quarter of New Orleans, "The Queen Of The South," before the crowds arrived for Mardi Gras. Luckily, he was able to phone in a reservation beforehand, and he got just the room he wanted at the same hotel. Pete Amirault was still rooming across the hall and the two men greeted each other like long lost buddies. Oliver felt happy; *here is where I belong*, he thought. With the repeal of Prohibition, the Monique Cafe had reopened and the same men had their jobs back.

"Can you fill in for Jake again, Oliver?"

"Sure, but I thought he was your regular drummer."

"He's even less dependable since Prohibition has been repealed . . . he's a real alcoholic! We need someone to show up regularly. Jake is too far gone."

"I feel sorry for the guy. Is he getting any help?"

"A guy has to want to get out of that kind of stupor. He simply refuses help."

The nightclub crowds had increased greatly, and Oliver was in his glory drumming away with the intricate rhythms; he had a talented sense of what Norm Cartier and Pete Amirault were feeling in their jazz performances, and the men were happy to have Oliver become one with their group again.

During one of their gig breaks, Oliver remarked, "This state seems so flat . . . no hills. There must be a lot of flooding."

"It's a thing of the past. Early in this century, floodwaters from the Mississippi were rerouted into Lake Ponchartrain . . . north of here," Norm offered.

"Sounds good. How did this business of Mardi Gras get going?"

"It all started over a hundred years ago. Now, it's perpetuated by wealthy families, keeping up a tradition they wouldn't want to let go of."

"You mean just the rich accomplish that? How so?"

"They pour lots of mazooma into it . . . time, too, preparing for the celebrations. The parades and balls are extravagant shows, produced by businessmen's clubs."

"How does it pay off for them?"

"Of course it pays off! The tourist industry generates millions of bucks—making their efforts worthwhile."

Pete added, "A king and queen are chosen from the families of importance . . . the New Orlean elite."

"Sounds like the elite can't be beat," joked Oliver.

"Well, they have the loot to boot," countered Pete.

"After 'Fat Tuesday,'" Norm chimed in, "the tourists go home, but we still get to play at the club . . . mostly weekends, though."

"What do you do when business slows down?" asked Oliver.

"We're right near the elbow of the Mississippi River great fishing . . . and then, we occasionally play poker, and still have our jam sessions . . . we keep busy."

"Sounds like my kind of life."

"We'd better get back on stage," announced Pete.

The heat of their jazz had patrons dancing, or tapping their feet while drinking beer.

Oliver stayed with his cohorts for the 1943 Mardi Gras, enjoying life, feeling young, until Frank's phone call about Mama Azilda's death. He was sad to lose his mother, and sad to leave the place where he felt the warmth of friendship—also the warmth of the weather.

"It's a shame that it takes something like this to happen to get the whole family together," Frank said.

The wake was held in the parlor of Eva Gagne's home. Flowers surrounded the bier, on which was placed the open casket. There was much weeping by Azilda's many grandchildren, as each one knelt before her body to say good-bye to Grand-mama. True to Canadian customs, a buffet of sandwich meats, breads, and cakes was laid out in the kitchen.

Most men visitors stayed in the kitchen eating, drinking, and telling jokes, which struck Oliver as being disrespectful of his mother, who was lying dead in the parlor. It was difficult for family members to try to dismiss these partying leeches.

"Some day," said Joe, the youngest Janvier, "this type of send-off of a beloved one will change . . . to a place other than a person's home. It would show more respect to show up for the purpose of expressing condolences . . . and then leave at a decent time . . . not at two in the morning!"

All family members agreed. "But this is the custom," exclaimed Sister Marie Gerard.

"Custom, custom . . . who's the authority to say that it has to be this way?"

There, now they know how I feel, thought Oliver. Why do people feel the need to follow custom . . . like a bunch of sheep? Maybe I'm the black one.

Oliver got Frank aside, handed him his diamond ring and said, "I want you to have this, Frank. One never knows what's ahead of us. I've decided that since you're one of my youngest brothers, it should be yours."

Frank knew that the ring was Oliver's prized possession, but Oliver had such persistence that all Frank could do was to thank him.

"Where will you go now, Oliver?"

"I never did get to see my buddies at the Dayton Veterans Hospital. I'll visit them before returning to New Orleans."

After the funeral, he rode in Frank's Pontiac all the way to Fredonia. It was easier to get to Ohio from there.

Oliver rested for a couple of days with his brother's family, and then caught the train from Buffalo. He checked into a hotel in Dayton, only planning to stay one night. He felt good about his plan to cheer up his fellow veterans.

He was beat—pale and gaunt after his sad experience. I'll go see them in the morning, after a refreshing night's sleep, he told himself.

He awakened at seven-ten the next morning and found that he couldn't move; the right side of his face felt strangely numb—as did the whole right side of his body. He tried to call for help, but his muffled cries went unheard.

Oliver realized that he had a loss of speech, and loss of motor control. He could only lie there until help would finally come to him . . . but how long would it be, he wondered. He lay there for untold hours, occasionally drifting off into unconsciousness. His neck was stiff, he had difficulty focusing his eyes and nausea overtook him.

Occasionally, in a few waking moments, he imagined that he heard his sister, Eva, calling him Mr. Independence . . . Mr. Itchy feet. He no longer felt independent, and no longer could feel his Feet . . . He tried calling out again, but to no avail. He could hardly hear himself. How could anyone else hear me, he fretted. Night came again, and his sister's accusations kept repeating in his aching head. He also heard Hedda saying, "You're like a rolling stone, never gathering moss. It was your choice to gather no moss." I finally fully realize what she means. I'm so all alone.

✳   ✳   ✳

"That Mr. Janvier in room 26 hasn't checked out . . . he only paid for one night," the night clerk informed the incoming relief.

"I'll send the security guard up to his room . . . maybe he's still there," the day clerk responded.

The ambulance whisked Oliver off to the hospital in an unconscious state; when he regained consciousness, he wondered if he could ever regain his independence, and roving ways, but fate was not in his hands.

Afterword

Oliver experienced a stroke in 1943, which ended his roving days; his last years were spent in the Dayton, Ohio, Veterans Hospital. Though he was wheelchair-bound, his infirmity did not deter him from entertaining and cheering the other veterans.

Oliver took advantage of learning craft skills, which were new to him. He enjoyed making leather belts, wallets, and purses.

He was forever the admirer of pretty girls, and enjoyed teasing the attractive nurses, who thought of him as "cute."

He died January 11, 1951, at the age of sixty-five, and was interred in Dayton's National Cemetery, section 8, row 11, grave 10.

Frank lived to be 101 years old. Eva died at the age of ninety. Blanche, the nun, died in Waterville, Maine at the age of eighty-three. Joe, the youngest, died in 1992; he was ninety-six years old.